ROGUE WARRIOR®

ECHO PLATOON

Photo by Kelly Campbell

ROGUE WARRIOR®

ECHO PLATOON

Richard Marcinko
and
John Weisman

POCKET BOOKS
New York   London   Toronto   Sydney   Singapore

Free Public Library of Monroe Township
306 S. Main Street
Williamstown, NJ 08094-1727

9 4 4 8 3

This book is a work of fiction. Names, characters, places and incidents are products of the author's imagination or are used fictitiously. Operational details have been altered so as not to betray current SpecWar techniques.

 POCKET BOOKS, a division of Simon & Schuster Inc.
1230 Avenue of the Americas, New York, NY 10020

Copyright © 2000 by Richard Marcinko and John Weisman

All rights reserved, including the right to reproduce this book or portions thereof in any form whatsoever. For information address Pocket Books, 1230 Avenue of the Americas, New York, NY 10020

ISBN: 0-671-00070-5

First Pocket Books paperback printing May 2000

10 9 8 7 6 5 4 3 2 1

POCKET and colophon are registered trademarks of Simon & Schuster Inc.

ROGUE WARRIOR is a registered trademark of Richard Marcinko

Printed in the U.S.A.

In memory of Bently Toxvard
Master Gunsmith, Warrior, and Patriot

The Rogue Warrior® series by Richard Marcinko and John Weisman

Rogue Warrior
Rogue Warrior: Red Cell
Rogue Warrior: Green Team
Rogue Warrior: Task Force Blue
Rogue Warrior: Designation Gold
Rogue Warrior: SEAL Force Alpha
Rogue Warrior: Option Delta
Rogue Warrior: Echo Platoon

Also by Richard Marcinko

Leadership Secrets of the Rogue Warrior
The Rogue Warrior's Success Strategies
The Real Team

Also by John Weisman

Fiction

Blood Cries
Watchdogs
Evidence

Nonfiction

Shadow Warrior (with Felix Rodriguez)

Anthologies

Unusual Suspects (edited by James Grady)
The Best American Mystery Stories of 1997 (edited by Robert B. Parker)

The friend of my enemy, he is my enemy;
The enemy of my friend, he is my enemy;
But the enemy of my enemy, he is my friend.

—OLD AZERI PROVERB

THE ROGUE WARRIOR'S
TEN COMMANDMENTS OF SPECWAR

- I am the War Lord and the wrathful God of Combat and I will always lead you from the front, not the rear.

- I will treat you all alike—just like shit.

- Thou shalt do nothing I will not do first, and thus will you be created Warriors in My deadly image.

- I shall punish thy bodies because the more thou sweatest in training, the less thou bleedest in combat.

- Indeed, if thou hurteth in thy efforts and thou suffer painful dings, then thou art Doing It Right.

- Thou hast not to like it—thou hast just to do it.

- Thou shalt Keep It Simple, Stupid.

- Thou shalt never assume.

- Verily, thou art not paid for thy methods, but for thy results, by which meaneth thou shalt kill thine enemy by any means available before he killeth you.

- Thou shalt, in thy Warrior's Mind and Soul, always remember My ultimate and final Commandment. There Are No Rules—Thou Shalt Win at All Cost.

Contents

Part One

THE FRIEND OF MY ENEMY

Chapter

1

FIRST THINGS FIRST. THE TIME IS CURRENTLY 0230, AND THE SITUATION is currently FUBAR.[1] Now, having given you the complete (yet still Roguishly pithy) sit-rep, I can proceed with the confessional portion of this affair.

Here goes. I have often maintained that Getting There Is Half the Fun. But today, following the presidential example, I can finally admit the truth: I have misled you. It was all mendacity. Lies. Duplicity. Prevarication. After almost a decade of these books, here is the unvarnished, frank, candid, pellucid, and wholly unadulterated acronymic truth: GTINFFAA. Getting There Is No Fucking Fun At All. None. Nada. Bupkis. Zilch.

There is precious little merriment involved in jumping out of a perfectly stable fucking aircraft into minus-sixty-degree-Fahrenheit air, seven miles above the ground, so you can surprise some hostage-holding malefactors unaware. It is not blissful to leave a perfectly fucking sound rigid inflatable boat and insert by wallowing snout-first through several hundred yards of oozy, chest-

---

[1]Fucked Up Beyond All Repair.

deep mud, all the while fending off nasty, often lethal creepie-crawlies, so you can reconnoiter a village of no-goodniks and then withdraw without being seen. There is no ecstasy in humping several score miles across hundred-plus-degree desert carrying everything but the fucking kitchen sink on your back to blow up a motley crew of transnational tangos.

Indeed, the sorts of experiences I'm describing here can be summarized in a single, evocative, one-syllable word. I am talking, friends, about *PAIN*.

Not the cartoon pain of television dramas and Hollywood shoot-'em-ups, either. I mean the real thing. The kind of pain that *hurts;* hurts for days. The lingering agony of a badly hyperextended joint when you smack the water the wrong way at thirty miles an hour. The month of searing suffering when your chute malfunctions during free fall, a nylon line slaps you across the eyes, ripping your goggles off and tearing your cornea loose. The involuntary tightening of sphincter muscles as a ricochet from your own weapon caroms off a metal wall, bounces off the floor, comes hurtling back at you, and slices through your side, just below the brisket half an inch below where your bulletproof vest stops.

Now, let me say that all of the various varieties of pain encapsulated in the above activities: each and every ding, all the blisters, bruises, contusions, and concussions, the gashes, lacerations, and plain, no-frills smacks upside the head, all of them pale when compared with my current situation.

And what, precisely, *was* my current situation? All you Enquiring minds want to know, huh?

Let's put it this way: my current situation comes straight out of the BOHICA[2] handbook. I mean, I've been cracked, smacked, whacked, and hacked; I've been thumped, dumped, bumped,

---

[2] Bend Over, Here It Comes Again.

and whumped; I've been ground, crowned, browned, and drowned. But until tonight, I've never experienced it while *greased*.

Yeah, greased. Like a cheap French fry. I mean as thickly coated with petroleum jelly as the Herndon Monument the day the plebes at the Naval Academy climb the fucking thing as the last act of their first year.[3] I mean schmeared. Like a bagel. I mean daubed, as with lard. Like Gertrude Ederle on her first attempt to swim the English fucking Channel.

So okay, maybe if you're a Channel swimmer, and you're wearing a 1930s one-piece wool bathing suit, maybe it helps if you envelop yourself in pig fat, or Vaseline (or love-jelly or K-Y, for all I care). But me, I had a little more to carry than Gertrude did. I was wearing a wet suit, which was uncomfortably hot in the tepid water in which I was currently attempting to swim. Over the wet suit was a set of basic black BDUs, which as you all probably know after seven of these books, stands for the oxymoronic Battle Dress Uniform. I was also sporting the ever-popular Point Blank Class III-A Tactical bulletproof vest, with its six-pound ceramic chest plate Velcro'd directly over the ol' Rogue heart. Atop that, I wore my inflatable SEAL CQC[4] vest—and lucky I did, because with all this extra weight I'd have sunk faster than what my longtime Kraut *komrade* in arms, Brigadier General Fred Kohler, would refer to as *ein Backstein*.

Sink like a brick? Oh, yeah—I was carrying almost seventy pounds of equipment tonight. Cinched around my waist was a tactical pistol belt. Descending from it, and attached to the Roguish right thigh, was a ballistic nylon holster that held my sup-

---

[3]The climbing of the greased Herndon obelisk, named after Commander William Lewis Herndon, USN, is supposed to represent the three most important aspects of life at the United States Naval Academy: discipline, teamwork, and courage. Oh, that those were actually the values they taught there. If they were, we'd have a lot better Navy than we do.

[4]Close Quarters Combat.

pressed Heckler & Koch USP-9 and five spare fifteen-round magazines.

To balance things out, my left thigh supported six thirty-round submachine gun magazines loaded with 115-grain Winchester Silvertips. Strapped to my back was a scabbard holding HK's ubiquitous MP5 submachine gun in 9-mm, with a Knight wet-technology suppressor screwed onto the barrel, and a seventh full mag of Silvertips within easy reach. I had six DefTec No. 25 flashbangs in modular pouches Velcro'd to my CQC vest, along with a secure radio, lip mike, and earpiece, twenty feet of shaped linear ribbon charge on a wooden spool, primers, wire, and an electric detonator, a pair of eighteen-inch bolt cutters, an electrician's screwdriver, lineman's pliers, a short steel pry bar, and a first-aid kit. Since I am from the carry-the-coals-to-Newcastle school of SEALdom, I carried a pair of two-liter bladders of drinking water. My fanny pack contained a handful of nylon restraints, and a small roll of waterproof duct tape.

Strapped to my right calf I wore a Mad Dog Taiho combat knife with a nonmagnetic blade. Wound around my waist was twenty feet of caving ladder with modular, titanium rungs and stainless steel cable-rail.

With all that dreck attached to my body, swimming the thousand yards from my insertion point to the target would have been, shall we say, *difficult*, even under the best of conditions. But I had no choice. Besides, we were all similarly loaded down. After all, once we'd made the swim, there was no place to go for supplies. If there was a possibility we'd need to use something, either we schlepped it with us, or we'd have to do without when the time came.

Having just said all that, I must admit that tonight's conditions were, in the abstract, not intolerable toward me and my men. Many elements actually worked in our favor. The water was warm and calm, with a mere eight-to-ten-inch chop. The current flowed obligingly directly toward my target from our launch point. The cuticle-thin sliver of moon low in the east was intermittently obscured by high wispy clouds, which gave me and the eleven men swimming with me a certain degree of invisibility.

Which is why, I guess, Mister Murphy of Murphy's Law fame, decided that my task was too simple and my goal too easily reached. A twelve-man assault team, swimming roughly one thousand yards, should reach its objective in about forty minutes.[5] We had gone about half that distance in less than twenty minutes—and were therefore ahead of schedule.

And so, with his usual sense of the ironic, Mister Murphy came up with an additional element of difficulty to layer on the night's events. An unforeseen, unanticipated, and totally unappreciated oil slick coated the water through which I swam tonight. I hadn't seen it until I was six feet into it—enough time to wave my guys off, but too late for me. We're not talking about a lot of crude here. The scum was perhaps a thirty-second of an inch at its thickest. But let me tell you something about crude oil: it doesn't take a lot to fuck you over, and that thirty-second of an inch of oil fucked me over good. The goddamn stuff stuck to me. It coated all my equipment with sticky, foul-smelling goo. And it weighed me down—almost doubling the load I had to swim under.

Moreover, oil slicks come under the rubric of what the tree huggers at the Environmental Protection Agency refer to as HAZMATs, which of course stands for HAZardous MATerials. Indeed, according to the EPA's current Rules of Engagement (and I've read 'em), one must not come into contact with oil slicks unless one is wearing: 1: a set of EPA-approved HAZMAT coveralls; 2: an EPA-approved HAZMAT mask; 3: EPA-approved HAZMAT gloves; 4: HAZMAT footwear; and 5: an EPA-sanctioned hard hat (in visibility orange, or bright yellow only, please). Violators will be severely fined. Their names will be put down in The Book.

---

[5]According to current NAVSPECWAR doctrine, it should take no more than four minutes to swim a hundred yards under combat conditions.

7

But since there wasn't an EPA tree hugger within six thousand miles, and since I have devoted my life to operating in spite of whatever mischief Mister Murphy or any of his relatives strews in my path, I just kept swimming. Shit, a few years ago, I took a dip in a fucking nuclear wastewater pool. I cured the resulting luminescence (I'm probably the only Richard whose dick has glowed in the dark) with Bombay Sapphire—and I haven't noticed any incidences of lighted lizard syndrome since. So, if Bombay can treat the effects of a nuke wastewater pool, I had no reason to think a dollop or two (or three, or four), after this little exercise wouldn't do the trick, too.

Okay, okay, I'm digressing. You wanted to know about the evening's festivities. It's actually quite simple. I was currently attempting to sidestroke through the Caspian Sea toward oil platform 16-Bravo, the main rig of a five-platform operation sitting nine miles from shore, about fifty miles due south of the Azerbaijani capital city of Baku. The rigs were owned by SOCAR, an oil consortium controlled jointly by CenTex (that's the Central Texas Oil Corporation), and the Azeri government, and manned by a mixed crew of a dozen CenTex and expatriate Brit roustabouts.

But that wasn't why I was here. I was here because 16-Bravo was currently under the control of a group of eight terrorists. They'd taken over the rig twenty hours ago, using darkness as cover to slip aboard from a pair of bright yellow Zodiac inflatables that were currently tethered to 16-Bravo's northeastern hull column and bobbing in the gentle waves. The tangos captured the rig, took the roustabouts hostage, then used their own state-of-the-art cellular phones to call CenTex's home office in Houston, Texas. The message, once it had been translated from Azeri into English, was pretty straightforward: we are pro-Iranian Azeris who do not like the fact that you Infidels are exploiting our nation. Get out of Azerbaijan, or suffer the consequences.

By chance, two hours after the bad guys' phone call had been translated, I'd wheels-downed in Baku with a platoon of SEALs, on a stealth-grade training mission *q-u-i-e-t-l-y* undertaken at the behest of the secretary of defense and the Chairman of the Joint Chiefs of Staff. But the well-planned secrecy went out the door the instant Americans were taken hostage. The Azeris knew all about my capabilities in the hostage-rescue arena, skills not possessed by any local military or police unit (which was one reason for my coming to Baku in the first place).

So, the government of Azerbaijan wanted me and my guys to do the evening's dirty work. And to be honest, I was more than happy to oblige. The best way to teach, after all, is by example. And taking down this oil rig would serve as a real-life demonstration of hopping & popping & shooting & looting to our Azeri students.

That was the good news. Here's the bad news: someone had told the press I was coming, and there was a big contingent of cameras and lights at the airport. The American networks wanted pictures of me and my guys, and interviews, too. Probably so Christiane Effing Amanpour could use the footage when she charged me with using unwarranted violence of action, nerve gas, or some other illegal substance on the hostage takers.

No effing way, José. I solved that problem by asking the Azeris to throw the reporters out, something they probably had a lot of fun doing. But there were two additional impediments to my merry nocturnal marauding. They were, in order of appearance, Her Excellency, the Honorable *Mizz* Marybeth Madison, Ambassador Extraordinary and Plenipotentiary of the United States of America to the Republic of Azerbaijan, and his exalted dweebship, Mr. Roscoe Grogan, Vice President for Security (Central Asia), the CenTex Corp.

The Honorable Ms. Madison just plain didn't want me and my dirtbags in her bailiwick. We'd arrived on a JCET, an acronym that stands for Joint Combined Educational Training mission, sans notice, sans cables, sans anything. And as the ambassador put it so . . . diplomatically, yet firmly, to me: "No one, Captain,

9

not even with your manifest testosterone level, cuts me off at the fucking knees like that and gets away with it."

Since I understand that kind of language, I explained to the good ambassador that JCETs didn't come under her jurisdiction. I wasn't, I explained, heading a diplomatic mission. I was here to train my SEALs, because in point of fact JCETs are training for us, not the Azeris, even though the Azeris might indeed benefit from watching what we did and learning how we did it.

"That, Captain Marcinko, is a double trailer load of horse puckey, and we both know it," quoth the ambassador, shaking her perfectly coifed streaked blonde do. "I read the damn papers, and the damn cables too. I know what JCET missions are. No matter what you tell me, you're here to train Azeris, and unless you're gonna do it in Iran or Russia or the Republic of Georgia, or you're gonna fly 'em back to the good ol' Yew Ess of A, you're gonna be infringin' on my turf."

She was correct, of course. But that's never stopped me before. And it didn't stop me now. Indeed, after one phone call from me to the secretary of defense back in DC, and another from the Azeri foreign minister to the principal deputy assistant secretary of state for former Soviet something-or-others (who they finally contacted via cellular during a boondoggle somewhere way out in one of the Stans[6]), Ambassador Madison's fashionable scrawny-assed, Chanel-clad, Vuitton-clutching, perfectly manicured claws were removed from my back.

Security dweeb Grogan, a bolo-tie sporting former FBI Special Agent in Charge (read desk jockey) from Dallas, probably had his last meaningful relationship with law enforcement when Ronald Reagan was in his first term, Ambassador Madison was in grade school, and Tony Lama boots cost a mere two

---

[6]No, the Stans are not Maurice and his family. They are all those former Soviet republics that are now independent states, like Kazak*stan*, Turkmeni*stan*, Kyrgyz*stan*, and Tajik-i*stan*, to name a few.

hundred bucks a pair. He was more difficult to deal with than the ambassador. She, at least, finally realized, after some, ah, interface with Washington, that it was the Azeris' country, they'd asked me to help, and I had the backing of the Chairman of the Joint Chiefs of Staff and the secretary of defense. While she didn't like my presence here, the other political factors were nonetheless overwhelming. And so, being a realist, she bowed to 'em and stepped aside.

Roscoe wasn't hampered by such political or diplomatic niceties. This was his company's damn awl rig, and he was going to handle things his way.

And what was his way, you want to know. Well, it was Roscoe's considered opinion that if we let a local self-help organization slip the tangos a hundred thou or so in American greenbacks, they'd jump back into their Zodiacs and hightail it outta Bah-Koo, toot sweet.

You say you don't believe me? Hey, let's go to the videotape.

As you can see, Roscoe and I are standing on the tarmac, nose to nose, off behind the greasy ramp of the big, black, unmarked C-130 on which my guys and I had flown in, so the two of us could have some privacy. See how his thumbs are hooked in his belt loops, like some dime-novel cowboy?

Let's listen in. "Yo, Dick, I've been dealin' with all these friggin' assholes over here for the last two-and-a-half friggin' years and three friggin' American ambassadors by goin' through the friggin' Sirzhik Foundation. Turkish friggin' Mafia. Chechen friggin' Mafia. Georgian friggin' Mafia. Russian friggin' Mafia. Armenian friggin' nationalists. Azeri friggin' pistoleros. The friggin' Foundation deals with 'em all. It has a friggin' system, and here's how it friggin' works: I slip the Foundation a suitcase of greenbacks—it's a 501-C charitable organization back in the States, so everything's on the up-and-up and CenTex even gets a tax deduction. Then maybe the Foundation takes a cut, maybe it don't, I frankly don't give a shit, y'know? Then it pays out however much it wants to as a kinda self-help bequest to the parties in question,

RICHARD MARCINKO and JOHN WEISMAN

after which they friggin' disappear. I've done this a dozen times in the past six months alone, so I know something you don't. Even though these particular friggin' assholes decided to up the friggin' ante by takin' hostages, they ain't friggin' terrorists, Dick—they're friggin' bidnessmen."

Yeah, right. So, I friggin' explain to friggin' Roscoe in my quaint, Roguish friggin' way that the friggin' Naval Special Warfare technical term for friggin' people who take friggin' hostages, is "friggin' terrorists." I add (somewhat unnecessarily, I thought at the time) that we don't pay friggin' bribes to friggin' terrorists, and we certainly don't go through some friggin' bogus foundation.

See how Roscoe's right hand goes up like a traffic cop's? "Whoa, Dick—I'm not talkin' about a friggin' bribe. That would be friggin' wrong. In fact, it would be friggin' illegal. This is what we in the friggin' awl bidness call expeditin', and the friggin' ambassador over there, who as you probably know, has been in the friggin' awl bidness for the past twelve years herself, agrees with me."

It struck me as odd that said friggin' ambassador could have been in any business for the past twelve years. She didn't look more than twenty-five. Of course, according to the file I'd read on the way over (I may look the part of the knuckle-dragging Rogue, but believe me, I do more homework than the chief stock analyst at Merrill Lynch), she was thirty-seven, the widow of the twelfth richest man in Texas, and she ran a corporation with more value than the GNP of most of the countries in the Third World. The article about her in *Forbes* told me that she was tough as nails, just as likely to season her language with *F*-words as the Parisian-pure French she'd learned at Madeira and the Sorbonne, or the economics-speak she'd absorbed at Harvard's business school.

I should also admit that even the flattering photo spreads in *Town and Country* and *Architectural Digest* hadn't done credit to her. Marybeth Madison may have been thirty-seven. But she had the muscle tone and firm skin of a woman who worked out regularly with a private trainer, and so she looked ten years younger than she was.

But all that bidness experience, all those advanced degrees, all that ability to use the *F*-word, and all that muscle tone did her absolutely no good when it came to dealing with hostage situations. In fact, it had worked against her. Because, for some reason—maybe it was the fact that they were fellow Texans; maybe she was just incapable of making tough choices when it came to dealing with human lives—she'd allied herself with Roscoe Grogan and Roscoe's friends at the Sirzhik Foundation, whatever the hell that was (I made a mental note at the time to check it out). And Roscoe, as you have seen, was a government-inspected, Grade-A, Ruby Red, size extra-large Asshole of hufuckingmongous proportions.

Now, I could give you a blow by blow of my reaction to this RRA's chop-logic, but that would waste both my time and yours. Suffice it to say that the ambassador and Roscoe went back to her embassy in a huff (actually they traveled in her armored limo), and I went to work.

Over the next eight hours, my men and I moved fifty miles south of Baku. With the help of the Azeri Army, I quietly set up a base of operations on the awl platform closest to 16-Bravo. While my two sniper teams (and the four Azeri spec-ops wannabes I allowed to observe the situation close-up) began to assess the situation through their night-vision spotting scopes, I got on the secure cellular and jump-started my intel network back in the States.

It didn't take long for me to discover that the TIQs (look it up in the glossary) weren't Azeri at all, but Iranian no-goodniks. They belonged to an over-the-edge splinter group from the Revolutionary Guards and called themselves the Fist of Allah. According to DIA, they had infiltrated from Iran—in point of fact their strike emanated from the old American CIA listening post in the mountains above the Iranian town of Astara, which sits just south of the Azeri border. Who says fundamentalists ain't got no sense of humor?

I do—at least when it comes to murdering Westerners. Because the FAs had, over the past sixteen months, assassinated seven Americans, three Brits, a German, and a Frenchie. They hadn't limited themselves to action in Europe and the Middle East, either. One hit had come in Japan; two others in Canada.

Anyway, shortly after nightfall, we confirmed that there were eight bad guys on 16-Bravo. Not a huge force of hostiles—but enough to cause both us and the hostages considerable damage. We also knew from what the Azeris had told us, and what we discovered through our own monitoring of the situation, that these tangos were efficient, professionally trained, and well equipped.

And oh, yeah: unlike me, they weren't coated with crude oil.

I flicked goo from my face mask (I was swimming virtually fucking blind), released most of the air in my SEAL vest, dropped under the surface like the aforementioned brick, and kicked and twirled, trying to shed as much of the sticky, viscous crude as I could. I don't think it did me much good at all. In fact, it was kinda disorienting. But it was still better than swimming through the goo. I breast-stroked underwater, in what I thought to be the general direction of 16-Bravo for about thirty yards, then rolled and headed toward the surface for air, my fins kicking and my arms sweeping the water to break up the surface slick.

That was when Boomerang, who I thought had been swimming ten meters off my port side and six meters astern of my position, kicked me square in the face. My chin got in the way of his heel—and he got me good.

Smaaack! Oh, it smarted. Belay that. It fucking *hurt*. The blow knocked my mask off, and all the air out of my lungs. I breached better than most whales, sucked air—and in the process swallowed about a gallon of oil-soaked seawater. I retched the water back up, then dove again, clutching and snatching vainly for the mask—and got another extra-large, extra-stiff, extra-hard swim fin blow, this one right across my big Slovak snout. Instinctively, I grabbed the offending appendage and struggled back toward the surface.

Immediately, the fin wrenched out of my grasp and Boomerang's long, narrow face appeared in the periphery of my blurred vision, my mask in his gloved right hand. He held me steady as I washed the glass off as best I could, slipped the strap over my head, fixed the mask back in position, vented it, then seated the fucking thing properly on my big, hairy face. His eyes told me he felt my pain. My eyes, which were smarting like hell from the effects of crude oil and polluted Caspian, told him he had . . . no idea.

I settled into a vertical position, trod water, blew some air into my vest to keep me afloat, and took bearings. We were about three hundred meters from the platform, well outside the ring of ambient light from the amber sodium work lights, catwalk incandescents, twinkly rail safety lights, red and white flashers atop the derrick, and a greenish fluorescent glow emanating from inside the modular living quarters.

There were twelve of us making the assault tonight. The four remaining SEALs in Echo Platoon were on one of the other four platforms in this cluster of five, protecting our six with suppressed, 50-caliber sniper rifles capable of making a two-thousand-meter shot with their hand-loaded, 750-grain Hornady projectiles. Tonight, they'd be shooting at roughly half that distance.

0232. As long as I'm catching my breath, let me take a minute or two to explain what we're about to do. There are only three ways to take down an oil rig. You can swim in, climb up the skeletal frame, and swarm the bad guys. You can chopper in at wave-top height, then suddenly flare above the platform, fast-rope down, and swarm the bad guys. Or, you can jump HALO (high altitude, low opening) from a plane, fall five miles, pop the chute at four thousand feet above the water, parachute onto the platform, and swarm the bad guys.

Frankly, the HALO approach is the most risky, because HALO doesn't assure that you'll put enough shooters onto the rig simultaneously to do the job, e.g., control the platform and kill all the bad guys before they have a chance to waste the hostages. Fast-roping from a chopper is perhaps the most effective. In fact, if you combine a chopper assault with a waterborne (combat swimmer) operation, you can put a shitload of shooters on the platform all at once. But tonight, fast-roping was not an option because I'd been given to understand there wasn't a single chopper capable of holding more than four people anywhere in the whole fucking country. And so, we were going to have to do this the old-fashioned way, a technique I call HP/SL. In other words, we'd *Hump* our way in, and then *Pump* our way up, so we could do what SEALs do best: *Shoot & Loot,* i.e., kill our enemies before they could do any damage to the hostages.

0234. Finally clear of the oil slick, I kicked off and started side-stroking toward the platform. Boomerang kept pace with me, his long, narrow head bobbing in the gentle current. Fanned out behind us swam the rest of the assault team. The core of Echo Platoon—Boomerang, Duck Foot Dewey, Nod DiCarlo, Half Pint Harris, Piccolo Mead, Gator Shepard, and the SEAL smidge I call Rodent—have been with me for years. Terry Devine, who I named Timex, because he can take a licking and still keep on kicking (butt), busted his cherry status with me in Germany last year.

The rest of the team is new—but they're capable. Digger O'Toole, of Hollywood Beach, Florida, for example. . . .

Hey, just who the fuck is that out there making all that goddamn noise? Oh, it's the fucking editor. And he wants to know why I have a bunch of newbies on this mission.

I have two words for you, *ed.* No, not FUCK YOU—although the thought occurred to me. The two words are *retention* and *reen-*

listment. Both are down in this politically correct, zero defect Navy. And so a lot of my old shooters have gone civilian. But there are still a handful of WARRIORS left for me to pick from. And these guys were the crème de la brouhaha.

Like, as I was saying, Digger O'Toole of Hollywood Beach, Florida. Digger's the kind of can-do dirtbag you need on ops like this one. There's nowhere he won't go, and nothing he can't climb. Rotten Randy Michaels and a wiry little Brit I call Nigel (his real name is Rupert. But who the hell is gonna call anybody Rupert these days of don't ask don't tell?) round out the assault group. Rotten Randy is built like a defensive linebacker—e.g., big and burly, and he can move like lightning when he has to. We call him Rotten Randy because he spent ten years as an Army Ranger— and if that ain't a rotten existence, I don't know what is. Then, he made the right decision: he realized that life should be an adventure, not just a job, and he joined the Navy. He went through BUD/S, where they retooled him to shout HOO-YAH instead of HOO-AH, at the ripe old age of twenty-nine. Currently, he's an E-9. That's a master chief for all you cake-eating civilians out there.

I shanghaied him from SEAL Team Eight after I saw him operate. Randy, friends, is the kind of Warrior you want to put your back up against when the *merde* hits the *ventilateur* and you're outnumbered eight to one. It took him about half a second to volunteer for my Roguish band. His only demand was that I also take his E-5 swim buddy, Nigel, who weighs in at a mere 115 pounds. Nigel was born Rupert Collis in East London, down the Old Kent Road—and you can tell it from the way he talks. He is living proof that the only thing that separates us from the English is our common language.

Anyway, Nigel came here at the age of eleven; became a citizen at eighteen, and the first thing he did was join the Navy. He can run thirty miles in five and a half hours. That's not a lot you say. You're right. But Nigel can do it in the desert. While carrying an eighty-pound load of combat gear. And after he's run his thirty miles, he can whip your ass no matter how big and bad you say you are.

Back on the platform I was using as a forward base was my four-man sniper/intel unit. Mustang, the lead spotter, is a half-Sioux (I think the other half is mountain lion) Warrior who grew up in Montana. He's built sorta like a mailbox, which leads people to believe that he's clumsy. Big mistake. Mustang is teamed with Hammer Johnson, who learned his nasty craft in the Marine Corps before he decided to leave Uncle Sam's Misguided Children and become a SEAL. Hammer once made a twenty-six-hundred-yard head shot with the 50-caliber sniper rifle he helped develop for Desert Storm. The weapon he's shooting tonight is a fourth-generation rifle that's twice as accurate as the Mark-1, Mod-0 original.

Sniper Two is made up of Butch Wells, a smart-ass kid from Reading, Massachusetts, with a New England accent as broad as the fucking Haavaad Yhaad, and Goober. Goober (if he has a last name he's never told anybody, and if I ever knew what it was I've forgotten) is Echo Platoon's other sniperman. Goober is a boatswain's mate first class from Georgia, and he can shoot the fucking eye out of a housefly at a thousand meters.

0245. My dirty dozen secured to a long, tubular member that ran between the thick, vertical hull columns. We were fucking exhausted already—and we hadn't even begun the night's work. Timex and I unhitched the pair of two-liter bladders of water. I passed one of my containers to the Pick, and the other to Duck Foot, so they could drink. Timex handed one off to Digger, and drank from the other. I lay on my back in the water, trying hard to breathe. It wasn't easy. The water temperature was in the low eighties; the air was perhaps ninety-five, and the heat sapped what little reserves I had in the way of energy.

I waited until everyone had taken on water, then took one of the bladders and drained it. I'd sweat buckets during the swim—and as heavy as the water had been, I was glad I'd insisted that we carry enough to make sure each man got about two-thirds of a liter before we made our assault. Something I've learned over the years is that a dehydrated Warrior doesn't perform as well as a hydrated Warrior.

0249. The platform towered above us, skeletal, gigantic, and imposing; a melange of brightness and shadow, all mechanical angularity. Sixteen-Bravo sat in perhaps 180 feet of water. It was what's known as a fixed rig, which means it was secured to the Caspian's bed. If the water had been, say, a hundred fathoms deep here, the platform would have been a semi-submersible, which floats on huge pontoons and is kept in one position by long anchor chains.

You may indeed be wondering how we could swim in with such impunity, knowing that the bad guys were on their guard. The answer is simple. First, the platform itself is huge, bigger than a twenty-five-story building. It is also virtually impossible to see directly down into the water unless you're hanging off one of the catwalks suspended below the main deck. The arc lights play tricks on your eyes. The water's surface, eighty to ninety feet below that decking, is indistinct. It's damn hard to pick a swimmer out, even in becalmed conditions like tonight.

Second, there's a lot of ambient noise on an oil rig. The metal creaks and groans; the platform itself moves in the water. The modular sheds and housing units shift as the currents below change. And then there are all those generators that power the electrics, the derricks, and the drilling units themselves. Even when 90 percent of the fucking rig is shut down—like this one was—it is still a noisy, distracting, environment. It is an environment that I can and do use to my advantage.

0251. Time to move. But first, I had to deal with the oil. Since I practice the credo of Roy Henry Boehm, Godfather of all SEALs,[7] I'd hit the slick first and hence suffered more than the rest of my guys, most of whom saw what happened to me and swam under it. My BDUs were almost entirely covered by crude. So was my SEAL vest. But layered below, my modular body armor was pretty clean. So was the wet suit. I shrugged out of the vest, body armor, and BDUs. Then I pulled the body armor back on over my wet suit, peeled the modular pouches off the CQC vest and rigged them onto the Velcro surface of the body armor, reattached my pistol belt, thigh holster, mag holders, and combat knife. The scabbard that held my sub-gun was totaled. But the viscous goo hadn't penetrated to the compartment holding the MP5.

0256. We plugged earpieces and lip mikes into our waterproof radios and checked to make sure they were all working. Well, I guess eight out of twelve isn't bad, although I tell you, I'm gonna have some nasty things to say to the folks at Motorola when I get back to the States about the alleged waterproofness of their products.

I raised my snipermen, sitting in the darkness a thousand feet away, and told 'em we were going over the rail.

"Aye, aye, Skipper," Mustang's voice came back into my ear. "I can see you through the night vision. We're on the case. The cat-walk above is clear. I can see one tango on top of the doghouse. He's got a weapon with night vision. Goober's got another target on top of the monkey board—he's got NV too. Looks like he's holding a detonator."

I flashed on the sketch I'd committed to memory earlier in the day. Okay: one bad guy had command of the high ground, because the monkey board is where the derrick man sits. That put the tango about seventy feet above the deck. From that posi-

---

[7]"Leadership," growls Roy, "can be defined in two words: *follow me!*"

94483

tion, his field of fire could control access to the chopper pad, modular living quarters, and the majority of the platform deck areas. From what Mustang said he also controlled the explosives.

A quartet of *tsk-tsks* in my ear signaled message received.

0303. We swam under the rig and I silent-signaled for the assault to begin. Digger secured the twenty-meter length of thin, nylon rope he'd been carrying over his shoulder, hoisted himself onto a thick vertical brace, and began the long climb up. He was followed by Duck Foot Dewey and Rotten Randy Michaels. I watched as they wormed their way up the slippery brace. I do not like taking down oil rigs. I lost a man during an oil rig operation in the Gulf of Mexico a few years ago. But, as the SpecWar Commandment says, we didn't have to like it, we just had to do it. My climbers made steady progress. But I could see the energy they were expending to do their jobs—visible heat waves were radiating off their bodies.

As Digger, Duck Foot, and Randy climbed, Boomerang, Nod, and Rodent perched, their sub-gun muzzles pointed up toward the catwalk fifty feet above the water, scanning for targets. If one of the tangos decided to take a cigarette break or a piss, it was their job to neutralize the sonofabitch before he could raise any alarm or injure the climbers. We were real vulnerable until the first three shooters reached the catwalk. Then, with Duck Foot and Randy protecting his six, Digger would lower the line, bring the caving ladder sections up, link 'em together, secure the ladder to the rail, and lower it, so the rest of us could make our way onto the catwalk. Caving ladders are no fun. But they're less painful to climb than the vertical braces my trio of shooters had just scaled.

0311. Eight minutes is a long fucking time when you're vulnerable, and that's how long it took us to get up the ladder. I went up last. Yes, I always lead from the front. But I've got a bit more age than my shooters, and they can scamper up a caving ladder, while I have to fight my way rung by rung.

I waited until Nigel's narrow butt was ten feet above the water,

Free Public Library of Monroe Township
306 S. Main Street
Williamstown, NJ 08094-1727

then raised myself as high as I could, took hold of one of the narrow titanium rungs, pulled myself upward ounce by ounce, until I could get the toes of my right Rogue foot through the narrow opening. God, that hurt. And, yes, I press 450 pounds, 155 reps, every fucking day, rain, sleet, snow, or shine, on the outdoor weight pile at Rogue Manor. I have superior upper-body strength. In fact, I am one bodaciously strong motherfucker. But all of that doesn't mean shit when you have to muscle your way up a twisting, narrow, slippery, wet caving ladder under combat conditions.

It has been said that the journey of a thousand miles begins with a single step. And for me, tonight's journey would only begin when I took that first step up. I fought the fucking ladder as it twisted away from me; used my shoulders and upper arms to get some leverage on the contorted metal and cable, and—finally—thrust my fucking foot onto the rung.

Have I mentioned, friends, that I'd been swimming through an oil slick? You say you remember that fact. Well, good for you—because your memory is better than mine. Me? I'd forgotten that the bottom of my neoprene bootie was as slick as deer guts. My foot went skidding out from under me, my leg slid through the ladder, my hands lost their grip on the rail, and I dropped about two and a half feet, wedging myself—*ooooh*—up to my crotch on the fucking rung.

Let me be more explicit. All of my own weight—every stone, every kilo, every pound, ounce, gill, and gram, not to mention the combined weight of everything I was carrying—was now resting squarely on my right nut. The selfsame nut that was being squeezed into peanut butter by the titanium rung. Oh damn oh shit oh doom on Dickie, which as you probably know, means I was being fuckee-fuckeed in Vietnamese. Fuckee-fuckee indeed—if I didn't do something soon, I was going to perform the rest of this *fekokte* mission as a goddamn countertenor.

I uncrossed my eyes, gulped air, and struggled to pull one

hand over the other until I was able to extract myself and start moving upward once again. Except now, each step of that painful climb was accompanied by the tom-tom throbbing of my right testicle. Oh, let me tell you, by the time I finally pulled myself over the catwalk rail, I hurt in every molecule of my body and from the way my wet suit felt, I'd probably lost another four or five pounds of water weight. I'm not as limber as I was when I started playing the lead role in this series, friends, and it is climbs like this one that make the fact painfully obvious.

But as I have said in the past, and will say again, pain exists to ensure that I know I'm alive. And since I was very much alive, I unsheathed my MP5, loaded a mag, and dropped the bolt. It was about to be Show Time.

Our insertion point was the small catwalk at the flare tip end of an oil/gas separator line. Most platforms have two such flare devices. The catwalks, with one vertical and one horizontal gas nozzle, are affixed to the end of a seventy-foot arm similar to the long jib of a tower crane. In the "at rest" position, the flare catwalks sit about three yards below the lowest part of the platform. That made 'em accessible without exposing our flanks. And because it is possible to shinny along the jib, my shooters could remain invisible to anyone on deck until they reached the shelter of the tanks in the oil-processing area.

If you looked at this particular platform head-on, which is to say, with the helipad in the "twelve o'clock" position, one oil/gas separator flare cluster was at five-thirty; the other one was at eleven o'clock. We had swum under the rig and climbed at the little-hand-on-eleven position because it was completely shielded by the huge derrick superstructure and main engine heat-exchangers from the aforementioned tangos who were manning the monkey board and the doghouse roof.

Now that we were aboard, all that remained was to stay out of sight until we'd made it to our assault position, while praying that the rest of the bad guys—the ones we hadn't seen yet—didn't have night-vision equipment, infrared sights on their weapons, or thermal-imaging range finders like their two buddies.

The unfortunate and nasty truth, friends, is that these days tangos can obtain just about every techno-goodie that is used by Delta Force, DEV Group,[8] or any other cutting-edge special-operations unit. Maybe not the absolute latest generation, but still better than most of the world's armed forces carry on a day-to-day basis.

The good news was that given the heat—it was still in the high nineties—all the metal on the rig was just about as hot as our bodies. And that would help mask us as we moved into position if the bad guys had some techno-backup.

0313. Time to move out. We were real bunched up on the eight-by-twelve foot platform, and crowds make me nervous under conditions like this.

I rubbed the soles of my booties against the nonskid flooring of the platform until I was satisfied that I'd removed all the oil residue. Then I silent-signaled to disperse.

Boomerang and I, accompanied by Nod and Duck Foot, would balance atop the four-foot rail of the flare platform and pull ourselves up onto the rig's main deck, sheltered from discovery by a red-and-white-striped crane housing. From there, we'd scamper across thirty feet of unprotected ground, up a steel ladderway, around a corner, and along a narrow length of decking that led to the back side of the modular housing unit.

As we did that, the rest of the platoon would make its way along the jib. When they reached the end, Timex, Gator, Randy, and Nigel would move to port. They'd crawl under the oil storage tanks, slip behind the explosives locker, then secure the front end of the modular housing unit and wait for my signal to hit the

---

[8]That's what they're calling SEAL Team Six these days. In Navyspeak, there's even an acronym, DEVGRP, which stands for Naval Special Warfare DEVelopment GRouP.

main force of tangos and free the hostages. As they did that, Half Pint, the Pick, Rodent, and Digger would head to starboard, where they'd thread the needle between the outermost storage tanks and the modular drilling equipment sheds, then separate into two-man hunter-killer groups to neutralize any tangos in the commo shack and stowage areas. We had eight bad guys to deal with. We had pinpointed two—the lookouts. I knew from experience most of the rest would be in close proximity to the hostages.

Boomerang scampered around the vertical flare nozzle to the corner of the rail. He looked up at the platform bed, which was about ten feet above his head and perhaps two feet distant. He vaulted up onto the rail, and with the athletic balance of a ballet dancer, then jumped vertically, about eighteen inches, straight up.

His fingertips caught the steel edge of the deck, and he began to haul himself up, as if he were doing the last pull-up of a very long string. Then his left hand slipped. His gloved fingers lost traction on the platform surface and slipped off. He tried to regain his grip, but it was impossible. And he was wearing too much equipment to pull himself up one-handed.

I watched as he dropped back into space and fell. Yes, the vertical distance between the bottom of the deck and the top of the rail was only about eighteen inches. But there were two feet of horizontal space to consider as well. If Boomerang didn't thrust himself backward at the same time he dropped onto the flare platform rail, he was going to fall about eighty feet into the water. And with all the weight he was carrying, falling eighty feet into the water was going to be like hitting fucking concrete from the same height.

I watched transfixed. This was one of those moves in which time seemed to stand still. Boomerang was suspended in space. But he didn't descend. Instead, he turned his whole body 180 degrees. Then, like one of those goddamn circus trapeze geniuses, his body, facing the flare platform, kinetically impelled itself forward. Only then did he actually drop. He landed on the balls of his feet, right atop the two-inch rail. The only sign of exertion I could see was the tension on his face.

His lips moved. No sound came out, but I could read his lips as he mouthed, "Sorry, Boss Dude."

He reversed his position, gauged the distance one more time, removed his Nomex gloves and stowed them in his belt, then leapt. The second jump was a lot higher than the first. Boomerang's long hands wrapped around the edge of the decking. He drew himself up, up, up, and finally, one-handed the support railing at the edge of the deck. Then he swung to his right, which allowed his knee to catch the edge.

He pulled himself up and over the rail, dropped to his knees, crawled under the bottom rung of the railing, and held his arms out wide. His expression said, "C'mon, Boss Dude—I'll catch you."

My expression told him, "Yeah—right." When I was but a tadpole, the nastiest feature of the obstacle course at the Little Creek Amphibious Naval Base was a series of telephone pole sections, cut into different heights, and stuck in the sand dunes. We called it The Dirty Name. You had to jump from one pole section to another without falling onto the sand. But that was easier said than done. Because if you could make the vertical jump, the horizontal distance seemed too far to achieve. If you could make the horizontal leap okay, the vertical seemed too high.

Now, the grizzled, war-tempered UDT chiefs who first built the fucking thing long before I ever made it into training had done their jobs well when they put The Dirty Name together. They designed it, you see, with the high goal of making us stinking trainees realize that nothing is impossible. They wanted to construct the physical embodiment of a philosophical tenet basic to SEALdom. That concept is: if you set your mind on a goal and your spirit is the spirit of a Warrior, the word *impossible* DOES NOT EXIST.

And so, we assaulted The Dirty Name until we overcame it. Conquered it. Vanquished it. And, just as the chiefs wanted, we tadpoles finally came to realize by our victory that when we came up against an obstacle, whether that obstacle was in WAR or in life, we could make ourselves triumph over it by sheer will, pure tenacity, and absolute determination.

You don't have to like it, they told us—you just have to do it. So these days, whenever I come up against an impediment, whether it is a physical challenge, a bureaucratic roadblock, or a tactical obstacle, I hearken back to The Dirty Name, and I know deep in my Warrior's bowels that I *CAN* win the battle, and therefore I WILL NOT FAIL. NOT EVER.

And so, although I can honestly say that I do not like balancing on slippery metal railings, I Just Did It. I clambered up, balanced on the balls of my feet as best I could given my throbbing right nut, bent my knees, raised my arms high over my head, and launched myself into the void. My eyes were locked onto Boomerang's; my concentration was total. I fucking felt myself approach the deck; sensed its bulk and physical mass. And then Boomerang's hands clasped my wrists, like a trapeze catcher traps the flyer, and he swung me, a big Slovak pendulum, upward, toward my right.

I used my bulk to help, adding to my speed and angle of trajectory. I shouldn't have. I should have let Boomerang do what he was doing, because he was doing it very well. But I couldn't leave well enough alone. And so, as I propelled myself up, the point of my right knee—the tender ball joint known as the patella—caught the metal edge of the steel deck.

How hard did I hit my patella?[9] Hard enough to bring tears to my eyes. Hard enough so that I couldn't feel my toes. Hard enough so that I forgot how much my right nut hurt.

I started to fall back. I kicked and twisted involuntarily as I

---

[9] *Patella* is a silly-sounding word, isn't it? But lemme tell you, silly or not, it fucking hurts when you smack it the way I did.

did so. Bad move, because Boomerang lost his grip on my left wrist.

Oh, fuck, oh, shit, oh, doom on Dickie. He was one-handing me, now. And even that was fucking tenuous. It was a very, very long way down. I didn't want to hit that water. Remember: you drop eighty feet, and hitting water isn't much different from hitting concrete. More serious so far as I was concerned: *I really didn't want to make the fucking climb a second time.* I gritted my teeth, swung my left arm up, and grabbed his left wrist—which was still clamped viselike onto my right wrist—with both hands.

"Gotcha," Boomerang said through clenched teeth. The fingers of his free hand wrapped around my wrists, and, straining, he swung me, the selfsame big Slovak pendulum, up toward the deck once again.

This time I let *him* do the work, and allowed my body to go where he wanted to put it. My knee caught the lip of the deck correctly. I put my weight on the leg, extricated my right hand from Boomerang's grasp, reached out and up to the support rail, hauled myself up, and pulled myself under the dark tubular metal.

I rolled over onto my back unable to breathe, bathed in sweat, my vision clouded by phosphorescent blue and orange spots. Oh, fuck. Not only was I hyperventilating, I was in the goddam HoJo Zone. I fought against it; made myself breathe steadily. Concentrated on overcoming the pain. Slowly, I regained control over my body and my mind.

By the time I sat up and began to massage my sore knee, Boomerang, Nod, and Duck Foot were all staring down at me. I gave them the kind of dirty look battle-weary veterans reserve for smart-assed youngsters who've kicked ass all day, and want to chase pussy all night. I groaned audibly, and grimaced up at them through my pain.

Nod pointedly ignored me. "Now that the Skipper's had his nap," he stage-whispered to Boomerang and Duck Foot, "maybe he'll be ready to come out and play."

"Negatory," Boomerang shook his head. "He probably wants milk and cookies first."

I struggled to my feet feeling each and every year, month, and day of my event-filled life. "Fuck you all very, very much."

Chapter

2

0317. I TOOK POINT, MY MP5 IN LOW READY POSITION, SCANNING AND breathing as I heel-toed deliberately along the red-and-white-striped derrick housing. Behind me, Boomerang's MP5 covered my left flank. Behind him, Duck Foot followed, the snout of his weapon covering my right side. Nod, a fourteen-inch Benelli breaching shotgun in the low ready position, worked the rear-guard slot, the muzzle of his weapon moving slowly right/left, left/right.

It was six yards to the corner of the derrick housing, and we covered the distance without incident. I stopped at the corner, dropped to the deck, slipped my adjustable night-vision goggles out of their pouch, and slid up to the edge of the red-and-white housing. You do not want to present your enemy with a silhouette to shoot at, so moving at ground level's a lot more effective than sticking my big Rogue nose around the corner at a height of six-foot-plus.

Slowly, slowly, slowly, I crept forward until I was able to get enough of my head around the corner. I knew I couldn't see the doghouse roof from where I was, but I should be able to look toward the monkey board.

The hair on the back of my neck stood straight up. *There he was, the sonofabitch.* I could see him. He had an automatic weapon—an

AK-74 from the look of it—with a night-vision sight slung around his shoulder. And he wore what looked to be a current issue, Kirasa-manufactured, Russkie Army Model-5, mil-spec bulletproof vest, with the extra-extra-high neck and the thick, ceramic strike plates fore and aft. It would take every molecule of the big, 750-grain handloaded bullet to take that s.o.b. down.

The tango was hunkered chest-high behind the monkey board windscreen, a pair of big Russkie or East German surplus first-generation night-vision glasses scanning the area from the starboard storage tanks to the port-side chopper pad. There was something clutched in his left hand. I zoomed my night vision in to take a closer look. Yeah—it was a fucking detonator. Soviet Army issue from what I could see.

My group would be moving in his blind spot, because he'd have to look through the huge drilling derrick superstructure to see us. But we were going to have to take him out before he spotted the four SEALs moving around the modular drilling equipment sheds toward the commo shack.

I eased back around the corner, flicked the transmit switch on my radio, and told Hammer what I wanted.

"Got a prob, Skipper," his voice said evenly in my ear.

I do not like to hear about problems. Especially under conditions like the ones under which I was currently operating.

Hammer's voice continued playing in my ear. "Goober's drawing a blank," he said.

Since we were all broadcasting on the same frequency, I knew that everyone whose radio was working had heard what Hammer'd just told me. But as you know, I have learned never to assume anything. And so, I said, "Hold-hold-hold, acknowledge," into my lip mike.

The situation was beginning to concern me. Was Goober's TIQ[10]

---

[10]Tango-in-question.

off somewhere prowling and growling? Had he seen something and gone to investigate? Or was he just off draining his lizard? I wanted to know. But I wasn't about to ask. I don't like to use the radios too much on ops like this one. You can be overheard, no matter what the folks at Motorola say about secure transmissions. If you get too close to a TV set, your transmissions can cause ghosting and static on the screen—and the bad guys will know you're in the neighborhood. So I speak very little. And when I do speak, I do it in ambiguous terms. I never say, "Shoot the tango in the red shirt on the left side of the balcony." Because if said tango is monitoring my comms, he will duck out of the way and live to fight another day. I will simply say, "Go," which tells the bad guy nothing, or leads him to believe that we are staging a frontal assault. Sometimes, I will use the old SAS Colour Clock Code, which assigns a set pattern of colours (or colors, if we're in the USA) and numbers to a target. But I will not ever broadcast specific directions that can be understood by the enemy. Thus endeth the lesson.

Back to real time. I heard six *tsk-tsks* in my ear. The problem was, I couldn't remember how many of the radios were working.

You disbelieve me? Listen, there were hundreds of thoughts and thought fragments running through my mind simultaneously. I was playing out every fucking scenario possible—and most of 'em ended badly. Only in Hollywood or in the books written by wannabe assholes does everything work out every time sans problems, sans fuckups, and sans Mister Murphy showing his ugly puss.

What would happen if the tango draining his lizard ran into my SEALs and started shooting?

What would happen if one of my hunter-killer groups hadn't gotten the "hold" message and started the takedown before we were all in position?

What if Goober or Hammer missed the first shot, and the tango on the monkey board detonated his explosive charges?

What would happen if . . . well, you get the idea.

0320. Butch Wells's voice interrupted my series of dark night-mares. "Goober's G2," which I knew meant he was Good to Go.

"Roger." I eased forward again. My night vision focused on the monkey board tango. "Engage-engage."

You never heard the shots because they were using suppressed weapons and subsonic hand-loads. The target on the monkey board just dropped from sight, as if he'd been poleaxed. Well, poleaxed is just about what happens when you're hit by a 50-caliber slug bigger than a baby's fist.

I couldn't see Goober's target—the guy on the doghouse. But Butch's voice in my ear told me he'd been neutralized, too.

Yes, it is nice to know that some things *do* work the way they are supposed to.

And then Mustang's voice played in my ear. "Clear."

"Roger-roger." The lookouts had been taken down. Do you know the significance of what that signal meant?

You are correct. It meant we had no time to waste.

If the bad guys inside tried to radio the pair of lookouts and they couldn't raise 'em, they'd realize that something was wrong. They'd go defensive. They'd put up their guard. Since the two most vital elements of a hostage rescue are surprise, and violence of action, I didn't want these tangos forewarned. Because fore-warned, as you know, is forearmed.

By killing the lookouts, therefore, we had committed ourselves to immediate and (here's the good part) violent action.

0321. We moved forward. I led the way across fifty feet of open ground, scampered up the narrow ladderway that led around the perimeter of the modular housing unit, vaulted a low railing and scampered along the narrow outdoor passageway that led to the housing unit's rear hatch. Behind me, I heard the muffled scuff of Boomerang's booties as he followed in my footsteps.

I waited until he caught up with me. Then Duck Foot arrived.

And Nod. We formed up into a four-man train. Eased along a metal bulkhead. Ducked under a pair of shuttered windows (yes, they were closed and darkened but why take chances?) and stacked by the doorway. But now, our positions had changed. Nod, the breacher, stood opposite me. Duck Foot had taken up the rear-guard position. Boomerang and I would go through the doorway first, neutralizing any threats we found.

I pressed my ear to the metal of the door and listened. I heard nothing. I drew back, and *tsk-tsked* into my lip mike. I wanted to know that Randy, Nigel, Gator, and Timex were in position— stacked just like we were, outside the modular housing unit's front door. Again—no response.

I do not like getting no response. Getting no response makes me uneasy. Perplexed. Apprehensive.

I was somewhere between perplexed and apprehensive when I heard Rotten Randy's low growl in my left ear. "Problem, Skipper."

Have I told you I do not like to hear about problems? Well, I was serious when I said it a while back, and I am serious now.

I waited in silence. Randy's voice continued: "There's something nasty about the front door."

Without warning, the hair on the back of my neck stood straight up. This instinctive reaction to my surroundings has kept me alive for a long, long time. My body was telling me that something was very wrong here. Very extremely wrong.

First off, I told Randy to shut up RIGHT NOW, and thought about WTF was going on. First of all, we were spending a lot more time on the radio than we should have been. You already know I don't like to broadcast during ops. A couple of *tsk-tsks,* and we hit the motherfuckers is the way I work. But tonight, all of a sudden the situation has apparently deteriorated so much that my B-team leader has to exfuckingplain the new sit-rep in excruciating detail.

When the light bulb went off, I had to blink, because it was so fucking bright it blinded me.

They were monitoring our comms. They were listening to us. They knew we were here, and they thought they knew where we were. They were waiting in ambush.

Of course they were. It was so fucking obvious. And, having discerned the fact that they were lying in wait for us, I understood in the depths of my Roguish soul how to defeat them. Once you know there is an ambush, you can overcome it. You can turn it around, and kill your enemy before he kills you.

How? Watch, and learn, tadpoles.

The first element is deception. You must make your enemy believe that he is still in control of the situation. And so, I got back on the radio.

"Tell me about the front door problem, in detail," I said.

There was a pause. Randy'd never heard me ask for something like that in a situation like this. Then his voice came back at me five by five. "The goddamn thing's electronic and it's sophisticated, too."

"What's your guestimate about defusing it?"

"I dunno," Randy's voice buzzed in my ear. "It's gonna take me like half an hour to bypass the fucking thing because I gotta make sure they didn't screw with the interior side of the hatch as well as the exterior."

Of course, the folks monitoring my conversation knew we didn't have half an hour. They knew we had to act—soon. Why? Because they'd just heard me say, "go-go-go," and they knew I couldn't call a halt to the action once I'd committed my troops. I pressed the transmit button. "Can you blow it and then hit from the front end?"

"Not without causing a lot of casualties inside. The explosives are behind the hatch. If the hatch blows, the force of the charge goes inward—into the room. And my thermal tells me they've got folks in the front room."

"Good guys or tangos?"

"HTF should I know, Skipper? Thermal can't differentiate."

I already knew that blowing the door wasn't an option. Hostage casualties couldn't be tolerated. Not tonight. Not with the politics of this situation just as explosive as the tactical side. But I wanted to paint a certain picture for the bad guys, and so I played the scene out. "Okay—we switch plans. Can you bottle up the front of the unit?"

"Can do."

"Then have Gator and Timex bottle it up. You get your ass and your partner's ass over here double-time. We'll all hit 'em from the back end at once."

Randy came back right on cue: "Aye, aye, Skipper."

I shut my radio down, and silent-signaled Boomerang, Duck Foot, and Nod to do the same. Boomerang looked over at me quizzically. His expression told me that he had no fucking idea what I was thinking. All he knew was that we were about to enter what's known in the trade as a fatal funnel, and that the bad guys were waiting for us inside.

Indeed, the tangos were following the same course of action I would have taken myself if I'd been them: set the agenda for the attacking team. Make 'em come to you the way you want them to come to you. And then you ambush 'em with great violence, and kill 'em all.

They were trying to fuck me. Well, I've been fucked by the best, and lemme tell you I have learned my own fucking bag of tricks.

Here's what I knew. According to the plans faxed from CenTex headquarters, the modular living quarters had been constructed from two double-wide trailer units—that is, four separate sections covered by a single roof. The trailer that contained the dorm rooms formed the shaft of an irregular capital *T*; the common living area was the top of the *T*, except that the trailers had been set so that one side of the top *T* was longer than the other.

The vertical shaft of the *T* comprised eight double bunk rooms, four to a side, all sharing a common corridor. At the bottom end of the corridor was the outside door. At the top, or interior, end of the bunkhouse unit were two bathrooms, one on each side of the corridor. The bunk area was separated from the common room by a short L-shaped passageway, and a hollow-panel door.

The common room itself was wide open. The front entry was a hatch on the far right-hand side of the modular unit as you faced it. The front door opened directly into the galley, which had two long picnic tables and four benches, and a corner kitchen—a four-burner electric stove, a big double-size restaurant quality fridge, a food-prep area, and a microwave. The pantry—what there was of one—was a stowage area above the stove and food-prep area, and a series of deep cabinets below.

To the left of the galley was the big living-room area. That's where they kept the big-screen TV, with the theater-quality sound system, DVD and videocassette decks, and the rig's extensive library of girlie magazines. Creature comforts are important to people who work on oil rigs. Above the galley area was a huge air-conditioning unit, with a spider's web of insulated ducts that ran the cooled air into the living area, the sleeping quarters, and the heads.

Now, the keep-it-simple-stupid way to take this place down, according to the book, was this: we'd hit the front and back doors simultaneously, and swarm both living and sleeping areas, catching the bad guys in between.

But it was obvious that these assholes had read the same book we'd been using. That's why they'd been so fucking obvious about booby-trapping the front door.

Why? Because they thus ensured that we'd make our assault through the back entrance. Where, of course, they'd be waiting for us.

Not all of 'em. We had eight tangos to deal with. Two had been neutralized. That left six. For argument's sake, let's say that one man is a free-floater, who's roaming the rig. That left five. At a minimum, they'd have one or two with the hostages, so that he/they could start killing them quickly. That left three or four. Of those, they'd probably set one guy in the common room. He'd be the backup just in case Mister Murphy screwed with the booby traps and they didn't work. He'd probably have grenades and maybe even explosives. The others would set up in ambush positions so they'd have a free-fire zone as we hit the back door.

Whoa. Let's stop right here, and take the time to war-game this scenario, as it has been submitted.

Action: we hit the place and engage two or three of the bad guys. The remaining tangos wax the hostages—either by shooting 'em or killing 'em with grenades or other explosives. Then having done that, they try to kill as many of us as they could before we overwhelm them and send 'em on the ol' MCRTA—which as you can probably guess, stands for Magic Carpet Ride To Allah.

My friends, I didn't like the way the plot played out. I don't mind sending tangos to meet their maker. But I prefer to do it without allowing them the opportunity to kill hostages or my men and me, before we help them make that one-way trip Allahward.

That's why I had to rewrite the book they'd written. I wasn't going to get a lot of time to redraft their manuscript, but I hoped I had enough to make sure the denouement would come out the way *I* wanted it to end: HEA[11] for *moi*; MCRTA for them.

Randy and Nigel appeared. I used my hands to tell them what was going on. I watched as they turned their radios off. Then I shrugged out of my combat gear and body armor and motioned for Boomerang to do the same. Then, motioning Nod to join us, we crept back, double-timing around the side of the dwelling unit, back to the derrick housing where we'd made our ascent onto the rig platform.

There, I opened the emergency fire-response compartment at

---

[11]Happily Ever After.

the base of the derrick and plucked the business end of the small-diameter rubber fire hose from its reel retainer. I made sure the nozzle was shut down, then turned the water on, watching as the hose ballooned as the pressure built up.

I silent-signaled for Boomerang to head back toward the rear of the modular dwelling unit with the hose. My hands told him where I wanted it, and I received a thumbs-up in return.

He and Nod headed out. I made my way through the small hatchway into the derrick housing chamber and peered around. It was empty. I moved toward the helipad. Below the pad itself was a protected hideout for the landing crew. I slipped inside.

Bingo. There it was: a forty-gallon garbage can sat off to the side. I dumped it quietly, removed the crap inside, and checked the plastic bag used as a liner.

No holes. Perfect. Were there any more around? I ran a fast look-see around the area. Nada. Well, fuck it. This one would have to do.

I sprinted back around the chopper pad, and along the rail, bag in hand. Nigel and Randy were waiting with Boomerang, Nod, and Duck Foot at the back side of the housing unit. Boomerang and I grabbed our tactical equipment and reattached it.

Then I jerked my right thumb toward the roofline. Nod nodded—he understood what I wanted. He scrunched down, and made steps out of his legs and cupped hands. I put my foot on his knee then my other in his hands. He rose enough so that I was able to catch the edge of the modular roof, and pull myself up soundlessly.

Silently, I looked down and told Boomerang, Randy, and Nigel to come up and bring the hose with them. The nasty grins on their faces told me they understood what I was about to do.

Nod boosted his shipmates up. Boomerang pulled his size forty-four extra-long frame onto the roof. Nod handed the nozzle of the hose to the lanky SEAL, and then helped the other two shooters roofward. With the deadly, muscular agility of a pride of big cats on the savanna, the three SEALs crept forward, following in my wake. Proceeding slowly, so as not to make any noise or vibration, we made our way across the flat roof until we reached the seam between the dorm unit and the common room unit. Just beyond us and to our left, the big roof air-conditioning unit whirred steadily, its exhaust fan vibrating just enough to mask our movements.

I pulled the wide, thin wooden spool from its pouch on the rear of my CQC vest, unrolled about four yards of V-shaped flexible shaped charge, and laid it out on the roof in a rough circle, the V of the lead shielding inverted, so it pointed upward.

I secured the ribbon charge to the roof using short pieces of duct tape. Then I inserted one of the pencil primers through the lead sheath into the PETN explosive inside, attached a six-foot length of electrical wire to the primer, then ran the wire to the pocket detonator I'd been carrying all night.

I took the big, black plastic garbage bag I'd been carrying and carefully laid it atop the shaped charge. When it was exactly where I thought it should be, my eyes told Boomerang to turn the water on.

He put the hose nozzle in the garbage bag, and twisted the tip gently. We watched as the bag filled with water. I hoped that the fucking thing would hold and not burst under the weight and pressure, because I didn't have a second fucking bag. There was GNBN.[12] The GN was that I didn't need much water—about four inches would do it. I watched as the bag expanded as it filled and caught the BN, which was there were a couple of tiny leaks, and I didn't want 'em expanding. But I had to wait until the water-filled bag covered the entire outline of the shaped charge I'd taped to the roof. As soon as it did, I drew my finger across my neck, and Boomerang shut the water off.

---

[12]Good News and Bad News.

Show Time. I hand-signaled Randy, Nigel, and Boomerang, then pressed the transmit button on my radio. "Hit on my signal."

A chorus of *tsk-tsks* told me everyone else had gotten the message. I put two fingers to my eyes, and tightened the straps to my night-vision goggles, which would allow me to see in the darkened unit below. The goggles in place, I watched as my phosphorescent shooters did the same. I flipped the safety off my MP5, double-checked to ensure I had a mag in place. I watched as Boomerang, Randy, and Nigel mimicked my actions. When they were locked and loaded, I extracted a DefTec distraction device from its pouch on my chest, pulled the pin, and held the spoon firmly in place with my size-Rogue paw. With my eyes, hands, and elbows I made the assignments. Randy and Nigel would go toward the front door; Boomerang and I would go toward the back door.

Time to do the dirty deed. I gave my men a wide-grinned nod and a big, fat finger, just as if we were about to launch ourselves off the greasy deck of a C-130 at twenty-five thousand feet.

Nigel's raised middle finger told me I was number one with him too. Boomerang and Randy mimicked the nasty "ready to go" signal. And so, with nothing left to do except ACT, I twisted the handle of the detonator.

If you haven't figured it out by now, what I'd just done was build an IED[13] roughly patterned after what the late Arleigh McRae, that genius explosives expert from the Los Angeles Police Department, used to call his Arleigh-gram. He designed the fucking thing using an inner tube and flexible charge to blow holes in the roofs of crack houses, so his SWAT officers could literally drop in on drug dealers.

Well, tonight I didn't have any fucking inner tubes handy—but let me tell you that the goddam garbage bag had done its job. A clean, manhole-cover-size hole had been blown in the roof of the

---

[13]Improvised Explosive Device.

modular structure. And I didn't waste a millisecond of time. I tossed the flashbang into the hole, then dove through myself—just as the fucking thing exploded.

DefTec No. 25 distraction devices explode at 188 decibels, with a flash factor of just under two million lumens. To put it in non-technical terms for you, they are FUCKING LOUD and FUCK-ING BRIGHT. Which is as it should be, because they have been designed to distract bad guys in life-and-death situations.

There is a downside, however. It is this: if you, the hostage rescue guy, are too close to the fucking thing when it goes off, you end up almost as distracted as the tango you're trying to throw off balance. That is why we train as follows:

- Step One. Gently toss the flashbang into the center, or toward the far side, of the space you want to occupy. DO NOT simply drop it in the doorway.

- Step Two. AFTER IT EXPLODES, make entry.

Tonight, for reasons that will go unexplained right now, I forgot the two basic rules of flashbangery outlined above.

The DefTec No. 25 has a one-point-five-second fuse. But I was so wrapped up with getting me and my guys down into the unit below and swarming the nasties, that I didn't toss it in at an angle, and I didn't wait until it went off to make entry.

Not me. Not Dickie. Not tonight. I simply dropped the fucking thing down the hole, then jumped after it into the darkness below. Well, not right quite. I guess I waited about seven-eighths of a second to make my descent. Because the fucking flashbang went off in all its 1.8 million candlepower and 188 decibel glory as I was about four feet off the deck, in midair, falling directly atop the goddam thing.

The concussion blew me off course by about six feet. My umpteenth generation, state-of-the-art lightweight, all-season, wide-angle night-vision goggles skewed, dropped, and fell away on their retaining lanyard, I crashed into a wall, tumbled to the deck, and landed in a goddam heap, my right leg wrapped behind my shoulder like some fucking diagram in a book of esoteric Tantric positions, blinded and deafened by my own Roguish hand. All I saw were spots. All I heard was ringing.

Which, of course, is when one of the tangos decided that I was having too much fun and it was his job to add a note of solemnity to my evening's labors.

I didn't hear the shots (I was still too deafened), but I was finally able to pick out the muzzle flash of whatever the fuck he was shooting at me through the green and white spots in front of my eyes. Let me say that I am not overly fond of CQC, or close-quarters combat. It is dangerous and precarious work. If you are careless, you, the hostages, and your own men will die. But as the SpecWar commandment dictates, I didn't have to like it—I just had to fucking do it. In CQC, you neutralize the most immediate threat first. In my case, that would be the aforementioned ass-hole, who was shooting at me from a distance of less than three yards. I rolled right, kept going (you NEVER want to stop moving in situations like this one), jarred my leg loose from behind my neck, and wasted no time trying to sight-acquire-return-the-fire in the direction of the muzzle flashes.[14]

---

[14]Yes, I hear you, screaming about why the fuck wasn't I wounded, given that this bad guy was shooting at me from less than ten feet away. Well, the fact of the matter is that most CQC takes place at less than five yards (most rooms are small); and if you are not trained in CQC shooting, you will miss your target because you will forget every fucking one of the basics of stress shooting and your rounds will go wild. I know of one incident in Detroit, where a gunfight took place on a six-by-eight-*foot* balcony. The bad guy sprayed seventeen rounds out of his Glock at a cop. Said cop emptied his Sig Sauer 226—sixteen shots in all directed at the malefactor. And guess what? Neither one was fucking hit. The cop had to subdue the suspect with his fists—and in doing so, he broke his hand. Believe me, shooting is a frangible skill. That's why we train the way we do. Only by constant practice can we achieve the ability to hit what we shoot at under the sorts of stressful conditions I'm illustrating here.

Off to my left, another DefTec exploded, its concussion literally lifting me off the deck. By luck, I averted my eyes as it went off and didn't get caught by the flash. My target wasn't so lucky. The fucking thing caught him unaware. He whirled—I saw the silhouette as he turned—and I was able to stitch him with three two-round bursts. He went down.

I crawled over to him and made sure he was who I thought he was. Then I finished him off with a pair of quick shots to the head.

You say that sounds brutal? Fuck you—I didn't want him coming back to haunt me once I thought I'd finished with him.

Millisecond by millisecond I was regaining my faculties. I set my goggles back where they belonged, pulled the night vision's straps around my head, and yanked 'em tight. Now I could see. I started yelling for the hostages to get down-down-down. You don't want them popping their heads up and getting shot.

Behind me, Randy and Nigel had begun to clear the great room. Their firing was suppressed. But I could hear 'em shouting, *"Get down get down get down."*

By the time Boomerang and I linked up and galumphed toward the short, L-shaped corridor leading to the eight bunk rooms and the back doorway, Nigel had shouted, "Clear-clear-clear!" on the radio and I knew the great room was secure.

No time to waste. I kicked the door in. Or tried to. It was a hollow door, remember? So I kicked—and buried my right leg, up to the knee, in eighth-inch plywood.

Fuck. Shit. Doom on Dickie. To hell with it—I just punched through the fucking door, ripped it off its hinges, and shook it loose. Not an instant to spare, I cut the pie of the short side of the L, swung my MP5 up, and—motherfucker—two threats hunkered at twelve o'clock, back to back in the six-foot-long, three-foot-wide corridor.

The closest had a machine pistol with a tactical flashlight on its forearm. He screamed, jumped up, and turned the light on me.

The cockbreath would have blinded me if I hadn't been wearing my night vision. But this generation of NV irises down fifty times faster than the human eye can.[15] He was obviously surprised that I didn't freeze like a jacklighted deer—and so, he was the one who fucking froze.

April fool, motherfucker. Before he could do it to me, I did it to him. I caught him with a two-round burst and he fell back, toward his partner in crime. I charged over the sonofabitch, leaving Boomerang to head-shoot him, and rough-and-tumbled the second tango, whose attention had been turned toward the commotion in the back hallway (that's where Duck Foot and Nod had breached the door and started tossing flashbangs down the hall).

I got some good purchase on the rugged floor and tackled tango two as he spun around, catching him with my shoulder and knocking the muzzle of his AK-74 away from me. That didn't stop the asshole from pulling the trigger, however—letting loose a full mag (or so it seemed) of damn loud and damn lethal 7.62-×-39mm steel-core bullets about three inches from my right ear. They punched through the ceiling like the proverbial HKTB.[16]

T2 decided I was much too close for his safety and comfort. He slipped out of my grasp while trying to rake my face with the front sight of his AK. I blocked the stroke with my left hand,

---

[15]You want specs? Okay. The Specialized Technical Services (STS) Model 2722 is a generation III low-profile night-vision goggle. It has an unaided horizontal fov (field of view) of 165 degrees, a vertical fov of ninety degrees, and an intensified fov of forty degrees. The unit operates off of two independent lithium batteries, and has two levels of light-intensity controls. Two infrared illuminators give you the capability of operating in zero ambient light. You can wear the 2722 while looking through a rifle scope. You can wear them for parachute ops. They will withstand immersion in salt water for two hours at a depth of three meters. And they weigh a mere seven-hundred grams—just over one and a half pounds.

[16]Look it up in the glossary if you can't figure it out.

slapped the muzzle down, reversed, caught him with a forearm to the side of the head, and rocked him sideways.

I've got to say he was a persistent little motherfucker. He lost his grip on the AK, but with both hands free, he launched himself at me and managed to knock my night vision off. That's all right, asshole—I can fight in Braille if I have to. I caught his hands in mine, wrapped him up, bear-hugged him, took his feet off the ground, and using him like a battering ram, I took us both through the fucking lightweight wall.

We crashed—him on the bottom—into one of the heads. The impact knocked a fucking sink off the wall and it went smashing onto the floor, severing the pipe and showering both me and Mr. T2 with water. Even sans lights, I was able to catch a faint glimpse of the room in the ambient light of the flashbangs my guys were throwing—pissers and shitters to my left, showers to the right. Damn—the disinfectant reeked even more than the cordite. But frankly, there was no time at all to admire either the decor, or the smell.

Why? Because T2 broke contact, coiled back, and caught me upside the head with a roundhouse kick. The blow broke the lanyard on my NVGs and sent 'em flying—we'd see how shockproof they really were later. I staggered back, hit the wall, and bounced off, back toward the motherfucker. He tried the kick routine again, but I caught his foot, twisted it until he screamed, then shifted north and popped him twice in the knee, hyperextending it. He must have realized he was in trouble, because he tried to get away. But he couldn't. Because by now I had the little *sik*[17] by the straps on his bulletproof vest, and he wasn't going anywhere.

He was a wiry little asshole and he'd been eating garlic and *fül* beans and who knows what else, because when I kneed him in

---

[17]That's a dick (but not a Richard) in Azeri.

the balls just to show how much I cared, he let go a fart so potent that it had to have been on the UNSCOM[18] CW warning list. We're talking maggot-gagging lethal green cloud here, folks. It was bad enough that even *moi*, the puke-snorting, snot-eating Rogue geek, got knocked ass over teakettle from the stench.

But here's the difference between Warriors and wannabes: Warriors keep going no matter how bad it gets. And so, I took a big deep gulp o' stink, choked the cloud down, and body-dropped T2 onto the floor.

The scream he emitted told me I'd hurt the sumbitch. I jumped on top of him—and discovered I'd dumped him atop the sink we'd broken off the wall. Less work for me. But like I said he was a wiry asshole—and he fought back like a fucking dervish even though he was hurt. He never stopped. He bit my arm. He raked my face. He tried to claw my eyes out. I finally pulled a hand free and hammered him in the nose—which is harder to accomplish than you might think, given all the equipment I was wearing, not to mention the fact that my MP5 was suspended around my neck, and kept getting in the way as I tried my best to kill the tango.

He snorted blood or snot or both and let go of my head—only to grab my French braid with both hands, growl *"Bilach, Bilach"*[19] in my ear while he tried to use it to haul himself onto his feet. My neck snapped forward as if I'd been rear-ended—I could hear the cartilage popping in my neck. My nose hit the butt of my MP5 hard enough to make my eyes water. This nonsense had to stop—soon.

The old Zen masters will tell you that you can fight in absolute dark if you "see" your enemy in your head, conceptualize where

---

[18]United Nations Security COMmand. The guys who tried, despite Secretary of State Albright's meddling, to uncover Saddam Hussein's chemical/biological/nuclear weapons-manufacturing sites.
[19]That's how Iranians tell you to go fuck yourself.

he is, and strike. Yeah—right. Let me tell you how it happens in real life: I head-butted the sonofabitch to make him let go of my braid.

Big mistake. Head-butting is something that you should not attempt in total darkness, no matter what the Zen masters tell you. I missed him completely—maybe he rolled out of the way, maybe I just fucked up. Either way, I scored a perfect ten for Mister Murphy, slamming my thick Slovak forehead straight onto the broken sink.

It was then I realized I wasn't on a fucking oil rig at all (or, at awl). Uh-huh. I was at the Academy fucking Awards. And *why* was I at the Academy fucking Awards? Because all I fucking saw was stars. Big stars. Lots of stars.

I guess I was distracted, because T2 wriggled out of my grasp. He rolled over and smacked my head between his hands, sending shock waves down to my toes, and making my ears ring louder than Big fucking Ben. I fell back. He seized the advantage, grabbing at the sink so he could pick it up and smash me with it.

No fucking way. I jerked out of the way, rolled, and caught him with a lucky kick to the face—heard the blow connect, and the nasty snap of his neck. That was a good sound—but I'd put myself in an awkward position. I was stretched out and vulnerable, and whether or not I'd hurt the motherfucker, he realized it.

He struck out at me blindly, catching my coccyx with his knee and sending a paroxysm of pure, unadulterated pain up my spine and into my brain. Oh, *that* fucking *hurt.*

I struggled to turn myself over so I could get hold of him again, but he understood by now that the closer I got to him, the worse off he'd be. We grappled some more, and he head-butted, and kicked, and twisted, and wrenched this way and that, but in the end I managed to crawl on top of the little cocksucker, and immediately latched on to his bulletproof vest.

Now here's the truth: I am a big, bad motherfucker. I weigh more than two hundred pounds. I can do five hundred finger-tip push-ups, and a thousand ab crunches without breaking much of a sweat. I also lift a huge pile of weights every day at Rogue Manor, my two hundred-plus acres of snakes and lakes that abuts the Marine base just outside Quantico, Virginia. All of the above makes me, in addition to being big and bad, a v-e-r-y strong motherfucker.

So, once I'd laid my hands on him there was no fucking way he was gonna get away from me—until I decided to let go of his corpse. Uh-huh. No way at all. Oh, he struggled and wrestled kicked and bit and screamed a bunch of rude imprecations at me in a language I couldn't understand.

But I didn't give a shit about any of that. See—I knew something. I knew it was time for him to die. Time for Mr. T2 to take that magic carpet ride to the Tango's Valhalla—the place you and I call HELL.

I pulled him close. *"Kuz Emeq,"* I whispered to him. "Fuck your mother's hole." And then, to show him how I really felt, I bit about half his ear off.

He screamed like crazy when I did my Mike Tyson imitation. Didn't like it at all.

C'est dommage. Too fucking bad. I spat the gristly chunk and its attached ear wax out. Hadn't this cockbreath ever heard of Q-Tips? Shit, it was gonna take a gallon of Dr. Bombay Sapphire to get *that* taste out of my mouth.

Au revoir, motherfucker. I took his head in my size ten paws, and wrenched it clean around. All the way. Three hundred and sixty degrees. I could hear his neck bones snap, a uniquely satisfying sound. At least *I* thought so.

I dropped him on the puddled linoleum. As I did, I heard Boomerang shout, "Clear-clear-clear." That was followed by Duck Foot and Randy, calling loud enough for me to hear through my ring-a-ding-dinging ears: "Hostages secure."

That was when the lights started to come on, one by one, and I realized that (as usual) I'd spent the last couple of minutes rolling around some fucking shitter chasing a piece of anonymous shit, and I'd missed all the fun.

Chapter

3

0332. WE SECURED THE RIG. AND DISCOVERED HOW LUCKY WE'D ACTU-ally been. Oh, my plan had worked just the way I knew it would. The Arleigh-gram allowed us to surprise the bad guys, spoil their ambush, and take 'em from behind. Nigel and Rotten Randy had cleared the front room—it was empty—then come around and backed up Boomerang. Nod and Duck Foot breached the rear door, and were able to kill the pair of tangos guarding the hostages before they'd had a chance to do any damage to 'em.

And Half Pint, Pick, Digger, and Rodent had taken out the lone tango hunkered in the commo shed right in the middle of his transmission. That made eight—which was the night's bag limit.

The surprise came when we tracked the wiring from the detonator on the monkey board. I'd assumed (a mistake right there) that the tangos had set the explosives to ambush us. I had been wrong. We went over the rig top to bottom. They hadn't set any antipersonnel charges at all. Nowhere. Instead, they'd run the wires back into the modular dwelling unit. There were three kilos of Semtex in the bunk room where the hostages lay hog-tied. If Goober had missed that first shot, and the bad guy had managed to turn the handle on the detonator, the hostages—hostages hell, the whole fucking modular dwelling unit—would have been vaporized.

Goober and Hammer, who'd arrived on the tender, hoisted themselves onto the roof of the doghouse and checked the corpse of target number one. Hammer was happy to see that he'd made a clean kill—entry just behind the ear and the entire opposite side of the sphincter's skull blown away. Not bad for government work, especially at about a thousand meters. Then they climbed up the derrick to the monkey board and examined Goober's handiwork. Goober had made an eye shot, exploding the tango's head like a fucking melon. I can and do recommend the Hornady 750-grain projectile and the 50-caliber sniper's rifle when a target absofuckingposilutely has to be disintegrated on time.

Then they unwired the detonator, brought it back down to the deck, and dropped it into my calloused palm. "I'm glad you didn't tell me about where this led, Skipper," Goober said, jerking his thumb toward the hostages. "That would have been a lot of pressure to handle."

I examined the device. It was the current Russkie SpecOps model—the one currently used by Spetsnaz maritime units. "Yeah, well twixt thee and me I *would* have told you—if I'd known." You bet I would have. After all, Goober is paid all that big money to take heavyweight pressure, isn't he? (I'm being ironic here. Chiefs, who make life-and-death decisions on a daily basis; who run and oversee billions of dollars' worth of high-tech equipment, make a paltry salary—less than half of your first-year law firm associate.)

I detailed Nod, Goober, Randy, and Mustang to collect intel. I wanted everything the tangos had on 'em bagged and tagged. We didn't get much. These guys had emptied their pockets before they'd launched. But we got all their fingerprints, and took their photos with the digital camera we'd carried in a waterproof bag. Surprising what the well-equipped CT unit will carry these days, huh?

The rest of us spent just over an hour debriefing the roustabouts before we loaded everyone aboard our tender and headed for shore. It's important to debrief ASAP after an incident. You want to know everything you can about your enemies, and hostages can often supply crucial information. They may not think it's important—but it can be crucial. And so, we cracked open the beer locker, sat the oil-rig crew down, and took the time to talk.

I discovered that the tangos who'd taken over 16-Bravo spoke Azeri, Russian, and English in addition to their native Farsi. They came aboard with engineer's diagrams of the rig. That meant they had an inside source somewhere. They'd secured the crew up with the same kind of nylon restraints and duct tape that I carried. And they didn't do any talking in front of the hostages. Indeed, they'd TTS'd 'em,[20] wired them with explosives in the bunk room where they were being held, and left 'em alone to die. All of the above told me the nasties we'd sent to Allah weren't your everyday tango cannon fodder, but an elite crew who'd been sent to do a specific job.

That fact became even more clear to me as I sorted through the equipment they had brought with them. It was all high-tech stuff. You already know the bulletproof vests were current Russian Army issue. So were the AK-74s, which are to AK-47s what the CAR-15 is to the M-16.[21] Their comms were better than ours—secure, digital French manufactured satellite phones. And the tango atop the doghouse had been equipped with a state-of-the-art portable scanner/unscrambler that had allowed him to listen in on everything we'd said. He might have caused us a lot of problems, too, if Hammer hadn't put a bullet through his head.

Indeed, the only precautions the bad guys hadn't taken were

---

[20]Tapped, Tied, and Stashed.
[21]The CAR-15 is the short, carbine version of the .223 caliber M-16; much more suited to SpecOps than the bigger weapon.

countermeasures against extra-long-range sniping. But that was to be expected. It was more than a thousand meters from 16-Bravo to the closest platform, and I guess they assumed it highly unlikely that anyone could make a first-shot kill that long, at night. Well, April fool, motherfuckers—you should have known about my SpecWar Commandment on the subject of assuming.

And oh, yes, there was a significant fact about the dead tango in the commo shed that I guess I should pass on to you. The TIQ was blond. He had gray eyes rolled back in what was left of his skull. He had a Spetsnaz Afghanistan tattoo on his right shoulder.

That was significant. Belay that. It was a lot more than significant, especially in light of the secret mission I'd been given here in Azerbaijan.

You say you don't know anything about any secret mission? You say you thought I'd been sent here simply to teach counterterrorism to the Azeris. Well, you weren't cleared, you assholes—no one was, including, obviously, Ambassador Marybeth Madison. But since she's nowhere close, I guess I can explain, if you'll raise your right hands and swear you won't tell anybody.

Since this book began with one confession, I guess it's time for a second soulful, Roguish revelation. Here goes: my JCET mission to Baku was a cover for a more substantial and altogether clandestine assignment. I was sent here to appraise what the Pentagon calls the politico-military situation in Azerbaijan. I was to scope the place out, see which of the political alpha males had the best shot of becoming the china-shop bull in the new millennium, and try to target a few Azeri military types who the United States could count on in the future. See, we sometimes actually can and do learn from experience. When we had all those problems with the Serbs marauding in Kosovo back in 1999, the United States basically had to operate blind. The CIA had no agents on the ground in Kosovo, or any recruited from within the Serb military. The State Department had no accurate assessments of the Kosovar leaders. So, when the ethnic cleansing started in earnest and large gobs of *merde* hit the *ventilateur*, we were totally unprepared. We had no contingency plans, and so we fucked things up a lot more than we had to.

Why did things go from SNAFU to TARFU to FUBAR? Because the politicians running the show and the generals working for them all forgot (or more likely had never heard) the old Navy Chief's PRECEPT OF THE SEVEN Ps. Which goes: "Proper Previous Planning Prevents Piss Poor Performance."

That's really why I was in Baku: to make sure that all our Ps would be covered. That way, if things ever went sour here in the Caucasus, we'd understand the dynamics of the place—and have some idea about who to deal with. That was Part One of my assignment.

Part Two was to assess the degree of overt/covert Iranian and Russian meddling in Azeri affairs. Oh, we know that the Russians are working a two-pronged approach. They have been trying to undermine the Azeris for years by supporting the Armenians, and running provocative naval exercises in the Caspian Sea, while simultaneously engaging in joint ventures with the Azeri oil consortium. And we know that Iranians look at Azerbaijan the way Saddam Hussein looks at Kuwait, which is, as a province that needs to be recaptured. And to help make that dream a reality, they've been supporting fundamental Islam in the crescent surrounding Azerbaijan. But because we're going to have to make a final decision soon about how we ship all that Azeri oil to the West, there have been lots of questions lately about what the Ivans and the Mullahs are *really* up to in this part of the world, and no one seems to be answering them, at least answering them to SECDEF's satisfaction.

The CIA just shrugs and says, "We dunno." Well, it should

shrug. I checked with my best contact at Christians In Action, Jim Wink,[22] two weeks before I left for Baku. He rolled his eyes, groaned, and said that this administration's handling of intel matters couldn't have been worse if Russian or Chinese agents had actually been put in charge of the American intelligence apparatus—something he didn't consider completely out of the realm of possibility.

Oh, we still kept more or less abreast of the Ivan's overt moves. Like the S-300 ground-to-air missiles they deployed to Armenia last year. Or the fact that they upgraded the Russian air arm stationed in Yerevan from MiG-23s to MiG-29s. But as for their long-term goals, Wink told me—incredibly—Washington had nary a clue. "Sure, we know that the Russians want to expand their sphere of influence, ever since the Azeris canceled the bilateral defense agreement with Moscow back in ninety-nine," he said. "And so, we track the military stuff, and we try to follow who's doing what to whom. Same thing for Iran. We use overhead, and No Such Agency[23] sends me reams of intercepts. But it's getting almost impossible to find people on the ground who can report good, solid, inside information to us."

"You're not serious," I said.

He wagged his head to say, yes, he *was* serious, drained his Corona, looked at the bottle as if he was seriously considering sucking the lime out, then gave me a sad, Huckleberry Hound look.

As if Wink's information wasn't already depressing enough, the three monkeys I spoke to at the State Department (because of the libel laws I will refer to them as Seeno, Hearno, and Speakno) refused to admit there was any problem whatsoever in the Cau-

[22]No, his name's not really Jim Wink. If his name was Jim Wink, it wouldn't have an asterisk next to it in the index. Asterisks are reserved for pseudonyms.
[23]That's spook-talk for the National Security Agency.

casus. Seeno actually said, "So far as we know it's all hunky-dory over there." He really used those words.

And as for the rest of the Cabinet agencies, well, they didn't know fuck-all either. One twentysomething assistant secretary at Energy (and you have to go through Senate confirmation to become an assistant secretary, but of course this was the current Administration) had no idea where Azerbaijan even was. He thought it was somewhere in the Gulf States. "Isn't that next to Qatar, maybe—or is that Onan?"

Jerk-offs aside, how the hell you make policy when you are in an info-vacuum, I don't know, and I guess neither do SECDEF and the Chairman. Which is why, to get a little real-world input, they sent *moi* here to do what SEALs do best, e.g., sneak & peek and snoop & poop, without making even a tiny ripple as I did so. And when I'd finished with the sneaking and the snooping, I'd submit a full report to the Chairman, giving him a no-shitter sit-rep about WTF is going on here in Azerbaijan—who is doing what, and to whom, and why.

Let me add that General Crocker had been very specific about my ROEs. First, I was not to ruffle the embassy's feathers. I was to keep it smooth and quiet. Second, I was to tread very carefully when it came to Ivans. "Azerbaijan," he reminded me, "used to be a part of the Soviet Union, and despite the current situation the Russians still have very proprietary feelings about the place. Moreover, we are engaged in some very delicate political moves with Moscow right now and I do not want things to go awry." So, third, I was to watch, and to look, and to listen. But I was not to act. "This is an information-gathering mission, Dick," he reminded me. "Keep it that way."

There was something odd about the Chairman's orders. I'd never known him to shy away from a fight. And we both knew that the Azeris were being meddled with. But he wore all the stars, while all I wore were scars, and so I saluted, and said, "Aye, aye, sir," and meant every word of it.

But as we all know, situations change. And *since* my cover had been blown before we'd even wheels-downed, and *since* the embassy was already pissed, and *since* I'd managed to kill one Ivan and seven Iranians, and I hadn't even been in-country two days yet, all the Chairman's well-meaning ROEs had been shattered. I had the unsettling feeling that I'd probably have to muscle my way through the rest of this mission. Which of course meant I would not be as stealthy in the sneaking & peeking department as General Crocker might have liked (and was *that* ever an understatement).

But as all of us—even a Chairman of the Joint Chiefs of Staff— must realize, life doesn't always go according to the plan you've made. You want an example? Take Bosnia. Take Kosovo. Take Mogadishu. And, when plans don't work out, one has to adapt. My way of adapting is to become aggressive. Very, very aggressive.

So much for ruminations. Let's get on with the story. The fact that I'd just discovered a dead Ivan along with a bunch of Iranian tangos told me that the Russkies—at least some Russkies—were working alongside the mullahs. I went over his body with the proverbial fine tooth comb. He had a wad of notebook paper with Cyrillic writing on it in the pocket of his Russkie-issue utility blouse. I took the papers and shoved 'em in my fanny pack. I'd deal with whatever they were later.

Randy and I wrapped the Russian corpse in twenty yards of chain and dumped him over the blind side of the rig. I didn't want anyone—especially the Azeris—discovering him. The fact that there'd been a Russkie in this assault was going to be my little secret.

The other question mark I was left with, was who the Ivan had been talking to. He'd been using the rig's radio. It was tuned to the frequency used by the security detail at the American

Embassy. Why? Obviously, I didn't know. But my guess was that he was listening to the chatter to see how the embassy was reacting to the incident.

But he hadn't been broadcasting. Let me rephrase that. He hadn't been talking on the rig radio. I knew that because the microphone wasn't even plugged into the system. But he had been talking to someone. He'd been chatting on a Russian-made, latest generation cellular phone ripped off (the Russkies like to rip off American technology) from the Motorola Star Tac. In fact, he'd been in the middle of a conversation just as Rodent and Half Pint got close to him. Then, the s.o.b. must have heard something, because he grabbed his AK, and fired half a mag in their direction.

They waxed his ass *sans pitié*. But in doing so, they also shot the hell out of the little cell phone on which he'd been chatting. And, since the Star Tac knockoff was nothing but plastic shreds and wires right now, the phone number (and the party attached thereto) to whom he'd been speaking just prior to his untimely demise remained a mystery.

But if that single unanswered question was the only wrinkle to the night's events, I was ready to take "yes" for an answer and haul ass back to shore. The hostages were all alive and well. I had one destroyed Russkie cell phone, and a workable state-of-the-art Russkie scanner to add to my inventory of souvenirs to turn over to Tony Mercaldi at DIA when we got home. And aside from the usual minor dings, pings, and scratches, my guys and I had come through unscathed.

We towed the tangos' Zodiacs behind the tender. Just offshore of Glinyannyy Island (Ostrov Glinyannyy to those of you who speak Russkie), I asked the Azeri captain to full stop the engines. I scanned the shoreline with Hammer's long-range night vision. Yup—just as I thought. The whole goddam dock was brimming with people. There were TV lights and camera crews. There was a fucking three-car convoy of big Mercedes limos, each bearing magnetic signs on the rear doors showing the CenTex map-of-Texas-and-awl-rig-in-a-big-white-circle logo. At the end of the quay, bathed in halogen security lights, was a white Aérospatiale Dauphin-2 with civilian numbers and small American and Azeri flag emblems painted next to the cockpit.

WTF. I'd been told that there wasn't a goddam chopper capable of holding more than three people in the whole country. Listen, the Dauphin-2 can carry twenty-two shooters—even a couple more if they don't mind a little intimacy—for hundreds of miles. I wondered whose it was.

I'd find out, but later. For now, it was time to pull a disappearing act. I took my guys, and all of our equipment, dropped into the inflatables, and headed toward the shelter of the island, so that the Azeris could ferry the hostages the rest of the way to the quay at Alät.

Why, you ask, did I do that?

The answer is simple. First, I didn't want a repeat of the Mogadishu landings, where the fucking Marines were outnumbered by the fucking photo-dogs ten to one. Second, our job wasn't to look good on camera, or give chatty one-liners to the reporters on scene. Our job was to kill terrorists. Which is exactly what we'd done. Moreover, as you already know, while I'm not shy about taking credit for creating Warriors in my own image, I don't give a shit about puffing out my chest and looking good on the nightly news. That's not part of my job description.

So we stayed behind, and watched from the wings, as they say in the the-*ater*. And when I saw the TV lights go out, and the chopper lift off, and the motorcade of limos depart, we gunned the motors, and tally-ho'd toward the dock.

0614. I hoisted myself over the edge of the empty quay, received the line from Mustang, and made us fast to a heavy cleat. The sun wasn't even up yet, and it was already close to a hundred degrees.

"Captain Dickie—"

I turned at the sound of my name. A tall, mustached officer in a sweat-stained, dust-streaked uniform came around the corner of a two-story concrete warehouse, his arms outstretched to give me what my Cuban friends call *un gran abrazo*.

I was enveloped in an Azeri bear hug and the odor of stale tobacco and alcohol. I squeezed back. "Araz. Good to see you." Araz Kurbanov, the field-wise officer who'd helped me set up the hit on 16-Bravo, was the titular head of Azeri special forces. We both knew *that* was an oxymoron. The Azeris have no special forces—except on paper. That's why we'd been sent here: to give Araz's company-size unit some basic training, so they could operate in crisis mode and not get themselves—or the hostages they'd be trying to rescue—killed.

"God, you SEALs really do like all that touchie-feelie stuff, despite all the macho psychobabble you sell the public, don't you?"

I released Araz, stepped back, and turned toward the sound. A tall, lean, redheaded Jarhead major in well-worn green cammie BDUs and spit-shined boondockers, carrying a black ballistic nylon briefcase and a holstered sidearm on a lanyard stepped warily around a pile of dry donkey dung. "Out a little early, ain't we, Major Evans?"

"Hell, Captain Marcinko, I'm a diplomat—and dontcha know, we diplomats work the regulation United States Marine Corps twenty-four-hour day, twenty-four hours the day, seven days the week, three-hundred sixty-five days the year. We diplomats are very dedicated to our work."

The major smiled, brightening the dusty morning with her perfect teeth. "Besides, the ambassador ordered me to keep an eye on you people and make sure y'all stay out of trouble." She wrinkled her nose as she drew within arm's length of *moi*. "Geez, Dick, you're pretty ripe. Maybe I should do my watching through binoculars."

"Ripe? Hell—this is the real smell of battle. You've been living the soft life too long, Major. All those mess-dress dinners. Receptions. Cocktail parties. What you need is a good, long deployment to someplace like Lagos."

She shook her head. "Negatory, Dick. BTDT. Been there, done that."

Actually, there wasn't too much that Major Ashley Evans, USMC, hadn't done. She'd grown up in Tennessee, then gone to the U.S. Naval Academy, where she'd won a varsity letter in small-bore rifle. As a Marine intelligence specialist she'd come under fire in Somalia, Nigeria, and Sierra Leone; she'd survived a chopper crash in the mountains behind Split, Croatia. And she'd run interference for the plain-speaking, pocket rocket commandant of the Marine Corps as a congressional liaison. These days she worked for the Defense Intelligence Agency, as one of two assistant defense attachés here in Azerbaijan.

As such, she (like all attachés) came under the ambassador's chain of command. And the boss had ordered her to make sure I didn't commit AFR, which as y'all can probably gather, stands for Any Fucking Roguery.

But luckily for me—and for this book—Ashley Evans was imbued with the Warrior Spirit. She'd let me know that she was on our side as soon as we'd met back at the airport when I was still a sweet-smelling SEAL. She'd quietly gathered as much tactical intel as she was able to and passed it in my direction. She'd funneled telephone numbers, whispered answers to logistical questions, and made sure I knew that Araz Kurbanov was one of the few Good Guys I could count on out here in the Azeri hinterlands.

Within minutes of our first handshake, she'd also made sure I understood—with a series of nods, hitches of shoulder, and other miscellaneous body language—that any working relationship we might enjoy had to be clandestine in nature. I grasped her point instinctively. I know from personal experience (I may not seem the type, but I was actually a naval attaché once) that while attachés are detailed by the Defense Intelligence Agency, they work for the ambassador, and if an ambassador gets pissed off at an attaché, the attaché's work can become hard, even impossible to do. And while I didn't mind Ambassador Madison's looking to put *my* pigtail on a platter, it did me no good if she saw one of her staffers as a turncoat.

So much for what we in the literary profession call backstory. Let's get on with it. "What do you know, Ashley?"

"Not a hell of a lot. I drove down with Grogan. Geez, that was real hardship duty. If that sleazebag tries to grope me one more time, I'm going to break his fingers in six places."

We all watched as the second Zodiac tied up. Then Araz put two fingers in his mouth and whistled. Half a dozen soldiers, in uniforms even more sweat-stained and dusty than his, double-timed around the corner. The Azeri barked at them in his native tongue, and they set about helping my guys unload the boats.

He joined Ashley and me as we stood up close to the warehouse. "You missed the beeg three-rings circus show," he said in heavily accented English. "Big times show. CNN alive broadcast and the whole nineteen yards."

"We didn't need our faces all over the TV."

He shook his head in agreement. "I understand." He paused. "Besides, that *tolkatch da'ma'ak*[24] from the oil company. He was giving all the. . . ." There was another pause as he searched for the right word in English. "The . . . the in-ter-*views*, and taking authority for the whole things, and of course, the ambassador too." Araz spat through his thick, Stalinesque mustache onto the dusty concrete of the dock to show what he thought of Grogan's performance. "He is saying that if he had been allowed to do

---

[24]Russian slang for *fixer* and Azeri for *asshole*

things his way, through Sirzhik Foundation"—Araz spat once again, letting me know what he thought of that organization, too—"then all the how you say hostage takers they would have surrendered peacefully and no need for you for making such nasty violence."

Of course. It figured. Grogan was the type of executive who elbowed his subordinates out of the way to take credit for anything that went right, couldn't be found within miles when things went sour, and spent all his spare time second-guessing. I'm surprised he wasn't a retired four-star admiral instead of a retired FBI Special Agent in Charge.

"Whose chopper was that, Grogan's?" It would have been in character for him to stiff me.

The colonel's dark eyes scanned the pale sky, which was growing lighter by the minute, to the north. "Ah—the Dauphin," he said longingly. "*Pokh*[25]—I'd give my *Yaytz naprávo* for it," he said, tapping the right side of his fatigue-trouser crotch by way of simultaneous translation. Araz noted my smile, and the color on Ashley's cheeks. He withdrew a pack of cigarettes from the breast pocket of his uniform, tamped it on his palm, then pulled a half inch of a yellow-papered cigarette made of black tobacco out of the pack and offered it in my direction.

I faced my palms toward him. "*Нет спасибо*—no thanks."

He shrugged, took the cigarette out, placed it between his lips, lit it with a cheap butane lighter, inhaled deeply, and then exhaled dragonlike through his long nose. I noted the look of relief on Ashley's face when I didn't press for a quick answer to my question. But then, I knew perfectly well it would have been rude.

No, I haven't been here in Azerbaijan before. But it didn't take me more than a few minutes on the ground to understand that the culture here is more Middle East than European, and Middle

---

[25]Shit.

East is a mentality, a culture, a gestalt, that I understand as fundamentally as any Islamic fundamentalist. And so, one takes one's time in all things; one does not press one's hosts unnecessarily. One does not "step in front" and cut off a colonel. That's why Ashley, who knew all the answers to these questions, kept her diplomatic mouth shut, and was obviously gratified to see that I was doing the same.

More smoke. More wistful staring at the sky. "The Dauphin," Araz finally said, a longing tone to his voice. "It belongs to your ambassador Madison. She brought it with her from the United States."

Y'know, friends, it pisses me off when I discover that my life could have been made easier, not to mention less dangerous, if I'd been given an asset that was on hand.

Let me pause long enough right now to explain something about Warriordom. The Warrior does not look for death unnecessarily. He is not afraid to die, but he doesn't want to die without reason, or because of stupidity—his or anyone else's. And so, while danger and peril are both a part of the Warrior's life, the true Warrior will always look for ways to make his job less risky. The ambassador's chopper would have given me an alternative way in which to take the platform down. And it is always preferable to have alternatives—which add flexibility to an operation—than to be forced to use a single, rigid plan.

And so, from here on in, you will see that I'll be dealing with Ambassador Marybeth Madison carefully. I will treat her with the Roguish respect to which her rank entitles her, just as I will salute the president because he is the nation's commander in chief, even though I know that he is a lowlife, cowardly, draft-dodging, nipple-rolling, pussy-fingering, double-dealing, lying cocksucker (and those, as we all know, are a litany of Blow-Job Bill's best attributes).

Likewise, knowing that Madam Ambassador put the lives of my men at greater risk than necessary, I will still treat her with respect. But I will deal with her as if she were my enemy, not my ally. Full stop. End of story.

But now, it was time to get on with things. The hostages were safe, and we had training to do. "Araz," I said, "let's get the fuck back to Baku. I'm bone tired and the major here has already told me I stink. I'd like a hot shower and a cold beer—and not necessarily in that order." I didn't say what I was simultaneously thinking: that I wanted to get back to Baku to check out this Sirzhik organization, because it didn't sound very kosher to me. But that was for me to know, not Araz.

The Azeri looked at me strangely. I could see the translation forming in his mind's eye. Then he threw his head back and laughed, snorting cigarette smoke all the while. "Then we go— now," he roared. "I bring the trucks. We load. We go back to Baku. I hose you down. Then we drink much vodka, we eat grilled goat balls, then the rest of the goat, and then we drink much vodka some more."

He may not have been talking about Bombay Sapphire, but it still sounded good to me. "*Spaciba*—thank you," I said. Araz and his men watched as my guys sorted equipment, reloaded magazines, and put their gear in working order.

Not one unit in a hundred would do that so soon after coming through an op. But these were SEALs, and so their dedication was unmatched. They also knew that they were here in Azerbaijan as teachers—inculcators, who had to show by example that attention to detail, and a constant readiness, were a big part of what SpecOps is all about.

So, sure, they were exhausted. No doubt about it. But they also had the glow of accomplishment about them—the kind of can-do body language that told the Azeris there was nothing they couldn't do, even though they were bone weary, rung out, and overworked.

* * *

We were on the road by 0800, chugging at thirty-one kliks an hour (that's a whopping nineteen mph) in a trio of circa-1968 Czechoslovakian-invasion, Soviet Army surplus diesel two-bys. You've probably seen similar transport in all those Cold War–era documentaries on the History Channel. We're talking big, high, squared-off, ugly trucks with uncomfortable wood bench seats, drafty canvas tops, and no springs. I rode shotgun in the first truck. Major Evans sat in the middle. Araz drove, fighting the eight-speed, synchrosmash transmission and strength-sapping Stalinesque steering every fucking centimeter of the way. I thought about asking Ashley about the Sirzhik Foundation, but didn't want to do it in front of Araz. It wasn't that I didn't trust him, but I didn't know him well enough to allow him a hint of what I was thinking. That is the Warrior's Way: keep thy thoughts to thyself and thine enemies guessing.

We wound our way through the narrow streets of Alät, slaloming around the vegetable vendors with their donkey carts, and big-wheeled tractors pulling flatbeds filled with miscellaneous crap, and finally ground our way onto the main road headed north, a two-lane ribbon of concrete whose bullet-dinged road signs told me we were on the A-322, which paralleled the twin high-speed (okay—it was only relatively high-speed) electric-powered railroad line, running on a more or less north/south axis.

We hit Gobustan at 0935. I nudged Araz and pointed toward a small shed at the side of the road where a wrinkled old man in an embroidered skullcap was selling tea from a shiny samovar, and cakes from a brass tray. "Let's pull over and get something to drink."

Let me tell you something about Azerbaijan: it is hot here. Moreover, between the trucks (which were like ovens), and the dust (which was persistent), and the stench of raw petroleum (which was ever present), and the remorseless heat of the diesel engines, even I of the cast-iron constitution was queasy.

Araz nodded. He steered hard right rudder, hit the brakes, and we shuddered to a stop. I clambered down and stretched, relieved to ease the pressure on my spine.

1010. Back on the road. I let my head loll back against the hot metal of the cab and closed my eyes for a short combat nap. I hadn't even begun to relax when Ashley Evans smacked me in the chest. "Yo, Dick—reveille."

I shook myself awake and tried to get my bearings. I looked at my watch. It was almost 1100. "Where are we?"

"Near Sangachaly," Araz answered from behind a haze of thick, acrid cigarette smoke, as if the name would have meant something significant to me.

Ashley pointed east. "There—" She pointed ahead and off to the right, where heavy black smoke was coming from somewhere beyond the scrub-covered dunes that lay between the highway and the Caspian.

I gestured toward the plume of black smoke. "What's over there?"

"Old Russian airfield," Araz said. "Deserted now. Empty."

I scanned the road ahead of us. About half a klik away, I could see a detour sign had been set up on a wood post. The main road had been blocked off by a pair of heavy wood blockades, with the international road sign for "construction ahead" tacked to them. Burning flares were spiked into the black macadam of the highway. An arrow pointed to the right, directing traffic toward the sea. "I guess we take it."

"But that is the road to the airfield—not the way to Baku." Araz scratched his head. "It wasn't this way when we are driving to meet you, Captain Dickie."

"It wasn't like this when Grogan and I convoyed the limos down, either," Ashley said. "And that was two, three hours after Araz came through."

The little red warning light in my head—the one behind the

bullshit meter and next to the pussy detector—started blinking like crazy. The hair on the back of my neck stood straight up.

I wasn't about to drive blind down that fucking road. No way. "Pull over. We'll take a look before we do anything."

Araz's men removed the barricade and extinguished the flares. Then we hunkered down at the side of the highway while Araz drew a rough sketch of the airfield with a stick in the dusty shoulder of the road. He drew the highway we were on. Then the long runway, which ran parallel to it. Then the narrow, unpaved service road leading to the airfield, which resembled a capital L, with a single half kilometer approach from the south leading to the airfield. A second, slightly longer L-shaped road led to the airfield from the north.

I borrowed his stick and used it as a pointer.

As I spoke, Ashley provided simultaneous translation. "You go here"—I indicated the northern service road—"and head back toward the airfield. I'll work my way up the south road." I pointed toward the bottom of the L, where the northern road took a ninety-degree turn. "There's the point to be careful," I said.

Araz looked at Ashley and nodded. His finger traced the curve. "Bad ambush spot?" he asked.

Ashley and I nodded simultaneously. Then, she rattled thirty seconds of machine-gun Azeri, her hands speaking even faster than her voice. When she finished, Araz looked at his men. They all shook their heads in agreement and spoke to one another, expanding on Ashley's riff.

"What did you tell 'em?"

"I said it's much more effective to ambush on a curve than it is on a straightaway. First of all, you can employ two fields of fire. Second, I told them it's normal to slow down on a curve, which gives you more time to kill your enemies, so we have to be very careful as we approach that curve up there."

"Okay—then let's go to work already." Quickly, we unpacked

enough gear for a counterambush. Nod made sure our radios were working.

I looked at the force at my disposal. "Boomerang—take seven guys with you, and take all the Azeris, too."

Boomerang's long index finger pointed at Mustang, Butch, Goober, Hammer, Randy, Digger, and Nigel. "You dudes come with me."

"That means I'm going with him," Ashley said, her thumb jerked in Boomerang's direction. "Just in case we need some translation."

"Fine with me," I said.

"I'll need a weapon."

I unstrapped my tactical thigh holster with the USP 9, three extra mag pouches, and handed them over. "Go crazy," I said.

She withdrew the weapon, dropped the mag into her palm, ratcheted the slide back and extracted the chambered round, then secured the slide back and examined the pistol stem to stern with a practiced eye.

Happy with what she saw, she released the slide forward and listened to it as it shot home. She sighted, aligned, and dry-fired into the scrub alongside the road.

The USP passed muster. She locked the slide back, shoved the mag home, released the slide and chambered a round, then dropped the magazine, put the single round she'd first extracted back in it, slammed the mag northward once again, then attached the holster and mag holders to her web belt. When she was finished doing business, she smiled in my direction. "Nice piece. You have some trigger work done?"

It's always nice to work with a pro. "Good of you to notice."

She cracked a smile. "One thing—"

"Yo?"

"If I were you, I'd keep four of the Azeris here."

"Why?"

"To keep traffic moving on the road." She paused. "They like to rubberneck in this country."

"Good idea. You set it up."

"Aye, aye." She and Araz went back and forth in Azeri. He growled at a quartet of youngsters, who unslung their AKs and took up positions on the roadside.

The major gave the highway detail a once-over. "All taken care of."

Nu, what did she want, a fucking medal? "So what are you waiting for?"

I watched as Boomerang's detachment climbed into the first two trucks and headed north.

The rest of us hunkered down for about six minutes, taking cover alongside the road leading to the airfield, far enough off the A-322 to be out of sight. Then, when Boomerang radioed that he'd set up a security detail at the barricades they'd discovered at the north service road, and were in position, we moved off toward the coastline.

I led the way, staying off the service road so as not to raise any dust. We made our way through the rough bramble and thorn bushes of the dunes, moving slowly, our weapons ready. It wasn't hard to stay on track, because the heavy black smoke was hard to miss, no matter what our position was.

We covered the half klik in about fifteen minutes, making steady progress in the rough terrain. For most of it I could see the road below our position. Then, it disappeared, falling away and toward the sea, as we came up on a huge, long, ten-meter-high earthen berm.

I silent-signaled that I was going to take a look-see. Dropped flat. Crawled slowly up the berm, found a crenel that had been formed by erosion, and s-l-o-w-l-y eased my way up, and pushed my puss into the opening.

The old airstrip sat below me. It was deserted. I panned

left/right, right/left with my binoculars, examining the site intently. Nada. Zip. No one in sight. No signs of life at all. No ambushers—although they'd left ample evidence that they'd been around a short time ago. The concrete control tower complex, obviously destroyed by sappers, lay in ruins, its roof pancaked atop the collapsed walls. The runway itself had been blown up, too—cracked and cratered by demolitions. But that was old. Vegetation grew in the runway craters. Small, hardy wildflowers pushed their way through the destroyed terminal building, dotting the gray rubble with bright chrome yellow. Thorn bushes had taken root, too—and their bloodred buds stood out against the dark concrete and macadam.

Below me, I could see the ambush site. It had been a classic L-formation ambush. Textbook perfect. The targets—three 600 series Mercedes limos—had traveled along the L from left to right, approaching the old control tower and slowing down as they approached the ninety-degree turn.

That was when the ambushers had set off a series of Claymore mines and other explosives. I could read it like a fucking book. The first Mercedes had been disabled by an explosive charge that blew its front axle off. The rear limo had simultaneously been hit by a rocket-propelled grenade or a LAW, disabling it. With the trio of cars immobilized, the motorcade was subjected to a withering, lethal barrage of RPGs, LAWs, and automatic weapons fire. The occupants hadn't made it out—they'd been trapped in the big, bulletproof cars, which had been set afire by Willy-Peter[26] grenades—and incinerated. Flanking the three limos sat six other destroyed vehicles—two cars that once had been Peugeots, one ancient Renault station wagon, and three small Zil panel trucks. I could make out the charred corpses in some of them.

You know as well as I do what I was looking at. This was the

---

[26]White phosphorous.

motorcade carrying the same fucking hostages we'd rescued back to Baku. The other vehicles contained innocent bystanders who'd simply been in the wrong place at the wrong time.

There is something inherently cowardly about terrorism, friends, in that it purposefully targets innocent people. Believe me, I have no trouble killing. But the assholes I kill usually deserve it. And if I cause what's known in the warfare trade these days as "collateral damage," which means civilian casualties, that fact is not taken lightly by me, or my men. Now, I know all too well that you cannot make war without killing civilians. Often, lots of them die. That is war, and war is messy, nasty, bloody business.

But I do not kill civilians just to kill civilians—to terrorize. Terrorists kill blindly. I put terrorists, domestic or foreign, in a category with wife beaters, child molesters, and animal abusers. Anybody who beats women, rapes children, or abuses animals is a cockbreath pus-nutted pencil-dicked pussy-ass coward. Anyone who kills wantonly, who targets innocents without regard, is no better than the sort of human slime who rapes babies for fun. And don't give me any shit about mitigating factors. There are no mitigating factors. Terrorists are cowardly cunts who deserve to be killed—and it is my goal in life to kill as many of them as I can get my calloused hands on. Full stop. End of story.

I stood up and signaled my men that it was all clear, then got on the radio to Boomerang, gave him a sit-rep, and told him to make sure the north road was clear, then get his ass up to the airfield. I swept the place with my binoculars. The fucking tangos had left everything behind, as if they knew I'd eventually show up. It was their way of giving me the finger.

Fuck—we'd have to work carefully, because the bad guys had probably booby-trapped the site. Did I know that for sure? Of course not. But I wasn't about to risk losing anyone because I hadn't taken precautions.

* * *

1322. I made sure we'd gone over the location stem to stern ourselves before I let Araz alert the Azeri authorities, or Ashley call the embassy. Not that the bad guys had abandoned a lot of stuff when they'd exfiltrated. The tangos had come by sea—and they'd left the same way. I could see where they'd beached their three RIBs,[27] made their way up across the dunes, and set up positions alongside the service road. From the tracks, there had been a dozen, give or take one or two.

As for other evidence, there wasn't a lot. They'd left eight LAW tubes behind. I wrote down the lot numbers. They'd also expended a huge amount of ammunition—all of it 7.62 by 39, which is what is used in AKs. I took a handful of the brown, Chinese-made steel casings and dropped them in my pocket. They'd abandoned one unexploded Claymore, which Pick defused. It was a current-issue Russkie mine. I noted with some ironic amusement that it had been manufactured on the same day in November of 1995 that our commander in chief had received a blow job while he was on the phone lobbying a congressman to support military action in Bosnia. Yes, I do indeed keep trivia like that in my head. Don't you?

When Ashley called the embassy to report the carnage, she got put through to the ambassador's office. She reported what she'd seen, and described some of what we'd discovered. Then she stood, the phone to her ear, an ashen look on her face, as the ambassador obviously threw what is known in the diplomatic trade as a shit fit.

She finally turned the phone off and dropped it into her blouse pocket. "She's not very happy."

"I wouldn't be either."

Ashley scowled. "You don't understand. She's unhappy because she took credit on TV for rescuing people who are now dead. Now, if you want my best guess, she's going to try to blame all this"—she swept the area with her right arm—"on you."

---

[27]Rigid Inflatable Boats.

That would be par for the course, especially for political appointees like the Honorable Marybeth Madison. They get where they get because they have money, or influence, or maybe they've given a little head to the president (or one of his best friends). Congress goes along with their nominations, because that's the way Washington works—each branch of government greases the other branches of government. And the people— that's you and me—are the ones who really get screwed.

If you ask me, and no one ever has, ambassadors would be selected because they were professional diplomats who knew all about the place where they were going. They'd speak the language, and they'd make fucking well sure that they represented the United States, not their own narrow parochial political interests. No, I don't especially like or get along with the striped-suit, pocket change–jingling, heel-rocking, fudge-cutting crowd at the State Department. But they are better than most of the political appointees by a fucking mile. Why? Because even if they are bureaucrats, they are professional bureaucrats. And you can count on professional bureaucrats to act, well, like the apparatchiks they are. Which makes 'em easy to deal with, because I know what they will do, and how they will do it. With the Schedule Cs,[28] there's no telling how irrationally they'll act, which makes my life a lot more difficult, and accounts for much of the gray hair on my huge, Roguish balls.

Now, if I had been the ambassador, I'd be trying like hell right now to find out just how the fuck a bunch of tangos were able to divert and ambush a convoy of recently released hostages. How did they know the schedule? How did they infil? How did they exfil? Who tipped 'em off? Where did they launch from? And where did they go back to?

But so far as I knew, the Honorable Marybeth Madison, rich-

---

[28] A Schedule C official is a political appointee.

bitch Ambassador Extraordinary and Plenipotentiary, wasn't checking out any of the above questions. Instead, she was trying to figure out some way to pin the blame on *moi.*

Well, fuck her—let her try. I have big, wide, strong shoulders, and I've taken a shitload of blame in my time. So, whatever Madam Ambassador might try, there'd be nothing I haven't seen before—and very little I couldn't handle proactively.

Besides, I had more important things to do than worry about blame or political correctness. I wanted to know who these tango assholes were, where they'd come from, and most important, who'd put 'em into play. Multi-part operations like this one do not just happen. They are always a component part of a much larger and more complicated series of events.

Someone was developing an intricate, elaborate, and multilayered scenario here: a plan that had SpecWar Ivans (remember the blond corpse on the awl rig) and fundamentalist Iranians running joint terrorist ops. That fact alone could have serious national security implications for the United States. And me? I wanted to know who was involved, and where it was all going to end up. I'd need Ashley's help, too. When I took her aside and asked directly, she'd said she'd do whatever she could. But we couldn't communicate directly. Not without the ambassador finding out.

I thought about it. "You know an Air Farce bird colonel at DIA named Mercaldi?"

"Tony? Sure. He was my rabbi at spy school."

Good news. We could go through Merc. Ashley's head bobbed in the affirmative. "Works for me."

And so, we left three of Araz's Azeri gruntz at the airfield to watch the bodies, and six more to block the entrances of the service road. Then the rest of us climbed back onto those abominable Russkie trucks, and headed back to Baku.

Chapter

4

IT WAS JUST ABOUT 1600 WHEN ARAZ LED US INTO THE COOL MARBLE lobby of the Grand Europe Hotel, which was on the dusty airport road a couple of kliks northeast of Baku's old city. By then we were all beyond ripe. And any pretext of saving my clandestine mission got tossed completely out the window as we trooped through the thick glass doors. Why? Because as I recced the lobby I realized we'd walked into the middle of a fucking spy convention.

Over there—near port side—a pair of Turkish/Georgian/ Azeri/who-could-tell Mafiyosi muscle, pistol bulges under the armpits of their plaid zoot suit jackets, stood next to the souvenir kiosk, talking on cellular phones. Three stooges in boxy, ill-fitting KGB-model double-breasted suits tried to look inconspicuous, as if that was possible when they were jammed side by side on a single couch, legs crossed in triplicate, all reading identical newspapers. A local gumshoe idled by the reception desk looking like a bad imitation of Bogart, a maize-papered cigarette dangling from the side of his mouth. A Georgian pimp, hair slicked back like a 1930s flamenco dancer, herded half a dozen whores d'combat toward the neon sign entrance to the hotel bar which, according to the sign in the window, poured draft Bass Ale and served Cajun fried chicken.

So much for the multicultural local color. Then there were the half dozen spooks of various types scattered through the place, watching one another and everyone else. How did I know they were spooks? I knew because I've been in the business for a long, long time, and one develops a keen sense of whom is who. They had a certain look to them. They sent out vibes. Signals. So far as I was concerned, it was as if they'd had beacons implanted. I saw their reactions as we came through the doors, and I just knew that within half an hour, our arrival would be duly noted, logged, and registered with a dozen government agencies in a dozen countries, over a dozen time zones.

The spooks weren't the only ones putting out signals. I saw the expressions on the desk clerks' faces as we came through the door. One prim woman, hair in a tight bun, nose wrinkled in distaste, her blouse starched as stiff as an English upper lip, raised her palm in my direction schoolmarmlike and started to call out to us in language that was incomprehensible yet needed no translation. Quoth she: "Where the hell do you think you're going?"

But Araz paid no attention to her clerkish protests. He pulled up, dead center of the lobby, and indicated that everyone should drop his gear. Then, with Ashley and me following in his wake, he marched straight as a ramrod into the manager's office, dropped his AK on the man's desk, and started shouting orders.

According to Ashley, who speaks the local lingo, Araz and the manager were on a first name basis, which is to say he called the manager "Fazil," and the manager called him, "Colonel sir your excellency." Whatever Araz was telling the poor little guy, it brought an amused expression to Ashley's face. And about three minutes later, a horde of bellmen descended like Azeri locusts, and we were all whisked (relatively speaking; this *is* Baku after all) to the ninth floor and ushered into eight adjoining rooms.

Ashley headed back to her place to clean up. Araz went downstairs to the bar. And *moi*, I shed my piss-stained sweat-through ragged-ass wet suit and headed for the big stall shower in the big marble bathroom before Boomerang, who was sharing the room with me, had a chance to beat me to the hot water. Yeah, I always feed my men before I eat. And I always make sure they have something to drink before I get anything to slake my own thirst. But when it comes to hot showers, rank has its privileges—and it was my privilege to be a whole shitload more rank than Boomerang was.

While Boomerang scrubbed down, I threw on a pair of UDT swim trunks and went to work. I turned the radio on, loud, then called my old pal Tony Mercaldi at DIA on the secure CipherTac 2000 cellular and pulled him out of a meeting. I passed on the lot numbers from the explosives we'd found at the airfield ambush, asked for a sit-rep on the Sirzhik Foundation, whatever that was, then plugged the secure fax into the CipherTac's second line, sent him the six pages of Cyrillic notes I'd taken off the dead Ivan, and requested a translation ASAP.

Then I dialed up another asshole I've known for years, an old No Such Agency intel squirrel who's put his job on the line for me dozens of times. He's a former Marine O-4, and I call him Pepperman, because he grows hundred-thou Scoville-unit Thai peppers in the front yard of his huge Crofton, Maryland, estate.

"Yo, Pepperman, fuck you, you half load round-eyes."

There was a slight pause on the line. Then: "Oh, shit—I knew life was too good." Another pause. "How's it going, Dick?"

"Well, since you asked . . ." I gave him a thumbnail. I could just see him shaking his head as I spoke.

"Well," he finally said, "you didn't fuckin' call just to pass the time of day. You gotta want something. So you might as well tell me straight off."

What I wanted was a full court press. I wanted Pepperman to check NSA's computer tapes and tell me who the dead Ivan had been transmitting to, and what they'd said. I wanted blanket coverage of every fucking phone call going into, and coming out of, this part of the world from the day before yesterday, until further notice. And I wanted all that information, neatly sorted, categorized, ordered, and arranged, and then I wanted it delivered to me *RIGHT NOW*. I wanted the satellite routes changed. The tangos, I said, had come by boat—from the old CIA listening post at Astara, Iran. I wanted to know everything about their base. I wanted the fucking blueprints. I wanted so much laser-enhanced imagery that I could do a fucking pecker check on each and every one of 'em if I wanted to. And then, with up-to-date intel and computer-generated maps, I'd pay these cockbreaths a Roguish social call at zero dark hundred.

"Y'know what I like about you, Dick? It's that you're such an undemanding fuckin' soul," Pepperman said in his still-thick New Yawk accent. "Never ask for anything that'll make waves." There was a pause, and I could hear him slurp his ever-present cuppa cawfee. "I wasn't asked for this much info when we fuckin' bombed Usama Bin Laden in Afghanistan."

"That's because BJB[29] didn't want to kill anybody when they went after Usama baby. You know *me* better than that."

"That I do, boyo." He snickered and slurped. "Lemme gedonit. I'll call when I know something." The phone went dead.

Which was when, precisely on cue, the hotel telephone on the night table between the queen-size beds went *bring-bring*.

I turned off the radio and plucked up the receiver. "Marcinko."

"Velcome to Baku, *haver.*"

I knew that voice. I blinked twice—and came up empty. I

---

[29]SEALspeak for Blow-Job Bill, the Leader of the Free World.

blinked twice again. Still nada. Then the brain fart passed, and the mouth kicked in. "Avi, you sonofabitch, how the fuck are you and where the fuck are you?"

"I'm in the lobby. I'm coming up. B'bye, b'bye," he said by way of reply, and hung up his receiver. That was par for Avi. Israelis have never been partial to small talk, and Avi was all Israeli.

While he's on the elevator, let me introduce him to you. Avi Ben Gal and I met back in the mid-1980s, when he was a young captain working for AMAN,[30] the Israeli military intelligence organization. We were assigned to a joint mission in Syria, where we became friends and have been ever since. Last year, he was promoted to *tat aluf*, which is Hebrew for brigadier general. I flew to Tel Aviv for the ceremony. Belay that. I flew to Tel Aviv for the party he gave afterward. It went on for three days, during which time I had managed to have a short yet extremely mean- ingful relationship with a svelte, young, raven-haired Yemenite lieutenant from AMAN named Rahel. That's Israel for you: every day a holiday; every nite a Yemenite.

Anyway, Avi is the kind of operator I'm willing to put my back up against anytime, anyplace. He's short, and probably doesn't weigh in at more than 120 pounds. But he has the soul of an Old Testament Warrior, and the courage of a, well, an Israeli. There's no place he won't go, and nothing he won't do if the mission requires it. And that includes jumping out of planes, something he happens to hate. He speaks English, Span- ish, Russian, Arabic, Farsi, German, French, and Turkish in addition to his native *Hevrit*. And, oh, yes, he's married to one of the most beautiful women in the world, the beautiful Miriam, who towers over him like Sophia Loren towered over Carlo Ponti.

I'd tell you about how he won his three *Tzalashim*—the tiny

---

[30]AMAN is the acronym for Agaf Modiin, which translates out from the Hebrew as Intelligence Branch of the General Staff.

crossed daggers that are Israel's second highest military decoration, but I hear him rapping at the door and he's modest when it comes to talking about his own accomplishments.

I peered through the fish-eye to make sure who was knocking, then opened the door, pulled Avi inside, and grabbed him in a Rogue-size bear hug.

He hadn't changed much since I'd seen him last. Maybe a little bit grayer around the edges. But he was still the small-framed skinny *marink* I'd met in Lebanon more than a decade ago. He stepped back, looked me up and down, and before I could get a word in, said, "So, boychik, you've been here less than a day and your own ambassador is ready to deport you as persona non grata."

I shrugged. "I guess it's my natural charm at work."

Avi threw back his head and laughed. "Well, you can always seek asylum in Israel. We'd take you—after a small bit of surgery, of course."

I crossed my legs in mock horror. "I'll remember you said that if I ever want to defect." I headed toward the minibar. "You want something to drink?"

"Sure—a bottled water would be great." Avi tossed his thumb in the direction of the bathroom door. "Who's in the shower, Ambassador Madison?"

The mere thought sent shivers down my back. "Yech—I wouldn't touch her. Not even with *your* schwantz." I opened the minibar, found a half liter of Evian, tossed the plastic bottle at Avi, and gave him a thumbnail on Boomerang while he broke the seal and took a swig.

Then he set the bottle on a glass-top coffee table and got to the point. "So, Dick, what brings you to this neck of the woods?"

I gave him the cover story, but judging from the look on his face he didn't buy a single word of it.

Then it was my turn to pry. The last time we'd worked together, in Moscow,[31] Avi had been operating under political cover as an agricultural attaché. I asked what position he'd been given here in Azerbaijan.

"Things have changed," he said with a smile. "Here I am what I am: the defense attaché. I have a nice flat in one of the new high-rise apartment houses. I rate a car and a driver twenty-four hours a day. And best of all, since all the kids are out of the house and she gets diplomatic rates on El Al so she can go home and visit them whenever she wants, Mikki decided Israel could spare her for three years, and she joined me on this assignment."

I grinned. "Mazel tov. That is really great news."

"*Todah rabah*—thank you, and yes it is."

"How's the job, Avi?"

The diminutive Israeli shrugged. "It's a challenge. You probably know we have a close relationship with the Azeris. One nonstop El Al flight a week between Baku and Tel Aviv, even. Not to mention a security agreement, since you Americans won't help in that area. And we're helping them clean up the environmental mess the Soviets made for so many years."

Environmental mess? That was an understatement. I hadn't been here long, but I can tell you that Azerbaijan is an ecological disaster zone. For sixty years, the Soviets drilled for oil, and every bit of waste matter from the process, every noxious chemical they used, was left to drain into the Caspian Sea. Even the earth of Azerbaijan smells polluted. It stinks of rancid petroleum and chemicals. Tens of thousands of tons of broken Soviet equipment has been left to rust and disintegrate. Hundreds of square miles of Azeri territory is uninhabitable: a vast, barren, ravaged, desolate, toxic wasteland.

But Avi wasn't here to clean up oil spills, which is exactly what I told him.

---

[31]You can read about it in *Rogue Warrior: Designation Gold*.

85

He reached up, put his hands on my shoulders, and drew me toward him. "Right you are, boychik. But you're not here to teach Araz Kurbanov how to climb an oil rig, either," he whispered.

I shrugged Avi off and pointed toward the ceiling. I wasn't going to talk about anything like that in a place like this.

So I walked over to the TV and turned the set on. It took a while, but CNN International finally faded in.

Avi squinted at the screen, slapped a hand to his right cheek, and wagged his head to and fro. *"Oy, vay iss mir,"* he said in mock Yiddish, a mischievous grin on his round face, "it's Voolf Blee-tzair. He's vatchamacallit, you-*biq*-vit-us. We can't escape him—even here." Avi picked up the remote control and pressed the volume button, turning the sound way up. Then he beckoned me over to where he stood, silent-signaling me that the walls probably had big ears.

I nodded in agreement and motioned for him to turn the TV even higher. He complied. Then, with Voolf blitzing about the latest White House scandal, I gave him the sheaf of Russkie writing I'd taken from the corpse on the oil rig, he read the material quickly, a look of grave concern on his face as he did so, and then the two of us engaged in what could only be called a quiet, earnest, and totally honest conversation.

I could recount to you all of what we said. But I won't—it would take too long, and besides, the dweeb editor wants me to move on to the next action sequence. Suffice it to say that Avi and I agreed that we'd team up again. Why? Because our objectives weren't all that dissimilar. Avi, for example, was interested in making sure that however things in Azerbaijan ended up, Israel would be assured of getting a permanent source of Caspian Sea oil. That meant keeping both Russian and Iranian hands off the valves that controlled the pipelines. So far as I was concerned, that wasn't a bad idea at all.

He was also worried about the spread of weapons of mass

destruction, which the Russkies had a bad habit of selling to whoever had enough greenbacks. The thought of Russkie nukes, or chemical/biological weapons being sold to Iraq, Iran, or one of the tin-pot dictators in the Balkans was frightening to me, too.

And Avi was also worried about the bigger picture. Both the Iranians and Ivans were already working hard to destabilize the region. In the nine months he'd been in Baku, Avi said, more than a dozen political leaders, journalists, and businessmen had been assassinated. Four car bombs had killed scores of Azeris. The oil rig takeover, he told me, was just the latest in a nasty series of terrorist events. There had been a half dozen incursions from Iran, and twice that number from the Armenian separatist strongholds in western Azerbaijan. On a more personal level, six of Avi's best sources— which was his way of telling me he was running at least one network of agents—had been murdered in the last four months.

"And," he added, "I'm not the only one. I've got good reason to believe that the CIA's single net in the region had been rolled up, too."

I'd thought CIA was blind in Baku, but if Avi believed they'd had a net and it had been rolled, I was willing to believe him. Of course, if it *had* happened, there'd been absolutely no reporting on it, or even RUMINT. Because I'd gone around the system to get a no-shitter from my old friend Wink, and Wink hadn't said anything about agent nets being rolled up here in Baku.

But even without the loss of intelligence assets, it was obvious that the Azeris were being squeezed from two directions. And no one was doing anything about it.

In fact, according to some of Avi's remaining sources, the American Embassy, he said, wasn't reporting most of the incidents.

I asked if he knew why.

He shook his head. "I can give you vatchamacallit, RUMINT," he said.

"And?"

"Look," Avi said, "The ambassador is in the oil business. Oil is big money. If this region is known to be unstable, then the oil companies will not invest as much capital as they might do in a stable environment."

I nodded in agreement. Do you see what Avi's getting at? If not, allow me to give you a little geopolitical background that'll help you understand the dynamics of what's going on, and what's at stake. First, you should understand that the entire Caspian region is basically Muslim. It was in Avi's interest, and ours, too, to make sure that the Muslims in Azerbaijan, Tajikistan, Uzbekistan, and Kazakstan (all of them potentially as oil-rich as any Gulf emirate) maintained balanced, even cordial relations with the West, so that all their oil and natural gas could be piped westward and used in Europe and the United States.

The Iranians, however, saw the Caspian region as an extension of their brand of fundamentalist Islam. To Iran, the vast Caspian petroleum reserves were a political fulcrum to be used against the West. And so, Avi said, Tehran had engaged in a systematic program of espionage, subversion, and intimidation to keep the Caspian region Muslims in line. On the overt side were the editorials in Tehran newspapers. Avi pulled a photocopy of a news clip complete with yellow highlighting out of his briefcase. "Look at this leader[32] from the *Kayhan International*."

I did—and guess what? It was all very Farsi-cal to me.

Avi, who speaks fluent Iranian, did the honors. " *'It is not in Baku's best interests',*" he read, his finger moving along the highlighted type, " *'to annoy its giant southern neighbor. Iran is not willing to see any foreign powers stationed along its borders.'* "

That was the Iranian point of view. Here is the other: the Russkies still consider the whole Caspian region as a part

---

[32]"Leaders" are how many Europeans and Middle Easterners refer to editorials.

of a Greater—and decidedly non-Islamic—Russia. They have worked diligently for the past half decade or so to keep the former Soviet republics destabilized, and out of the Iranian camp, by using various surrogates to wage guerrilla war on the indigenous populations.

Evidence? You want evidence? Well, the papers I'd just shown Avi, all that Russian ordnance left at the ambush site, and the state-of-the-art Russian communication devices used by the tangos were all pretty strong evidence of Russkie involvement. Avi agreed. The circumstantial evidence, he said, indicated that the Ivans were helping to equip and train a force of Iranian irregulars, who would be used to harass the Azeris from the south, while Russian-supported Armenian nationalists attacked from the west.

The fact that the Russians and the Iranians were working together was confusing to me at first glance. Because it appeared—on the surface at least—that Tehran and Moscow had very different objectives for the region, and no reason at all to cooperate with each other. But, my friends, what appears on the surface is usually not the real story. The Russians have historically appeared to do one thing when in fact they are doing just the opposite. So, while they might appear to be helping the Iranians, I realized that they were in fact probably operating in their own narrow national interest.

And what was that national interest? To be succinct, it was the two hundred billion—that's right, *billion*—barrels of oil and uncounted cubic tons of natural gas that lay buried beneath the surface of the Caspian. Those oil and gas reserves and the trillions of dollars they would generate, the Russians understood, would re-establish the former Soviet Union as a strategic player on the world stage. Historically, we know that the Soviets allied themselves with many of their enemies, from Hitler's Germany, to Iraq, Iran, and even China, if it was deemed politically advantageous to do so. Well, I had no doubt that what tactics Russkies have followed in the past, they would repeat now.

And right in the middle of all this, Avi volunteered, was the Sirzhik Foundation.

My nose must have twitched, because he took notice. "You've heard of Sirzhik?" he asked.

"Grogan wanted to use it as an intermediary."

Avi nodded. "That makes sense," he said, "knowing Grogan."

I looked at him. "Spill, Avi—what's this fucking thing all about?"

"Ah," he said, "Sirzhik is ver-r-r-y interesting, Dick. Very interesting indeed." He explained that the foundation had its fingers in almost every pot from Moscow to Baku. Officially, Sirzhik was an NGO (NonGovernmental Organization) headquartered in New York, in the old Whitney mansion on upper Fifth Avenue. From there, as well as from its network of offices in Washington, London, Paris, Moscow, Prague, T'bilisi, Baku, and Yerevan, Sirzhik's CEO, Steve Sarkesian, bankrolled economic and social development all across the former Soviet Union and Warsaw Pact.

"Sarkesian? The guy I'm always reading about in the financial pages?"

"*Biduk*—precisely."

That added a new wrinkle. Steve Sarkesian was a rich s.o.b. who'd made his money who-knows-how. All I knew was what I read, and what I read was that the newspapers referred to him as a Washington power player of the liberal persuasion, although it was always pointed out that he had friends in high places in both political parties. He was always writing op-ed pieces in the *Wall Street Journal* and *New York Times* about economic affairs, usually slamming the free market. Well, that's liberals for you. They support school busing but they send their own kids to private schools; they oppose investing any Social Security money in the stock market, but investments are how they fund their own retirement plans. They set up offshore corporations to escape the tax laws and other financial controls, then hire some ghostwriter to put together a series of op-ed pieces for them demanding market controls and higher taxes.

But Avi didn't give a shit about Sarkesian's politics. It was his friends that disturbed the Israeli. Unofficially, so far as Avi was concerned, Sirzhik was a money-laundering organization that had ties to organized crime all over the globe.

"Can you prove it?"

"No," the diminutive Israeli answered matter of factly. "But that's what my instincts tell me."

Avi's instincts were good. They'd kept him alive all these years, operating in hostile environments. And the thought of a nonprofit foundation serving as a conduit for laundering money was fascinating—and had real possibilities. But without proof . . .

The Israeli broke into my train of thought. Forget about Sirzhik right now, he was saying. We have more immediate things to deal with.

And we did. Like the fact that my arrival hadn't gone unnoticed. I hadn't been here for two full days yet and already Avi's networks had picked up ripples. The Russkies and their surrogates were working overtime, gearing up for something. Mafiya goons were coming in from T'bilisi and points west. The Iranians were also on the move, although their progress was much harder to track than the Ivans

Given the time factors and the inevitability that sooner or later (and sooner was obviously more distinct a possibility than later), some nasty miscreant would try his hardest to wax my ass, Avi wondered aloud how we should deal with this potentially dangerous situation. My answer was Keep It Simple Stupid. We would go proactive. We would take the initiative. We would kill them before they killed us. And by so doing, WE WOULD NOT FAIL.

Let me give you the Rogue's First Rule of Engagement: WHEN YOU ARE ATTACKED BY EIGHT BOGEYS, THE ONLY QUESTION TO ASK IS, "WHICH ONE DO I KILL FIRST?"

The tangos who'd attacked the oil rig and ambushed the hostages had staged the raid from northern Iran. Even now, Pepperman was working on finding out where they'd come from. I suggested that once we discovered that location, we go and pay the bad guys a visit on their home turf. That would send the proper sort of message to Tehran—and the Iranians would back off for a while.

Then, we'd go after the Armenian separatists who'd been killing foreign targets—and send a similar cease-and-desist message to Moscow. We'd hit 'em both on their home turf. Hit 'em hard and mercilessly.

"You want to *hock* everybody's *choiniks*," Avi said, using the Yiddish phrase for rattling teacups.

"You got it. We hit 'em as a way of saying 'Fuck you—strong message follows.' Then we watch. We see who blinks. Who reacts. We watch how they play. And then we kick it up a couple of notches. We work our way up the chain of command, and when we get to the top, we cut the head off."

From the look on Avi's face, he liked the idea. "I can work on getting tactical intel through my channels," Avi said. "But frankly, Dick, from what I've seen, your embassy would never allow what you're suggesting."

I wriggled my eyebrows in a more than passable imitation of Groucho Marx. "My embassy? Who said anything about telling anybody at my embassy?"

Chapter

5

"DECEPTION," THE GREAT CHINESE WARRIOR GENERAL TAI LI'ANG once wrote, "is the key to all warfare." And, since I always take General Tai's lessons to heart, I wasted no time setting up a series of deceptive ruses that would mislead my enemies.

First, I used the hotel telephone to call the embassy's RSO—that's the Regional Security Officer—and asked for a one-on-one briefing the following morning at 1000 hours. That would give whoever was in charge of keeping track of me lots of time to set up a surveillance. Then, I dialed Araz Kurbanov. I explained that we'd begin his training the next morning at 0600, and that the course would run two weeks in length, seven days a week. I said that while I would be around to oversee the instruction, Master Chief Rotten Randy Michaels would be in actual charge of the day-to-day inculcation.

That done, I summoned my most senior people, Boomerang, Randy, Pick, Half Pint, and Duck Foot, to give them their instructions. We communicated on paper, and with sign language, with both the TV and the radio going full-tilt boogie. By the end of our fifteen-minute conversation, my squad chiefs understood exactly what I needed them to do.

For two weeks, from 0600 until 2000 hours every day, the Azeris would be run through an exhausting, concentrated tactical team-building course that would give them the rudiments of SpecWar—everything from dynamic entry and CQC, to tracking, setting ambushes, and basic EOD work with improvised explosive devices. They'd learn maritime operations, airborne assault, and survival skills. And while they were learning, we'd be watching. That way, when we got back to Washington, Rotten Randy would be able to put together an operations manual about how the Azeri special forces worked. So that if we ever had to operate against 'em, we'd know how they waged war. That, friends, is what the JCET program is REALLY about.

And while the training was going on, Avi and I, with the help of Boomerang, Duck Foot, Gator, and Nod, would v-e-r-y quietly set up two separate covert strikes. One in Iran, and the other in Armenia.

How would we do that? By taking a lesson from my own experience. We would use the Azeri training as cover for our own very covert, and deadly, operations.

Now, the truth can finally be told about how I was able to run more than two dozen successful covert counterterrorist ops when I commanded the infamous Red Cell at the behest of legendary Admiral James "Ace" Lyons.

Red Cell's mission, on paper at least, was to conduct FXs—field exercises—at naval installations worldwide. The exercises were designed to raise the Navy's overall consciousness about terrorist infiltration and hostage-taking techniques. Red Cell operators, most of whom were in fact experienced shooters from SEAL Team Six, would surveil Navy installations. Then they would conduct mock terrorist attacks, exploiting the weaknesses they'd discovered, and illustrating for the on-site security personnel how those weaknesses could be modified and the targets hardened, making life for any real tangos much more difficult and costly.

In truth, however, Admiral "Ace" Lyons had designed Red Cell as a cover op. Oh, we ran our FXs all right—my men terrorized dozens of one-, two-, three-, and four-star admirals with lots of scrambled eggs on their hat brims (not to mention lots of shit for their brains). And I'm proud to say that we taught an entire generation of sailors how to become sensitized to terrorism and guard against it.

But that wasn't our *real* mission. Our *real* mission was to kill terrorists. And so, virtually every time we conducted an exercise, both here in the United States and abroad, I would disappear for a short time and lead a small nucleus of shooters in a well-coordinated and totally covert hit against real tangos. If we'd ever fucked up, it would have meant the end of Ace's career (mine was already in the toilet). But Ace didn't care. To him, ridding the world of a few dozen world-class bad guys was worth the risk of a court-martial.

You want examples. Okay. When we tested the security at the Groton, Connecticut, nuclear sub base, my real target was a certain sailor who was selling secrets about our sub cruise schedules to the Soviets. According to the New London, Connecticut, newspapers, he fell into the water, hit his head, and drowned, poor guy. *Sure* he did. I was delighted: we pulled off such a clean hit that the Sovs never realized I'd neutralized one of their best sources. I was less concerned about leaving a mess in the Philippines, where Red Cell spent three weeks at Subic Bay. In fact (and on videotape!), we actually took an aircraft carrier out of action by proving that terrorists could ram its unguarded flank with a speedboat filled with high explosives, rendering it unseaworthy. Another of my Red Cell units took two hundred officers and men prisoners at the base's O-Club. We kidnapped dependents at the McDonald's. We "blew up" a radio tower and shut down all the base communications networks for eight hours.

And while all that confusion was taking place, much of it simultaneously and a lot of it covered by the local press, three of my best operators and I dropped out of sight for twelve hours and made our way into the slums of Manila. There, operating in mufti, and sans any backup, we tracked down the five leaders of the Alex Boncayao Brigade, the main assassination squad for the New People's Army, which is the military wing of the Communist Party of the Philippines.

Three months previously, a sparrow team[33] from the ABB had murdered U.S. Army Colonel Jim Rowe. I'd known Jim since Christ was a mess cook. He was a real hero, a combat-seasoned Warrior; a man committed to the ideals of democracy and freedom. Jim was one of very few Americans who'd actually escaped from a VC prison camp during the Vietnam War. He could have retired. He didn't. Instead, he volunteered for duty in the Philippines. His reward? Two hitmen from the ABB assassinated him as he left his job one day.

But fortunately (if there can be a fortunate aspect of this incident), his murder took place when George Bush was president. George Herbert Walker Bush may have looked like a WASP banker. But believe me, the man had balls of U-235. The day he was told that Jim had been murdered, he personally called Ace Lyons and told him, "Ace, this cannot stand. You deal with it."

So, Ace ordered me to set up an FX at Subic Bay. My prep time was ninety days—barely enough to develop the kind of tactical intel necessary to pull off a hit in absolute stealth.[34] We carried all

---

[33]That's how the ABB designated its assassination squads.

[34]Hits like this one cannot be accomplished on the spur of the moment. You want evidence? Okay. When the Israelis went after a notorious Hamas capo named Haled Mesha'al in Amman, Jordan, back in 1996, Mossad put the mission together too quickly. The intel was faulty. The team didn't stake out the subject long enough to track how he moved, and who went with him. They didn't work long enough on their extraction routes, or war-game the Murphy factors. The unhappy result was that the Mossad assassins were chased by Haled's bodyguards, waylaid, and captured by the Jordanians, causing the Israelis a profound political problem with their one true friend in the Arab world, the late King Hussein. As is usual in these sorts of fuckups, the top people in Mossad's ops division, who'd allowed this travesty of an operation to go forward despite the fact that they were putting their own officers' lives at risk, kept their jobs.

our equipment in specially built Red Cell Conex boxes, which had secret compartments that allowed us to carry sanitized weapons, ordnance, and other specialized killing equipment.

My intel—and great intel it was, too—was developed by my old shipmate Tony Mercaldi, who was one of maybe three people in the world who knew what Red Cell was really about. And Tony always came through.

He certainly did in Manila. It took him sixty-eight days of working without creating a single ripple to do it, but he was finally able to identify the safe house where the ABB leadership met once a month. We hit it. And yeah, we killed them all. Messily. With what the Hollywood writer-assholes call "extreme prejudice." Then we decapitated the corpses and left the tangos propped up against the wall, holding their own heads in their lifeless hands as a sign to their comrades that we Yankees were serious fuckin' dudes. Then we hauled our butts back to Subic, in plenty of time for me to get a new asshole reamed by the pussy-ass can't-cunt sit-down-to-make-wee-wee four-star who thought my Red Cell "tangos" had played too rough with his poor sailors. If he'd only known.

Here and now, I would run a similar game in Azerbaijan. Since my stealth arrival had been blown, I'd use the JCET mission to provide cover for us. And Araz's troops would be our unwitting camouflage. We'd schedule our JCET exercises in the border areas we would be using to stage our real-world hits. The Azeris would proposition equipment for their training—and we'd use much of it ourselves. Sure, it would be complicated. And if Araz was as smart as I believed him to be, he might get a little suspicious. But he wouldn't be able to prove anything and neither would anyone else.

Of course, the schedule I was designing meant precious little sleep for me and my band of shoot-and-looters. But then, you don't become a SEAL for the light schedule and the ease of operations.

* * *

97

Bright and early, I detailed Boomerang, Randy Michaels, Nod, Half Pint, Pick, Mustang, and Goober to meet with Araz and begin preliminary work with his troops. While they did that, I sent Rodent, Gator, Butch, Nigel, Digger, Timex, Duck Foot, and Hammer to recce the city. I wanted to see who was following whom. My boys were good street operators. And because I allow 'em to look like your everyday dirtbag, they looked no different from the thousands of expatriate Brits and Americans, Frenchies, Italians, Norwegians, and Turks who'd come here to work the oil fields and make a bundle of tax-free cash. And me? I used my first twenty-four hours to gather intel in the Iranian/Russkie alliance.

I didn't have to worry about the Armenian angle. Avi already had the goods on everything going on in that AO.[35]

How come? It's because the Israelis are tight with the Turks as well as the Azeris. Turkish pilots train in Israel. So do elite Turkish troops. And as you probably know (if you don't, you should pay more attention in your geography classes), Yerevan, the Armenian capital city, is no more than twenty kliks from the Turkish border and just about sixty miles due north of the place the Turks call Büyükagri Dagi, and we call Mount Ararat, where Noah's Ark is supposed to have landed after the Flood. That area, close both to Armenia and Iran, is where the Israelis have established half a dozen listening posts, where they suck TECHINT, SIGINT, and ELINT[36] out of the air. Moreover, using small, virtually undetectable sixth-generation Kevlar-skinned UAVs (Unmanned Aerial Vehicles) outfitted with FLIR (Forward-Looking InfraRed) and high-resolution television lenses, they regularly reconnoiter a two-hundred-mile radial arc that stretches from the Armenian enclave of Mountainous Karabakh, to the Iranian city of Khoy.

---

[35]Area of Operations.
[36]TECHnical INTelligence, SIGnals INTelligence, and ELectronics INTelligence.

See, unlike us, the Israelis don't give a shit about violating Armenian or Iranian sovereignty. They need information—and they are willing to do what they have to do to get it. Without good intelligence, they could be overrun; their country destroyed before they could react. And so, they operate proactively in their own national interest. In fact, they sometimes piss us off mightily, because from time to time, the Israeli national interest has nothing whatsoever to do with the United States' national interest, and the United States comes up holding the short end of the stick. We tend to think of the other guy in situations like that. The Israelis don't. If it comes to a question of us or them, they will take them—and I can't blame 'em. In fact, we could learn a few lessons about acting like WARRIORS, instead of pussies, from the Israelis if you ask me.

But this wasn't the time for one of my sermons about how the politicians and the bureaucrats make messy pudding out of national policy. It was time to get some intel on the Iranian tangos. And let me tell you, I owe my pals Pepperman and Mercaldi big time. You already know that the FA[37] tangos we'd waxed on the oil rig had been based at the old CIA listening post at Astara.

Well, Pepperman risked his job and faxed me some interesting imagery. From the look of things, there had been a Spetsnaz Alpha Group training mission on site. How could I tell? I could tell because they'd set up the obstacle course, the kill houses, and the sniping ranges in the very same pattern I'd seen during the Cold War when I pored over satellite imagery of Spetsnaz training facilities in the Soviet Union. Just to be certain, I secure-faxed the images back to Tony Merc at DIA.

Merc called me on the secure phone not sixty seconds after the fax had been transmitted. "Holy shit," quoth he, "why the fuck hasn't anybody sent this stuff over here before?"

---

[37]Fist of Allah.

A good question. Why hadn't this significant development become apparent to our army of qualified analysts at Langley, Fort Meade, and Bolling Air Force Base? The answer is that those analysts were never given the imagery in the first place. The administration's orders were that satellite imagery was to be concentrated on monitoring the tense situation in India and Pakistan (where they have not a single HUMINT source), keeping tabs on the North Korean nuclear program (ditto), watching drug growers in South America (ditto, because the CIA has been forbidden to utilize agents who may have committed any crimes), and using our 2.3-million-bucks-a-day-to-keep-'em-in-orbit surveillance devices to help keep the peace in Northern fucking Ireland, where the political situation has, of late, turned into the proverbial goatfuck.

Now, you know and I know that using a multi–billion-dollar Lacrosse satellite to monitor the situation in Northern Ireland is a total waste of money. We'd be better off if the CIA had half a dozen agents in IRA splinter groups and Protestant paramilitaries. But that might mean recruiting someone who has, at one point in their lives, done something naughty. And the zero-defect CIA wants only the purest of the pure as agents these days. Maybe they could recruit a bunch of two-year-olds. But BJB wants to show his Brit pals how "committed" we are to the Good Friday peace agreement. And so we spent twelve billion dollars last year flying a bird over Belfast. Then there's the pair of Keyhole-13s we have sitting twenty-two thousand miles above Colombia and Peru. Guess what—the twelve billion bucks they cost us don't mean that we allow one gram less of cocaine into the United States.

"Those birds are nothing but political priorities," is how Pepperman put it. "The administration cut our budget by forty percent over the past six years. Now we're being told we gotta give 'em only what they ask for an' no more, or we get cut back some more. It's like they don' wanna know nuthin' about nuthin'."

Kinda makes you want to puke, doesn't it? So far as I am concerned, it's almost as if our intelligence-gathering agencies are being misdirected on purpose. It's almost as if our foreign policy is being directed by agents of our adversaries.

Which is not out of the question. You already know about all those Chinese campaign donations to Clinton and Gore. You already know that Chinese military officials were given access to the White House and its secrets. You already know that hundreds of thousands of dollars were donated to the 1996 Clinton/Gore campaign by quiet emissaries of the Colombian drug cartels. You don't? Then you should start reading the newspapers. Because there's more: agents of other foreign countries, from Thailand to Lebanon, realized early on that they could buy access and influence to the highest levels of the United States government simply by putting large amounts of what's known in politics as "soft money" into organizations that then channeled the funds into Clinton/Gore coffers. Shit, many of my friends in the intelligence community believe that the whole Monica Lewinsky mess was brought about to distract the country from the real damage being done, i.e., the subversion, the leaks of TECHINT, and other traitorous acts allowed by this administration.

So I had good reason to believe that attention was being drawn away from this area of the world on purpose. Could I prove it? Not yet—but if you know me, you know that I will ultimately ferret out the traitors, then kill 'em.

But first things first. I'd scheduled a meeting with the RSO for 1000 hours to discuss the general situation, and get his read on the local players.

At 0730, said RSO called and cancelled the meet. He was apologetic. He was sheepish. I knew from the way he danced around the subject that he'd been ordered not to see me.

So, to make absolutely sure I'd read the situation correctly, I suggested we meet for a quiet, private drink at the Filarmoni

Club, a seafood joint on the corner of Milari Gashai Prospekt (that's the Russkie word for *avenue*) and Nizami Street, after he got off from work.

There was a long, and very awkward pause, which I allowed to go on, and on, and on, at his end of the line. Then he said, "I'm real sorry, Captain, no can do." There was another pause equally as painful. Finally, he sort of whispered: "Look, Dick, it's just impossible. We can't do any business. That's just the way it has to be. Sorry." And he hung up.

Message received. Loud and clear. And so, it was time for Plan B. I made contact with Ashley Evans on the secure cell phone, by working through Tony Mercaldi, who just loved playing "telephone" at zero dark hundred Washington time, and asked for a meeting, ASAP.

By 0820, we'd made our arrangements. For obvious reasons, we both needed to keep our rendezvous private. And so, after checking for static surveillance outside her flat and finding none, Ashley had suggested I come over to the apartment she occupied on the fourth floor of what Merc described as a five-story rococo, 1920s apartment house on Evendiyev Street, about a fifteen-minute walk south and east of the embassy compound on upper Azadiyg Avenue, and a twenty-minute ride through Baku traffic from the Grand Europe Hotel, where I was staying.

But I knew my trip to Ashley's would take a lot longer than twenty minutes. Before we could meet I'd have to deal with whoever the fuck was surveiling me.

Surveiling? You bet. You already know my room is bugged. And my guys had already alerted me to the fact that there were surveillance teams, countersurveillance teams, and counter-countersurveillance teams outside the Grand Europe Hotel. A CNN producer was lurking in the lobby. A *Washington Post* reporter was sniffing around. The word was obviously out. I had two questions. First, who'd leaked information about JCET to the press, and second, who was doing the watching: Russkies, Iranians, spies from Ambassador Madison's office—or all of the above.

I slipped on my HK P7-M13, adjusted the inside waistband holster to just where I wanted it, and dropped two extra thirteen-round mags into the left-hand back pocket of my jeans. Then I pulled on my photographer's vest,[38] took my cellular phone and a few other goodies, and decided to find out.

First, let me give you a little geography lesson. The city of Baku sits on the southern rim of the Apsheronskiy peninsula, which juts out into the Caspian. The peninsula itself looks like a short arm, and Baku's downtown is in the armpit position, which is appropriate enough, given the constant stink of petroleum, sweat, and dirt in the always dusty air. The city itself is an eclectic mix of architecture. There's old Azerbaijan: the mosques, and the sorts of two-, three-, and four-story houses with louvered windows and marble floors that are common from Damascus to Kabul. There are scores of ornate palaces and hotels from the days of the 1920s' oil boom, most of which have deteriorated over the years. There are the boxy relics of the Soviet Union: massive, ugly fortresslike apartment blocs and office complexes. And there are the spanking new glass and steel towers of the post-Soviet era, evidence of the new capitalism that has made millionaires of the hundreds of Azeris who know how to get things done—what the late and unlamented Roscoe Grogan would call expediting—in this rapidly metamorphosing society.

I came out of the hotel, pressed a five-dollar bill into the doorman's hand, elbowed a proper businessman in a three-

---

[38]The photographer's vest is a wonderful garment. It hangs low enough to hide most weapons from sight. It has eleven pockets into which all sorts of goodies can go. And because my vest was custom built by my friends at the CIA's Technical Services Division, it has inside pockets that can hold Class III-A ceramic armor plates, although I wasn't wearing any ceramic plates today.

piece striped seersucker suit, straw boater, and two-toned shoes out of the way, and jumped into his waiting taxi. "Hyatt, *pazhalstuh.*"

The driver swiveled, looked me over, rubbed his left forefinger back and forth over a thick, handlebar mustache in which the remnants of a recent meal could be discerned, then grunted, *"Da."* Then we both went to work. He eased his old Peugeot station wagon into gear, or a reasonable facsimile thereof, and sputtered down the driveway, while I scanned the area for hostiles. And it didn't take long to find 'em. A Mercedes coupe with two round-faced, heavyset men inside pulled away from the curb on the opposite side of the road, U-turned, and swung into the knotty traffic flow half a dozen cars behind us.

Mark one.

The next pair of hostiles was just as easy to spot. The driver was a kid with long, slicked-down hair pulled back from a face so pockmarked it looked like the fucking Sea of Tranquility, wearing wraparound Oakley knockoffs and sitting astride a big Kawasaki at the end of the hotel driveway. Either he was wearing a black radio earpiece, or he had the worst case of ear wax known to medical history. I double-checked the Mercedes, looking closely. Yup: Moonface took directions from the goon riding shotgun in the Mercedes, who was talking into a small transceiver.

Moonface kick-started the bike, and veered into traffic, weaving in and out as he maneuvered close to me. His armed passenger held on to a strap with his left hand, like a practiced bronco rider. Moonface's rice rocket was quickly followed by a second greaser wannabe, a kid in a UCLA tank top and black Levi's knockoffs, who was riding a dinged, black BMW 750 that needed a lot of muffler work.

How did I know the passenger on the rice rocket was armed? I knew it because he was wearing a three-quarter-length leather coat, zipped up to his throat. You do not dress like that in hundred degree-plus weather unless you are carrying your own brand of heat.

Now, as we embark on this sequence, allow me to tell you a few things about surveillance, my friends. Surveillance is a tough job. The best surveillance crews in the world are from British, Frog, and Israeli units. The Brits have a bunch of operators (the unit was formerly known as 14 Intelligence Company[39]), which made its bones working Northern Ireland. Unlike most other surveillance units, the folks at ███████████ are shooters as well as sneak & peekers. They were able to put a dozen people on an IRA bomb maker while she was working an SDR, or surveillance detection route, without her suspecting anything. Then, when she'd led the team to her bomb cache, they waxed her ass and retrieved two hundred pounds of plastic explosive.

The Israelis have *Shabak*[40] (Internal Security) units capable of close-tracking Hamas tangos in the safe havens of the Gaza Strip, or Palestinian-controlled towns like Nablus or Jenin. Like their Brit brethren, the Israeli units do double duty as shooters if they have to. The Frogs are good too. They use single-purpose teams from the DST (the Directorate for Surveillance of the Territory, the organization that is responsible for counterintelligence on French soil), known as Groupes Chasse, or more commonly, GC, pronounced Jay-Say, which may entail as many as 150 people, to surveil a single target, if the threat is high enough.

I've operated with DST. My old *compagnon d'armes* Jacques Lillis is an *inspecteur* with the GC. If the target is important enough,

---

[39]Intelligence Company has a new designator, ever since its cover was blown a couple of years back. But I'm not going to tell you what it is, because the folks there have asked me to keep their identity secure. And if you don't like that, well fuck you very much.

[40]Shabak (sometimes also known as Shin Beth) is the Hebrew acronym for *Sherut ha-Bitachon ha-Klali*, which translates as, "The General Security Service." Shabak's overall mission includes counterespionage, counterterrorism, and protective security.

he'll use multiple automobiles, vans, trucks, and mopeds. DST Groupes Chasse have operators dressed as street people, students, tourists, priests—you name it. And the French understand the subtleties of surveillance. When DST agents change their clothes, they also switch shoes. Because the easiest way to check on whether or not you are being followed is not by looking at someone's face, or their clothes. It is by watching for the same pair of shoes or boots.

Today, I was being watched by amateurs. Zero-class gumshoes. Twerps. G&G (Goon and Gunsel) wannabes. They did it by the numbers—and from the look of it they'd all flunked math. The Mercedes stayed three cars back, following the taxi with the obviousness of an old KGB tail. Moonface and his passenger dawdled along the curb lane, to make sure the ancient taxi didn't pull a fast absquatulation down some alley or side street. The Greaser wannabe handled the hammer lane, just in case my driver knew how to pull off a bootlegger's turn and skedaddle back the way we'd come.

They were so fuckin' obvious I was surprised they didn't have toilet paper stuck to the heels of their shoes (maybe they did—I just couldn't see). I settled back in my seat to enjoy the ride. This E&E was going to be APOC.[41]

We'd made it about two-thirds of the way to the Hyatt, where I planned to shake these clowns, run a long SDR, and link up with Ashley, when events took a definite turn for the worse. Until then, it hadn't been a bad ride. The driver knew how to stay out of traffic. He'd run west on Karl Marx Strasse, then took a hard left onto Khan Shushinski Street, where he drove past a squat bloc of government apartments that could have been lifted from 1950s Albania, or 1930s Moscow. Then it was another left, followed by another right.

---

[41]A Piece of Cake.

That was when we encountered Murphy Avenue: a crowded, anonymous four-lane boulevard leading south toward the croisette and (ultimately) the Hyatt. Except, now traffic moved *comme un escargot* (that's the way my *copain*[42] Jacques Lillis from the Jay-Say says, "at a snail's pace"), enhanced by carbon monoxide–enriched, diesel-fume-intense, stop-and-go, bumper-to-bumper traffic.

---

[42]*Copain* is Frog for *pal*.

Chapter

6

WE STOP-AND-WENT THREE BLOCKS, WORKING OUR WAY METER BY SUL-fur-enriched meter until we reached what was obviously The Problem. I stuck my head out of the window to see. I didn't see a damn thing. So, I climbed out and stood on the rear bumper to increase my perspective. What I saw reminded me of Cairo on a bad traffic day, or Mexico City on a good one. We'd obviously arrived at the intersection from hell. Sixty feet ahead of where we sat, our four lanes of roadway were bisected by a six-lane avenue, which came at a bizarre angle. I went to my tippy-toes and craned my neck. Holy shit. There, on the far side of the intersec-tion, was a third, one-two-three-four-lane avenue. It, too, was gridlocked.

That made a total of fourteen lanes of traffic with nowhere to go, compounded by double and triple parkers, pedestrians, don-key carts, and bicycles. Oh, yeah—the traffic signals were all non-operational, and, no, there was not a single cop on scene to direct vehicles.

I swiveled so I could check our six. Guess what: the Mercedes was nowhere to be seen.

Which struck me as odd. As you already know, it had stuck to our bumper like fucking glue since we'd left the Grand Europe Hotel, dutifully maintaining a two-car distance.

Well, that's Baku traffic for you. We'd shaken our tail without even trying. I climbed out of the diesel fumes and smoky exhausts, back into the taxi, and slammed the door shut. The driver shook debris out of his huge, thick mustache and shrugged helplessly. He wasn't telling me anything I didn't already know. I sat back, sucked on the fumes, and thought about the headache I was going to have by the time I rendezvoused with Major Evans.

I closed my eyes and lost track of the time. When I opened them, I saw we hadn't moved more than twenty meters. But at least we were within two vehicle-lengths of the intersection.

I closed my eyes again. Then I blinked 'em open. Because, through the carbon monoxide fog in my addled brain (and as if from a great distance away), I heard the unique, distinctive sound of a rice rocket accelerating, its high-pitched throttle growing louder and louder above the ambient traffic noise. And then, as has happened so many times before, the hair on the back of my neck stood straight up, and the Klaxon horn in my brain went *ougah-ougah—dive, dive!*

I threw myself over the front seat just as the big red bike, its engine screaming, threaded the needle between the beat-up bus behind us, the huge tractor trailer truck on our right flank, and the car full of native costumed Azeris directly behind us. I rolled to my left, yanked the driver out of his seat, threw him across me, and rudely, crudely, lewdly slid behind the wheel and took control of the taxi.

I guess the driver was screaming and yelling but frankly I didn't hear anything. Right then, everything was happening in the sort of slow motion under which most combat takes place.

The cycle braked, veered sharply, and came up on our starboard side, the driver working his way dangerously close. Then it pulled abreast of the rear window. I glanced back and right and looked into Moonface's mirrored, wraparound sunglasses. He didn't react noticeably, except to edge forward. That was when I stared right into the boyish face of the leather-coated passenger. And into the muzzle of the suppressed .32-caliber Skorpion submachine pistol he one-handed, level with my face. With the sort of meticulous attention to detail that is common to trained observers and those who are about to die, I noticed that Leather Boy chewed his fingernails.

And then I realized that this was no time for focusing on shit like that. To hell with all traffic lights. Belay that. To hell with all traffic. I threw the car into gear, stomped the accelerator, smacked into the car in front of me, pushing it ahead. Then I backed, smacking the car of screaming Azeris behind me. And then into first gear again, yanking the wheel to my left and cutting into traffic, heading blindly into the intersection just as the rear passenger window disintegrated. I heard the bullets impact the undercarriage as they tore through the seat cushions. But I didn't give a shit about the upholstery.

I sideswiped a small truck coming the other way. Too fucking bad. Hit the brakes; double-clutched. Backed off, tried to smack the rice rocket with my front quarter panel, but the sumbitch had pulled off just enough to save himself. At least the fucking gunman was holding on for his life. Which meant he wasn't shooting at me.

Oh, shit—I slammed on the brakes just in time to avoid broadsiding a big lorry. I jerked my head to the right. Oh, shit again—the rice rocket was staying with me—and the *scheißkerl*[43] with the machine pistol had brought the fucking weapon up one-handed for a second go-round.

I reversed, K-turned, went left. Hit a dead end. Backed up, reversed, then edged my way around the truck in a herky-jerky, smack-the-horn, stop-and-go manner so as not to fucking get shot. I wedged the taxi between a car and a truck and steered left

---

[43]That's Kraut for *shithead*.

and right into their side panels as a way of hinting that they should keep the fuck outta my way.

Oh, fuck me. My peripheral vision told me that motorcycle man had maneuvered around to my six again and was about to align himself for another try.

I swung the wheel to the right, forcing him to disengage, or vault a tank truck. He chose to disengage, stopped, backed off, then veered wildly to the right and jumped ahead of me by eight, nine, ten yards and three cars. The kid with the Skorpion swiveled and swung the gun barrel over his shoulder toward my windshield. He wasn't worried about aiming—he was gonna spray and pray, and if he killed half a dozen bystanders, then it was too bad for them.

That's the thing about fucking kids today. They got no respect. They don't mind wasting ammo—or innocent people.

In that single careless instant, Leather Boy had signed his death warrant. He was no better than the scumbags who'd killed all those innocent people on the road to Baku yesterday morning.

It was time to stop these assholes. So I threw the taxi in reverse, backed for about ten feet pedal to metal, then braked, shifted into first, popped the clutch, and fucking stood on the accelerator.

Now, Peugeots—especially old diesels like the taxi I was riding in—have notoriously slow acceleration. But that didn't matter. I wasn't even thirty feet from the motorcycle, and didn't hit the sumbitch at more than twenty miles an hour.

But twenty miles an hour was enough, believe me. I drove the rice rocket forward like a fucking croquet ball. The driver panicked and stood on the brakes, which caused him to slide and veer and smack—splat—into the undercarriage of a big, long truck.

Was it perfect? No—because I didn't kill the pair of 'em right then. But given the traffic, it was good enough for me. I reached into my pocket, found a bunch of greenbacks, yanked the driver out of the front seat well, and pressed the bills into his hands.

Then, as my cop friends are fond of writing in their reports, "Subject rapidly exited the vehicle so he could commit further violence and mayhem." Translation: I hadn't finished the morning's work yet.

By which I mean, I reached around and unholstered the P7. There was a crowd gathering around the downed bike. Good news was that Moonface was in pretty bad shape—he'd sheared most of his scalp off as he'd gone under the truck bed, and he was bleeding profusely.

Bad news was that the gunman was down, too—but he wasn't out.

We made eye contact as I came around the nose of an old Zil sedan. Leather Boy may have hurt. But he was ready to go. He pulled himself out from under the downed bike, waved the Skorpion around to scatter the crowd, shouted a whole passel of words I couldn't understand, and pointed the tiny weapon in my direction.

You couldn't hear the shots, but I could sense the impact of the rounds as they hit all around me. I swept a young woman out of the way with my left arm, pushed a pair of men to the ground, stepped in front of another Azeri and shoved rudely to make her hit the deck, then brought the P7 up, up, up to get a sight picture, and squeezed off three, four, five, six, seven rounds of the 147-grain Hydra-Shok ammo the pistol likes so much.

The noise fucking scattered the crowd. Leather Boy may have had the automatic fucking weapon—but no one could hear it going off. My pistol, however, made a shitload of noise. So I was the one who caused all the pandemonium.

But do not forget what part I play here: I am THE sole, official, authenticated, gin-yew-whine, and legally trademarked Rogue

Warrior®. I love confusion, chaos, and turmoil—shit, I'd trademark *them* if I could. So, anyway, my shooting wasn't range-perfect. But it was combat-efficient.[44] I hit him in the legs and the groin—a particularly painful place to get shot. Leather Boy obviously didn't like what I'd done because he rolled into a ball and tried to hide behind the downed rice rocket.

That was what we SEALs call a BMOLBP—Bad Mistake on Leather Boy's Part. If someone is shooting at you and you are armed, SEALs understand that they must use every molecule of their energy to shoot back. Because if you don't return a withering barrage of suppressive fire and kill the asshole who's shooting at you, you're probably gonna die.

Just like this asshole was about to. I kept advancing on him: six yards, five yards, four yards, my sight picture getting better by the second.

Pedestrians were scattering. I could sense them running, blurry shadows in my peripheral vision. But all I could really *see* was Leather Boy, getting larger and larger through my front sight.

Big mistake. Humongous-as-my-Marcinko-dick mistake. I was tunneling. Which is the quick way of saying that I'd become a victim of tunnel vision. I wasn't scanning left/right, right/left. I wasn't breathing, forcing oxygen into my lungs. I wasn't doing any of the things that one is supposed to be doing when one engages in CQC. And let me say right now, that CQC doesn't have to always take place in a small room, or on a plane or boat, where there are hostages. CQC can take place anywhere. And I should have remembered that. But no one's perfect—even *moi*. And so, I wasn't the least attuned to my environment. I'd become

---

[44]Let me tell you that there are a lot of perfect score shooters who can't do fuck-all in combat. That is why I train the way I do, emphasizing stress shooting and nasty conditions and moving targets that fuck with the ol' Rogue mind. That way, when the merde hits the old *ventilateur*, I'll be able to kill my enemy, while the guy wearing the "Expert" marksman's medal will be lying dead.

fixated. All I wanted was to wax this asshole's behind, and then get the hell outta Dodge.

Except, I'd forgotten where I was (in a hostile environment), and what I was supposed to be doing (checking on the surveillance). Most critical, I'd completely forgotten about Beemer Man, as well as the two goons in the Mercedes.

I remembered about Beemer Man when I heard the big Kraut bike's muffler-less engine bearing down on me, whirled, recognized the kid's UCLA tank top and black jeans, and realized (lightbulb!) who he was and what he wanted. He'd fought his way through the gridlock, walking his bike, gesturing rudely and pushing people aside. Now he was twenty yards away and heading in my direction, a nasty look on his pockmarked face and a small pistol clamped atop the right handlebar grip by his hand.

Do you remember the Rogue's First Rule of Engagement? I did—and I knew exactly which target I wanted to engage. And so, I held my ground and pumped four quick rounds into Leather Boy's head, just to make perfectly sure he stayed where he was. Then and only then did I turn to deal with the no-goodnik on the Beemer.

There are times, friends, when I become clairvoyant in situations such as this one. There are other times, like my present situation, when I become, for one reason or another, negligent, heedless, even oblivious to the basic facts of life and truths of existence. Now, let's pause just long enough for me to give you an overview of my predicament.

I was standing in the middle of a fucking intersection of the capital city of a country in which I do not speak the language, holding a loaded weapon with which I had just shot a native-speaking individual. The gravity of my dilemma was made immediately apparent when, instead of shooting at me, the kid on the Beemer waved his pistol in my direction and screamed something at the crowd of shocked pedestrians and gridlocked drivers.

What did he say? Since I don't speak Azeri I have no fucking idea what he said. But I knew the gist of it as soon as the words came out of his mouth. The gist was: "That ugly sonofabitch with the big flat nose and the long French braid just killed my brother/cousin/uncle/friend, so we should hang the mother-fucker from the closest lamppost. But before we string the cock-sucker up, let's beat the shit out of him and tear him limb from fucking limb to teach him a lesson he won't forget."

Y'see, right then, all of a sudden things came to a complete stop. Like—*whoa*. S-t-o-p. Total freeze frame.

And then, and then, the whole fucking crowd turned on me. And started to scream. And come toward me.

Oh, fuck, oh, shit, oh doom on Dickie. This was not going to be any fun. None at all.

Some fucking bearded Azeri put his hands on my shoulders. I swatted him away. Two more grabbed at my vest. I elbowed them aside. I tried to talk my way out, but no one was listening. This had gone from crowd to mob by now—and all they wanted was a chance to lay their hands on me and do some damage.

I pushed back, hard, straight-arming the chests of a trio of guys who, judging from the clumps of old food in their mustaches, were probably related to my taxi driver. They gave way and I started working my way toward the relative safety at the far side of the intersection, beyond the wreckage of the rice rocket. But it was like trying to run the forty-yard dash inside a crowded New York subway train. There was just no place to go. No wiggle room.

A pair of big, burly guys smelling of garlic tried to double-team me, wrapping me up in a simultaneous headlock and a body lock. I smacked the first one with my elbow, catching him in the nose. He slapped his hands to his face and backed off just far enough so I could use the heavy steel slide of the pistol on B^{2}G.[45] I smacked him pretty hard. He staggered back, releasing his grip,

---

[45]You can probably figure out that it stands for Big Burly Guy No. 2.

too. But by then there were other hands on me, grabbing, gripping, clutching at my clothes and various extremities. My vest was ripped. My shirt pocket was torn. A hand yanked at my French braid, snapping my head back painfully. Then some cockbreath took hold of my left hand and wouldn't let go. I tried to disengage, but all I succeeded in doing was getting him to release his grip on my hand, take hold of my pinky, and try to head south with it. I struggled to free the fucking digit, but he wasn't about to let go. Maybe he wanted a souvenir. Who knew—and who cared. Well, *I* did. It was *my* fucking finger after all. Then an arm in a rough peasant shirt wrapped around my neck, squeezed tight, and pulled me in the opposite direction from the one I'd been more or less going in. Another set of arms grabbed me around the torso and pulled me in a third direction. All of a sudden I heard an ominous pop, and an icy shaft of pain radiated from my hand into my brain. Oh, fuck me—the asshole had dislocated my fucking pinky.

I was getting mad. I began to flail, swat, elbow, and claw my way out of the mob. I didn't necessarily want to hurt any of these people, but I wasn't getting a vote here, and they sure as hell wanted to nail my ass.

The only thing to do was get out of the intersection and outrun 'em. Except outrunning is a hard thing to do when you have a couple of dozen people trying to tackle you. I screamed, "Back the fuck off—" It didn't do a bit of good.

Time for a diversion. I fired the P7. Two, three shots went into the black macadam of the street. And then the slide locked back and I was out of ammo.

Oops. Bad move. Remember all those times I told you about counting rounds, and how hard it is to do under combat conditions? Well, now you see how right I was. Fuck. I squeezed the cocker, slid the slide forward, jammed the pistol back in its holster, and hoped that no one would try to grab it.

And all the while, the crowd was getting nastier and nastier and more and more aggressive. I cold-cocked one motherfucker who came at me with a club. Somewhere in the background, I could hear the electric hee-haw of a police siren. It was getting closer, too. I didn't want, or need, to deal with the cops.

I screamed, "Back the fuck off!" in what's known as Command Voice. It worked—kinda. The dozen or so folks closest to me hesitated—a few even stepped backward.

I tried it again. This time with much more menace in my Command Voice. Shit—it worked. They backed away some more. And then, I spied a single narrow venue for escape opening up. To be precise, the big, heavy truck that had destroyed the rice rocket was only eight or nine feet away. If I could make it to the truck and squeeze underneath, I'd have a fighting chance of getting away. I headed for the truckbed.

But just then, the damn dam must have broke, because the fucking mob came collapsing on me, and damn near all of 'em had their War Faces on. The pair of Burly Guys, both of whom had murder in their eyes, led the charge. It was T2A—Time To ACT before they shut me down completely. I flailed, and slapped, and kicked, and finally scrambled under the big, high-bed truck.

Wild-eyed, I emerged on the far side, scrambling on my hands and knees. GNBN. The good news was that it immediately became apparent to me that the folks on *this* side of the intersection hadn't heard Beemer Man's exhortation. Or, if they had, they hadn't understood him, so they didn't quite know what or who to look for. The down side was that I was the only guy running from the angry, hell-bent mob on the other side of the truck.

Except these folks didn't know that. Not really. I whirled and pointed back at the first B^2G, whose puffing, red, determined, puss poked out from the truck's undercarriage. "He did it," I bellowed. "That's the guy—he's the one. That's the motherfucker who did it. Kill the cocksucker!"

Did they understand me? No. But, just as I'd been able to

grasp the underlying substance of what Beemer Man had shouted to incite the mob against me, what I'd just shouted was instantly understood—and acted upon.

Angry hands reached for him. B²G was pulled out, stood up against the truck, and pummeled, all the while protesting his innocence. Me? I didn't waste a millisecond. I backed away, slowly, trying to attract zero fucking attention, until I'd managed a total and completely successful exfiltration from the nasty AO.

Total? Completely successful? Well . . . not quite. I wasn't alone. Mister Murphy, who can obviously pass for Azeri when he wants to, had followed me as I'd snuck away. I picked my way south and west, moving contrapuntally to the sounds of the approaching sirens. But somehow, Beemer Man had managed to thread his way through the gridlock, squirt past the mob, and head for the exact same thoroughfare I'd chosen to make my escape on.

And Beemer Man wasn't alone any more than I was. He had a passenger on the back of his big black bike—the goon who'd been riding shotgun in the Mercedes. And said goon didn't look very happy at all. In fact, he looked pretty much like a POG, which as you can probably figure out, stands for Pissed-Off Goon.

I checked for anywhere to cover and conceal—and came up dry. Off to my left was the yawning entrance of a metro stop. But I knew better than to head toward it. I didn't have any tokens, or whatever the fuck they use here in Baku, and I wasn't about to try to figure out how to use the fucking system sans a map, or a diagram. Ahead and to starboard I saw a jam-packed Irish pub theme-bar. I rejected that, too. I've learned the hard way that if you go into some bar or restaurant or café in a strange city, you can simply bottle yourself up inside—and moreover, the bad guys can call for reinforcements.

There are times when you are being followed that you want to attract attention to yourself. This was not one of them. So, my pinky now swelled to the size of a half-dill, I left the main drag and headed into what looked like a working-class neighborhood, half-walking, half-jogging against the traffic flow, moving up a narrow, one-way street, heading away from the bad guys. My ploy didn't bother Beemer Man at all—he simply followed me, taking his time and working the bike along the curb, its engine growling noisily, while the POG peered over his shoulder and scowled a War Face scowl.

But he didn't take any hostile action. Why? For the same reason I didn't want to attract attention: there were just too many potential witnesses on this lower-class side street. Look, Baku may be a big, congested city with a lot of skyscrapers that look as if they've been transplanted from Paris, or Tel Aviv, or Tulsa, Oklahoma. But don't let all those glass and steel towers fool you. Baku's not a rich city, yet. Even though the oil business has brought a lot of money into the country, there's still a lot of poverty, much of which takes the form of hundreds of thousands of unemployed Azeris who have nothing to do but park themselves on the sidewalks in front of their dilapidated, grimy Soviet-era slum apartment houses, and sit in the stifling heat on broken-down chairs, with folding tables and *shesh-besh* boards (which is how they refer to backgammon in this part of the world), between 'em. No—neither Beemer Man nor the POG wanted to kill me publicly.

And I could use that to my own tactical advantage. But first, I needed the sort of environment that would help me—and impair the opposition. I moved at a steady pace, scanning left and right. On impulse, I cut through a narrow alley. Beemer Man and the POG crawled up to the entrance, perhaps sixty, seventy feet behind me.

I turned—and saw the smile on Beemer Man's face as he realized the alley dead-ended, and I was apparently trapped.

Except, from where he was, Beemer Man couldn't see what I saw: the alley didn't dead end. It came to a T. And off to the right, about thirty yards away, I could make out the back side of a small, shabby, under-inventoried, but nonetheless bustling street market.

So far as I was concerned, that was like Brer Rabbit finding the fucking briar patch, when hungry Brer Fox was on the wily bunny rabbit's heels. I tossed the bird toward Beemer Man and the POG, then whirled, and ran like hell for the street market. As I ran, I extracted one of the spare magazines in my back pocket, reloaded the P7, reholstered it, and made sure my ripped vest still covered the weapon.

Thus armed and dangerous, I slipped between a couple of vegetable carts, then paused long enough to get a sense of where I was. And guess what—just as I'd hoped, this block-long cluster of rickety carts and rattletrap stalls and makeshift counters was no different from poor folks' street markets all over the world, from Philadelphia to Cairo; from Damascus to Shanghai.

They're all laid out roughly the same. The sidewalks have rows of jerry-built stalls, or chocked-wheel carts. Behind the stalls are small stores, where butchers, bakers, and cheese dealers ply their trade. At one end of the street, you'll always find dry goods—everything from disposable diapers to the kinds of plastic kitchen goods common to all Second, Third, and Fourth World countries. At the other, are the vegetables, legumes, and spices.

I'd landed between the veggies and the dry goods. I dropped low and made my way past crates of tiny cucumbers and radishes whose green tops lay withered in the heat, slipped behind a kiosk that sold towels and soap, then scampered across a narrow break between stalls to take up a defensive position behind a small, shriveled pyramid of past-their-prime Jaffa oranges. I stuck my big Slovak snout over the top of the orange pile, snuck a look, and liked what I saw. Which was that Beemer Man had stopped before committing himself to running the gauntlet of the market, and sat astride his bike, idling and gunning his engine, at the head of the street.

The POG climbed off the cycle and scanned the crowd of shoppers, his face reflecting both confusion and aggravation. He turned back and shouted something at the driver, gesticulating angrily, then stalked off in my direction, in obvious exasperation.

The bike pulled away, burning rubber as it did—no doubt heading around the block to cut me off at the far end of the market. It was a move that made sense, assuming I was going to actually go to the far end of the market. Of course, I had other ideas. But Beemer Man didn't know that.

I eyeballed the opposition. The POG was squat—built like a fireplug. He had a round face, and wore his hair short on top and white-walled around the sides, like a Ranger or Marine recon grunt. He was dressed in double-knit trousers and a scruffy, soiled short-sleeved band-neck shirt, over which he wore a long, sleeveless photographer's vest very much like my own.

Before the POG did anything else, he unzipped the vest, which I understood only too well gave him quick access to whatever weapon he was no doubt concealing beneath it. Next, he felt at the top left-hand pocket of his vest, his thick fingers working around what appeared to be a small, rectangular item. That told me he was carrying a cellular phone. Then, satisfied that everything was properly stowed, he started down the far side of the street, working his way around the stalls in a classic squared-off search pattern. The way he moved plus the hair style told me he was no Mafiya wannabe, but a military professional, probably Russkie or German.

Oh, but God loves me. Yes, He does. Why do I say that? Because He divides my enemies for me, and thusly divided, I can (and most certainly will) conquer them.

I stood up, put two fingers to my mouth, and whistled. Loud.

The sound brought the POG up short. He looked in my direction. I grinned and tossed him the bird. A nasty look came over his round, ugly face, he snorted like a fucking bull in heat, put his head down, and charged, bowling over a poor babushka in his haste to get to me.

I sprinted away from him, broken-field running around the

stalls; slaloming past the carts, until I spotted what I'd been looking for—an open door that led to an interior courtyard.

I turned on the speed, and burst through the doorway, into the courtyard, took my bearings, then fled up a narrow flight of stairs that led to the apartments on the second, third, and fourth levels of the building. I could hear the POG huffing and puffing as he proceeded at flank speed in my wake. Great—we were all on schedule. I charged noisily up the stairs, then at the first landing, I took a hard left and clattered down the hallway, my feet thumping boldly *pa-whap, pa-whap.*

Abruptly, I stopped. I listened to the sound of the POG in pursuit. Then I whirled and, silent as a fucking jaguar, I quickly retraced my steps and positioned myself at the corner of the hallway, just out of sight of the stairwell, and coiled to spring

I listened as the soon-to-be-posthumous POG came huffing up the stairs, paused to get his bearings and his breath, then charged headlong into the hallway. I drew back and, using every ounce of strength I could muster in my legs, my torso, my shoulders, and my arm, I sucker-punched him just as he turned the corner.

Except—the sonofabitch stopped short. Maybe to take a breath. Maybe to fart. Maybe to—well, who knows and who cares. Well, I do. Why? Because my roundhouse missed, my momentum carried me forward, and I caromed rudely off the wall in front of him.

This POG knew how to *carpe* the *diem,* believe me. He used the small, stainless steel pistol in his left hand to swat me upside the head as I came off the wall. The blow brought tears to my eyes. But it was a small pistol, and it caught me on the back side not the up side of the ol' Rogue haid. Oh, I was gonna have a chestnut-size knot back there tomorrow. But at least I was going to still have a head on my shoulders.

I shook the spots out of my eyes and flailed, to give myself a second to recover. Shit, he'd hit me harder than I'd thought.

Well, fuck the pain. It was time to show this asshole how

things were done. I reached around, caught him by the wrist, dropped, turned, kneed him in the chest, and twisted. *Voila*— fucking textbook. The gun came loose and went clattering across the tile floor and down the hallway.

Being a pro, he knew better than to worry about the weapon. Instead, his hands flew up into a defensive martial arts stance, and he swiveled, turned, feinted, then came back under me and delivered an elbow to my gut that made my eyes cross.

Ooh, that *hurt*. But I had no time to think about pain, because this sumbitch was trying to kill me. From the way he was handling himself, he'd been to Spetsnaz school. They teach a martial arts style that relies on lots of blows being delivered quickly—the optimum number is just over two hundred blows a minute. I can guar-on-tee that this asshole had done his best to get an A+.

But as you all probably know, for every measure, there is an active countermeasure. In this case, I used an old UDT martial arts technique taught to me by Roy Henry Boehm, the Godfather of all SEALs. The technical nomenclature for this Froggish martial art is known as PFW/PFD, which stands for PURE FUCK-ING WILL and PURE FUCKING DETERMINATION.

Roy once took on four Marines, all of them fifteen years younger than he, at the bar of the Little Creek Virginia Amphibious Base O-Club. I see you out there, asshole, scoffing because Roy didn't take on eight or nine Marines. Well, the only place you see that kind of horseshit is on TV shows or in movies. In real life, taking on four Marines—shit, taking on four bikers, or longshoremen, or four cops—can get you killed. But not Roy Henry Boehm, who was—and is—a man in ten million.

Anyway, Roy was a sarcastic sonofabitch, and he'd probably made some nice-to-see-you comment like, "You know why God gave Marines one more I.Q. point than horses? It's so Marines can march in parades without shitting on the street." Anyway, whether he started the fun, or they did, is unimportant. Here is the bottom line: Roy didn't demolish this quartet of younger, faster, and better-conditioned opponents because he was more skilled than they were. He demolished 'em because he wanted to win more than they did. He was meaner and more vicious and didn't give a shit about fighting fair. As Roy was always fond of telling us tadpoles, "Remember, you worthless scumbucket assholes: the Marquis of Queensberry was a *fag*."

That night at Little Creek, Roy's pure will and his sheer determination gave him the edge. He simply could not conceive of losing—and so, he fought with such wild ferocity that his opponents had to give way. HE COULD NOT FAIL. Thus, when he'd finished, not one Marine was left standing.

Now, this here POG was just as big as I, and just as strong. And his technique was pretty fucking good. But all of that didn't mean shit. Because, thanks to Roy, I've been taught the key to victory. I knew, deep in my Roguish soul, that I wanted to kill the POG much, much more than he wanted to kill me.

And so, as he kept up his rain of blows, I enveloped him, smothered him like onions on liver, and shut the motherfucker d-o-w-n. He fought me off; he came back with elbows and knees and fingernails and teeth. I answered him with a head butt that rocked him back on his foot, followed by a wide, sweeping kick that caught him behind the knees and took us both down to the floor.

I rolled on top of him and we grappled hand to hand. He tried to keep me away from him. Tried to struggle to his feet. But I wasn't about to let him up. See, I know that most fights end up on the floor. And if you're not comfortable on the floor, you're gonna lose. I've been a floor brawler all my life. This asshole? He was in good shape so long as he remained on his feet. But now, rolling around on the dusty landing, he was out of *his* fucking element—while I was in *mine*.

He tried to use his weight to muscle me onto my back while

holding on to my wrists with his hands. I twisted and broke my left hand free, brought it up, and hammered my fist at his face with as much power as I could muster.

He saw what was coming, twisted away at the last minute, and my fist smashed into the tile of the hallway floor.

If you recall, you will remember that someone had very recently dislocated my left pinky. I'm glad you remember, because I hadn't. And the pain of striking the swollen digit on that hard floor shook me to my toenails.

The POG wasn't about to let me recover, either. He grabbed hold of my French braid and yanked, snapping my neck back. He thrust his fingers, spearlike, toward my Adam's apple. I parried the blow with my arm, catching his fingers and bending them backward, making him scream. I wriggled out from under him, and using every fucking ounce of energy I had left, body-blocked him with my shoulder, then used my forearm to slam his head against the wall.

That stunned him some—but not quite enough. He rolled off the wall, scrambled to his knees, then launched himself toward where the pistol lay, about two yards down the hallway.

I shoestring-tackled the cocksucker. But like a good running back, his legs just kept churning and churning, and he reached out, grabbed the pistol by the muzzle, then tried to work it around in his fat hands.

No fucking way. I slammed him in the small of the back with my right fist hard enough to make him gag. He used the pistol butt to open a nasty cut on my forehead, then tried to open my forehead itself.

Big fucking mistake. I sensed the second blow, reached up, and trapped the pistol in my extra-large paw.

That didn't fluster the POG at all. He worked the gun so that the muzzle was pointing vaguely in my direction, then tried to work his thumb into the trigger guard so he could fire the fucking weapon. I don't think he gave a shit where the round might go, either.

But I did—and fuck, the muzzle was getting too close for comfort. I wrestled his arm, caught it under mine, and hyperextended it with enough power to break the elbow.

The goddam joint didn't break, but it must have hurt like hell. He screamed at me in Russkie, but he didn't let go of the fucking pistol. In fact, he worked even harder to squeeze at the trigger.

I fought back, and finally was able to jam my thumb, right up to the joint, behind the fucking trigger. Now, if he tried to pull it, nothing would happen.

My strategy kept the pistol from firing—but it took my right hand out of the fight. So it was time to end things before the situation deteriorated any further.

I raked his eyes with my left hand—which hurt me just about as much as it hurt him. He tried to swat me away with his one good arm. That opened him up—took his free hand out of things for just a microsecond. It was enough for me. I caught him with an elbow, then a knee, then twisted him up and around, using the pistol as the fulcrum. As he went over the top, his right wrist snapped.

Oh, that must have wounded the sumbitch one whole lot because he screamed, and nasty froth came out of his mouth. Holy shit, I hoped the cockbreath wasn't rabid.

I used all my strength to wrestle the pistol away from him. Reversed it. Extracted my thumb. Got my paw around the grips, and my finger on the trigger, then brought the gun around so the business end was pointed in his direction. He saw it coming out of the corner of his eye, and he fought against it real hard. But there was no escape. I had this asshole, and I was gonna waste him. I knew it—and he knew it, too, because I could see the fear in his eyes.

That look meant he was *mine*. I pushed the pistol up into his armpit and let him feel the pressure of the muzzle. I looked at his sweaty, round, red, soon-to-be-dead face, and whispered, "*Zamochit, baklan.*"[46]

I pulled the trigger three times as he struggled, wild-eyed, against me. The trio of shots was muffled by his body. He fought back another few seconds. I put another round into him and he then went limp.

He dropped in a messy pile, facedown. I put the muzzle of the pistol to the back of his neck, kneeled, held him at arm's length to keep myself out of the blood spray, then sent a final round into his brain, just to make sure he stayed where he was.

I pulled myself to my feet, exhausted. The one positive aspect of the past few minutes—aside from the fact that the POG was dead—was that, at some point during the fracas, my left pinky had snapped back into proper alignment. It was sore as hell, but at least it was working again.

Well, to be honest, "working" is a relative term. Frankly, friends, I used to be able to do this sort of thing with fewer detrimental aftereffects when I was closer to the tadpole stage of my life cycle. That was when there was never too much beer or too much pussy, sleep was an unnecessary impediment to one's existence, and my dick was hard all twenty-four hours a day. Ah, but youth, my friends, is wasted on the young. And—

I heard a noise behind me and looked up, alert for a new threat. But it was only the fucking dweeb editor, blue pencil in hand, who'd snuck up into the hallway to tell me, "Enough with the *fürshtunken* rhapsodizing already. Get on with the effing story line."

I guess he's right. Time was a-wasting.

Okay, first of all I was a little surprised that not a single door had cracked open to see WTF was going on. Then I realized that this was Baku, the first boomtown of the twenty-first century.

---

[46]That's Russkie slang for "I piss on your grave, punk." To paraphrase Spencer Tracy, I may not know much Russian, but what I *do* know is cherce.

And in boomtowns—Dodge City and San Francisco in the nineteenth century come to mind—you don't stick your schnozz into other people's business unless you're Wyatt fucking Earp and carrying a bad-ass Buntline Special. But just to make sure Mister Murphy or the Azeri equivalent hadn't called the cops from behind some closed door, I got down to work. I wiped the POG's blood off the little pistol—it was an old Sig Sauer 230—and dropped the weapon into my vest pocket.

Moving quickly but efficiently I rifled the POG's pockets. There wasn't much. I used my dirty handkerchief and his clean pocket handkerchief to staunch the bleeding on my forehead. I took his wallet, riffled through it, and discovered that the POG was named Feliks Maximov. He had an old Russian Army ID, a CIS driver's license, neither of which I could read, and an American Express Platinum card, expiration date 03/02, with his name embossed in English. A disorderly bunch of business cards were stashed in the wallet's inside compartment. I pocketed the billfold, as well as his thick ring of keys. And I plucked out of his vest pocket the little cellular phone that had somehow survived the battle. In fact, I was on my way down the stairs—gingerly, given my dinged condition—when the fucking thing rang.

I kept going, taking the phone out of my pocket as I hobbled, flipped it open, and growled, in the most authentic accent I could muster, "Pree-_vet_?"[47]

I was answered with a flood of polysyllabic Russkie, a language that, as you know, I do not understand, all spoken in a resonant and uniquely mellifluous tone. It was like . . . *Da Voice* speaks *RUSSIAN*. No, really. It was like listening to one of those unctuously lubricious announcers from Radio Moscow introducing the weekly broadcast from Moscow's Tchaikovsky Concert Hall. And, boy, did

---

[47]Hello.

this asshole like to talk uninterrupted. He provided a monologue long enough to carry me down the stairway, out the front door, through the courtyard, and back into the bustle of the street market.

As I moved onto the sidewalk, I checked quickly but carefully to port and to starboard, peering down to the end of the line of stalls and carts. Beemer Man was nowhere to be seen.

I suddenly realized that Da Voice had paused, as if waiting for an answer. Well, why not give him one.

"I'm sorry, but Feliks can't come to the phone right now. Can I take a message for him?"

I heard intake of breath, so I continued. "Not that he's in any condition to hear it."

Now, there was nothing but shocked silence. But what's one shock without a follow-up? So, I gave Da Voice a wake-up call in Russki: *"Otsosi, pedik*—blow me, you miserable cocksucker."

The connection was suddenly broken with an electronic *bleep.* Rude sonofabitch, wasn't he?

I looked down at the phone. I pressed the "end" button, then AutoDialed the first number in the phone's memory. It went through a nine number sequence, then started to ring. After nine double rings, and no answer, I fiddled with the phucking phone until I found the second stored telno, and dialed it up.

I listened as a long, long sequence of numbers beeped off. Then two raucous *bring-brings,* the double rings you hear when you dial up European phones. Then: *"Pree*-vet?"

Ah, the sweet sound of success. It was . . . *Da Voice.* And even from that one-word response I could tell he was PIC'd, which is pronounced piqued, and stands for Pissed, Irritated, and Confused. Good for me. I love it when I can PIC on assholes like this one.

"I asked if you wanted to leave a message for Feliks, and you fucking hung up on me, you rude motherfucker. Maybe I should come around and kick the shit out of *you,* cockbreath."

I gave the Russkie ample time to answer. When he didn't,

when all I heard was breathing, it was my turn to slap the receiver shut. *V pizdu*[48] with him.

I dropped the cell phone into my vest pocket, got my bearings, then turned southeast toward Ashley Evans's flat, periodically checking my six as I limped along, working my throbbing, swollen left pinky, and wondering what the politically incorrect Azeri idiomatic for *Gimme a fucking Rogue-size bottle of your most effective extra-strength painkiller* might be.

---

[48]Russkie idiom for "To hell." Literally, "into the cunt."

Chapter

7

"GEEZUS, YOU LOOK LIKE HELL." ASHLEY'S EYES WERE SAUCER-WIDE AS she stared at me through the half-opened door to her flat.

"You gotta do something about the road rage in this city, Major," I deadpanned. "Say, you got any aspirin in this here joint?"

"*Aspirin?* You want *aspirin?* Dick, you're a candidate for a Syrette of morphine and about thirty stitches."

We caught up while I dealt with my newly acquired dings and dents. Since Ashley had her flat swept twice a week for bugs by the embassy techies, she felt secure about talking. Even so, I made sure we had the radio and TV turned on full blast. Never, ever assume, right? Anyway, she told me that there were two developments she thought I should know about. First, about two hours ago she'd heard through an Azeri military source with close ties to what's known as the *chornye smorodiny*,[49] or Caucasian Mafiya, that a contract might have been put out on me.

"I could have told you that."

---

[49]The literal translation is "black currants." It's Russkie Mafiya slang for *vori* (Mafiyosi) from Georgia, Chechnya, Azerbaijan, and Armenia.

"Yeah, well you weren't around to confirm it. I called the hotel, but you'd already left. I didn't want to leave a message." She looked critically at my collection of black-and-blue (not to mention purple, green, and raw-meat-red) bruises as I applied Betadine liberally to my torso. "I will upgrade that particular source from a B to an A," she said, dutifully jotting a reminder to herself on the legal pad on which she'd been keeping notes.

I worked on the long cut that ran from my forehead into my hairline, wincing as I moved my sore-as-hell left pinky. "Any idea who ordered the hit?"

"Not really. If it was a Mafiya job it could have been anybody—Azeri, Russian, Iranian, Armenian. Hell, Dick, you're so politically incorrect it could have been the Pentagon Gay Women's Support Group."

I considered that particular possibility then dismissed the thought: "Nah. The crew looked Russkie."

"That doesn't tell me anything. You can hire ex-Spetsnaz Alpha Team specialists for fifty bucks a day in these parts."

"What about the guy on the phone?"

She wrinkled her nose. "Maybe significant, maybe not. Problem is there's no way to tell who he was, because we have no way of checking cell phone numbers here. There are so many black-market cell phones, faxes, wireless transmitters, and other stuff, the one you took off Maximov's body might have been stolen in London, or Rome, or who knows where. They blue-box everything out here." She hooked her thumb in the direction of the plain-paper fax on her desk. "That's probably one of the few legally acquired faxes in Azerbaijan."

I nodded. Another dead end.

Her face brightened. "One piece of good news is that you can check on the Amex card. There'll be records. Maybe someone paying the bills."

"I'll get Merc on the case as soon as I get back to my secure phone." I squinted into the mirror, evaluating my handiwork, and was gladdened by the results. I turned to face Ashley. "So—how do I look?"

"Like someone tried to beat the crap out of you."

"Killjoy."

"Yeah, well truth is truth." She paced nervously back and forth. "There's something else you should know," she said.

"Shoot."

"You've been declared persona non grata at the embassy."

I'd sensed that from my brief chat with the RSO, and told Ashley as much. She explained that even though Ambassador Madison couldn't force the Azeris to have me declared persona non grata and tossed out of Azerbaijan, she could box me out so far as the embassy was concerned. So, she'd put a memo out to the embassy staff, and I was now officially an untouchable. No one was to have anything to do with me, or my men. No support. No assistance. No nothing.

I shrugged. "What's your point?"

"Well—"

"Look, Major—" I told Ashley in RUT—Roguishly Unvarnished Terms—what I thought of Ambassador Madison and her way of doing business. And since I don't give a damn about Article 88,[50] I also told her what I think of the current administration, and our commander in chief. Oh, I will salute his ass if I am in his presence, because the office, if not the man, has my respect. But when I salute, and I say, "Aye-aye, sir" to this commander in chief, I'm spelling sir *C-U-R*. That's because, so far as I am concerned, this slimy sphincter is a traitor who has sold this country—and its armed forces—out for his own political gain.

---

[50]Article 88 of the Universal Code of Military Justice forbids anyone in the military from making disparaging comments about the civilian leadership of the armed forces. The bottom line is that I may die defending *your* First Amendment rights, but while I wear the uniform of this nation, *I* don't have any First Amendment rights.

Then, having made my views clear, I made sure Ashley understood that we SEALs don't need a lot of support from people like Ambassador Madison. Hey, we are force multipliers. We develop our own networks for operations, intel, supply, and logistics. Bottom line? What the ambassador did, or didn't do, frankly didn't concern me one iota.

At the same, time, I knew that I couldn't work in a vacuum. It's dangerous to do so, because on this mission, everything had political ramifications. And while I'm not political, my big Slavic butt could be scorched pretty bad if I wasn't plugged in. Bottom line? I would need someone inside the embassy to toss me infobits and political intel. Someone I could trust to watch my back.

Ashley threw up her hands. "Gee, Dick, given the long list of possibilities, I guess that person would have to be me."

"You don't have to volunteer—I can probably find someone else to help me out."

She made a dismissive gesture. "You don't believe that any more than I do. Look, Dick, I'm sure you and I don't agree on everything—my feelings about the president, for example, aren't as, ah, extreme as yours. And maybe I'm not altogether fond of your methods, either. But we are soldiers. We are military people. Now, the ambassador thinks that buying off the enemy works. 'Expediting,' she calls it. I know better—and so do you. Most of the political people at the embassy think that talking is an end in itself. It's kind of like diplomacy by way of Montel, or Hey-Raldo. They think that simply by *negotiating,* they'll solve problems. Well, you and I know from experience that all that talk, without some kind of political muscle to back it up, is meaningless. Look at the way Saddam Hussein walked all over Kofi Annan. Look at how the Serbs screwed Richard Holbrooke. There are dozens of examples."

She paused to catch her breath. "And in this part of the world? Political muscle means military force—or the very real threat of it. You know what they understand out here in *dikiy dikiy vostok—*

which in case you didn't know, means the wild, wild east? They understand that power comes either from the barrel of a gun—or from a barrel of oil. The Russians know that, and they're trying their best to muscle in on the action. So are the Iranians. And so, frankly, are we, although we're not quite as brazen about it as the Russkies or the Iranians. So, it's not a good situation." She took a gulp from her can of Coke. "Anyway, this is a long-winded way of saying that I think we have serious problems here, and I'm willing to help."

It gratifies me, friends, to see youngsters like Ashley Evans; young officers who are willing to put their butts on the line for what they believe in. That kind of grit, pluck, fortitude, is growing rarer and rarer in today's military. And I know when to take yes for an answer. "You're on. And I'll keep you out of it as much as I can."

We spent the next couple of hours working out the essential elements of information I'd be needing from the embassy, and figuring how Ashley could get 'em for me. I didn't tell her about my plans to hit the Fist of Allah camp with Avi Ben Gal, because the less she knew about what I was up to, the further out of trouble she'd be when the shit hit the fan.

I had a string of messages as long as my dick waiting for me when I got back to the Grand Europe Hotel, just after 1600. I thumbed through the thick pile of pink slips and counted eight from one caller alone. Starting just after midday, a Miss Ivana from the Sirzhik Foundation had called repeatedly, asking me to get back to her as soon as possible. There was also a pair of messages from Avi Ben Gal.

Yes, I wanted to learn all I could about Sirzhik. But Avi came first. I dialed his private number and he picked up directly. "Ben Gal."

"*Lech ti-Zedayeen*—go fuck yourself."

"Gee, I wonder who this is." He laughed. "Where the heck have you been?"

"I'll tell you when we're face-to-face."

I heard him groan in mock horror. "Listen—I called to say two things. One is that I have some of the information we'll need to move ahead on our joint project."

That was great news. "Terrific. I'd like to move as quickly as possible on that, Avi. Maybe as soon as tomorrow or the day after."

"That's going to be a problem," he said.

I don't like hearing about problems, and I let Avi know it in my customary RUT.

"This has to do with you," he said. "Don't you realize that you're already a celebrity here in Baku."

"Oh?"

"Oh, absolutely," he said. "You are bona fide vatchamacallit, glitterati, Dick." I could hear bemusement creeping into his tone "You're even having a party thrown for you."

I was? That was news to me.

"The Sirzhik Foundation office in Baku has decided to honor you."

Oh, c'mon. This was unreal. It was like manna from heaven. It also explained all those calls from the mysterious Miss Ivana.

And Avi made sure I knew why I had to accept, even on this obviously tapped telephone. "Take it from me, you'll want to get a good look at Sirzhik's offices."

I paused before answering. Then: "Oh?" I know Avi pretty well, and he was trying to pass me a message.

"I mean, *professionally*," Avi said. "You'll want to check out . . . the decor."

Message received, loud and clear. "Will you be there?"

"Oh, *absolument*," Avi said. "*Mais bien sûr*. And I'll even bring Mikki with me."

"Then count me in. I don't give a shit about you. But seeing Mikki will be a real treat."

"*Hasta luego*," Avi said. I heard his receiver slap down and the line went dead.

I hung up, then punched Ivana's number into the phone and waited while it *bring-bringged* three times. It was picked up.

I said, "I'd like to speak to Ivana, Please."

The sexiest, smokiest, whisky-barrel voice I've heard in years, responded. "Sir*jeeek* Foundation. This is Ivana. How may I help you?"

Here is what I thought: "*How about a Full Lewinsky, right now?*" But I must be getting old, because here is what I said: "Ivana, this is Dick Marcinko. You called."

"*Cap*-ten," she murmured warmly. "So good of you to return my call. I was *van*dering if you would be so kind as to attend an exclusive black-tie reception ve are having tomorrow evening here at the Foundation's office, to *vel*come you to Baku. We are a small but we like to think qvite effective self-*halp* organization that is trying to better the quality of life for all peoples here in the Caucasus. We read of your arrival and our chairman, *Stephan* Sarkesian, would very much like to meet you. He will be flying in from Paris especially to do so, so it would be lovely if you will agree to come and meet with him."

Would I ever. I wanted to stare this guy in the eyes. Check him out. My instinctive reactions to people are very, very well honed. And besides, with a voice like that I wasn't about to turn Ivana down. "Will *you* be there, Ivana?"

"Most assuredly, *Cap*-ten."

"Then you can count on it."

In response, she purred. No shit, gentle reader. She fucking *p-u-r-r-r-r-r-e-d*. Okay, it may not have been the Full Lewinsky, but it still counted as aural sex so far as I was concerned. Then—reluctantly—it was back to business. I wrote down time, place, and directions. I hung up, her voice still smoldering in my ear, thinking about all the ruler-carrying, knuckle-smacking nuns back in parochial school who told me I'd get hairy palms if I . . .

And then the phone rang, and Boomerang's distinctive singsong voice said, "Yo, Boss Dude, let me sit-rep you on how it's goin' with Araz and the boyz," and all—okay-okay-okay, *most*—lewd thoughts dissipated from my Roguish brain.

I spent nine of the next twelve hours on the computer. Oh, yeah, my sleeve length may be three inches longer than my inseam. And yeah, my scarred, thick knuckles are hairy and there is perpetual grime under my fingernails. And yeah, my eyebrows grow all the way around my face down to my mustache. And yeah, I look like the Rogue Neanderthal, and occasionally speak like him, too. Big fuckin' deal. It doesn't mean I *think* like a caveman.

In fact, I speak five languages at level-four fluency, and another three passably. I have a master's degree in political science from Auburn University. Sure, I have killed scores of men in hand to hand combat. Yes, I have slit my fair share of throats. But I have also one-on-one briefed the president of the United States, the secretary of defense, and the Chairman of the Joint Chiefs of Staff. I have made face-to-face presentations to the director of Central Intelligence, the British undersecretary of defense, the director of MI-6, the head of the Bundesamt für Verfassungs-schutz, Germany's top-secret counterintelligence apparatus, the French minister of defense, the president of Egypt, the late King Hussein of Jordan, and the director of Mossad. What I'm trying to tell you is that being The Rogue Warrior® means more than the ability to kill at whim, or will. I must also have other, more subtle tools at my disposal. Which, these days, means knowing how to find exactly what I need on the Internet, and understanding how to run complicated programs on a computer.

What was I doing? Two things. First, I was running scenarios for our hit in Iran. I'd received enough intel from Tony Merc and Pepperman to start the mission planning process.

Yes, the mission planning process. SpecWar missions are not seat-of-the-pants, "Hey, let's go off and kill some Japs . . ." affairs. We may be *unconventional* warriors, but we spend a shitload of time working on our ops plans. I call it the Satchmo approach to killing.

Louis Armstrong, known as Satchmo, was the greatest jazz trumpet player this country (or any other) ever produced. His solos were ineffable, inventive flights of creation that soared and sang and pushed the edge of the musical envelope way beyond where it had ever been taken, just as my own thousands of real-world operations have pushed the SpecWar envelope further than anyone else has taken the Warrior's craft of breaking things and killing people.

But Armstrong's solos weren't off-the-top-of-the-head jam sessions any more than my ops are improvised hop & pops. He worked out each solo—every nuance of it—during long hours of practice. He improvised, revised, adapted, reworked, and refitted his performance so that, in the end, it fit perfectly and completely into the Armstrong artistic and technical musical universe. And then, thus shaped, buffed, and polished, he played the hell out of that solo in public. The result was that the audience believed what they were hearing was total improvisation when, in fact, they were listening to an artistic and technical genius whose compositional capabilities were on the level of a J. S. Bach.

And so, I scratched notes on legal pads, and played with my rational databases on the computer, dealing with EEIs (Essential Elements of Information), working out the limitations and special conditions under which we'd be operating, diagramming the six mission phases,[51] then identifying within each of those six phases

---

[51]The six phases of any SpecWar mission are: Premission, Insertion, Infiltration, Actions at Objective, Exfiltration, and Postmission.

the most likely times that Mister Murphy and his family would make an appearance, and work out the solutions to either prevent him from showing up, or putting the sumbitch out of action right after he made his appearance.

Under normal circumstances, my senior enlisted men would do much of this planning. I'm a firm believer in what might be called "bottoming up." That's when you let your senior noncoms, who know the men in their platoons best, design the nuts-and-bolts of an op-plan.

But today, my senior enlisted men were training Araz Kurbanov's troops, and it was up to me to do all the work. And so I slaved over the keyboard and the legal pad until I got it done. No—I didn't necessarily like it. But I did it. That's what being IN COMMAND is all about.

And when I finished, I did not go straight to the minibar and pour myself a Dr. Bombay Sapphire on the rocks. I did not pop a six-pack of Heinekens. I closed down the mission planning files, logged onto the Internet, found a good search engine, and typed Steve Sarkesian's name into it. After I downloaded a humongous number of files, I typed "Sirzhik Foundation" into the search engine, and tapped the left mouse button. It didn't take long to get lots of hits on that subject, either.

And here, *mit einem Wort, kurz gesagt,* as my old shipmate, KSK commander Brigadier General Fred Kohler[52] would say "in a nutshell" in his native Kraut, is what I found out after some three-plus hours of staring at the screen and downloading.

As you already know, the Sirzhik Foundation was what they call an NGO, which stands for NonGovernmental Organization. NGO is a twenty-first century way of saying that it was a hybrid organization, somewhere between a pressure group and a nonprofit charitable association. Whatever it was, Sirzhik certainly had a lot of

---

[52]Fred runs the newest Kraut CT strike force, known as KSK, or Kommando Spezialkräfte. You can read about him—and it—in *Rogue Warrior: Option Delta.*

money to dole out. And I already knew it was headquartered in the old Whitney mansion on upper Fifth Avenue in New York City. But I learned that in that particular neighborhood, real estate goes for about half a mil per square *yard*. I also knew Sirzhik had a network of offices in the high-rent districts of Washington, London, Paris, Moscow, Prague, T'bilisi, Baku, and even Yerevan. On paper, Sirzhik was devoted to economic and social development all across the former Soviet Union. A glowing article in the *Wall Street Journal* less than three months ago described the Foundation's programs in Armenia, the Republic of Georgia, Turkmenistan, Kazakstan, and Azerbaijan. There was nothing in the article about Sirzhik taking bribe money, so I guess the reporter didn't spend much time talking to the late and unlamented Roscoe Grogan. Nor was there any material about Sirzhik's possible ties to transnational crime syndicates. But then, as Avi had said, it was only a suspicion on his part.

But by reading between the lines, I also understood that the organization used its financial clout to achieve political goals. For example, it had lobbied strenuously to prevent the Azeris from receiving any security assistance from the United States—and it had won that fight by making sure that several of its projects were directed toward the states and districts where key senators and congressmen were from. And where did Sirzhik get all its money?

Let me quote from the *Journal:* "Thanks to the huge stock market run-up of 1995–1998, the Sirzhik Foundation's endowment is currently in the hundred-billion-dollar range, which is more than twice the United Nations' budget. That huge fiscal clout makes Sirzhik CEO Steve Sarkesian a world-class socioeconomic and political power broker."

The same Steve Sarkesian who is head of the Armenian National Foundation. The multibillionaire who ranks number five on the *Forbes* magazine Four Hundred Richest People in the World list, but still takes kickbacks from oil companies in Baku. The one who's throwing a party so he can meet me. *That* Steve Sarkesian.

You, the one waving your hand out there, interrupting *moi*. What the fuck do you want? You say you don't know anything about Steve Sarkesian, and I should fill you in.

What's the matter with you, do I look like some fucking intel squirrel with a plastic fucking penholder in my fucking shirt pocket and dweebish black-framed glasses with fucking Coke-bottle lenses?

You what? You say you paid good fucking money for this fucking book and I should do my fucking job and fucking tell you who the fucking characters are.

Well, fuck you very much, too. But since you asked the way I like to be asked, here's what I know courtesy of my research. Sarkesian came to the United States as a twelve-year-old Armenian orphan named Sirzhik Sarkis—ergo the name of the foundation he currently heads. He made his fortune in the 1970s, 1980s, and 1990s in New York's volatile real estate market, along with forays into venture capitalism (he bankrolled three of Silicon Valley's most profitable software companies and currently holds four hundred thousand shares of Amazon.com and six hundred thousand shares of AOL in his personal portfolio), and hard-nosed international currency speculation in deutsche marks, British pounds, and yen. In fact, according to a clip that I found in the *New York Times* archive, Steve-o single-handedly collapsed the British pound on the world currency markets back in 1992. That was just after the Tory prime minister dissed him in a House of Commons speech as "nothing more than the tarted-up, bespoke-suited, nineties vision of the itinerant rug peddler."

The self-styled Armenian nationalist also allocated his own money to political causes and to politicians who do things his way all over the world. According to materials I discovered at the Jane's Information Group Web site, he allegedly contributed more than a million dollars to the current Russian president's campaign, bypassing Russkie election laws by providing political advisers and media consultants instead of cash. According to a top OSINT[53] service I subscribe to, he has been active in the Caucasus, too, financing projects that made him popular with the region's leaders, most of them former Communist officials, or what was obliquely referred to as "new-style capitalists." When you read about "new-style capitalists" in this part of the world, friends, you're reading about gangsters. Full stop. No wonder Grogan had been so impressed. I wondered if Roscoe'd been taking kickbacks skimmed from the money he'd been paying out to Sirzhik. He'd struck me as the type who would.

Another article, this one at BusinessWeek.com mentioned that Sarkesian had spent more than six million dollars in the past year, donating half of it in "soft" money to both Democrat and Republican national committees, and the rest to Armenian causes. The guy was a regular fountain of cash.

"And so," gushed some slavish split-tail in the Style section of the *Washington Post*, "when he's in Washington, Steve Sarkesian meets regularly with the president and vice president, with the speaker and the minority leaders of the House, as well as with leading senators and the national political chairmen of both parties. And according to one Capitol Hill observer, they pay attention to what he says, too. Like those old E. F. Hutton TV commercials went, when Steve Sarkesian talks . . . people listen."

Sounds too good to be true, don't it? Yeah—I think so, too. I'm not a cynic by nature, but I have to say that I instinctively mistrust folks like Steve Sarkesian, even without meeting 'em, when I read such a huge quantity of breathless, uncritical drivel.

Because, let's be RP—Roguishly Plain—about what we are talking about here. We are talking about fixers. Influence peddlers. Folks who pay bribes but call 'em "expediting." Bribes?

---

[53]Open Source INTelligence.

Yeah, bribes. They bribe congressmen and senators with political contributions, and in return *they* get to write the laws that affect us all. You say that's undemocratic. Fuckin' A. But to this unelected group of grease-the-wheels motherfuckers that doesn't matter. They believe they know what is best for the USA—that's the unruly, unwashed, unsophisticated assholes out there—in other words, you and me.

But the old bottom line is that these rent-by-the-hour power brokers are no more and no less than whores. In fact, hookers are more honest about what they do. Oh, they may call themselves lawyers, or public affairs counsels, and they may consider themselves to be Washington's own God-given Brahmin class, because they spend their days and nights kissing up to the nation's alleged leaders, throwing them fund-raisers, and taking 'em for all-expenses-paid weekends. What I detest most about 'em, however, is their cynicism. It is absolutely unbounded. By that, I mean this moneyed, limo-riding, bespoke-suit wearing bunch of vermin believe that their money can buy them anything, or anyone. I have seen it in the past. Assholes like the late and unlamented Clark Clifford of the BCCI scandal, who got too big for his Guccis and skimmed a few mil here and a few mil there just because he felt like it. Or former SECDEF Grant Griffith, whom I had to wax when he thought he could get away with selling nuclear missiles because it would be too politically embarrassing to bring him to justice. Lemme tell, ya, the list is as long as my *szeb*.

And so, with my instincts at odds with all the profusely fawning prose in the public press, I turned up the radio and the TV sound, and got on the secure cellular to that intel safety net of mine, back in the States. It only took me a few minutes, because Jim Wink was able to pull up a shitload of info almost as if he'd had the stuff sitting on his desk waiting for me to call. And half an hour after I'd reached for the phone I had the REAL and unvarnished skinny on Steve Sarkesian and the Sirzhik Foundation. And believe me, what I learned from Wink and a couple of others like him was a lot more helpful than the fluff I'd been reading.

RUMINT had it, said Wink, that the foundation had been trying to form relationships with the big multinational oil companies who were planning exploration in the Caucasus, but without any positive results. The corporate lawyers were chary because bribery is illegal, no matter what you call it. So Steve Sarkesian had been reduced to making deals with the smaller consortiums in Azerbaijan, Kazakstan, and Tajikistan.

He added that Steve Sarkesian might be overextended financially, even though there were billions and billions of dollars in the foundation's coffers. Several Paris banks had lately put "holds" on Sarkesian's personal checks. And the Swiss had, only last year, refused to open any new accounts from Steve Sarkesian, and had asked him to remove all his funds from Zurich and Geneva. Why was that? Because last year was when the Swiss banking laws had been changed, making it much, much easier to track money laundering.

Finally, Wink told me that even the White House, which as we all know, will do almost anything including sell the nation's secrets for campaign funds, had been holding Steve Sarkesian at arm's length recently. Did all of the above prove that Steve Sarkesian was dirty? No, it didn't. But the signs sure led me to believe that this sumbitch was no patriot.

I was putting other pieces of the puzzle together as well. Pepperman had been able to lay his hands on what's known in the trade as a Whiskey-Number intercept[54] log. There was no way he could ever see the message itself. But sometimes, just seeing the

---

[54]Whiskey-Number is the code word designator for the National Security Agency's highest-priority intercepts. Whiskey-Numbers go directly to the president's desk, eyes only, by way of the DCI. It occurs to me that there will probably be taps put on all my phones because I told you about their existence.

log can help. And in this case, that's what happened. According to one of the log entries, the Russkie I'd waxed on the awl rig had been on the phone to Paris when we hit the place. Paris was where Steve Sarkesian was flying to Baku from. It occurred to me to wonder why NSA had been targeting that specific cell phone, but Pepperman has limits about what he can tell me and what he can't, so I didn't even bother to ask.

Second, the Amex card I'd taken off the POG belonged to a dummy corporation in the Seychelles, which belonged to a dummy corporation in the Bahamas, which belonged to a shell corporation based in Liechtenstein and run out of the British West Indies, which belonged to an Iranian corporation headquartered in Paris, which in turn was half-controlled by . . . Steve Sarkesian's wife.

This guy was dirtier than Grant Griffith, Bentley Brendel, and Werner Lantos all put together. That was when I realized what I had to do. Which was exactly what the POG had done earlier, and *cårpe* the old *diem*, take advantage of the situation, and use the trip to the Sirzhik Foundation not only to gather as much intel on Steve Sarkesian as I could, but also to simultaneously rattle the sumbitch's cage long and loud enough so that he'd do something careless.

Why? Because intel gathering and cage rattling was what my *real* mission to Baku here was all about. Remember my real mission? I'd been tasked to assess what the Ivans and the Iranians were doing, so SECDEF could formulate the right security policy for the Caucasus. And from what I'd just learned, old Steve-o was up to his armpits in Russkies and Iranians.

Oh, yeah. I knew the Sirzhik Foundation had about 180 permanent employees. Guess what: about 65 percent of those were either Ivans, Iranians, or Armenians, with the rest about equally divided between Frogs, Krauts, Brits, and miscellaneous Eastern Europeans. There were only two Americans employed by the Foundation—and they were in low-level security positions at the Foundation's London office, Sirzhik's least active and smallest outpost.

And guess what else. According to my pal Tony Merc, someone was rustling the bushes back in the States, working quick and hard to assemble as much info on *moi* as possible. Tony'd run a Standing Order Seventeen[55] on the inquires, and discovered that before they'd caromed around Washington, they'd originated at the Sirzhik Foundation.

"I figured they'd want the good stuff," Tony giggled. "So, I made sure they got it."

"The good stuff?"

"Yeah—your troubles with the White House. Your alcoholism. Your many brushes with the law. Your prison record. I tell you, Dick, you are in deep doo-doo with the Navy. Your career is almost over—again."

I love my friends because they are so fucking devious. "Great work, Merc."

"Fuck you, asshole, you owe me."

Okay, now I was forewarned. And so, while Steve Sarkesian was trying to check me out (and not doing very well at it), I'd be doing the same thing to him. But I'd be doing my body cavity search up close and real personal. And lemme tell you: I was about to give this rich, self-important asshole a real Roguish proctoscopy—sans any lubricant whatsoever.

---

[55]Major Robert Roger was the first American SpecWarrior. He led a band of buckskin-clad, flintlock-and-hatchet-carrying commandos during what's come to be known as the French and Indian War, and he tore the French and the Indians some new assholes with his unconventional tactics. Anyway, in 1759, Roger wrote nineteen Standing Orders to his troops. They are the original Commandments of SpecWar, and they're as valid today as they were when Roger wrote them. Standing Order Seventeen goes like this: "If somebody's trailing you, make a circle, come back on your own tracks, and ambush the folks that aim to ambush you." Well, the technique works whether you're on a trail in the woods, or the trail of someone trying to track down information. Ergo, Merc made a figurative circle back onto his own track, and was thus able to pinpoint where the queries were coming from.

Chapter

8

I WASN'T CARRYING MESS DRESS WITH ME ON THIS TRIP. AFTER ALL, I'D come to Baku in full stealth mode, and formal wear isn't generally required for sneaking & peeking. But I have been around long enough to follow my own SpecWar Commandments, and so, never assuming that all I'll need are BDUs, jeans, Velcro, and Kevlar, I habitually pack one set of dress clothes, and a Class A uniform.

I decided on the civvies, because they make me stand out less in a crowd. Since I never go anywhere where there will be single women without carrying the proper sort of protection, I slipped a .32-caliber P7-K3 into a suede, inside-the-waistband holster, tucked the holster into the small of my back, and secured the clasp to my belt.

I checked my watch, picked up the secure cell phone, and made contact with Boomerang and Randy. We went over the progress they were making with the Azeris, and I was happy to be told that Araz's training was all on track. I was even happier to learn that the covert preparations for our little cross-border excursion were all taking place on schedule.

"I'll see your butts after the reception," I told Boomerang. "Save me a beer." Then, sit-repped to my satisfaction, I fluffed a foulard silk square, stuffed it into the breast pocket of my custom-made, Seoul, Korea-tailored, double-breasted blazer, then dropped a set of custom-made, New-York-tailored lockpicks behind it. Then I thought about what I'd done, removed 'em, and slipped the slim package into my shoe. Was it uncomfortable? You bet it was. But I've learned over the years that discomfort is tolerable if you have a goal. And I had a goal: stealth.

Major Ashley Evans, who *was* wearing mess dress, picked me up at 1945. She was driving her very own vehicle, a humongous, four-door blue-and-white Chevy Suburban Silverado 2500 with oversize tires. It was a relic, she explained, from her stint a few years back in Sarajevo. A gift from a DIA countersurveillance team. "See?" She pointed out a trio of well-preserved bullet holes in the rear quarter panel. "That was from my last trip up Mount Igman, on the drive out of town."

I looked at the spacing of the three holes, stuck a finger atop one, and guesstimated. "Light machine gun?"

"You got it," she called out to me. I stepped back and took a second look. Not bad—she'd gone to the trouble of overpainting the metal to keep it from rusting. "Nice souvenirs. I'll bet you're glad he missed the gas tank."

"How do you know it was a he? There were female snipers in Sarajevo, too, y'know."

Never fuckin' assume, right? "Guilty. I don't," I said. I continued around the rear of the big vehicle, making sure she saw me unbuttoning my blazer ostentatiously through her side-view mirror as I went.

I stopped next to the passenger door and looked at Ashley through the half-open window. "Hey, maybe you'd like to see *my* scars?"

She hit a switch and the electric door locks opened with a loud *thwock.* "Don't even think about it."

I opened the passenger door, hoisted myself up, climbed in, locked up, buckled down, and shut the window so we wouldn't lose any more air-conditioning than we had to. "Thanks for being my date tonight. Of course, I'm not sure the ambassador would approve."

The major reached forward, turned down the volume on the Garth Brooks the local country-music station was playing, and turned up the air-conditioning fan to Full Tilt Boogie. "We'll find out soon enough if she does or she doesn't," Ashley said, "because she'll be there." The major smiled at my expression, twisted around to better check on the traffic flow behind her, and then pulled out carefully into the street. "Hey, don't worry. Taking her abuse is all in a day's work. Besides, I've wanted to see the inside of this place since I got here. But I've never been on the Sirzhik Foundation's A-list." She paused. "Heck—I'm not even on its B-list.

"You travel first class when you travel with me, Major."

We stopped at a traffic light and she took the time to look me up and down critically. "Well, I must say, you clean up pretty well, given your reputation, that is."

"Don't believe a word of it."

"What—that you clean up pretty well, or your reputation."

I grinned. "Both."

That brought a smile to her face. She stepped on the accelerator and the big truck moved forward.

I reached down, straining against my seat belt, and slid the seat back to get some leg room, then stretched expansively. "So what's the drill?"

"Your guess is as good as mine—hold on a sec." She signaled, turned right onto a one-way street, braked, then cruised slowly, checking our six in her outside mirror, her expression serious. "Looks as if we're running in the clear," she finally said.

"That would be a change—for me."

"I bet it would." The Suburban swerved left, then right, then left again—it needed some suspension work if you ask me—as Ashley drove down a series of unlit streets bordered by decrepit, Soviet-era housing. "There are some parts of this city that are just plain depressing," Ashley said. "And this is one of them."

I nodded in agreement. "Relics of the Cold War." I peered out the window at the housing bloc. Many of the windows were dark. Behind some, I could make out flickering lights.

"Candles," Ashley said, anticipating my question. "Ironic, isn't it—that in the oil capital of the Caucasus, most of the people can't afford power."

I shrugged and said nothing. We drove on in silence for some minutes.

Finally, Ashley half-turned toward me. "So, how do we play this, Dick?"

I scratched at my beard. "Well, to be perfectly honest, at some point I want to get a look at the Foundation's offices," I said. "Just a short sneak-and-peek—nothing outrageous."

Ashley nodded. "I think that's doable." She hesitated momentarily. "*If* we're careful."

"I'm always careful."

She snuck a look at the long cut on my forehead, which was still visible, reached out, and touched it. "Oh, yeah?"

I shrugged. "Well, almost always."

She looked at me evenly. "Okay, let's say I'm in, if the situation arises. Do you have a way to deal with locked doors?"

I wiggled my fingers in her direction. "These," I said, "are educated."

She gave me a skeptical look. "That's not what I asked."

"I can do what I have to," I said. "What about you—did you take the locksmith course at spy school?"

"Why, Captain," she said coyly, "how would you ever know about that sort of thing?"

"Because I took it myself." What I didn't say is that in addition to taking DIA's spy school course when I was a tadpole, I'd had further inculcation when I ran SEAL Team Six. Back then, I hired a Noo Yawk professional known as Eddie the Burglar, who showed me and my guys not only where to find the best cannoli on the face of the earth, but also how to pick any lock we ever came across. Eddie was—still is—a scholar, and a gent, and a patriot, too, because he didn't charge us a cent for his week-long course of instruction.

Ashley turned left now onto a wide avenue. "This is an interesting part of town," she said as she saw my expression turn inquisitive. "Most of the houses were built in the nineteen twenties by the first group of oil barons."

I looked. I've seen pictures of Fifth Avenue when it was all four- and five-story private houses owned by folks with names like Rockefeller and Carnegie, and I have to admit that it was pretty close to what I was looking at now. The avenue was broad—six lanes wide. On either side, set well back from the curb, was a row of large stone mansions. On some blocks, they were separated by only a few feet. On others, one house sat alone, behind formidable walls and high gates. The assortment of architectural styles was staggering. Some of the mansions were baroque in style. Others were rococo. And still others had been built in the sort of push-mepullyou quasi-neoclassical, pseudo-Renaissance fashion that I refer to as Nouveau Mafia. But whatever their diverse styles, they were uniformly well kept. "They're in real good shape."

"Most were bought up right after the collapse of the Soviet Union, by the first Azeri capitalists."

"Who were . . ."

"The same people who'd been running the country for the Sovs."

Business as usual. "That figures."

"Talk about your insider trading. Anyway, they knew all about Western interest in Caspian oil. So they bought property at pennies on the dollar, held the mansions until the oil rush, then they sold 'em to Western oil companies, banks, venture capital firms, and so on."

I laughed. "Underneath every Commie was a decadent capitalist trying to get out, right?"

She nodded in agreement. "And that's only half the story. Guess who controls the construction industry here in Baku? The same people who owned the houses, of course. So every damn nail, every pipe, every fixture and shingle costs three, four, five times what it should have cost. And guess what—when the oil companies tried to import their own materials, the Azeris charged a thousand percent duty on the stuff to teach 'em a lesson."

"Nice hustle."

"It was a hustle that worked, too." She pointed a quarter klik down the avenue. I followed her finger and saw a lot of lights and a knot of traffic outside a huge one-to-the-block estate. "That's where we're headed."

I looked closer. "Impressive." And it was—if you liked your homes to be ostentatious. As we pulled abreast, I could see one-two-three-four-five stories of intricate hand-carved stonework topped by a frieze depicting the labors of Hercules. Above the framed upper windows, the keystones featured the faces of goddesses. The whole structure was surrounded by a ten-foot wall topped by ornate, electrically controlled wrought iron double gates that reminded me of the ones outside the Hôtel de Ville, Paris's city hall. It looked like a movie set. Indeed, the whole estate had been professionally illuminated by soft but powerful floodlights, giving it a charming, magazine cover appearance.

But, I noted, the storybook look was only surface patina. This place had been fine-toothed by someone who understood security. Why? Because despite the fact that the house had been lit up so artfully, the grounds were also—and much more brightly—bathed in bright, white light. There was no place to hide while making an approach. No shadows to work. No bushes to scamper between. I quick-checked for security cameras, and found half a dozen, on motorized gimbals, covering all the angles. I squinted at the windows on the ground floor, and saw that except for four tiny bathroom vent windows partially obscured by thick well-watered ivy vines, they had been sheathed with the latest generation of anti-grenade screens. The basement windows—at least the few I could see—were plated over in steel, and covered by heavy bars.

We drew abreast of the entry, and a uniformed security guard, perspiration drenching his light blue uniform, waved Ashley through the gate, and onto the half-moon driveway. A second pair of sweating rent-a-cops holding flashlights directed us off the driveway and onto a broad courtyard, where perhaps two dozen vehicles were jammed door-to-door and bumper-to-bumper on white pea-gravel.

We scrunched our way across fifty feet or so of stones so hot I could feel them through the soles of my shoes, and climbed six wide stairs, up to a set of double glass and mahogany doors. A liveried footman standing next to the right hand door opened it for us and nodded deferentially as we passed him.

Once inside the crowded entryway, the temperature dropped by about twenty degrees. We bumped along at the end of a slow-moving knot of black-tied guests until our way was blocked by a short, extremely stocky woman in a sequined, tasseled ivory and gold evening dress that gave her the look of an antique lamp shade with legs. She scanned her clipboard, then gave me a VTVE—that's a Very Thorough Visual Exam, checked her clipboard again, peered over her half-glasses, and broke into an apple-cheeked smile. *"Cap-*ten Marcinko," she oozed. "I am Ivana. We are so *vary* pleased that you could be with us tonight."

I clicked my heels together and bowed in her direction, all lustful thoughts dismissed. "It is my pleasure, Miss Ivana." I nudged Ashley forward. "Allow me to introduce Major Evans of the United States Marine Corps."

Ivana's eyes chilled. She nodded formally. "I am pleased to meet you Major Evans. Velcome to Sir-jeek Foundation." She presented her hand, took Ashley's, and worked her arm once, up/down, like a pump handle. Then she stood aside and beckoned us through a narrow portal that led into the huge foyer area itself.

I urged Ashley to precede me. I followed. As I stepped through the portal, I heard a soft gonging sound.

A footman blocked my way. "Excuse me, sir," he said.

I put some distance between us. I don't like to be crowded, and this guy was crowding me. "What's the problem?"

He stepped up close again. "I'm sorry, sir, but we will have to have your weapon."

No fuckin' chance of that. "What weapon?"

I sensed a second body behind me and turned. Ivana had glided up. "I am sorry, *Cap*-ten, but we do not allow weapons to be carried here at Sirzhik. Our purpose is peaceful, and that is the image we insist that our guests present. It is a procedure that everyone here has been happy to honor, and it would please me very much if you, too, would conform to our custom."

"Since you asked so beautifully . . ." I reached behind me, and placed the pistol in its soft holster atop Ivana's outstretched palm. "Do I get a claim check, or will you remember whose gun is whose?"

Ivana giggled and batted her eyes at me coyly. "You will never need a claim check, Cap-ten Marcinko. Not with Ivana." She looked down at the diminutive K3 with a look of amusement on her face. "I should have imagined that you of all people would have something . . . larger," she said suggestively.

I grinned back Roguishly. "You probably don't know the old SEAL saying, Ivana—'the bigger your pistol, the smaller your gun.' "

Ivana thought about what I'd said, lips pursed, forehead wrinkled. When it finally translated properly, she threw her head back and roared with delight. "I vill re*mamb*er that the next time I go looking for a man," she said. She hefted the little piece, examined it, then gave my crotch a v-e-r-y penetrating stare. She looked down at the pistol once more, laughing as she did so. "Thank you, Cap-ten," she said over her shoulder. "I vill have this waiting for you, *van* you leave." With that, she wheeled, and waddled, thighs rustling, back toward her station at the entrance.

We wandered to our left, made our way through the high-ceilinged foyer, and were directed toward a long, marble-floored corridor that ran almost the whole depth of the mansion. The marble was topped with a series of antique Shusha, Jebrail, Kazak-Lambalo, and Shirwan tribal rugs; the walls lined with ornately framed sixteenth- and seventeenth-century oil paintings from the Flemish school. I noticed rest rooms to our left, halfway down the hallway. A small library that would have done justice to an English club opened off the right-hand side of the corridor. At the far end, a quartet of butlers stood sentry duty at a set of paneled hand-wrought wood-and-glass double French doors. I could hear violins beyond, and the muffled tone of a big crowd as we drew closer.

We ambled up. But instead of beckoning us inside, the butler with his hand on the right-hand door stood his ground, and looked at me inquisitively.

I stood my ground and looked at him inquisitively. I mean—WTF.

Ashley, the professional diplomat, the ossifer who'd been to spy school more recently than I, realized what he wanted. "Captain Marcinko and Major Evans," she said, a formal tone to her voice.

The butler cracked the door and stage-whispered to someone inside, "Cap-ten Marchenko and *May*-or Ewans."

I guess it was close enough for government work, because after a couple of beats, the butlers swung the double doors open, and we were allowed to Make Our Entrance.

Here's the Slo-Mo version: it was like walking onto a fucking movie set of one of those 1950s costume extravaganzas. The room itself was all white and gilt and high, beam ceilings. At each end of the huge chamber I could see a long table, heavy with food. Starched waiters passed trays of hors d'oeuvres and champagne to the huge crowd of formally dressed guests. On a raised dais, a string quartet in white tie was doing a very credible job of one of Beethoven's middle quartets. (I'll bet you didn't know I went in for those sorts of things. I'll bet you thought I liked vintage rock and country music. Well, I do—sometimes. But Beethoven, Schubert, Bach, and Brahms are all good for the Warrior's soul, which is why I've come to know 'em.)

And there, just inside the door, a security man shadow just behind his left shoulder, stood Our Host.

He was tall, slim, sharp featured, and distinguished looking. His face was lined around the eyes and mouth. His whiter-than-white teeth were small, and the canines were extremely pointed, giving him a vaguely predatory look that was amplified by short, black, flecked-with-gray hair spikily moussed to perfection. I noticed that his double-breasted tuxedo lapels were done in understated grosgrain, not showy silk, and that all the buttons on his jacket cuffs buttoned.

At his shoulder stood the missus, a slim woman with no bra, tiny aroused tits, and upswept hair, sporting an off-the-shoulder, form-fitting dress that must have cost more than most people make in six months. Oh, I knew them from their pictures, just as his eyes told me he knew me from mine. A half-smile crept across his face, then he turned the charm rheostat up all the way to overload, and the half-smile transmogrified into a hospitable, warm expression as he beckoned us forward.

He gave Ashley a quick-flash-of-teeth-nice-to-see-you-so-delighted-you-could-come shake of the head, then passed her off to his wife with the sort of professional, horizontal-motion hand-shake common to those used to being in long receiving lines.

Then he fixed me with his baby violets. Yes, friends, he had purple eyes. I know—people don't have purple eyes. So I guess he was wearing contacts. Why? Don't ask, because I sure don't know. But it did give him a distinctive, wolfish aura, when you combined the eyes with the spiky black-going-silver hair, the thick eyebrows, and the thin, sharp features. I wondered whether his nose was cold and wet, but suppressed any inclination to find out.

He looked me square in the face, his unblinking eyes probing my own, his cool, dry hands sandwiching my right hand, his long, aristocratic fingers reaching as far as the pulse in my wrists.

That was when he growled in one of those generically unidentifiable European-type accents, "I am Stephan Sarkesian, and I am truly delighted to meet you, at long last"—he paused—"face-to-face, Captain."

Oh, yes, oh, yes, oh, yes. He was speaking English now, but it was . . . *Da Voice*. That same distinctive, deep, mellow, unctuously lubricious tone I'd first heard on the late and unlamented POG's cell phone. Now, the pieces fell into place: he knew that I knew that he'd sent a team of Rogue Russkies out to kill me. And he was gauging just how I was going to digest that info.

Okay, now, since this is all going on in Slo-Mo, let me explain what Stephan Sarkesian, aka Steve-o, who is pretty fuckin' smart, had just managed to do.

What he'd done was that he'd put me on the polygraph. Oh, not, perhaps, so elaborate as the lie detectors that Christians In Action use to double-check their agents. But I was being given a flutter, just as thoroughly as if I'd been sitting in a chair and with the straps around my chest and wrist, and rubber cups on my fingers.

But he was doing it all manually. He was checking my eyes for the sorts of micromomentary fluctuations that signal mendacity in answers. Simultaneously, his hands were monitoring my pulse, and my sweat, and my tactile reactions.

Was it perfect? No. But I had to hand it to him (literally!): he'd wrapped me up pretty fuckin' good and I hadn't seen it coming.

But here, my friends, is where the ol' rubber really meets the road; where we separate the Warriors from the also-rans and the wannabes. The Warrior, you see, is Always In Control. In control of his body; in control of his mind; in control of the whole fucking situation. When my chute malfunctions at thirty-seven thousand feet—seven miles above what Chief Gunner's Mate/Guns Butch Wells calls *terror firmer*—I may be surprised by the malfunction itself, but I am not surprised by the situation. Why? Because I have already war-gamed what I will do. I will take control and defeat the malfunction.

When my body is immersed in fifty-three-degree water sans benefit of wet suit, and I still have to make my way across six hundred yards of frigid chop, I WILL PREVAIL because I will control my body; I will not allow myself to become hypothermic. Now, could I do that for an hour, or more? The answer, as you can probably guess, is a resounding NO. The laws of physics can be challenged, and they can be bent, by dint of sheer will, or sheer adrenaline. But in the end, they are natural laws, and natural laws cannot be permanently altered.

Here and now, in this situation, with Steve Sarkesian's eyes boring into my own, and his hands, sensitive as any surgeon's, waiting to perceive any minute change in my physical state, I used every molecule of my existence to MAINTAIN CONTROL OVER MY MIND, MY BODY, AND MY SITUATION.

And so, I looked directly back at him, my eyes hooded as a cobra's, so he could not see what I was thinking, my hand absolutely steady; the pulse in my wrist and my heart all as controlled and slow as I keep 'em when I'm on the range working out at eight hundred meters with a Remington PSS sniper's rifle, and an errant heartbeat can cause a missed shot. Oh, no—I gave him NOTHING.

I said: "It is a pleasure to meet *you* face-to-face, too, Sirzhik. I have learned a lot about you and your organization in the past day. Your employees leave a lot to be desired when it comes to efficiency and thoroughness. But a small part of what I discovered has been helpful to me and to my colleagues back in the United States, as well."

That's right—it was MY turn to put him on the spot and see how he handled it. I'm sorry to have to report that Steve-o flunked lunch. How did I know that? I knew it because I was watching the expression on his face. It was changing as quickly as one of those fucking dime-store kaleidoscopes I used to play with as a kid. The ones whose patterns changed when you twisted the cardboard cylinder in front of your eye. Well, Stephan Sarkesian's expression went from charming, to rage, to confusion, to bewilderment, to horror, to the final comprehension that I'd just performed a classic "Gotcha" on him—all in a matter of about a half-second (let me remind you again that this is all happening in Slo-Mo).

I smiled. "Just kidding."

He knew I wasn't kidding. I could tell by looking into his eyes. The eyes really are the doorway to the soul, my friends. And among the things they told me was that this particular asshole had no soul. None at all.

But he was a game player, and so, he played his game gamely. "Really," he said.

"Really," I replied.

He took me by the arm, turning to Ashley as he did. "I hope, my dear Major Evans, that you will not mind if I steal Captain Marcinko for a few minutes."

"Not at all, Mister Sarkesian."

He looked at me with his violet eyes, took the back of my arm, and guided me toward the door of a small antechamber. "Captain . . ."

I shrugged. "It's your party, Sirzhik. You want to talk, I'd like to listen."

He closed the door, leaned on it, and frowned. "I do not use that name anymore, Captain."

I grabbed a quick look-see. There was probably a couple of million bucks' worth of art in this room, which didn't measure more than ten by twelve. The guy obviously had good taste. Or at least his decorator did. "But you named your foundation the Sirzhik Foundation."

"That," he said, his face growing serious, "is to remind me who I was; and where I came from." He paused, as if searching for the right words, even though he struck me as the kind of guy who never, ever, had to search for the right words.

"Captain," he finally said, "I'd like to lay out for you a few realities about this part of the world."

"I'm listening."

And listen I did. The monologue lasted about a quarter of an hour, and it would take up far too many pages in this book for me to give you the whole, unexpurgated text. But let me play Thos. Bowdler for a couple of minutes, and give you the short version of what he said.

He claimed that NGOs[56] now play a quasi-official role in diplomacy and finance, especially in emerging economies such as Azerbaijan's, and that, as such, he considered the Sirzhik Foundation to be an equal of the United States, or any other government, when it came to encouraging diplomacy in the Caucasus, because of the sheer amount of money he was bringing into the region. "This office," he told me seriously, "is like an embassy. My chief of staff here is the equivalent of an ambassador. And what we provide is foreign aid."

He explained that as a European, he understood, much better

---

[56]Remember, those are NonGovernmental Organizations.

than anyone in Washington, what Azerbaijan needed in order to develop its natural resources. He insisted that the Americans, being market driven, operated in their own narrow political interest, while he and his foundation tried to operate in the interest of the entire region.

He insisted that missions such as mine only served to divide the host nations. Why? Because I was dealing with the military, and in places like Azerbaijan, the military was seen as callous, brutal, and repressive by most of the population, a throwback to the days of Soviet control. Only NGOs, he said, could bring the Azeris forward into the twenty-first century by encouraging the "right kind" (as he put it) of controlled market economy.

He gave me a real concerned look as he told me he knew about all my current problems with the Navy, and the White House, and how my career was hanging on a thread, all of which had exacerbated my drinking problem. He told me there was a real good place he could get me into if I wanted to dry out without anyone at the Navy knowing about it. I gotta tell you that Tony Merc had laid it on kind of thick when he slipped all that disinformation to the folks who were looking for dirt on *moi.*

But I guess it worked, because the next thing I knew, he was hinting that there could be big bucks in it for me if I was to share some of the "wisdom," as he put it, I was gaining during my visit here, with him. He was careful never to mention the words *intelligence,* or *spying,* or anything like that. In fact, I gotta tell you that he was smooth, and practiced, and entirely professional. That's what made him so fucking dangerous.

Well, friends, I listened to him as he piled the manure higher and higher. And it was indeed all horse puckey. Every bit of it.

Now, I wasn't going to let on that I knew about his ties to all those crime organizations. Or that I suspected he was using his NGO to launder money. Or that I thought he was as dirty as any double-dealing, pond-scum-sucking sphincter I'd come across in a long, long time. I also knew that it was time for me to give him the sort of wake up call that would rattle his teacup. But I had to do it carefully. If I didn't play the part right, he'd take me seriously. And I didn't want him doing that. Not yet. Not until I'd had the opportunity to take a real close look at his operation—and his office. Not until I had the goods on him, put him in the crosshairs, and was s-q-u-e-e-z-i-n-g the trigger.

"That's all very interesting, Sirzhik," I said. "But in point of fact, people like you can't do fuck-all."

He looked at me as if I was crazy. "Now, Captain—"

I didn't allow him to continue but stepped in, took him by the lapels, and let him see into the depths of my WARRIOR's soul by giving him my War Face, up close and personal. "Y'see . . . Sirzhik," I said, "let's take a fucking NGO like your foundation. Oh, you have economic clout. And you know a bunch of people who can pull strings. But that's it. You can't make policy, because you don't have a military to back it up." I paused. "You got a few goons here, a few goons there, but they don't mean shit. Now me? I'm here as a fucking projection of America's strength and power." I lifted his feet clear off the deck and shook him like a shaman's rattle. "See what I'm talking about, *Sirzhik?*" I asked, shaking him some more. *"That's* fucking power."

He tried to wriggle away, but I held him close to me. I knew he spoke French, so I told him, "Jap bed, scumbag."

He looked at me as if I were crazy. *"What?"*

"Fut-on. Get fucked, asshole." I shook him some more. "Lemme put that in Russkie. *Yob tvoy mat*—fuck you." He struggled, his feet tap-tap-tapping the floor as I held him. But I wasn't about to let him go. No way.

Then I gave him the Crazy Roguish Biker Gangster Jesse Ventura Look—the one where I cross my eyes and spew saliva when I speak. "They sent me here because I'm a fucking killer, Sirzhik."

He tried to pull back, because he was getting wet. Oops. He

couldn't move. Now it was time to set the hook. He knew I was dangerous. His body language told me that. But now he had to think I was a complete fool, so he'd leave me alone and let me do my job. I let his feet touch the floor, but I kept hold of his tux. "Now what really makes me mad is your saying I have a drinking problem. I don't know where you heard it, but it ain't fuckin' true. Got that?"

His head bobbed up and down.

"Good. Because lemme tell you, the next time you talk about my fucking drinking problem, Sirzhik, which is a problem I DON'T FUCKING HAVE AND NEVER FUCKING DID, I'm gonna come visit you and disassemble you, piece by fucking piece."

I started to let him go, and then, as if I'd just remembered something else to say, I grabbed him and pulled him even closer. "Because nobody tells me I have a fucking drinking problem. Nobody." I squinted at him to make sure he was receiving my message loud and clear. "Got that, Sirzhik?"

From the look on his face, he had indeed Got It. He realized that I was an alcoholic in full denial; that I couldn't handle being confronted with my problems; and that when I was confronted, I became belligerent and violent. And from the pace of his pulse, which I could feel through his tux, he didn't like having Got It one fucking bit.

Then it was my turn to take him by the back of his arm. Except I applied some real Roguish pressure. Enough to make him wince.

"So, now that we've had our little tête-à-tête, maybe we should go back and join the ladies." I elbowed him in the ribs hard enough to make the cartilage crack. "Mine's a real piece of ass, ain't she? And hey, yours ain't so bad for a broad without tits. Maybe we switch, huh?"

His eyes went all crazy on me. He struggled in my grip, but there was no way he could escape my grasp. Not until I decided to let him go. "And Steve—"

He looked over at me, his face contorted in pain. "No sweet speeches about me tonight, okay? I kind of like my privacy."

His expression told me I didn't have to worry about that one iota. Good. I opened the door with my left hand, and walked him through. His feet were barely touching the floor. We rejoined the receiving line, The missus gave him a nasty glance for deserting her. But Sirzhik wasn't looking at her. He was searching the crowd.

I held him close. "Thanks for the conversation, *baklan*," I stage-whispered, and then I licked his ear in the Hells Angels style just for emphasis.

He yanked himself away from me, turned, pulled a handker-chief out of his pocket, and rubbed his ear. He saw that people were staring at the two of us, and self-consciously he stuck the hankie back in his pocket. But he was out of my clutches, and obviously feeling safer now.

He backed toward a pair of his security guards and stood between 'em. "Our conversation was . . . very instructive." He looked at me with undisguised repugnance. But he was every inch The Diplomat he considered himself, because he managed to clench his teeth and say, "Please, go and enjoy yourself, Captain." He put another three feet of space between us. "I expect," he said through clenched teeth, "that we will have a chance to deal with one another in a . . . less public venue in the near future."

Steve Sarkesian paused, and cocked his head like a hunting falcon who's just noticed raw meat nearby. "I have just decided to remain in Baku for the foreseeable future," he said to no one in particular. His violet eyes caught the light from a chandelier and flickered brilliantly. "There is so much work to do here."

"You got that right, Sirzhik—that's what I always say: 'So many assholes to kill, so little time.' Right, huh?"

He started to give me that kaleidoscopic look again. But I moved on, giving Mrs. Sirzhik a Roguish leer as I passed.

Ashley took my elbow and steered me toward the bar. "What was that all about?"

"Mind games," I said. "I'm up one set to nil." I looked across the mansion-size blue-on-red Azeri beneath my feet, saw a familiar figure, and waved. "Yo, Avi—"

The little Israeli waved back. He was in what passes in Israel for a dress uniform, although it's a lot less "dress" than most Park Avenue doormen wear on a regular basis. But that's always been the case with the Israelis. They prefer killing to cocktail parties, and their uniform reflects that fact.

But more important than Avi, there was Mikki, his wife. She stands six inches taller than Avi—and she's a lot better looking, too.

We shouldered our way through the crowd and I picked Mikki up off the floor, whirled her around, kissed her on both cheeks in the French style, and then made the proper introductions.

Avi looked approvingly at Major Evans. "You know this crowd, of course," he said offhandedly. And when Ashley demurred, and hinted that she'd been left out of the social loop by the ambassador, Avi grinned and spread his arms wide. "Then let me tell you all about the who's and who's and vhat's and vhat's of this magnificent Baku intelligentsia," he said, a playful twinkle in his eye.

Ashley interrupted him right then by tapping her index finger below her own right eye in the French sign of skepticism. "Baku intelligentsia? Isn't that an oxymoron, Avi?" she asked.

That broke the ice. It wasn't five minutes before Ashley and the Ben Gals were chatting as animatedly as any old friends. I brushed up between Ashley and Avi and told them I'd be back in a few minutes, after I'd scoped the place out. But first, I went in search of succor—which I found at the bar. Lots of it, in fact. Standing at the end of the room, an old-fashioned glass of Bombay Sapphire on the rocks in my paw, I had a good opportunity to eyeball the party for a while, gauging the ebb and the flow of the place. I saw where the surveillance cameras had been placed. I noted the likely locations of hidden microphones. Then I ambled back up the main corridor toward the loos, stuck my head inside both, to take note of their layout as well (shocked the shit out of a bejeweled dowager socialite when I emerged from the stall next to hers, too).

Then it was back to the bar for another Bombay, and a tactical overview of the room. It didn't take long for me to pick up on the rhythms, either. In fact, it was kinda like looking at the ocean off the bridge of a big carrier. I watched eddies of socialites easing their way up and down the long, wide space, making sure they'd covered their bases by making contact with as many folks as they could, spending a few seconds with each—a kiss on each cheek, a smile, a knowing wink—then leaving 'em in their wake. There were half a dozen corner huggers, who'd come STO—simply to observe. There they were: drinking it all in, hungrily. But they wanted no part of full-contact party-going. And so they remained close to the reassuring safety of the walls and corners, watching from afar. There were lots of politicians and diplomats. Ambassador Madison, for one. She made her entrance like the fucking queen of the night, and spent a long, long time in earnest conversation with Steve Sarkesian, her fingers intertwined with his, playing the fucking "Moonlight Sonata" on his palm.

I watched their faces as they played handsie-handsie. Then I saw the look on Mrs. Sarkesian's face as she watched her hubby and Ambassador Madison try to play out their petit charade.

Of course. Eureka. It was obvious from the look on her face. Wifey knew what was going on. Wifey knew that Steve-o was getting a little on the side. A little . . . foreign aid . . . from our benevolent Ambassador Extraordinary and Plenipotentiary, Marybeth Madison.

Then, having played fuckee-fingers and probably given Steve-o a nice stiff dick, Ms. Madison proceeded to work the room like a pro, displaying her ten-grand dental work and her twenty-grand tits to all and to sundry. You had to hand it to her. She was just as smooth and polished as any senator up for reelection as she smiled and tittered and laughed her way through the crowd, a quartet of tuxedoed Diplomatic Security Service agents surrounding her in a rough diamond pattern, clearing the path.

Oh, she was a piece of work.

But I didn't have time to admire our good ambassador, because I wanted to eyeball the professionals here tonight. How did I know they were pros? I knew it just like I knew it in the Grand Europe Hotel lobby: because I am a fucking pro myself, and it takes one to know one.

And it didn't take me long to pick 'em out, either. Steve Sarkesian had his security people on duty. He'd brought 'em in from Paris, and they were smooth. Then there were the clods. To be precise, a TOC—a trio of clods—in badly tailored formal wear, who were elbowing and shouldering their way around as if they owned the place. By their moves, they obviously worked for Sirzhik, and they'd been assigned to keep an eye on *moi*, although they weren't doing a very good job of it.

The other two floaters *were* pros. One was a Sov—to be precise, a retarded[57] KGB brigadier general named Oleg Lapinov. He was wearing civvies, and he'd shaved his head, making him look almost like a malignant Mister Clean®, what with his puffy cotton-ball eyebrows and thick white handlebar mustache. But I still recognized his face, even from the ten-year-old DIA surveillance photos I'd been faxed. And lemme tell you, Oleg was no Mister Clean®. Not by a long shot. He was RBN—real bad news. He was in his seventies now, but he still had the stone killer look on his beat-up, round, perpetually red face. As a young KGB hood he'd actually worked for Uncle Joe Stalin, making political dissidents disappear in East Germany just after World War II. Later, he'd

---

[57]That's SEALspeak for retired.

been part of the KGB's advance group infiltrating Prague just before the Soviet invasion of Czechoslovakia in 1956. In the 1970s, he'd run training camps for transnational terrorists right here in the Caucasus. In 1979, he'd been in charge of the Spetsnaz Alpha Team that assassinated the president of Afghanistan just prior to the Soviet invasion. In the 1980s, he'd directed a ruthless policy of extermination against Afghan mujahideen leaders.

Now, he'd turned up once again—this time as the Kremlin's chief advisor on oil policy in the former republics. Which is to say, it was his job to notch the trees out here in Baku so they'd fall in a direction that would benefit Moscow, not Washington or anyone else. To do that, according to the CIA's RUMINT, he was Moscow's liaison with the *lovrushniki*—which is KGB slang for the Georgian, Azeri, and Armenian Mafiyas. He told 'em how far they could go collecting *dan,* or protection money. He set the limits on how big a *tusovka,* or piece of the action, they could slice themselves. At least that's what Jim Wink had told me when I'd asked who my opposition in Baku was.

And where was Oleg baby? He was playing yin to my yang. When I went right, he went left. If I did the port side thing, he did starboard. When I went fore, he mirrored the move. It was like we were two magnets, working in polar opposite. I decided to have some fun with him, but before I could manage anything, one of the Parisian security guys pulled him out of the crowd and ushered him over to the edge of the room, where Stephan Sarkesian stood, a serious expression on his wolfish puss.

I could tell from Oleg baby's body language that he didn't like being summoned. Well, that was in character. Generals, whether they're KGB or USA, like to give orders, not take 'em.

Hey, too fucking bad, Oleg. At least now I knew who really wore the stars on his shoulders. And then, as I looked on, Oleg and Steve were joined by the evening's second heavyweight, a slightly built Iranian scumbag named Ali Sherafi, whose dour demeanor, monochromatic black clothes, thick dark beard, and greasy hair gave him the forbidding bearing of an Islamic fundamentalist funeral director. Which wasn't actually too far from the truth.

Oh, yeah. I recognized Ali Sherafi from his DIA mug shots. As a young "student," Ali-baby had been part of the 1979 takeover of the American embassy in Tehran. But he was about as much of a student then as he was now. In point of fact, Ali Sherafi was one of the original members of Ayatollah Khomeini's militant Sepa-e Pasadran—the Iranian Revolutionary Guard Corps. He was alleged to be in disfavor in Tehran. Only last year, the intel reports said, he'd tried to mount a coup against the current Iranian government because he thought its policy of rapprochement with the West was evil and antirevolutionary. But he still had a few rabbis left amongst the mullahs, and they had, according to the stories Iranian sources were floating, saved him from prison, and sent him into a kind of exile, as an "agricultural expert," to consult with the governments of the Caspian region about improving grain exports to Iran.

And if you believe *that* cover story, I have a real nice piece of oceanfront property to sell you. It is just outside Grenville, New Mexico.

Something was rotten here—and we weren't even in Denmark. And being of the enquiring mind personality type, I wanted to find out what that something was. But I wasn't gonna do it by working the crowd. I was gonna do it, as you already know, by breaking into hostile territory, in this particular case Steve Sarkesian's office, for a recon; a sneak; a peek; and a quick look-see, followed by a speedy burglary and a rapid escape.

Now, if you are a student of these books, you know that it has been my experience in the past that assholes like Sarkesian are the sorts of egomaniacs who spend hundreds of thousands of dollars on security but then leave the computers in their offices turned on and unprotected by passwords. They have state-of-the-art electronic locks on their office safes—then stow important papers in their briefcases. But before I could accomplish any foray into hostile territory, I'd need to get rid of the TOC.

How? By use of a ploy; a ruse; a machination? No—I'd need something more . . . subtle than that. I'd need a Roguish diversion. And some hot intel, too.

Chapter

9

WHICH IS WHY I SAUNTERED BACK TO AVI AND, UNDER THE COVER OF making nice-nice with Ashley, asked if he had any idea where our host's office was. Avi gave me one of those "you're not really gonna do this" looks, and when he realized I was serious, whispered the info I needed. You got to hand it to folks like Avi, who take their jobs seriously. The look on Ashley's face told me that she wanted in on this little op. But I gave her a quick negatory glance. This had to be a solo excursion. She was unhappy with the news, but being a pro, she took it as well as could be expected.

Show Time. Intel in hand (okay, so it was in my head, but I'm being figurative), I hit the bar and requested a water tumbler full of Bombay on the rocks from the bartender. Then I slurped it loudly enough to cause nasty stares from the folks Avi'd called who's and who's, and nervous frowns from all the what's and what's in the vicinity. Then I shouldered (slurping all the way) to the buffet table and meandered down its considerable length, asking for (and receiving) huge portions of pasta, bloody rare roast beef, Beluga caviar, smoked Caspian sturgeon, and that ever-popular mayonnaise-based potato salad beloved by folks all over this region.

I grabbed one of the huge, starched linen napkins arranged at the end of the table, unfurled it, shook it one-handed, and tucked it into my collar so I wouldn't dribble anything on my tie in an ungentlemanly fashion. I sunk the water tumbler of Bombay right in the pile of perfectly prepared al dente spaghetti alla carbonara that sat dead center on my plate. Then, I plucked a large and very *au jus–s*y chunk of roast beef from the platter and got most of it into my mouth before the blood started—oops—dripping *jus* down my chin.

No matter. I jus' chewed away as, balancing the top-heavy plate somewhat precariously, and nodding and smiling all the way, I pushed back into the center of the room, right in the smack-dab middle of the crowd of black-tied swells, socialites, and pols.

Which is where I began to eat my dinner. Have I mentioned that I hadn't bothered to obtain any silverware? Well, I hadn't. And so, making polite yet Roguishly risqué conversation to all and sundry as I went, I proceeded to consume everything on my plate at flank speed, nodding and smiling and inhaling my food, all the time watching as guests around me scattered in horror.

Why were they scattering? Because they didn't want to be covered in the food I was inhaling.

Yes, inhaling. Yes, literally.

Now, as those of you who have been with me from the very start already know, I spent my youth as an enlisted geek in the Teams, which is shorthand for what used to be known as Underwater Demolition Teams, or UDT. There, as a member of Everett Emerson Barrett's Second (to None) Platoon, UDT Team 21, one of my duties was to make sure that our platoon always ate together. This was not always possible aboard ship during our six-month deployments. You see, there is a rigid caste system onboard ships under way. (Shit, there is even a rigid caste system onboard ships at anchor.) And that caste system put us Frogs at the bottom of the food chain. Which meant we slept, showered, shit, and ate only after everyone else, including the

Marines, had done so. And you know how Frogs feel about Marines, don't you?

No? Well, Frogs *love* Uncle Sam's Misguided Children. They love to make olive drab–colored toothpaste out of 'em. They love to wipe floors with 'em. You get the idea.

Now, so far as eating goes, the fact that we were LTWS[58] meant we couldn't take our meals as a group but had to squeeze ourselves in one by one at whatever table at the enlisted men's mess deck was partially open. Chief Barrett didn't like that at all, and so he hinted very strongly that I, and another Second (to None) platoon sailor, Mr. Mugs, regularly clear out a table on the enlisted mess deck so that our entire platoon could eat together.

Mr. Mugs and I developed the following Froggishly understated routine. We'd grab our plates, piling 'em high with food—specifics and food groups unimportant just so long as there was a lot of it—and then we'd sit down and eat. Sans utensils. Sans manners. Sans any civilized behavior whatsofuckingever. For example, it didn't take long until I got adept at sucking peas up my nose, and slurping spaghetti through my nostrils. If that didn't gross the tablemates out, we'd move 'em out by snorting honkers into each other's coffee and drinking 'em. The desired result took only a few days. In fact, by the end of the first week at sea, all I had to do was walk onto the enlisted mess deck and pick up a tray, and a couple of tables would just fuckin' clear out—even the Marines.

I can report to you that the art of sucking spaghetti through the Roguish nose is like riding a bike: once you learn how, it's easy to pick up again, even after many, many years.

And so, I worked the crowd. It didn't take too long—not more than ten minutes or so—until my diversion began to take its desired effect. Of course, I played the innocent. I adopted a puzzled glance as who's and what's melted away at my approach.

---

[58]Lower Than Whale Shit.

Finally, I cornered a woman in a strapless, sapphire blue evening dress, draped in the sorts of diamonds you see in fashion magazines that cost about ten bucks a copy. Now, for the life of me I couldn't understand why she looked at me so weirdly. I mean, what was so bad about three inches of spaghetti No. 12, dripping with raw egg and cheese, sticking out of my left nostril?

Well, if she was going to react like that—I simply snorted the offending pasta up and out of the way, put my finger to my opposite nostril to shut it down, then cleared the excess egg and cheese by blowing 'em ("Oops, sorry, lady") onto the ample bosom of her gown.

I reached over to wipe the egg off, but the goo on my hands did even more damage.

Her hubby, a short rotund number who had a face like a pug dog I know named Tuffy, stepped between the wifey and me, his pushed-in face all red and offended, and said something I couldn't quite understand. I think he was speaking Turkish. WTF. He could have been speaking Greek.

I shrugged, smiled as broadly as I could, stuffed a pair of peas up my nose, and inhaled. "Hey, food's great, huh?"

No answer. Well, according to Miss Manners, when there's a lull in the conversation, it's high time to move on.

I saw another target of opportunity across the ballroom and fired a shot across her bow. "Madam Ambassador—"

I watched her as I hove to. Even though I don't find the woman attractive, I gotta tell you, I can see why there were rumors for years that Marybeth Madison and the Leader of the Free World have been making the Beast with Two Backs (as Iago once called it) whenever the first lady was out of town and Mizz Madison found a way to leave her billionaire husband back in Texas and visit her pal BJ Bill in Washington. The woman is tall, well put together (even statuesque), and has the sort of command presence common to four-star flag officers, *Fortune* 500 CEOs, and Park Avenue doyennes. The problem was, that beneath that artfully crafted and well-maintained veneer of aristocracy and obvious wealth, lay a much thicker stratum of something else; a dark, manipulative, perhaps even vicious nature that made her— at least to me—sinister, repulsive, and forbidding.

As I approached, she regarded me with the sort of penile-withering arched eyebrow sneer that actually does render some types of men impotent for days. But her face darkened in anger as she realized that she was looking at someone with a much more permanent hard-on than Clinton. That's when the ambassador took in the whole package of *moi:* the soiled napkin tucked under my beard, the glass of Bombay Sapphire with greasy fingerprints all around shoved in the pile of pasta, and the many fragments of food woven into my facial hair. Her expression was even more fucking kaleidoscopic than Steve-o's had been. As she observed each messy element of my appearance, her face transmogrified: displeasure morphed to aversion; aversion was transfigured to repulsion. And repulsion became simple, cold hatred.

I, of course, paid no outward attention whatsoever. I smiled— my teeth covered in crushed Beluga—and wiped egg from my nose. "Is this a great fuckin' party or what?"

That sent her over the edge. "You are a total disgrace to your country," she hissed as she slowly and carefully backed away, putting distance between us. "And I will make sure that Washington learns about this . . . performance." With that, she turned on her heel and stalked off, her security detail parting the crowd so that she could make her escape.

In response, I shrugged, lifted my messy tumbler of gin, and drained it, allowing a fair amount of Bombay to run out the sides of my mouth, down my chin, through my beard, and into my collar. I wiped at my face with my sleeve. I'd been at this game for almost half an hour now, and frankly, it was getting OLD. Not to mention the fact that getting all this shit cleaned off my bespoke blazer was going to cost me the old arm and the old leg. But expenses be damned. I was also getting the desired results, to wit, I was being pointedly ignored by the crowd of swells, who turned away whenever I drew close.

You want more evidence my act was working? Okay, right now, even as I'm speaking, the TOC Steve Sarkesian had detailed to watch me was breaking contact. In fact, they were being waved out of the room by Miss Ivana, who now looked at me with undisguised loathing. I waved at her and blew a food-stained kiss. She chose to ignore my messy-faced smile, whirled on a Miss Piggy ankle, and departed.

And what about Steve Sarkesian? I worked my way to starboard. He was deep in conversation with Ambassador Madison. There is a SEAL technical term for her emotional state. It is, *pissed off*. She was reading him the fucking riot act. And guess what: he was taking it. That's what pussy will do to you, friends. It will whip your ass. And Steve Sarkesian was obviously pussy-whipped, when it came to matters Madison, because he was simply nodding his head up and down like one of those toy dogs you used to see in the rear windows of Buick sedans and Olds 98s.

Then, all of a sudden, Ambassador Madison was done—done with Steve, and done with the evening's programme. She gathered her security minions around her and swept into the night, leaving him standing there like a fool, sputtering.

His reaction, when he realized I was looking at him cross-eyed, was to motion Oleg Lapinov and Ali Sherafi up close, and gesture in my direction. From the expression on his face, he was probably saying something negative about me.

Or maybe not. But whatever he'd said, the former KGB general didn't like it. He was shaking his big, shaved head in disagreement. He tried to interrupt Sarkesian, a big, thick finger in the Armenian's face, but got cut off with a quick look that was downright scary.

The slim Iranian had a smirk on his face. He stood with his

arms crossed petulantly. His body language told me that whatever the Russkie was saying, or trying to say, Ali Sherafi wasn't buying it. He was siding with Steve-o.

Then the Russkie turned, his face flushed with anger, stomped off, and headed for the exit. Probably looking for the vodka truck. Ali Sherafi put both of his hands on Steve Sarkesian's shoulders, hugged him, and kissed him, thrice, in the Arab Terrorist style common to such folks as Yasser Arafat and Abu Nidal. Which I found somewhat funny, because Iranians ain't Arabs.

Well, whatever the fuck they were into, it didn't frigging matter. Not right now, anyway. Because I'd achieved what I'd set out to do: the shadow-goons had been pulled off the case. So, it was time for me to go to work.

First things first: unzipping my fly as I went (there's nothing like really making sure people really understand the sort of character you're playing), I lurched toward the head, bifurcating the swells in my path as I did so. The men's john was off the outer side of the long hallway, about halfway between the foyer and the ballroom. It was what my friends from West By-God[59] call an uptown two-holer: two stalls and a sink. And it had an outer door that locked with a dead bolt.

A gent with a bunch of ribbons on his tux already had his hand on the doorknob. I tapped him on the shoulder (leaving finger smudges), pointed to my unzipped fly, and nudged him out of the way. "I'm gonna be a while," I said.

Inside, I put the plate in the sink, twisted the heavy bolt closed, then double-checked to make sure the door was secure. I didn't want Mister Murphy interrupting anything.

I hit the elapsed-time counter switch on my little-watch-big-dick-watch, opened the right-hand stall, climbed atop the com-

---

[59]That's the way we SEALs refer to West Virginia.

mode, and cranked the small, frosted glass window open, and poked my big Slovak snout through. Damn—just beyond the frame was a thick knot of ivy vines. I cranked the window until it wedged against the ivy, squeezed my head and right shoulder through the opening, and tried to move the green foliage aside.

It wouldn't budge. But I could still muscle my way through. I forced my left shoulder through the window, and wrestled with the dense vines, which abutted the narrow bathroom window like jail cell bars. Then, with both arms, I rent the pair of thicker-than-my-dick vines that blocked my egress. Shit—they weren't just thicker than my dick, they were harder, too: as stiff as fucking steel. But I'm a big, strong motherfucker, and thick or not I muscled them far enough apart to poke my head through, and grab a quick look-see.

Seven feet below me sat a thick, dark hedge. Beyond it lay a wide swath of lawn, which ran up to the tree line just behind the mansion's outer wall. I swiveled my head and looked for the security camera. I guess I loosened my grip as my attention was distracted, because the fucking vines came out of my hands, snapped back, and caught my head between 'em as firmly as if I'd been locked in a set of Puritan stocks.

But I don't press 450 pounds, 155 times a day for nothing. I took the offending pair and, straining as I did, forced them back apart, and extracted my head. I lost a fair amount of skin on my cheeks and ears as I pulled through, but WTF, it was only skin.

Okay, on to Plan B. I closed the window, dropped onto the tile floor, moved to the left-side stall, opened the window, and checked for obstruction. Here, the ivy was less dense—more tendrils and fewer dick-thick vines. I pushed my shoulders through, pulled myself out and stood, partially concealed by the bulky vegetation, on the narrow window ledge.

Now I could really do some recon. Eight feet or so above me was the bottom of a narrow balcony. And over there, sixty feet away, at the corner of the building, the surveillance camera pivoted on its gimbal, sweeping from the wall of the mansion with its thick bushes, out across a wide swath of lawn, toward the graveled parking lot, and back again.

I ticked off seconds in my head as I watched the camera go through two full observation cycles. My guesstimate was that I had thirteen seconds in which to jump or pull myself up the ivy high enough to grab the bottom of the balcony, work myself up, hoist myself over the rail, and drop down flat, before the camera swung back far enough to catch any possible movement.

No, that is not a lot of time. But it was all the time I had. And so, I watched and waited another full cycle, and then, as carefully as any surfer times the way he catches the Big One, I reached up, grabbed a handful of ivy vine, tested it, and when I knew it would take my weight, I heaved myself out of the window, put my foot on the sill, and pulled myself up-up-up.

Which, of course, is when Mister Murphy disengaged all the fucking ivy tendrils from the fucking stonework, I lost my balance, my feet slipped off the windowsill, I fell backward and tumbled ass over teakettle, landing face first on the nicely watered, densely packed lawn, just outside the neatly trimmed hedge.

Here is the good news: I did not break my neck. Here is the bad news: I hit the ground hard enough to stun myself, and I lost count of how many of those thirteen fucking seconds I'd used up by falling. Wild-eyed, I looked over and saw—fuzzily—that the camera had hit the apogee of its arc, and was heading back my way.

Oh damn, oh shit, oh, doom on Dickie. Cover—I needed cover. Which meant the hedge. I rolled over, scrambled to hands and knees, and hurled myself toward the bushes, which were dense with small dark green and purple leaves.

And thorns. *Beaucoup* thorns. Big, spiky, prickly, *sharp* thorns. Nasty, body-piercing, skin-lacerating, pain-inflicting thorns.

Oh, that fucking *hurt*.

I lay quietly, trying not to move, because every time I moved, another quadrant of the ol' Rogue body was impaled. I had so many things sticking in me I looked like one of those fucking fourteenth-century Florentine-school martyr paintings. And don't fucking ask how I felt.

But guess what: I couldn't just lie there and take it. That's not the SEAL WAY. The SEAL WAY is to OVERCOME ALL OBSTACLES AND FUCKING TOUGH IT OUT.

And so, thorns be damned, I rolled over far enough to be able to make out the position of the security camera. Then, when it had swiveled far enough out of the way, I began my count (*one thousand, two thousand*) and quick and quiet, pulled myself up against the wall of the mansion and clawed my way up, up, up (*three thousand, four thousand, five thousand, six thousand, seven thousand, eight thousand*) past the bathroom window. My fingers found the edge of the balcony ledge (*nine thousand, ten thousand, eleven thousand*), I chinned myself, muscled my body over the low wrought iron railing (*twelve thousand, thirteen thousand*) and collapsed, silently but completely exhausted, on the cool tile floor.

There wasn't a part of me that didn't hurt. But as you know, I have a very special relationship with pain. Pain was created so that I know I am alive. At that moment, I knew I was very much alive. My crisp white shirt was neither crisp nor white anymore. Well, sure, it had been somewhat food stained. But now it was flecked with blood. My blazer was pierced and ripped where the thorns had pulled against the fabric. My grass-stained trousers were shredded too.

But that was all cosmetic shit. Cuts and bruises heal quickly, given a long soak between warm thighs and enough Dr. Bombay. I checked the elapsed time on my watch. It showed 00:02:01 since I'd locked the bathroom door. God, how time flies when you're having fun.

I reached down and untied my shoe, extracted my set of lockpicks, checked to make sure the French door windows weren't wired, and when I'd ascertained they weren't, I went to work.

00:02:57. Inside—no sweat. I eased the doors shut behind me, and looked around. I'd let myself into some sort of drawing room. There were no alarms, no motion detectors, and nothing of interest either. I could see light under the double doors on the far side of the room, which is where I made my way carefully (no creaking of floors allowed).

I tested the right-hand door. It was not locked, and so I cracked it ever so slightly. I could hear the buzz of the party going on downstairs. The string quartet was playing a very passable Mozart.

Okay, the question was, where the fuck was I going. You know, in all those pogue Rogue action-adventure flicks Hollywood puts out or you see on the TV, the Good Guy just abso-fuckingunswervingly heads for the Bad Guy's HQ, or the secret room, or whatever the fuck, without having received one god-dam iota of tactical intel about where the goddamn room is.

Well, that is what's known in the real world as horseshit. People like me don't like to operate without intel. It doesn't make sense.

Which is why I'd asked Avi if he knew where Stephan Sarke-sian's office was, and why Avi, being a sneaky, manipulative, and altogether thorough intelligence operator, had told me (in his lovely, Israeli accent), *"Fairst floor, bleck eleven."*

" 'Bleck eleven,' " you ask.

Yeah, bleck eleven. Like me, Avi Ben Gal uses the SAS Colour Clock to provide physical location in structures.

You say you forgot how the SAS Colour Clock works.

Well, fuck you, you have bad retention. What the fuck do you suffer from, ADD?

Okay, I will explain. But this is the last fucking time.

The SAS Colour Clock is a designator by which we SEALs (and lots of other SpecWar operators, too) can define where a location within a structure is, without having to be redundant or confusing. All structures are divided into four quadrants. The back side is black; the front is white; the left-hand side as you face it is green, and the right-hand side is red. Then, starting at the rear center, you overlay a twelve-hour clock. Thus, when Avi told me I'd find Steve Sarkesian's office at bleck eleven, he was telling me that I should head toward the rearmost left-hand corner of the mansion.

Now, since the men's loo was about a third of the way back along the mansion's port side, I knew where I had to go. I turned left, and made my way down the corridor.

You had to hand it to the fella who used to be called Sirzhik—he did have taste. The marble floor was covered in more of those beautiful, antique Azeri rugs, rich antique patterns that featured robust reds and rich blues and delicate ivories. The walls, which reached ten feet to the ceiling, had been stripped and replastered to give them the look of old bleached stone. On the walls, huge Persian wooden gates and narrow, antique Arab olive-wood doors, inlaid with ornate patterns made of mother-of-pearl, had been artfully hung so that they appeared to be suspended in space, sans any support.

But I wasn't here to admire the fucking scenery. I was here to commit burglary. And so I started paying less attention to the decor, and more to the environment.

00:03:29 The corridor went left. I peered around, to make sure it was empty—and it was. I stepped around. In front of me was an antique double door made of paneled, burled walnut. Instinctively, I tried the ornate brass knob. It was locked. I looked for a keyhole, so I could jimmy the damn thing—but there was none.

And then I saw the fucking keypad sunk into the wall just to the right of the door frame. An electronic lock. The motherfuck-er'd had an electronic lock installed.

Now, I can bypass electronic locks—if I have the right equipment. But all I had tonight was my fucking set of lockpicks. I shook my head in disbelief, and looked to see where the hell Mister Murphy was lurking, because I knew the sumbitch was somewhere close by. The clock was ticking, and I was not getting anywhere. This was not Good News.

Now, here is a bit of SpecWar sooth, as provided to me many years ago by Roy Henry Boehm, the Godfather of all SEALs. I'd gone to visit Roy down in Florida, to get some Froggish advice about a problem I was having with a tight-assed three-star. We were sitting in a bar on the wharf about a mile and a half from his house, nursing a couple of brewskis, and I idly asked him how he problem-solved when he was stuck in the middle of a tactical goatfuck.

Quoth Roy: "Listen, asshole, when you've been butt-fucked by Mister Murphy, you have to butt-fuck him back ASAP. So just fuckin' railroad crossing, and the solution will come to you."

I chugged the last of my beer and ordered another round. "Railroad crossing?"

Roy slapped his glass on the table so loud that everyone in the whole frigging bar turned toward him. He waited until they turned away, then stage-croaked, "You worthless, shit-for-brains pencil-dicked tadpole pukes don't know fuck-all, do you? Yeah, railroad crossing: fuckin' stop, fuckin' look, and fuckin' listen. And if you take the fucking time to take a deep breath and assess your situation—and it generally doesn't fucking take much fucking time at all to do it—you'll realize exactly how to fuck the fucking fuckers."

As you can see, Roy is a very direct fellow. And his advice is always good. And so I stopped futzing. Then I looked—really looked—at the door. And I listened to the sounds of classical music wafting down the empty corridor, freeing my brain from all the stress of the moment. And sixteen seconds later, staring me in the ol' Rogue puss, was the solution to my problem.

I'd had tunnel vision. I'd been fixating on the lock. Well, *fock* the lock. When I looked, really looked, I realized that Steve Sarkesian's office doors opened outward. I'd been staring straight at the goddam door hinges, but I'd never really *seen* 'em until I'd stepped back, took a deep breath, and followed Roy's advice.

Chapter

10

00:03:51. I USED THE POINT OF A PICK TO POP THE HINGE BOLTS. I POCK-eted 'em, pried the door open without disturbing the electronic lock mechanism, then e-a-s-e-d it back (more or less) into position from the inside.

That had been easy. I looked around the office. It was dark, but there was enough light coming from outside so that I could see pretty clearly. And, when I opened the drapes all the way, the visibility improved some more.

He'd done the place in a kind of French château style. Lots of hand-carved wood, and rich carpets. There was the Washington style "OH, FUCK, BUT I'M IMPORTANT" wall, which featured warmly inscribed pictures of Steve Sarkesian shaking hands with a panoply of world leaders. But I wasn't there to admire the scenery. I was there to gather intel. And I wasn't going to be altogether subtle about it either. Remember, I wanted to *hock* the ol' Sarkesian teacup. And so I headed for Steve-o's desk, and when I discovered it was locked, I pried it open with a convenient letter opener.

I fumbled around. There was a cellular phone—the same model I'd taken off the POG. I thought about pocketing it, but decided not to. I had one of Steve's phones, I didn't need another. But way back

189

in the drawer my fingers came upon a computer disk. I slid it forward, then looked it over. It was unlabeled, but I took it anyway.

I went through the rest of the office, but found nothing of interest. Finally, I rifled the credenza, a nice, eighteenth-century, French burled walnut piece. Not a lot there, either. I found half a dozen notes scrawled in Russkie and stuffed 'em in my pocket. And another computer disk, which I also took, and a bunch of Sirzhik Foundation letterhead—thick, expensive stuff from Cartier in Paris. But basically, this office was a showplace, not a working area. There were no files; no business correspondence; no nothing. I even tried tapping the walls but could discover no secret compartments.

Well, in the intelligence business, sometimes what you don't find is as important as what you do find. And in this instance, I'd learned that Steve Sarkesian either kept all his work with him at another location, or didn't do much work at all in this office.

Except . . . I had this nagging feeling that I was overlooking something significant. Just like outside the door, I was tunneling. I sat on the edge of the desk and let my mind wander.

That was when I realized what I'd missed, and missed, and missed. I reached into the kneehole under Steve Sarkesian's desk. There, where I'd seen it without seeing it, was his thin, black leather attaché case. I retrieved it, put it on the desk, and examined it, running my fingers over the mottled surface of the leather. Geezus—the fucking thing was made of crocodile. I flicked at the combination locks with my thumbs, but they didn't open. Well, time was getting short, and I wasn't in the mood to screw around, and so I took the letter opener, pried the brass flanges from the frame of the case, and flipped the lid up.

Inside lay four bundles of papers. I looked at the top sheaf, and saw it was a photocopy of an official U.S. government document. The cover sheet bore the seal of the National Security Council, and the stamped notation TOP SECRET.

That got my attention fast enough. I leafed through the ten-

page report. It didn't take long to figure out that what I was looking at was a draft briefing paper detailing our negotiating positions about the oil pipeline that the United States wanted to build
between Baku and Turkey, and outlining our public and private
stances toward Iran, Russia, Armenia, and Azerbaijan.

The paper provided an inside look at how we would proceed;
it summarized potential fallback positions; it was undiplomatically direct in its political assessments of the region, and the
regional players. Obviously, it hadn't been put together by the
folks at State, because the prose wasn't sufficiently wishy-washy.

Judging from the date on the cover page, it was an early draft.
But early or not, it had no business being in Steve Sarkesian's
briefcase, unless he was a fucking NSC staffer, which we all
know he wasn't.

I flipped through the other three documents. One was a draft
of a long memo from Ambassador Madison to the secretary of
state, suggesting ways in which the Sirzhik Foundation could be
used to help further American goals in the region. Here is the bad
news: the memo hadn't been written by the ambassador; it was
on the Foundation's letterhead. Here is the good news: there was
a Post-it note attached to the last page. It read:

> Dearest—this sort of thing won't fly back in Washington, so, I'm
> going to have to respectfully decline to allow it to go forward
> in any form. But I can't wait to see you again and hope my
> negative reaction to this draft won't spoil what we have. —M.

Okay, so the fact that Ambassador Madison could separate her
personal life and her professional life gave her a check in the
"plus" column of the ledger I carry in my head. That—and a
buck-and-a-half token—would get her on the subway in New
York. Quickly, I examined the rest of the papers. There was a

long, detailed document handwritten in a language I couldn't decipher, And there was a final report of some kind, twelve pages in all, written in Cyrillic, with what had to be TOP SECRET stamps on the top and bottom of each page.

I speed-read the ten pages of the NSC draft. Shit—the fucking thing had enough raw intelligence data in it to point toward some of the United States' holy of intel holies, its sources and its methods. And having that kind of document in one's possession, my friends, is a no-no. In fact, it is fucking illegal, because disclosure of top secret material (and this is the official definition), "could reasonably be expected to cause exceptionally grave damage to the national security of the United States."

And when exceptionally grave damage to the national security of the United States takes place, then I get the green light to shoot and loot and take no fucking prisoners whatsoever.

Now, let's look at what's happened in the past couple of days. A bunch of folks have been murdered. A bunch of no-goodniks working for Stephan Sarkesian have tried to kill *moi*. And now, I discover that this self-same Sarkesian not only has a couple of world-class killers (e.g., Oleg Lapinov and Ali Sherafi) as his honored guests here at the Sirzhik Foundation, but he is also in possession of a document that would get him locked up if he were back in the U.S. of A. and the FBI knew what he had.

00:05:59. Shit—how time flies when you're having fun. Quickly, I folded the reports and thrust 'em into my jacket pocket. I went through the case to be sure he wasn't hiding any more classified material. He wasn't—but I removed the rest of the letters and memos and Post-it notes, which were in English and French and Cyrillic and Azeri and Armenian and what looked like Farsi—just to be on the safe side.

I closed the now-empty briefcase and slipped it back under the desk. If what I'd just done didn't rattle the Sarkesian teacup, nothing would. Nobody likes to be burgled. Especially folks like Steve-o.

Especially when what's been purloined is valuable information that he probably had a hard time obtaining in the first place.

But, just to make sure he knew who'd done the deed, I took a sheet of that thick Cartier letterhead from the credenza, grabbed a pen, and scrawled, "Yo, Sirzhik, FYVM," and left it dead center on his desktop. I hoped he'd find some significance in the "dead" part of the positioning.

00:06:34: I eased the door shut and replaced the hinge pins, snuck back down the hallway, went out onto the balcony, down the ivy, back into the head, and emerged from the head at 00:07:24. To be honest, it wasn't as good a time as I could have managed ten years ago, but it was still pretty fuckin' respectable for a guy with as many dings, nicks, dents, and dimples as I have on my fenders.

Avi's, Mikki's, and Ashley's eyes all went wide as I crossed the crowded room toward them, the crowd parting for me as I proceeded. Maybe it was the blood, egg, and caviar on my shirt-front; maybe it was the knee-shredded, grass-stained trousers. Maybe it was—well, it didn't matter. I draped one arm around Avi's shoulder, and the other around Ashley's, and whispered a nutshell sit-rep.

Major Evans was undiplomatically direct: "Holy shit," she said, drawing a stare or two.

Avi Ben Gal betrayed nothing. He looked up at me, and mouthed, "Can you let me have the non-American documents?"

I thought about it. Here is the Rogue's most basic rule of intelligence gathering: NEVER GIVE UP AN ORIGINAL DOCUMENT, EVEN TO YOUR BEST FRIEND. Especially if it is the only copy. "What about I make you some Xeroxes tomorrow?"

"No problem." The Israeli shrugged. "But the sooner the better." He paused, then put his hand in the small of his wife's back and nudged her toward the door. "*Yalla,* Mikki, let's go home. *Hava na-mova.*"

Avi and Mikki took point. Ashley and I followed. Across the

room, Steve Sarkesian stood, his mannequinlike wife draped on his arm, deep in conversation with Ali Sherafi. Still, he took note of us—and of the way I was comporting myself, which is to say, normally. It was immediately apparent by the look on his face that he realized he'd been had once again—good—and it was a look that told me he didn't like being had. Didn't like it at all.

I guess I was in one of my stop-me-before-I-kill-again moods, because as I passed in front of him, I couldn't resist demurely tapping atop the inside breast pocket of my messy blazer, where the slight bulge of papers gave me a Roguishly D-cup appearance. Then I discreetly pointed toward the ceiling with my gnarled index finger, indicating where I'd just been playing. Then I tossed him the bird, just so he'd know he was number one with me.

The color drained from his face. His expression turned absolutely homicidal. There's no other way to describe it. Believe me, I know homicidal, and there was murder in Steve Sarkesian's eyes. He took two steps in our direction. But there was nothing he could do, not with this crowd of whoses and vhatses milling around. Not without betraying the real Steve Sarkesian. The asshole who hangs out with tangos and stone killers. And he was too much of a pro for that. I could see him trying to stabilize: to steady and brace himself so he would remain outwardly cool. It took a lot of effort, but he finally brought himself under control. Still, the look he gave me as we went through the door told me that this episode wasn't over. Not yet. And not by a long shot.

Part Two

THE ENEMY OF MY FRIEND

Chapter

11

THAT LONG SHOT CAME AT 0840 THE FOLLOWING MORNING. I HEARD
it—a dull explosion that reverbed the window of my hotel
room as I was using the secure satellite phone and scrambler
fax to transmit both a report of my activities and the top secret
documents I'd taken from Steve Sarkesian's briefcase back to
General Crocker. As soon as I'd gotten in after Ashley'd
dropped me off, I'd called him at Quarters Six back in Washington to tell him what I had discovered. Fortunately, he was
more pissed at my news about finding the big DIQ[60] than he
was upset with me for causing what Ambassador Madison had
already called his office to describe as a damaging diplomatic
incident involving a drunken and out-of-control U.S. Naval
officer, i.e., *moi.*

The Chairman groaned. Yes, friends, he actually groaned. Then
he sighed. I'd never heard him do either before. "You really took
the documents?" he asked, as if he wanted to hear a different
answer.

---

[60]Document-In-Question, and of course pronounced "Dick."

I told him once again that I had—and that I had 'em in my possession.

My voice was followed by a long and uncomfortable period of silence. Then General Crocker instructed me to give him a full report on the situation. He wanted my read on the situation regarding the relationship between Ali Sherafi, Oleg Lapinov, and Stephen Sarkesian. He wanted the full details about what I'd done, and precisely how I'd done it. "I want the whole damn nine yards, and not a detail spared" is the way he put it to me. When I'd finished, I was to roll my big DIQ, the Russkie document, the handwritten memo, the Sirzhik Foundation draft, and my report into the fax machine and send 'em directly to the secure comms shack in his office, where he'd see them first thing in the morning.

It had taken me the rest of the night to accomplish what the Chairman had asked for. I looked away from the fax at the sound of the dull thud. Even with the air-conditioning going, I knew I was listening to the impact of a sizable chunk of high explosive. Five seconds later, the hotel building itself shuddered slightly from the aftershock. I went to the window and peered out. It was a great view—looking southwest, with the center of the city fanned out in front of me. The room was on the ninth floor—high enough to see much of the skyline. In the hazy distance, was the light blue water of the Caspian.

Off to my left, at about ten thirty, I saw a thick plume of dirty black rising into the morning sky, coming from the part of old Baku that houses many of the city's diplomatic compounds and residences. The nasty color of the smoke confirmed for me that what I'd just heard was high explosive. The pattern and distribution—after all, this was Baku and there was no wind, just heat—was similar to the initial aftermath of car bombs I've seen in Lebanon, Northern Ireland, and Turkey, to name a few of the sites where Mister Murphy has steered me to the wrong place, at the wrong time.

As an aside, let me state for the record that I detest fucking car bombs. They're too goddam random. Oh, there are occasions when I've used 'em, like the time I was able to vaporize Islamic Jihad's master bomb-maker in the late 1980s as he made his way north on a little street called Farid Trad, just past the old UNESCO compound in Beirut. Sometimes, they're the only way to hit a target and make it look like it was a local job, not a U.S. Navy SEAL hit. But the problem with car bombs is that they cause a lot of what the Pentagon likes to call collateral damage, i.e., innocent (or at least not guilty) civilians. In Beirut, for example, I killed my intended target. But in the process, sixteen other folks were vaporized, too—a real nasty case of wp/wt.[61]

But then, war itself is a messy business. It's not precise. You can't wage war by taking polls, or worrying about "collateral damage," because if you do, you will end up getting a lot more of your own people killed—and making fewer of the enemy into corpses. You have to make the moral choice in war that killing some enemy civilians, or bystanders, or poor folks who are in the wrong place at the wrong time is a lesser evil, because you have decimated your target and saved a lot of other lives in doing so. Perfect? Far from it. But it is a moral choice I, for one, can—and do—live with.

I called the U.S. embassy for a sit-rep. Yes, I know I am persona non grata there. But I didn't call the RSO, or the ambassador's office, or even Ashley. I called the gunny at the Marine Security Detail's Post Number One, identified myself, and asked if there was anything he knew about the explosion we'd both just heard.

There was a slight pause as the name recognition hit. Then, because he was a Marine gunny, and he was more concerned about solving problems than he was about playing politics, he told me the answer was no, sir. Then he said, "Wait just a second, please, sir," and put me on hold. Two minutes later he came back

---

[61]Wrong place and wrong time.

on the line and said that according to his scanner, there had just been an incident involving an Israeli diplomat, and he had to go right now, because his boss, the detail's master gunnery sergeant, was about to ratchet the embassy's security profile up one notch, to Threatcon Charlie.

I'd just dropped the receiver on the cradle when it rang again. "Marcinko."

"Dick, it's Ashley."

"What's up."

"Are you okay?"

"Sure. Why?"

"Your friend—"

I had only one friend in Baku, and it wasn't Steve Sarkesian. "Avi."

"Avi. I've just received a report that says his car was ambushed as it left his flat on the way to the Israeli embassy."

Oh, that was not good news. "Did they get him?"

"We don't know. It's pretty crazy out there. The Israeli embassy's buttoning up, and so are we."

"What's the location of the bombing?"

She told me. I hung up before she could say anything else, grabbed a pistol and a flak vest, and launched toward the door.

I had it open when I realized I still had eleven pages to fax.

There are times when doing your duty is painful—and this was one of them. But life is made up of priorities, and getting my material to the Chairman took precedence over everything else.

I finished transmitting, and was securing the documents in the lockbox when the phone rang again. I reached out and grabbed the receiver.

"Dick—this is Avi."

I can tell you, my friends, that I have seldom, in a life of War, destruction, and death, been happier to hear a voice. "Avi, what happened? They said—"

"I'm okay, I'm okay" his voice came back shaken but steady. "But my driver is dead and Mikki needs medical attention. Needs it badly."

Oh, fuck, oh, shit, oh Goddammit. "What happened?"

"Some *b'nai zonim*[62] put explosives in a car half a block down from our flat. We live on Abbas Sikhat Street, which runs one way, so we can't make a turn until we come to the Azadiyg Prospekt. That's the only part of the route to the embassy I can't vary. They detonated as we drove up to the intersection. There's a big wall right there on the left side of the street—some big corporate estate—and the wall amplified the blast."

He took a deep breath. "They knew what they were doing, Dick. It was as good an op as we ever ran in Lebanon against Hezb'allah." The Israeli gulped for more air. "But Mikki was with me this morning—she wanted to buy groceries at the embassy commissary, and she was sitting on the left side of the car." He paused. "That was the side that took the brunt of the blast." His voice started to waver. "She's not in good shape, Dick. Not in good shape at all."

"What can I do? Where do you need me to be?"

He heaved a huge sigh, then started talking in rapid-fire bursts. "Okay, I need you to keep going on what we've discussed between us. The . . . vatchamacallit . . . thing down south. I am convinced what happened today and last night are interrelated. You remember last night? You know what I'm speaking about?"

He was referring to what I'd done at the Sirzhik Foundation. "I do, Avi, I do—take it easy."

"I never got the materials, Dick. You keep them until I get back." He stopped as suddenly as if he'd been switched off, and I heard him consciously trying to wrestle himself under control. When he'd calmed himself, he breathed deeply, then continued:

---

[62]That's a Hebrew idiom for sons of bitches. The literal translation is "sons of whores."

"Look, there's an El Al flight to Tel Aviv in two hours, and if the damn *fürshtunken* doctor who's working on her manages to get her stabilized by then, we'll be on it. I'll commandeer first class and use it as a sick bay. Damn it, Dick, twenty-eight years without a scratch, and now this. This . . . This . . ." The energy drained from him, and suddenly he became exhausted. Drained. Empty.

Not surprising. He was in shock and running on adrenaline, and his adrenaline had just stopped pumping. Now it was as if he could barely summon the power to whisper. "Dick, she needs the kind of attention she can only get at home. I have to take her home. Have to take her home."

There are times when words won't do. This was one of 'em. I thought about what I'd just been thinking about collateral damage, and suddenly realized there are two sides to that coin: the sending side, on which I usually find myself, and the receiving side, which is where I was now. It is not fun to be on the receiving side. And that is a colossal understatement. "Avi—"

"I know, Dick," he said, cutting me off. "I know. B'bye, Dick, b'bye. Keep me vatchamacallit, up-to-date. You have the number in Herzlyya." And then the phone went dead.

Now, callous as it may appear, I didn't sit around and daydream about all the good times I'd had with Avi and Mikki Ben Gal. Instead, I went to work with the kind of vengeance-driven energy that I can summon up in times of stress. I put together lists containing the essential elements of information our covert strikes would need; I did target assessments. I pored over the satellite pictures that Pepperman had faxed me on the secure fax. I calculated distances using a Magellan GPS unit and the file of Defense Mapping Agency aeronautic maps I carry with me. And I used a magnifying glass to examine the minute details of the blueprints of the place we'd be going, blueprints Jim Wink had dug out of the CIA's archives and faxed to me.

And fourteen hours later, give or take a few minutes, I'd come up with what I thought was an effective and reasonably Murphy-resistant mission profile. I handed my pages over to Boomerang, Duck Foot, Nod, and Rotten Randy for their input, because in that quartet of senior noncoms lies decades of real-world combat experience. I watched as they attacked my op-plan, trying to poke holes in it, find the weaknesses, and make it better and more deadly. I opened the minibar, drank a single beer, then walked into the bedroom, lay down atop the bedcovers, and closed my eyes for a short combat nap.

I was roused by the phone *bring-bring*ing next to my left ear. I rubbed at my eyes, and looked at the luminescent dial on my watch. 0412. I'd been asleep for six and a half hours. The loud music coming from the suite's living room told me that my senior noncoms were still working on the op-plan.

I rolled over and grabbed the receiver. "Marcinko." I heard my voice reverbing on the line, as if I were in an echo chamber.

"Dick, this is Avi, can you hear me?"

I could—in fact I told him there were about half a dozen of him. "How's Mikki."

He got straight to the point. "She died two hours ago, Dick. There was nothing anybody could do."

I started to say something, but Avi cut me off. "Look," he said, "I know how you feel, and that is great comfort to me right now. But we have to put her in the ground before sundown tonight, and then I am here for thirty days of mourning."

"I'll be on a plane to be with you even if I have to fly the fucking thing myself, Avi."

"No," he said. "You stay where you are. You do the work you began. That is most critical. I'll take care of the sons of bitches who killed her. I can handle that. I know who they are, and I will deal with them."

"Dammit, Avi—"

RICHARD MARCINKO and JOHN WEISMAN

"Do your job, Dick," he said. "You finish your work—I'll finish mine," he said. And then he hung up.

I sat on the edge of the bed, staring blankly at the window for I don't know how long. I have known Miriam Ben Gal for almost two decades now. I watched her children grow up, marry, and have their own kids. I have fallen asleep on the couch in her home and awakened, covered in a hand-knit comforter, that she laid over me. We have laughed together. And now some anonymous tango had detonated a car filled with high explosive and ended her life.

Except, the TIQ wasn't anonymous at all, so far as I was concerned. I'd seen the homicidal look on Steve Sarkesian's face as Mikki and Avi and Ashley and I left the Sirzhik Foundation reception. I knew I'd provoked him. And I knew, deep in my soul, that no matter what his alibi might be, he'd uttered the words that had set the plan for this . . . incident in motion. Whether he'd said them to Ali Sherafi, or Oleg Lapinov, or another of his TOCs, none of that mattered. All I knew was he'd given a command that had left Miriam Ben Gal dead.

And so, despite what Avi had said, his name went onto the execution list I carry in my head.

But, for the moment, that was all. One of the critical elements of Warriordom is carrying on. If your swim buddy gets killed, you carry on. You do not sit about and mope, or snivel, or get all touchie-feelie and weepy. You take your revenge for his death out on your enemies. You kill them. And the more of them you kill, the more you avenge your swim buddy's Warrior spirit. Killing is what he would do for you. Killing is what Avi wanted me to do for him. And so, killing is what would happen. The white heat of my rage would radiate toward my enemies, the scum who'd murdered Mikki Ben Gal. I WOULD NOT FAIL: I would kill them all.

Chapter

12

WE SLIPPED OUT OF BAKU AT ZERO DARK HUNDRED, USING ARAZ'S
wheezing trucks to hide our presence. I'd waited all day to hear
General Crocker's reaction to my messages, and get new instructions. But I received not a word from him—nothing. I tried his
private number, but was told by some officious-sounding aide
that he was in meetings and could not be interrupted. By
midafternoon I began to feel that I was getting the runaround.
And so, shortly before we pulled out, I sent him an UNODIR
message, explaining in terse language that I was going to reconnoiter a possible tango-staging area that presented a clear and
present threat to me and my men. I explained that the operation
would take between two and three days. I closed by letting him
know it would be impossible to get hold of us, but that I would
make contact as soon as I got back, so he could tell me how he
wanted me to deal with the materials I'd sent.

   As I went out the door, there were five messages from Ashley
Evans, all marked "urgent," sitting shredded in the wastebas-
ket. I hadn't returned her calls. I didn't want her to know what
we were doing, and didn't want to have to lie. The less she

knew about what I was up to, the better it would be for her career.

We were able to travel light because Boomerang and Nod had already overseen the prepositioning of our equipment in a dense, ten-acre patch of thorny overgrowth convenient to the highway, on the Azeri side of the Iranian border. The border itself was fortified. There were both passive and active sensors, and while sensors can be penetrated, we'd take the path of least resistance and do the infil by water. My guys had been teaching Araz's shooters the basics of waterborne operations, and so two RIBs lay beached on the oily sand, three kliks north of the Azeri port of Astara.

Thanks to the surveillance pictures that Pepperman provided, and the blueprints of the old CIA listening post I'd received from Jim Wink, I'd been able to construct the following mission plan.

- We'd use the RIBs to take us around Astara. Five kliks south of the town, we'd make our way ashore just south of a line of tall electrical towers. Pick and Butch would then exfil and make their way back to the Azeri side of the border, where they'd wait at a little roadhouse run by a friendly Azeri named Mahmoud on the outskirts of the seaside town of Shakhagach. We'd discovered the place during our training sessions with Araz and it had become our unofficial living room. We provided Mahmoud with copious amounts of American greenbacks, and Mahmoud provided us with plates of kebab and pilaf, cases of cold beer, gallons of hot coffee, and a couple of cots where we could grab combat naps.
- Meanwhile, the fourteen-man strike force would move inland through the thick scrub on the dunes, then climb from sea level up, making our way parallel to a winding stream, into the hills the Iranians called the Kuhe Asbinasi.

- We'd set up a covert observation post before daylight, and watch the bad guys all day. We'd count them, make note of their activities, check their weaponry, and learn their behavior patterns.
- Then when it got dark, we'd slip inside the camp, cut their throats, fingerprint and photograph 'em so we could trace their identities, grab all the intel we could carry, and set explosive charges to vaporize the place. Then I'd call up the boats to come across the border, and we'd exfil down the foothills a lot more quickly than we'd made it up 'em, extract off the beach before sunrise, and return to Baku just in time for a long, hot shower, and a hearty Cajun breakfast at the hotel restaurant.

I was somewhat uneasy about running this mission in two stages, with that fourteen-hour hole-up during the daylight hours. I don't like stop-and-go ops. I believe that operations should flow, like a single knockout punch. One single, powerful, decisive, kinetic motion from start to finish. But here I had no choice. The old CIA station was eighteen kliks inland—just under eleven miles—and all of it was uphill, through some of the roughest landscape God (and/or Allah) had ever created. And so, I'd built a fair amount of Murphy time into the op plan, and my senior guys had seconded the opinion, because they knew we'd need every second we could get.

The reason you want your senior noncoms to work on your op-plan is because most of 'em, if they're worth anything, have BTDT many more times than any wet-behind-the-balls junior officer. All of my senior chiefs have been blooded in battle. And there isn't a terrain on which they haven't fought. So they looked at the maps, and pored over the surveillance pictures, and understood immediately that the old listening post sat at an altitude of eighteen hundred feet, in a two-hundred-by-two-hundred-yard earthen pocket that had been bulldozed clear of boulders. They saw the camp was shielded to the west by a ridge that climbed as high as three thousand feet in some places. They knew that to the north lay a series of jagged, three-hundred-foot cliffs that would make an approach from that direction much too time-consuming, given the operational constraints and the amount of gear we'd be carrying.

They knew that the main road from the listening post ran due south, up, through a series of precarious ravines that S-curved inland, heading toward the high Iranian plateau town of Nara, and from there, on to Ardabīl, where the CIA's old single-runway airfield (altitude: 4,317 feet above sea level) was still used these days by the Iranian Air Force.

And so they, just as I, determined that the most effective way to hit the tangos was through the unprotected back door, which meant coming from the east. And to come from the east, we'd have to schedule this op over two days, not one.

But in one step or two, the denouement would be the same. We'd blow the site (and the bad guys) into the well-known smithereens, and then skedaddle outta Dodge.

The six cinder block buildings on the site had been cleaned out by the Agency when it pulled out of Iran shortly before the shah fled into exile in 1978. But the shells remained, and judging from the satellite pix I was looking at, they were being put to good use by the Fist of Allah tangos.

UHF and VHF antennas had been mounted on the roof. There was a satellite dish, too. They'd built two Spetsnaz-type firing ranges, one twenty-five yarder for pistol, the other, a two-hundred-meter rifle course. There was an outdoor weight pile and a hand-to-hand combat pit that looked like the ones I'd seen the Sovs build in Afghanistan. There were a row of junker cars and trucks that the bad guys could use for target practice—I could make out impact marks on the windshields in the enhanced satellite pictures.

But what most fascinated me were the stakes pounded into the ground on a football field–size clearing. There were hundreds of them, in a random pattern. Some were plain wood. Others were painted white. Others were painted black. A few were painted red. Still others were orange.

Pepperman's people knew the tangos were doing something bad, but they'd been stymied about their true objectives. That's because most of the people working for Pepperman these days are kids. They may have advanced degrees, but they're still kids. And most kids don't know shit about history.

What does history have to do with a lot of stakes in the ground? Well, lemme tell you a story. Back about twenty years ago, the Israelis decided that Saddam Hussein's nuclear weapons program was within months of producing a nuclear weapon, and they decided to put a stop to it. And so, in the high plateau of the Sinai Peninsula, above the Gulf of Aqaba, near a top-secret Israeli Defense Forces airbase they used to call Moon Valley, they built a full-scale model of Saddam's nuclear reactor at Tiuwatha, which was also known as Ossirak.

Well, they didn't actually build the whole thing. They just laid out the floor plan on the plateau. They made it out of wood stakes, with different-colored plastic tape, like crime-scene tape, run between the stakes, to show the outline of the buildings, the position of the reactor core within the BURT,[63] or containment building, the cooling tower, and all the other elements of the huge facility.

The Israelis used the tape so their pilots could get used to hitting a precise spot within the Ossirak compound during their dry runs, which they performed with inert training bombs. When they finished the session, they removed all the tape, leaving a mass of stakes, planted in what appeared to be a random pattern,

---

[63]Big Ugly Round Thing.

on the plateau floor. That way, the KeyHole satellites that we had flying over the region in those days picked up nothing significant. And the Israelis went on to flatten Ossirak, and stymie Saddam Hussein's nuclear weapons program for almost two decades.

So the minute I saw those stakes, I knew what the bad guys were doing. They were using 'em to simulate targets.

I had six sequential pix from Pepperman—and the colored stakes were being moved around, which told me that the Japs were working on a number of hits. The fact that the most recent image was less than twelve hours old was good news, too, because I didn't want to pull a Son Tay, which is to say, stage a balls-to-the-wall raid and come up dick-handed empty, with no results. Uh-huh. Negatory. I wanted to find these Fist of Allah sons of bitches and their Russkie-pusskie advisors right where they were supposed to be: in their goddamn beds. Then I'd kill them. Every fucking one of 'em.

Chapter

13

0102. THE TRANSITION TO SHORE WENT ALTOGETHER FAR TOO SMOOTHLY. The new moon made us all but invisible with our blacked-out faces and black BDUs. We didn't lose any equipment. Nobody sprained an ankle or hyperextended a knee. That perfection made me nervous. Well, I didn't have to worry: Mister Murphy made his presence known about three and a half kliks inland.

We'd worked our way across the rocky beach, camouflaged our tracks, crossed the two-lane highway that paralleled the coast, then began the long trek up into the foothills. The going was rough. What topographic maps don't show you are things like thorns that shred BDUs. Or heat. Or the creepie-crawlies—in this case a repulsive mix of attack-trained sand fleas, vicious brown gnats, malevolent horseflies, and thirsty mosquitoes, which combined to make our lives downright unpleasant, since no one had thought to bring insect repellant. But being SEALs, and therefore used to discomfort, we pressed on, humping the sixty-pound packs, weapons, water, and rations we were carrying, unmindful of the insect bites, the thorn pricks, and the ninety-plus degree weather.

Duck Foot had the point, with Nod in the number-two position. In the old days, Nod would have counted paces so we'd know how far we'd come. But now, thanks to an endless supply of double-A batteries and a network of global positioning satellites, we knew within six meters where we were, how far we'd come, and how far we had to go. I'd programmed the information into our three Magellan GPS units. But like topographic maps, GPS position finders can merely show you where you are and where you're going. They can't deal with situations.

It was 0258. We'd made good progress—until now. In front of us was a sheer, vertical rock wall, about fifty feet in height, which stretched north and south as far as we could see. It hadn't shown up on the topographic map. It hadn't shown up on the satellite photo. But it was here nonetheless.

I dropped to one knee, extracted my map, and put my red-lensed flashlight beam on the pertinent section. Nada. Bupkis. Obviously, then, this cliff did not exist. Yeah—right.

Had we brought the climbing ropes? No, we had not brought the climbing ropes. And so, we'd have to go around.

I checked the map again. About three-quarters of a klik north of us, I made out a thin, wavy broken line, which signified a mountain stream, or creek, or wadi, or whatever the fuck they called those things in this part of the world. I squinted and looked closer at the wrinkled paper, tracing the wadi with my index finger. The line wove its way through the hills, descending to the Caspian. Okay. We'd head toward the wadi. If the rock face didn't dissipate soon, we could work our way up its bank, then go south again.

0410. Our detour cost us precious time. Now there was less than an hour and a half until dawn, and we were still three kliks—just under two miles—from where I wanted to be. Now just under two miles may not sound like much. And if you're hiking the Appalachian Trail, even the toughest parts of it, that distance can be covered in a relatively short period of time. But those same three kliks become a long, grueling, arduous fucking hike when you are in the middle of hostile territory, operating blind, and trying not to make any noise that would alert the various Iranian military, Revolutionary Guard, Ivan and/or fundamentalist tango units who might happen to be out prowling and growling and searching for people like us.

And so, we proceeded meter by meter, moving cautiously through the dry streambed, climbing the rough rock outcroppings, picking our way so as not to leave the sorts of tracks that security units look for.

Did I know for sure there were hostiles operating in the area? No, I did not. But I wasn't going to assume there weren't. Assumptions like that can get you killed.

0455. The sky was quickly metamorphosing from black to dark blue. Which meant it was way past the time for us to dig in. I didn't want the opposition waking up and scanning the area with a set of binoculars and discovering a bunch of gringos trying to make themselves invisible.

Now, as we're working to conceal ourselves, let me give you a concise primer about the problems of concealment in this sort of terrain. It is: it's fucking hard to do.

In heavily wooded areas, you can use the natural, thick vegetation to help you conceal your positions. The same goes for jungle venues. Thick forest is a great help because it allows you to augment your ability to camouflage yourself by using the natural lighting and shadows—to advantage. Here, the light during daylight hours was direct and strong, and the lack of vegetation would make camouflage difficult.

But I have seen SEAL snipers who've managed to create what my Brit friends at SAS call a LUP, or lying-up point, on a sandy beach that doesn't have a single fucking piece of vegetation within sixty yards, and do it so artfully that the unsuspecting natives walk right over 'em.

And so, because nothing is impossible, and because every once in a while you can fool Mother Nature, I'd anticipated the problem, and we'd brought an assortment of helpful materials with us.

But first I had to select the right spot for our hideout. I shrugged out of my pack, dropped most of my equipment, and then started exploring.

0514. The God of War must have been watching out for me tonight, because after about nine minutes of crawling, climbing, and clambering, I found a cave whose opening actually faced the old CIA site at an oblique angle from a distance of about three-quarters of a klik, making it perfect as an observation post. The cave's mouth was partially covered by a short outcropping of rock, and large irregularly shaped boulders added to the concealment possibilities. I dropped behind the natural cover, took my night-vision glasses out of their case, and scanned the tango camp. There was nothing moving. I rolled over and peered inside the cave.

From what I could see, it was perfect. Perhaps fifteen to twenty feet deep, with a ceiling that was just over three feet high at the mouth, then opening up to five feet for much of the chamber, closing back down to roughly eighteen inches at the rear. The width of the chamber was nine, perhaps ten feet. Oh, we'd be crowded inside. But we'd be hidden—and we could observe the enemy all day. I crawled inside, scanning closely. I ran my hand along the wall. It was cool—and dry. That was a good sign.

I used my elbows and knees to make my way toward the far rear corner of the cave, my night vision probing as I proceeded along the rough floor. About halfway back, something dropped onto the back of my neck. Instinctively, I swatted at it. Too late: whatever it was bit the shit out of me. I slapped at the fucking thing, knocking my night vision off, and sending the goggles clattering to the cave floor. The noise echoed slightly in the chamber, and instinctively I stopped moving. Then, I reached onto my H-harness and grabbed my red-lensed flashlight, switched it on, and swept the cave floor.

I reached down to pluck my night-vision goggles off the deck.

The fucking things moved. I drew my hand back, then carefully reached down and lifted the goggles by their strap. Underneath was one of the largest damn spiders I've ever seen. Who knows what color it was, because the red lens made colors impossible to see. But it had a rough hourglass-and-diamond pattern on its back. This was not good news.

I held the goggles out of the way, then smashed the fucking thing with my boot. It struck me that the dead creepie-crawlie might have friends or relatives, so I directed my flashlight beam toward the chamber roof, just to make sure the place wasn't filled with other sharp-mandibled nasties.

All I saw was rock. So this little mother and I had been brought together by Mister Murphy. The bite didn't itch, but it had a slight burning sensation to it. And it began to swell almost immediately. Well, I know how to deal with insect bites: I reached into my fanny pack, found an alcohol swab and scrubbed the bite clean, then pulled a well-used OD doo-rag out of my pocket and wrapped it around my neck to cover the slight swelling, and Just Kept Going.

0522. I pronounced the cave habitable—and we went to work. The sky was deep royal blue now—and the sun's glow was beginning to insinuate itself. The fact that it was growing light was bad news. But the good news was that our lie-up position was east of the camp, and anyone who might look in our direction was going to get a blast of sunlight in his eyes.

No time to waste. From their packs, Timex and Randy pulled a length of black hessian screening material, which they stretched between the gap in the rocks where we were going to do our work. As long as it remained dark, the screen, which does not show up on IR, would shield us from being seen. By the time it was light, we'd have camouflaged ourselves sufficiently to pull it down.

Gator, Digger O'Toole, Nigel, and Rodent had all packed desert-colored camouflage netting. I had matching poncho material, as well as collapsible plastic stakes. Boomerang, Duck Foot, Nod, and Hammer had trenching tools, with which they started to quietly pick away at the loose rocks and earth near the cave mouth.

0538. We laid the camouflage netting, working the few sparse sprigs of thistle we could find into the material. If anyone came up close and personal to check the cave out, they'd know someone was in residence. But at a distance—or through binoculars—we'd be invisible.

Although it was still in the low seventies, I'd sweat completely through my BDUs. I hunkered down, put my back against the cool rock, and tried to get my breath. To be honest, I wasn't feeling too good. The spider bite on my neck had swelled to about the size of a golf ball, and it burned like hell under the doo-rag. My tongue was dry; I felt as if I had a ball of cotton fluff in my mouth, and my joints ached.

Hey, so what else is new, right? Dick and pain—a matched pair, just like Pete and repeat, or muck and mire, or gonorrhea and diarrhea. I fought against the pain and the heat, and the sudden chill in my joints, and kept on keepin' on.

0547. It was light by the time we were ready to pull back into the cave. I told Hammer, Nigel, Duck Foot, and Mustang to pull the first two shifts of observation duty. I wanted their keen, snipers' eyes on the target. My eyes? They were just about useless. I mean, things were kind of out of focus, and I'd started to see a big field of white spots. Tiny white spots. I tried to shake 'em off, but I couldn't. Then I tried to stand up, but my legs wouldn't work.

Randy Michaels looked at me strangely as I tried to pull myself to my feet. Then he put his hand on my shoulder to keep me from rising, knelt down, and put the palm of his hand up against my neck, his fingers caressing the skin just below the right ear.

I swatted his hand away. "I like you, too, asshole, but not *that* way."

His big, tanned, shaved head dropped, so we were nose to nose. I noticed that his mustache twitched as he spoke, and for some reason, I suddenly found that fact absurdly, preposterously, funny. I pointed in his direction and laughed, but Rotten Randy didn't get the joke. No, he was serious through and through. "Skipper, you are about to be in bad shape. I figure you've got a fever somewhere around a hundred and three right now."

I watched the ludicrous movements of the hair strands at the ends of his mustache, giggled, and said, "Bullshit."

He wasn't paying attention. "What was it, Skipper? Snake? Spider? Scorpion?"

Now his mustache was quivering furiously, which I found even more hilarious. "Look, Rotten—"

"Fuck you, Skipper." He unwrapped the doo-rag, pushed me sideways, turned my head so he could see the back of my neck, and whistled softly. "Spider," he pronounced. "Nasty big one, too."

He spun me around—or at least that's the way it felt—grabbed me by my H-harness, and dragged me into the cave, unmindful of the rough rocks smacking at my coccyx. He pulled me out of the light, leaned me up against an interior wall, and asked nobody in particular, "Anybody bring any antivenin? From the way his neck looks, Skipper here decided to get bit by one hufuckingmongous black widow–type spider."

I started to protest. C'mon, I've been bitten by hundreds of fucking spiders over the years, not to mention assorted ticks, mites, fleas, bedbugs, and horseflies. Shit, I've even chugged cobra venom. But I had to admit that none of those experiences had done as much damage as quickly as this one had. At least I thought about admitting it. Problem was, that when I opened my mouth, nothing came out.

I stared dumbly at Randy. I saw Boomerang's long, narrow face looking down at me, a concerned expression on it. Behind him, Nod, Rodent, Duck Foot, Timex, and Gator stared down at me, their faces neutral masks. It occurred to me right then that they were watching to see whether or not I'd died on 'em. Well, fuck me. I tried to reach down and come up with some sort of Roguish riposte, but then the fucking spots got bigger and bigger, and then everything went black.

I came to just after 1600, bathed, as they say, in my own sweat and puke and who knows what else. I felt like a misused horse—rode hard and put away wet. I probably smelled like one, too. I rolled onto my right side, and into a body—Nod—who mumbled something unintelligible, then nudged me back onto my left side. I rolled, bumped into another body, finally remembered where I was, and groaned.

The body I'd just jostled belonged to Boomerang. "Hey, Boss Dude, just stay cool and you'll be okay in no time." Boomerang spoke softly, pushed me gently back onto my back, and repositioned the alcohol swab on my neck.

I tried to get myself up, but frankly I didn't have the energy. "WTF, Boomerang?"

"Looks like you're allergic to certain kinds of spider bites, Boss Dude. We got some antihistamine in you. And Randy spiked you with some morphine, too."

Morphine? Morphine? I'd never heard of using morphine to deal with spider bites, and managed to croak that opinion out loud.

Boomerang shrugged. "Yeah—I was skeptical, too." He cracked an uneven smile. "But it seems to have worked. I mean, you lived, right?"

You call this living? "Kinda."

He raised my head, cradled it, and put a canteen to my lips. "Try some water, Boss Dude."

I sipped. God, that felt good. I sipped some more. After I managed two, three, four greedy swallows, Boomerang pulled the canteen back. "Little at a time, Boss Dude."

"Thanks." I lay back and closed my eyes. "I'm just gonna lie here for a couple of more minutes."

I was in the middle of one of those incredible dreams that tie together all the nasty experiences of the past five years in one hu-fucking-mongous nightmare, when reality intruded, in the person of Rotten Randy Michaels's growly basso profundo, which cut into my subconscious like the fucking Klaxon horn on a sewer pipe.

I cracked an eye open, but didn't see anything until Randy turned his red-lensed flashlight on so I could make out his shaved head and nasty-looking War Face, which was covered with dark cammo cream. He looked down at me with the sort of paternally bemused look senior noncoms reserve for dumbass junior officers. "I hate to disturb your beauty rest, Skipper, because if you ask me, you need every fucking minute of it you can get. But it's getting late, and we gotta move, and you're the one who's always telling us *sympathy* is between *shit* and *syphilis* in the dictionary. So roust your ass, hoist your gear, and let's go the fuck over the rail and kill us some Japs."

0112. Oh, I didn't have to like it—and I didn't like it at all. But I had to do it. And so, do it I did. I took five quick gulps of water, struggled to my knees, then my feet—cracking the ol' Rogue skull on the four-foot ceiling of the cave. Then, since everything was normal (meaning I was in pain), I got down to business. I listened to Randy and Boomerang's sit-rep, so I knew where the bad guys were and how my senior noncoms had fine-tuned the op-plan. Then I hunkered down and pulled my equipment on. First came the bulletproof vest. Then over that, the tactical load-bearing vest. I shifted until the goddam things felt more or less comfortable, and then double-checked to make sure that the buckles were buckled, the snaps were snapped, and the Velcro was Velcro'd. I focused on my magazines, made sure they were topped off and that the rounds were facing the right way. Don't laugh. I've seen experienced shooters load in the dark, and stick a fucking round in the magazine backward. The joke's on them when the weapon jams.

0119. I was ready to go—at least as ready as I was gonna be.

Yes, I was shaky. Yes, I felt like shit. Yes, I hurt, and stank, and my vision was fuzzy to say the least. But when you are a Warrior, and you lead Warriors into battle, how you feel, and how you smell, and how many aches and pains you may have—these things do not count. What counts is leading by example. What counts is showing that no matter what happens, you will persevere. You will go on. You will fulfill the mission, and your men can count on you to bring them back alive and victorious.

Now, this here book is pure fiction, but the sort of Warrior leadership I'm talking about can be found in real life, every now and then.

Like the example set by Master Sergeant Roy Benavidez. Master Sergeant Benavidez was attached to Fifth Special Forces back in Vietnam. Here, quoting from the citation for his Medal of Honor, is what he did—and how he led by example. And don't skip over this section, because each one of you out there owe Roy Benavidez, who died in November 1998, at the age of fifty-three, a shitload of respect. He was the kind of soldier I've always tried to pattern myself after.

On the morning of 2 May 1968, a twelve-man Special Forces Reconnaissance Team was inserted by helicopters in a dense jungle area west of Loc Ninh, Vietnam, to gather intelligence information about confirmed large-scale enemy activity. This area was controlled and routinely patrolled by the North Vietnamese Army. After a short period of time on the ground, the team met heavy enemy resistance, and requested emergency extraction. Three helicopters attempted extraction, but were unable to land, due to intense enemy small arms and anti-aircraft fire.

Sergeant Benavidez was at the Forward Operating Base in Loc Ninh monitoring the operation by radio when these helicopters returned to off-load wounded crewmembers and to assess aircraft damage. Sergeant Benavidez voluntarily boarded a returning aircraft to assist in another extraction attempt.

Realizing that all the team members were either dead or wounded and unable to move to the pickup zone, he directed the aircraft to a nearby clearing where he jumped from the hovering helicopter, and ran approximately 75 meters under withering small arms fire to the crippled team. Prior to reaching the team's position he was wounded in his right leg, face, and head. Despite these painful injuries, he took charge, repositioning the team members and directing their fire to facilitate the landing of an extraction aircraft and the loading of wounded and dead team members. He then threw smoke canisters to direct the aircraft to the team's position. Despite his severe wounds and under intense enemy fire, he carried and dragged half of the wounded team members to the awaiting aircraft. He then provided protective fire by running alongside the aircraft as it moved to pick up the remaining team members.

As the enemy's fire intensified, he hurried to recover the body of, and classified documents on, the dead team leader. When he reached the leader's body, Sergeant Benavidez was severely wounded by small arms fire in the abdomen and grenade fragments in his back. At nearly the same moment, the aircraft pilot was mortally wounded, and his helicopter crashed.

Although in extremely critical condition due to his multiple wounds, Sergeant Benavidez secured the classified documents and made his way back to the wreckage, where he aided the wounded out of the overturned aircraft and gathered the stunned survivors into a defensive perimeter. Under increasing enemy automatic weapons and grenade fire, he moved around the perimeter distributing water and ammunition to his weary men, reinstilling in them a will to live and fight.

Facing a buildup of enemy opposition with a beleaguered team, Sergeant Benavidez mustered his strength, began calling in tactical air strikes, and directed the fire from supporting gunships to suppress the enemy's fire and so permit another extraction attempt. He was wounded again in his thigh by small arms fire while administering first aid to a wounded team member just before another extraction helicopter was able to land. His indomitable spirit kept him going as he began to ferry his comrades to the craft.

On his second trip with the wounded, he was clubbed from additional wounds to his head and arms before killing his adversary. He then continued under devastating fire to carry the wounded to the helicopter. Upon reaching the aircraft, he spotted and killed two enemy soldiers who were rushing the craft from an angle that prevented the aircraft door gunner from firing upon them. With little strength remaining, he made one last trip to the perimeter to ensure that all classified material had been collected or destroyed, and to bring in the remaining wounded. Only then, in extremely serious condition from numerous wounds and loss of blood, did he allow himself to be pulled into the extraction aircraft.

Sergeant Benavidez's gallant choice to join voluntarily his comrades who were in critical straits, to expose himself constantly to withering enemy fire, and his refusal to be stopped despite numerous severe wounds, saved the lives of at least eight men. His fearless personal leadership, tenacious devotion to duty, and extremely valorous actions in the face of overwhelming odds were in keeping with the highest traditions of the military service, and reflect the utmost credit on him and the United States Army.

That, friends, is leadership in the Roy Boehm tradition, and heroism in the tradition of America's greatest Warriors. And so, unmindful of puke and sweat and blurred vision and everything except the blood-and-pure-guts examples set for me by real-life

Warriors like Master Sergeant Roy Benavidez, I slung my MP5, daubed my face, neck, and the backs of my hands with blackout cream, gritted my teeth, stowed my boots in my pack, and crawled on my hands and knees out of the cave into the hot night air.

Chapter

14

0126. Maybe it was me, but the heat was damn oppressive, even at this hour. I could make out the cluster of buildings below us and to the west, all outlined neatly by the orange glow of the sodium security lamps that were positioned at regular intervals high above the ten-foot-high, chain-link perimeter fence topped with coiled razor wire—standard KGB design. From where I stood to the fence line was perhaps eight hundred yards of open lunarlike landscape. Randy and I made sure our watches were reading the same time. We tested the radios, and made sure our lip mikes and earpieces were working.

Then I started the countdown, silent-signaled for dispersion, and Echo Platoon broke up into two prearranged strike groups. I took the Alpha squad: Boomerang, Nod, Duck Foot, Timex, Gator, and Hammer. Randy led Bravo squad: Half Pint, Digger, Rodent, Mustang, Nigel, and Goober.

My team would circle south, go over the fence, and at 0300 we'd hit the two main buildings at the southern end of the camp used as dorms and classrooms by the tangos. The hit would be complicated because in addition to the two one-story buildings, which were about the size of double trailers laid out in a rough L shape, we had a single corrugated steel cargo container that looked as if it was being used as an armory off to the short side of the L, as well as a trio of smaller sheds, set up in an irregular pattern behind and to the right of the largest of the structures.

The bottom line was that if we didn't hit first and hit hard, and any of the tangos escaped, we'd have a hard time rooting 'em out of the nooks and crannies. And there was another complication as well: we'd have to hit 'em quick enough to ensure that nobody'd have the chance to get an alarm out on the cellular phones most of the bad guys carried on their belts. Oh, yeah. Welcome to the twenty-first century, where everybody has their own cell phone, even bad guys. Okay, while we were taking down the main force of nasties, Randy's squad would cut through the north end of the compound and disable the radio tower and the satellite dish. He'd clear the comms shed, remove every piece of intel he could get his hands on, then set timed charges to blow everything up. By the end of the evening, I wanted nothing left of this place but rubble.

If the sniper log was accurate, there'd be three Japs in the comms shed, and two pair of bad guys on roving security details. The good news was that the security detail stayed well within the perimeter fence line. So we were talking about a total of twenty-three bad guys. I asked if anybody'd seen any Ivans, and Hammer said the answer was no—they all looked like your typical full-bearded Shiite mujahideen. Not a single Ivan among 'em.

That meant sixteen easy targets for me and my squad, all tucked into their beds in the dorm unit, dreaming whatever sorts of nasty dreams that tangos dream. And while my squad did the fish-in-a-barrel number on the sixteen sleepers, Randy's shooters would take care of neutralizing the remaining seven.

Prisoners? You want to know about prisoners? Okay, that's simple: there would be none. I expected 100 percent enemy casualties tonight.

0127. My guys and I started moving south. The most important element of any night attack is noise discipline. Sound seems to carry farther at night than it does during daylight hours. In fact, it doesn't—it just appears to. The reason is because with eyesight diminished by the darkness, your hearing becomes enhanced. And so, we'd made sure that every bit of our gear was tied or taped down. I didn't want mags rattling, or weapons clacking.

To make doubly sure I for one wouldn't make any noise, I was working barefoot tonight. Now, don't try this at home, friends, because you'll tear the soles of your feet into bloody shreds. But the skin on the bottom of my size ten extra Rogue feet is tougher and more durable than what you'll find on most hiking boots. Remember that when I served my year in the Petersburg, Virginia, Federal Bad Boys' Camp and Mayoral Blow Job Facility in 1990, I used to run six miles a day, every fucking day, rain, shine, heat, cold, snow, ice, or fog, on the camp's six-laps-to-the-mile cinder track. Yeah— every single fucking day. And I ran barefoot. Oh, I bled like hell for the first two weeks. And then, my feet got tougher and tougher. By the time they released me, the half inch of callus on the bottom of my feet made 'em as hard and durable as the Vibram sole of a running shoe or a hiking boot. Even today, I seldom wear shoes when I'm out running the hundreds of acres of woods at Rogue Manor. Sure, there are thorns and thistles and sharp-edged rocks, but they don't bother me. In fact, I can move through the fucking woods as silently as any stealthy Algonquin, Iroquois, or Mohawk in a James Fenimore Cooper or Charles Brockden Brown novel.

I cut through a natural defilade that ran for perhaps two hundred yards, then emerged onto a long, wide, open field strewn with huge rocks and short, dry brush. When you move at night, you have to make the terrain work for you. Give the enemy nothing. Use the darkness as a friend: no silhouettes, skylines, or quick, jerky moves that attract attention. I like to have bow hunters in my units, because bow hunters learn young how to move so as not to disturb the game as they get into position.

Now the going got slow. I worked my way from cover to cover, keeping myself as low as I could, providing no S-3, which stands for shadow, shine, or silhouette. We were spaced out at eight- to ten-yard intervals, with Timex providing rear security, and Hammer just in front of him, sweeping the area in front of me with the night-vision sight of his suppressed sniper's rifle to make sure I didn't run into any surprises.

I'd made it to within a hundred yards of the perimeter fence when I heard a *"tsk-tsk"* in my left ear. I froze where I was, which was prone, just beyond an irregular pool of light from one of the security lamps, lying half in the shadow of a rock and half out.

I lay there for eight, nine, ten seconds, not breathing. Listening. And then the hair on the back of my neck stood straight up as I heard the crunch of boots on ground, approaching from my left. The sound was followed by the scent of cigarette smoke, garlic, and b.o. I guess that meant the enemy had arrived. So much for roving security patrols keeping inside the perimeter fence.

I dropped my face into the crook of my arm, so no light reflected by my eyes would betray me. I e-a-s-e-d the muzzle of my MP5 alongside my temple, so it could be brought up with almost no effort. And then I lay, as inert as a corpse, and waited, my heart beating a loud tattoo in my ears.

Why? Because I didn't want to have to kill this asshole. Not now. Not yet. We were still way outside the fence line, and dispatching him, as pleasurable as it might be, given my mood and the way the day had gone, would give away the fact that hostile visitors—i.e., *us*—had come a-calling. More to the point, it is mainly in Hollywood pictures that up-close-and-personal killing is accomplished sans any noise whatsoever. In real life there is always the possibility of ambient sound—a body collapsing onto the ground; the chance that the kill won't be completely silent and your target will manage one bloody scream; or the sudden appearance of Mister Murphy (or one of his damn relatives) to gum up the situation.

And so, I lay there and waited. Because I knew that unless this asshole had night vision, or thermal, or he was an accomplished fucking hunter, he wouldn't see me, even if he looked right at me.

Why? Because at night, you don't see the same way you do in daylight. In daylight, you look directly at an object to see it. That's because you use the cone cells of your eyes, which are concentrated in the center of the retina. At night, you use the rod cells, which are grouped around the cones. I've taught my guys that at night, they should never look directly at anything. Instead, they should skew their vision by about the width of a human fist. And by doing that, they'll see their enemy before their enemy sees them.

But not everyone knows that trick. Obviously, the tango who was out for a stroll didn't know it. Moreover, his night vision was spoiled by the cigarette he was smoking. So he ambled on past, oblivious to *moi*, and got to live for a few more minutes, enjoying what would probably be his last cigarette.

0201. Fifty-nine minutes until Show Time. I lay up against the chain-link fence in the partial shadow between the security lights, fumbling for the wire cutters in my fanny pack. And fumbling. And fumbling. In point of fact, I could have fumbled all fucking night, because the fucking wire cutters weren't in my fanny pack. Where were they? you ask. Good question. Ask Mister Murphy, because I know goddam well I'd stowed 'em there when I'd loaded my gear in Baku.

It took me six minutes to wriggle and slither my way back to where the rest of the squad lay behind cover, only to discover that I was the one fella carrying the wire cutters tonight.

Now the Naval Special Warfare technical term for what's just happened is "goatfuck." Why? Because redundancy is supposed to be built into every mission. Put simply, if I get killed, my men have to be able to complete the mission, and they can't do that if I'm the OFACWC—only fucking asshole carrying wire cutters.

But I was the OFACWC tonight. So doom on me, because now

we were nine minutes behind the schedule that was scrolling in my head.

And we were still outside the fence.

But not for long. I silent-signaled that we'd go up and over the top. I pulled off my flak jacket. I'd use it to go around the coil of razor wire. I looked at Nod and mimed a slingshot. Nod gave me an upturned thumb, patted himself down, then reached into his left-hand cargo pocket and displayed a slingshot and a bag of ball bearings. He made the return trip with me, lay on his back, and shot out the closest security light with his first shot. At least some things were working tonight.

Have I ever told you to never think like that? Well, never think like that. Because when you assume everything's going right, then something will always go wrong.

Because just as I was giving Nod a big grin for his job well done, I heard a quick *tsk-tsk-tsk* in my ear. So did Nod. We froze— because that triplet was the trouble signal. We lay on our backs, trying to become invisible in the darkness. That was when I heard the crunch of approaching boot-falls on the gravel, coming from just inside the perimeter fence.

They slowed, then stopped. I didn't dare look, because looking would mean motion and motion is what gives you away. But the hair on the back of my neck was standing as fucking straight as it ever had when my body is telling me I am in extremis. And then, the footsteps began again. Slowly. Deliberately. Evenly. Crunch. Crunch. Crunch. And then I heard the sound of a boot sole stepping on broken glass.

That's because Mister Murphy had made the fucking security lamp lens fall inside the fence.

The footsteps stopped. In my mind's eye I could see him, bending over, looking for what had caused that disparate sound.

I heard intake of breath as he realized something was wrong. And then, a soft *thwop*, as if someone had punched a pillow in the next room, and then the very welcome muffled sound of BCOD—body crumpling onto the deck.

No time to lose. I looked over to where the sentry had fallen. He was still clutching some kind of automatic weapon in his lifeless hand. I scrambled to my feet, clambered up the chain-link fence, molded my flak jacket over the sharp coils of razor wire, rolled over the top with the practiced motion of someone who's done this exercise hundreds of times before, and dropped down the eight or nine feet to the ground.

Directly onto a sharp, sharp stone about the size of a tennis ball. Yes, my feet have half an inch of callus. But sharp is sharp, and big is big, this one caught me right at the forward part of the arch, at the precise pressure point Chinese martial artists call *hsing hsüan*. A properly executed strike at *hsing hsüan* causes immediate spasm and loss of mobility. And since I execute nothing improperly, I fucked myself up but good.

I did not pass GO. I did not collect the two hundred fucking dollars. I went straight to PAIN. I collapsed as if I'd been suckerpunched. The fucking spasm shot up my leg, radiating from the arch of my foot, through my Achilles tendon, all the way up past my knee, into the semitendinous muscle at the base of my butt. I couldn't straighten my fucking leg out. I just lay there, the cap of my knee touching my chin, in perfect, complete, God given agony.

Nod was the first to get to me. He uncoiled my leg and pushed me down on the ground until I was stretched out on my back. Then he began to work the muscles and tendons in my leg. I looked up through unfocused eyes and saw Boomerang arrive. He took up a defensive position close to the body of the man Hammer had sniped. Then Duck Foot came over the fence, followed by Timex and Gator, who held his position long enough to retrieve Hammer's big MSG90 sniper rifle so my sniper-man could climb up and drop down unharried.

Enough of this shit. I sat up and tried to massage the spasm out of my foot. But it wasn't going anywhere. So I stood up, planted it on the ground—*hard!*—and grimaced, because the fucking thing still contained a big knot of absolute white-hot pain.

Which, of course, was precisely when the cigarette-smoking asshole who'd been patrolling the outside of the fence decided to make his repeat appearance.

We heard him before we saw him, because he started shouting at us in Farsi or whatever. I turned toward the sound. The sumbitch was coming from the gully we'd used, his AK up to his shoulder, the muzzle waving vaguely in our direction. Obviously he saw motion. But since the security lights were pointed outward, and we were in darkness maybe 150, 160 yards from where he was, he didn't know what he was looking at. All he knew was that we shouldn't be where we were, and he was gonna check us out.

Gator swung the fourteen-pound semiauto sniper rifle up to his shoulder, dropped into his half-crouch MP5 position, stuck the muzzle through the chain-link fence, squinted into the ten power night-vision sight, flicked the safety downward, and squeezed off three quick shots.

No, he's not a sniper, but he's a shooter—and he hits what he shoots at, even with an unfamiliar piece of hardware that was sized for Hammer's big frame. The first shot kicked up rock fragments just above the tango's left shoulder. The second and third shots scored—the bad guy went down, knocked back as if he'd been punched, but still moving. Now, his target immobilized, Gator took his time, and holding the big rifle rock-steady, got a match-quality cheek mold and put a fourth shot into the Jap's head, exploding it like a fucking melon.

I gave the kid a look that told him he'd just done great work. But there was no time for further Bravo Zulus. We had to move our butts.

0212. Let me pause here long enough to tell you about a highly important element of unconventional warfare. It is keeping quiet during the infil. Noise discipline is critical. You can't go up to a target making a ruckus, because if you do, the bad guy will hear you coming, and he will wax your ass before you can wax his ass. Now, I see you out there, protesting that what I've just said is such basic common sense I didn't need to say it. But you are mistaken. Even the best of us violates noise discipline from time to time. And so, as you make your approach, you must ensure that it is wholly silent, hushed, and quiet. No crunching of gravel. No stepping on twigs or leaves. No whispering. No nothing.

Now, that kind of technique takes time. You cannot just run up to the target, because running ain't silent. And so, we'd have to move slowly, cautiously, prudently, as we made our way across a wide, open graveled area, toward the long side of the L.

The larger of the two structures had a makeshift deck/porch about ten feet wide, running its entire length. There were two doors on the long side of the L, one door on the short side, and no windows. I hadn't been able to tell from the surveillance photograph, since the entire structure was under one roof. But now, I could see that the two sides of the L were not attached. That was good news, because it's easier—less complicated—to hit a pair of targets simultaneously than work your way through a long, double target, especially when you do not know what the interior layout looks like.

Last, between the perimeter fence and the structures, just shy of the seven o'clock position, was that big, tractor trailer–size corrugated steel container that, from the surveillance pictures, I'd concluded the bad guys used as their armory and equipment stowage facility. It would offer us protection and cover, and so we'd stage there, then go hit the motherfuckers.

Chapter

15

0227. WE PUT HAMMER IN POSITION FIRST, EASING HIM UP ATOP THE warm steel of the corrugated cargo container. He slithered across the top of the container, settled into a prone position, put the rifle to his cheek, then swept the area with his night-vision scope and pronounced it clear.

0233. I made my way inch by inch across the gravel, picking my way carefully, until I reached the deck area that abutted the larger of the two one-story buildings, and pulled myself underneath it. I lay there, sweating, the ache in my foot pulsing contrapuntally to my accelerated heartbeat, thinking about how much God loves me. I edged forward, only to smack my skull against a concrete footer. It is good to know that some things, like pain, are constant in my life. Thirty seconds later, I was joined by Nod, whose night vision was good enough so that he crawled around the thick, rough footer. Half a minute after that, Duck Foot and Timex made their way under the wooden planking. They were followed by Gator and Boomerang.

We lay on our backs, with half a foot between the tip of my much-mashed nose and the bottom of the unevenly spaced deck planks. There was no need to communicate: each man knew what he had to do.

I checked my watch. Nineteen minutes to go. Duck Foot and Timex kept moving, working their way deliberately toward the aft end of the deck, where they'd be able to stage their assault on the single entrance to the classroom building. As they hit their target, we'd hit ours. I lay on my back, running my hands over my equipment, making sure everything was where it needed to be.

Which was when I heard the door just above my head creak open, followed by the sound of feet on the creaky wood planks. All movement stopped. I lay there, my heart pounding in my ears. Talk about pucker factor; I don't think you'd have been able to get a fucking straight pin up my sphincter right then.

I heard the unmistakable scratch of a match swiping against wood, a secondary pause, an intake of breath, and the satisfied exhale/sigh of a serious smoker as he took his first drag of the day.

He stood where he was for about a minute and a half, although it felt like a fucking hour and a half to me. Then he ambled over to the edge of the deck (four more footsteps). There was rustling, and then the noisy drizzle of piss on gravel as the motherfucker stood at the edge of the deck and relieved himself. Then he farted long and hard—geezus, what the hell had he been eating?—shook off, flicked his cigarette out into the darkness, and walked back inside.

This was not good news. As I've told you, folks like me are at our most vulnerable when we are in the staging portions of our operations. That's when we're unprotected, and it is hardest to achieve the critical mass of surprise combined with violence of action that allows us to overcome the enemy's superior numbers.

And with at least one tango awake, surprise was going to be a lot harder. Not to mention the fact that our approach was now going to have to be even more silent than ever.

But what is life without a challenge every now and then, right?

0246. I crawled out from under the decking as far away from

the piss puddle as I could manage, the muzzle of my MP5 up and ready, my night-vision goggles turned on and secured tightly around my forehead.

I rolled onto my back, and signaled that it was time to go to work. Nod and Gator started toward the secondary doorway, some thirty feet away, moving sans sound.

Thirty seconds after they'd made their move, I crept six feet to the edge of the deck, slid out from underneath, hunkered, then climbed between the deck's rough-hewn posts and rails, c-a-r-e-f-u-l-l-y crossed the planking sans making any noise, eased on up to the building itself, and pressed myself against the outer wall, just to the left of the doorway, on the same side as the hinges. Boomerang followed—but obviously not in my footsteps. I winced as the deck creaked under his weight. If I hadn't been concentrating so hard I would have given him a dirty look. He knew how to move better than that.

Then it was Nod's turn. The former Green Beret moved like a fucking ghost. So did Timex. Their expressions told Boomerang they knew he'd fucked up.

Once they'd crossed the deck, we shifted position to the side of the doorway opposite the hinges. Boomerang stacked behind me, Nod behind him, and Timex played rear security. I could feel Boomerang's fingers patting, probing, and poking to make sure that everything I was carrying was secure and ready to go. As he was checking me, Nod was doing the same for him, and Timex checked Nod's equipment, pronouncing him ready with a squeeze on his right shoulder. Finally, Nod spun Timex around and made sure everything was where it was supposed to be. My quartet squeezed off from the rear, and when I felt the pressure of Boomerang's hand on my shoulder, I knew we were ready to go.

0254. I *tsk-tsked* twice to check on the rest of the team's preparation, and received affirmative responses. Shit, we were not only ready to go, we were even six minutes early. Well, isn't it nice that some things actually work out. Okay: *Show Time.* I eased up on the MP5 that was slung over my left shoulder on its worn canvas harness, my left hand on the extra-wide forearm to control the muzzle angle. My right hand went to the pocket on my CQC vest that held one of the three DefTec No. 25 flashbangs I was carrying tonight.

I eased it out of the pocket, and then, holding my hand securely around the spoon, I pulled the pin. Boomerang began tapping my shoulder. I shrugged him off, as if to say, 'I know, I know,' straightened the pin out, and hung it on my left pinky. You never want to drop a grenade pin because you might need the fucking thing again, if you decide not to toss the grenade and have to stow it. He didn't have to remind me of such a basic detail.

Okay, I was armed and dangerous; ready to hop & pop and shoot & loot. And Boomerang was still fucking tapping me on the shoulder.

Which was when the door opened by its own fucking self. Of course, we all know that the door did not open by its own fucking self. It was pushed open by another tango on his way to an early morning smoke 'n' piss.

He didn't see me, because I was pressed back next to the door frame as he pushed the door open. But he sure as shit sensed my presence, because he suddenly pushed against the door, whirled, and slammed me splat in the face with his fucking fist. My night vision went flying. His fist continued in its trajectory, smashing me in the nose. Yes, of course it hurt. It hurt like hell. But since I'm used to pain, I just absorbed it, held my ground, reached up, and swatted at his ugly puss, using the Def-Tec in my right hand as a brass knuck.

The body of the DefTec No. 25 is made of thick steel. It weighs almost two pounds. It makes a hell of an old-fashioned cold-cocker. And between the fucking spider, and my fucking foot, and my currently mashed Slovak snout, I was in the fucking mood to fucking kill somebody and do it soon—brass knucks or no.

I felt the welcome sound of steel on flesh, followed by a gurgle. I rolled on top of the motherfucker and brought him down to the deck. I saw the flash of Nod's knife and tried to get out of the way so Nod could slit this asshole's throat. But it was dark and it was complicated and we were all moving at the same time and trying like hell not to make any noise, and the fucking tango was tough and he was wiry, too, and he rolled away from Nod and me, and as he did, he bit me—hard—right through my black Nomex and leather assault gloves, and I reacted by dropping the fucking DefTec.

Which, of course, exploded just as I reflexively looked toward it.

Have I recently told you the specifications of the DefTec No. 25? Of course I have, but since you don't retain much information, you've probably forgotten the pertinent details. Well, here's a fucking refresher. The DefTec No. 25 has a sound level of 185 dB at five feet, a light level of 1.8 million candela, and a duration of nine milliseconds.

Here is what little good news I can give you: most of the energy of the explosion, which emanates from vent holes in the top and the bottom of the grenade, was absorbed by the unfortunate tango who'd caused me to drop it. It must have gone off pretty close to his face, because there wasn't a whole lot left of his head.

Not that I could tell. Not right then. Right then, all I saw was fucking dots and spots and a ball of white/orange/red/white light.

I did exactly what most people do when they are confronted by a distraction device: I fucking froze.

Which did not make the rest of the team's lives any easier. Perhaps the most basic tactical rule of dynamic entry is KTFM, or Keep The Fuck Moving. If you freeze in a doorway, you will get someone killed, and there I was, frozen on all fours, right in the fucking middle of the doorway, having just told every hostile within three hundred yards that there were visitors in the neighborhood, visitors who were boding them no good at all.

And so, Boomerang, Nod, and Timex, not wanting to become statistics, kept going. They didn't wait. They leapt over me, their War Faces on, screaming as they made their entry.

I wasn't about to let 'em go it alone. I might not have been able to see much or hear much, but there are times when instinct and the WILL TO WIN allow you to do 200 percent more than you ever thought you would be able to. And so, I made myself see; I forced myself to hear; I made myself scan, and breathe, and pay attention to the hostile environment.

No, I was not in good shape. But that was secondary to making sure that Nod, Timex, and Boomerang stayed alive tonight.

"I'm behind you," I shouted—at least that's what I think I said.

"Going left." That's what Boomerang's hand signal told me. Just to make sure I understood, he kicked the port-side door in and tossed a grenade.

The concussion lifted our feet off the floor. It was echoed by more explosions, coming from the other end of the hallway, where Gator and Nod had staged. Then Boomerang disappeared through the doorway. He'd already fired off two three-round bursts by the time I made entry, my back sliding along the right-hand wall, MP5 muzzle up and scanning.

Something at eleven o'clock—well within my field of fire—moved. I shot in its general direction. Heard a scream. Fired a three-shot burst toward the sound. Now more motion. Spray-and-prayed the opposite wall until I heard Boomerang scream, "Clear-clear-clear . . ."

He backed out, pulling me by the straps on my vest, making sure I stayed close.

More explosions. Nod and Timex were working the opposite side of the hallway, leapfrogging Boomerang and me. I began to be able to make out the sounds of return fire coming through the cinder block walls. Shit, the fucking cinder blocks were thin and porous, and rounds were cutting through 'em. Talk about your fucking second-rate government contractors.

I dropped to the deck and started crawling. War may be hell. But close quarters battle is worse than hell. We are talking pure chaos here, friends, coupled with the nasty reality that everything happens within a few feet, and takes only a few seconds.

I pulled myself around Boomerang, rolled over onto my back, and kicked in the next door, only to be greeted by what sounded like a fucking brigade of AKs spraying and praying. How many were really firing? Two, maybe three. But who the fuck cared. One's enough to wax your ass.

I backpedaled, sucked more concrete, turned around, stuck the business end of the MP5 around the door frame, and squeezed off a mag's worth of jacketed hollowpoint.

From the return fire we were getting, my fucking fusillade hadn't seemed to do any good.

"Motherfucker—" Boomerang's high voice cut through the noise. I turned to look at him. He'd been caught by a fragment of cinder block or a jacketed ricochet and was bleeding heavily around his Oakleys.

Then it was my turn. I'd just dropped the empty mag, shoved a new one up and into position and slapped the bolt forward when a fucking baseball bat whacked me in the left arm, knocking the subgun out of my hand. As I reacted to that, the business end of a church key slashed me from my right ear down to my chin. I tried to make the fingers of my left hand work—but I couldn't. Meanwhile, blood was beginning to obscure the vision in my right eye.

"Use the fucking Mark-Three, Boss Dude," Boomerang shouted in my virtually deaf left ear. He was right, of course— and now I realized what he'd been trying to tell me when he was tapping me on the shoulder outside. Well, fuck—wasn't I the fella who told you a few pages back that we wouldn't be concerned about taking prisoners tonight? Well, fuck—wasn't it time to get serious? Well, fuck—weren't we here to kill people and break things? So, fuck—why risk an entry into a room full of hostiles when you can Boehm 'em: fuck the fucking fuckers with a grenade, and then go in with a dustpan to sweep up the pieces.

Good question. Sometimes I am a dense fucking Rogue. But never for too long. I tore at my CQC vest until my fingers found one of the four Mark 3A2 concussion grenades I was carrying tonight. Mark 3A2s contain half a pound of TNT. They work wonders in enclosed spaces, like the interior of T-72 tanks, or small rooms. I forced my left hand up, inserted my index finger in the ring, pulled the pin, let the spoon fly, screamed, *"Fire in the hole,"* and rolled—rolled, not tossed—the fucking thing, around the doorway into the room.

Why am I emphasizing *roll?* You want to know that *now?*

Quick answer: because if I tossed it, Mister Murphy would probably catch the fucking thing and toss it back at me. By rolling it, I made sure it wouldn't bounce off anything and come back my way.

I dropped as close to the deck as I could and pressed my body over Boomerang's. Even so, we were both lifted off the floor by the explosion, picked up, then body-slammed onto the hard concrete.

But there was no time to complain. I struggled through the doorway, the acrid smell of high explosive permeating my nostrils, Boomerang in my wake.

Scan and breathe. Search for the threat. I wiped blood out of my eye, blinked, tried to focus, blinked again. All I saw was body parts.

Time to move. I backed away. Boomerang took point. Now it was his turn. He didn't bother making nice-nice. He started with the Mark 3A2. Pulled it from his vest, pitched it into the door he'd just kicked in, then dropped onto the deck. The earth moved once more, and the laws of physics prevailed, proving that TNT can be hazardous to human flesh.

0312. We mopped up. You can take that simple declarative sentence literally, because there wasn't much left of the opposition except for lots of small, bloody chunks of skin and bone and flesh. We'd managed to go through 'em like the proverbial shit through pig. But there was no time for high-fiving now. We began working at a double-time pace to sort through the camp, assess the situation, grab all the intel we could lay our hands on, set the explosives, and then haul our butts down to the sea at flank speed.

While the guys are doing their jobs, let me nutshell the most important thing I discovered. It was that the tangos we'd waxed were either the stay-behind force or the terrorists who hadn't been assigned their targets yet.

How did I understand that? Well, by looking over the clothes, supplies, equipment, as well as the creature features, bunks, and other accoutrements. All the signs I read told me that as recently as a week ago, this camp had been home to at least twice the number who were currently lying dead.

Couple that info-shard with the materials I'd discovered in Steve Sarkesian's office, as well as the fact that he and his foundation were tied in with Ali Sherafi and Oleg Lapinov, and I got real worried, real fast.

Moreover, the bad guys had made our lives difficult before they'd died. These hadn't been pussy-assed opponents who'd provided only token resistance. They'd fought with determination—and they'd extracted a high price for riding the magic carpet to Allah's side.

My left arm was virtually useless. I could hardly make my fingers obey my brain—which indicated some sort of nerve damage—and the dull constant pain between my wrist and elbow told me I'd jammed the bone in some new way. Boomerang could probably use a dozen stitches to close the nasty gash above his eyebrows. And if I'd had a staple gun, I'd have used it on the two inches of my right cheek that ran right up to the ear.

But all that was superficial compared to Rodent, who'd taken a round through the chest, and was bleeding the kind of bright red blood that told me he'd been shot through the lung. Yes, he'd been wearing his bulletproof vest. But the shot had hit him at an oblique angle at the armhole, ricocheted off a bone, gone into his chest, and punched out the back through the scapula. Digger and Nigel had stabilized him as well as could be done. They'd filled the tough little SEAL with morphine, inserted an IV, packed the wounds, started the procedures that would, I hoped, keep him alive. Then they'd improvised a litter so Rodent could be carried out. But once we got back to Baku, Rodent would be heading straight for the military hospital at Rhine Main for major surgery and who knows what else. As much as I wanted to believe otherwise, I knew his shooting and looting days were over.

The rest of us had assorted dings and dents, too—but nothing to compare with Rodent. Although Randy Michaels, who is as indestructible an asshole as you'll ever find, had managed to hyperextend his knee as he blew through the hatch of the comms shed. The joint had swelled to the size of a small melon. Oh, he was gonna *love* the exfil.

All the above was on the debit side of the book. On the credit side was the fact that we had twenty kilos of intel materials—journals, diaries, notes, and messages,[64] radio logs and frequencies. Two of the men—Nigel and Randy—read Farsi. Not perfectly, but well enough to be able to provide me with the gist of what we'd discovered. But the most valuable intel we were able to lay our hands on was a half dozen sheets of paper that looked like hand-drawn maps of streets and buildings, overlaid with tiny Xs in black, red, and orange. Yup—they were the diagrams the tangos had been using to lay out all those colored wood stakes.

---

[64]It has always surprised me how tangos tend to keep such copious records. If I was a bad guy I wouldn't want to have evidence around that could incriminate me. But from Che Guevara to Yasser Arafat, from Abu Nidal to Osama bin Laden, they just keep doin' it. Makes my work that much easier.

I discovered that one of those targets had been Avi Ben Gal. When I looked at the sheet of paper, with its hand-drawn map and overlaid pattern of small red, white, black, and orange Xs, it suddenly made sense.

Avi'd told me he lived on a one-way street—Abbas something or other street. And that he couldn't vary his route until he made the turn onto Azadiyg Prospekt. And he'd told me that at the corner of his street and Azadiyg, there was a big house with a high wall on the left-hand side. I looked at the sketched sheet of paper in my hands.

Fuck. They'd outlined the street Avi lived on. The position of the wall was highlighted. And the car holding the bomb was also highlighted. A row of black Xs depicted Avi's route. The position where the bombers would make ready was delineated in orange, and the detonation point was a red X. It was all there: they'd worked out the positioning; determined the placement of the explosive charges; laid everything out on paper. When I walked the compound, I discovered corresponding stakes—and pieces of burned vehicle. So they'd even tried it for real, using junked autos.

Oh, I was glad right then we hadn't taken any prisoners, because I wouldn't have trusted myself with 'em. Oh, I stared at the burned-out car in that desolate place, and I wept. At that instant my rage was absolute, and my hate was incendiary, as hot as white phosphorous. These cockbreaths had killed the wife of my good friend, and I would not have been gentle with them if I'd had the opportunity.

I stood on their range, holding the hand-drawn diagrams in my hand. Without a detailed map of Baku, they were useless. And who was to say that all the targets were in Baku. I might be looking at sketches of streets in New York or Washington. London. Paris. Geneva. Rome. Obviously, I'd have to get these docs to Tony Merc so he could use his computers to narrow the search. Because once I knew where the targets were, I could get to 'em first. And then I'd Boehm the assholes. Yeah, that's right. I'd fuck the fucking fuckers.

0355. We set the timers for 0420, and headed out, more than half an hour behind schedule. Timex and Hammer carried Rodent's litter. Randy'd built himself a makeshift crutch, and hobbled gamely as we picked our way up onto the ridge and moved east, down the bolder-strewn defilade toward the dry streambed, and the safety of the water, eighteen kliks away.

0500. I decided to break radio silence. The way I'd designed this mission, we'd scheduled to exfil the camp at 0330, then scamper back to the Caspian by 0700. But we'd made less than three kliks, because between Rodent's litter and Randy's knee, we were moving ahead at about one quarter of the speed we needed to make the rendezvous.

So I'd need them to hold for a while. I didn't want Pick and Butch bobbing offshore for almost a full day while we struggled out of the mountains.

I turned the power switch on, adjusted the squelch knob, then pressed the transmit button on the secure VHF transceiver. Let me be succinct about this. The fucking radio didn't work.

I pulled it from the pouch on my CQC vest to check the battery, and realized that perhaps—*ah-hah!*—perhaps it was the large shard of shrapnel, which had lodged itself in the radio's guts and mashed most of its transistors, that was causing the problem.

Of course, since Mister Murphy had helped me plan this mission from the git-go, he'd made sure that I was carrying the only secure VHF transceiver. Just like he'd made sure I was the only asshole with the wire cutters.

My friends, remember this advice: do as I say, not as I do. Because obviously, if you do as I do, you are going to be stuck in the fucking middle of fucking Iran without the means to get yourself out.

Okay. It was time to go to Plan B. Except we didn't fucking have a Plan B. And Plan A had just come apart at the seams.

That was when Digger kinda hemmed and hawed and scratched his boot soles on the rough ground, and looked at me all guiltylike because he'd forgotten something, and then displayed the dozen cellular phones he'd stashed in his assault pack. It was good intelligence gathering—by tracing the numbers and the billing, we'd be able to see who was funding the Fist of Allah tangos.

Okay, now I had a bunch of cell phones. Sure, it was better than nothing. Except Mahmoud's place didn't have a phone, and neither did Butch and Pick.

But Ashley Evans had a phone. And she'd be home now. I held out my palm until Digger laid a sample of his booty in it. I turned the phone on, flipped it open, and listened for a dial tone. Nada. I tried a second unit without success, and a third.

Gator surveyed our position. "Maybe we're in a dead spot, Skipper. I bet it'll work when we're closer to the coast."

That might be true, but it would also mean a long, long wait— and Rodent's condition wasn't improving as time went on. I tried a fourth phone. This one worked, but when I tried to dial Ashley's number, I heard a series of beeps, and instructions in Farsi.

"Nigel?" I handed him the phone.

He shrugged. "Try again, Skipper."

I dialed Ashley's flat, and handed the phone back. He listened and nodded. "It wants your access code," he said.

Well, I didn't fucking have a fucking access fucking code. I looked at Digger. "Couldn't you have fucking stolen a fucking satellite phone without a fucking security system, asshole?"

He had to check twice to see that I wasn't serious. Except, I was serious, and he knew it. He rummaged through his stash, then bright-eyed, came up with a Motorola, and examined it closely. "Hey, this is an Iridium," Digger announced proudly. He switched the damn thing on, watched as it cycled, then punched in about twenty numbers, and waited until he heard something on the other end. A huge, self-satisfied grin spread over his round face. "Yo, Skipper . . ."

He handed me the phone. This is what I heard: ". . . the weather forecast for New York City and vicinity. Today, partially cloudy with winds from the southeast, highs in the sixties, lows in the midfifties."

I disconnected quickly, then hit him on the arm hard enough to make his eyes water. "Good work, cockbreath," I said, using the universal SEAL term of endearment. "Now let's hope you didn't fuck the battery with that call."

I could spend the next twenty pages or so giving you a minute-by-minute description of our exfil. But that wouldn't do much to move the action of this book along, so I'm just going to skip it and tell you that eventually, we made it out sans too many more visits from Mister Murphy, and/or his relatives.

But we didn't do it in the single day I'd scheduled. Remember how I just knew that Ashley would be home? Well, she wasn't at home. It took me two hours to make contact. And then she informed me—very brusquely, now that I come to think of it—that it would be another five hours minimum before she could make the drive south, give Butch and Pick a cell phone that I could dial, and tell them what I needed 'em to do.

"You should not have gone off without telling me," she said, her voice deliberate, cold, and angry.

"What I'm doing is 'need to know,' " I told her.

"Screw 'need to know.' I have been trying to help you all along, and you left me in the dark. That was stupid, Dick. It was shortsighted."

"Shortsighted?"

"The situation here has changed dramatically."

"How so?"

"I'm not going to talk about it now. I'll explain when you're back up north."

It struck me she was being coy. I had a wounded man to look after, I hurt like hell, and I wasn't in the mood for coy.

"Tough shit," she said, very uncharacteristically. "Deal with it." And then the phone went dead.

And so, I dealt with it in the only way I know how: one fucking step forward at a time. We made our way slowly down toward the sea, moving carefully because it was daylight, picking our way meter by nasty meter. And then, we hunkered just west of the coastal road until it was dark, and the traffic let up, and we crossed carefully, obscuring our tracks, into the sandy, thorn scrub-and-sea-grass-covered dunes.

At 2140, I stood atop the highest dune I could find, my night vision on, my left arm throbbing like hell, and flashed Infrared out to sea. Three dots, four dots, one dot and a dash said it all, so far as I was concerned.

And of course I got no response. Yes, it was the perfect end to a perfect mission. And yes, I am employing the literary device known as irony here.

Sixty-eight seconds later (I was definitely counting, dammit), the signal was finally returned, in reverse. I flashed the light pattern once a minute for the next eighteen minutes until I could make the RIBs out as they cut through the chop, their faint wakes heading straight toward my IR. We loaded Rodent first. The rest of us clambered over the gunwales and hunkered down in the heat. The extraction took two hours, plus another four and a half in those fucking wheezing diesels chugging up the coast road to Baku. I rode in the back of the lead truck, splitting my attention between the satchel of intel we'd taken, and checking on Rodent.

The tiny SEAL looked tallowy, and he was running a fever. He'd lost a lot of blood—he was probably in the first stages of exsanguinary shock. But he was holding on—barely. Like all my men, he had so much sheer WILL and DETERMINATION that he would fight right to the end, no matter how badly he'd been wounded.

I checked to see the IV was dripping properly, mopped his sweaty forehead with a damp cloth, and lay my hand along his carotid artery to feel the pulse in his neck. It was weak. But it was regular. The way I looked at it, since Rodent hadn't died yet, there was no way I was gonna allow him to croak on me now.

Part Three

THE ENEMY OF MY ENEMY

Chapter

16

THE ONLY WAY TO DESCRIBE THE HOTEL LOBBY AS I CAME THROUGH THE doors was that it looked like the opening scene from a big Broadway musical. That was because the whole fucking cast was milling around waiting, looking as if they were about to break into the Big Opening Number. Ashley was there, in BDUs. So was Araz, and a squad of his shooters, all combat ready in camouflage BDUs and carrying automatic weapons.

And so was Oleg Lapinov, standing next to the reception desk, wearing a wide-lapeled, double-breasted pinstriped suit, a plaid shirt, and a loud tie with a knot bigger than Half Phil's fist that made him look like Mr. Clean® playing Good Ol' Reliable Nathan (*Nathan-Nathan-Nathan*) Detroitski in the Moscow summer stock version of *Guyskis and Dollskis*.

Except he wasn't good ol' reliable anything. He was the same no-load shit-for-brains pus-nutted pencil-dicked scumbag who'd been involved in killing the wife of my friend. That made him my enemy.

And that meant it was time for him to die. I pushed past Ashley and Araz, scattering bellmen, spooks, tourists, and Turkish Mafiosi as I plowed across the marble at flank speed. I went up to

253

the desk, took the big Russkie's lapels in my hands, and pulled him close to me. "You fucking pussy-ass cockbreath *opushchiny*," I whisper-growled by way of greeting, calling him a prison whore. Then I kneed him in the balls.

But the sonofabitch was just as fast as I. He deflected my leg, used my own momentum against me, turned my rib cage toward him, then swiveled and used the point of his elbow to smack me with a quick and nasty chop to the solar plexus as he bounced me off the counter edge.

The blow took the breath out of me, but my rage carried me forward and made me forget any pain I might have had from the previous days. I smacked his ears, grabbed the rolls of fat on the back of his neck then stunned him with a head butt.

His eyes rolled back for an instant, but then he was on me again like stink on shit. We struggled, each of us trying to gain the advantage as the lobby emptied. Then he wrapped me up in a bear hug and used his weight to drop us both onto the marble floor. We fell over like a couple of trees, caroming off the furniture.

Fuck—he kicked the outside of my sore knee, and the pain took my breath away. But then I saw Mikki Ben Gal's face and I fought back. I brought my fist down on his clavicle. He grunted and loosened his grip on me. That gave me an opening. I slapped his head toward the floor, trying to smack his big bald skull against the marble. But he was too fucking fast, and he twisted away from me, his hands moving *whap-whap-whap*, making me keep my distance.

I tackled him, my fists pounding paradiddles on his face and torso. I tried to get my legs around him, but he rolled away and escaped again, planting the sole of his shoe in my face as he did so. I grabbed the foot and twisted—and was rewarded with an angry bellow and an explosion of nasty Russkie. I pulled myself up his churning legs and hit him in the balls hard enough to make his eyes cross.

He might have been hurt, but he wasn't stopping. Shit—this

guy had to be seventy years old, but he was still moving like a fucking thirty-year-old Spetsnaz Alpha Group shooter.

Well, you know me. I'm an EEO kind of Rogue. Which means I'll kill a seventy-year-old just the same way I'd kill a thirty-year-old: by reaching down his fucking throat, tearing his fucking heart out, and fuckin' eating it raw.

I think he saw what I was thinking, because he backpedaled and tried to put some distance between us. I was having none of it, however, and I stayed close, elbowing and clawing and biting and gouging, trading blow for fucking blow until I knew I had the motherfucker on the run, and I could batter his fucking Ivan shit-for-brains out against the marble floor.

Which was when Boomerang, Gator, Hammer, Mustang, Nod, Digger, Nigel, Butch, and Timex gang-tackled the two of us and pried me off the asshole, just as I was beginning to make some progress disassembling his face.

Boomerang sat on my chest. "Chill, Boss Dude."

"Fuck you." I tried to wrestle out from under him. Believe me, I was white-hot. I wanted no part of chilling.

Ashley. It was fucking Ashley who'd ordered Boomerang to break things up. I gave her a dirty look—and when I got my hands on her I'd do worse.

She stared down at me with derision. "I told you the situation had changed," she said. Then she went over to Oleg Lapinov and started to help the KGB one-star off the deck.

Oleg Lapinov brushed her hand away and waved her off with a throaty growl. He shook off the SEALs holding him down, pulled himself to his feet, and began to brush the lobby dust out of his clothes. He spat blood onto the marble floor and looked over at me. "Not bad for an old man, eh?" he said in decent enough English.

I was in no mood for cuteski fucking banter with this Ivan asshole. "*Yob tvoy mat*—Fuck you."

He looked down at me, laughed contemptuously, and answered with a torrent of AK-47 full auto Russian.

Of which, of course, I understood not a word. "Huh?"

The big Ivan looked down at me. Then he gestured to Boomerang in a way that told me he knew how to command. Boomerang rolled off me, and Lapinov's big, heavy hand took my wrist and pulled me to my feet. "So, Captain, you only learn the good words from the mother of all tongues, is that it?"

I guess he was asking a rhetorical question, because he didn't give me a chance to respond. Instead, he looked me squarely in the eyes, and said, "We must talk. It is important for the interests of both our nations that we do so."

"The interests of both our nations?" What was this highfalutin' shit all about. Now, as you know, I trust Russkies about as far as I can toss the Empire State Building. But there was something about the way that Lapinov was talking—plus the fact that neither Boomerang nor Rotten Randy was protesting—that gave me pause.

"I'm listening," I told him, warily.

"Not here. In private."

That made sense—unless he wanted to get me outside so some Alpha Team shooter could snipe me. But I had to deal with a couple of more important issues before I spent a second of my time talking to some fucking Russkie.

I waved Ashley over, and jerked my thumb at Rodent's litter. "We have to get him taken care of ASAP. He took a bullet through his lung—he's got to be evac'd to Rhine Main, stat."

Ashley didn't need to hear any more. She flipped open her cell phone and got on the case. Then I dealt with my men. I put Boomerang in charge. He knew what had to happen without being told.

With my men taken care of, I could confront new business— i.e., Oleg Lapinov. I looked over at Araz. "Can you and your guys make a little breathing room for Oleg and me outside?"

The big Azeri colonel nodded. "Can do, Captain Dickie." He wheeled, and barked a series of orders. His shooters surrounded Oleg and me, putting us in a rough approximation of what the Secret Service calls The Diamond. As Oleg and I moved toward the hotel doors, the Azeris moved with us, keeping us inside a protective bubble.

I looked back at Araz. "They're learning," I said.

He gave me an offhanded salute cum wave. "Thank you, Captain Dickie."

We started down the long, curved driveway, Araz's squad giving us more and more room as we moved farther from the hotel. Across the four lanes of traffic, opposite the hotel entrance, was a small park. I gestured toward it.

Lapinov scowled and shook his head once up, once down, in considered assent. "That will be good," he said.

We crossed the avenue and made our way into the little park. Lapinov swept the area with practiced eyes, then gestured toward a bench that faced away from the hotel and the traffic. "We can sit there."

We strolled over. Araz silent-signaled his people, who set up their perimeter six yards from us. I looked around. Our backs were to the hotel. Across the park was a row of apartment flats. The sun reflected off the windows.

Lapinov settled himself on the bench and beckoned for me to join him. From the pocket of his jacket he extracted a newspaper. He unfolded it carefully, then handed me one edge of the page while he held the other.

"Now we have a privacy curtain," he explained, "just in case anybody is watching from the flats on the far side of the park and reading our lips."

Okay, so he understood security procedures. BFD.[65] I didn't

---

[65]If you can't figure it out, look it up in the glossary.

have the time, or the patience, for nicey-nicey. I was in the revenge mode, and he hadn't said or done anything to make me change my mind.

He turned his face slightly toward me. "I had nothing to do with the murder of the Israeli woman."

"Who did?"

"It was Ali Sherafi's operation," he said matter-of-factly. "Ali Sherafi and the IRGC[66] control the Fist of Allah."

This *szeb* was just stating the obvious. "With help from assholes like you, Oleg. The fucking camp is set up like a goddam Alpha Team base, and there was a fucking Ivan shooter on the oil rig."

"He was not one of mine," Lapinov insisted. "And my people have never worked with Sherafi." He rustled the newspaper. "Just like in your country, there are political factions in Russia that operate at cross purposes with the government."

"So?"

"The Iranians turned to Sarkesian for help," he said matter-of-factly. "And certain elements of my government encouraged him to help them, because they believed Sarkesian works for them, and they could control him. Or at least that's what they wanted to believe."

Have I mentioned that I wasn't in the mood for coy? "What's this we-they shit, Oleg?"

He looked straight ahead into the newspaper and scowled, then continued in a monotone. "I do not like you, Captain," he said. "When we had the Cold War, I would have liked to—how is it said?—go up against you. I would have killed you, too. And it would have given me great pleasure to kill you." He paused. "But I am a soldier. And while I may disagree with what my government does, I cannot work against it the way some people do."

---

[66]Iranian Revolutionary Guard Corps

At least in that aspect of life, I understood where he was coming from, and told him so. Warriors cannot operate outside society. When they do, they become terrorists, or worse. The Warrior must operate from within a defined chain of command. He may not like it, and he may occasionally skirt it—but in the end, he must submit to it.

"Sarkesian works for the Iranians and he has worked in the past for us. But mainly, we have recently discovered much to our great regret, he works for himself and himself only. Currently, he is playing my country against your country, by employing both Iranian terrorists and renegade Russians, and trying to shift the blame for what they do to my government." A cold-eyed expression came over the Ivan's red face. "And he almost succeeded, until he was pushed over the brink, and panicked, and ordered Ali Sherafi to assassinate the Israeli and killed his wife in the attempt."

"Oh?"

"His conversation was intercepted by Moscow, and the information was passed on to me." He paused. "It was also shared with your people."

"My people?"

"Your intelligence apparatus."

That piece of information rocked me. I mean, if we knew how dirty Sarkesian was, then why the *F*-word wasn't I informed, since General Crocker and SECDEF dropped me into this confusing pile of merde in the first place. "By whom?"

"That is, as you say in English, above my pay grade." Lapinov's tone told me he was ending that particular part of the discussion. Then he continued. "Very recently, Sarkesian also managed to obtain a set of very sensitive diplomatic documents from our foreign ministry," the Russian said, his face coloring in what appeared to be discomfort, "and I was tasked with retrieving them."

"So?" I knew exactly which set of diplomatic documents he

259

was talking about. They were, of course, the top secret docs I'd purloined from Steve Sarkesian's briefcase at the Sirzhik Foundation. But I wasn't about to make Oleg's job any easier—or offer to give 'em back.

He looked at me in a way that told me he realized exactly what I was doing. "I am not in the mood for childish games," Oleg Lapinov said, a nasty edge creeping into his voice.

"Then fuck you very much, asshole." I brushed the newspaper out of his big hands and stood up. "See you around the playground, Oleg." Frankly, I didn't need this creep. I had other things to do. Like hit the Armenian nationalists, who were being supported by the Russkies. Russkies just like Oleg. In fact, it occurred to me right then that maybe I should kill him right now and save myself the trouble of doing it later.

He stood up, the veins in his big thick neck pulsing. He was as big as me, even a little bigger—and even with the suit and tie, I could see that this seventy-year-old worked out. "I am not asking for your help getting the documents back," he said, reaching down to pluck the newspaper without taking his eyes off me. "That is not the point of this exercise." There was blood on his teeth when he spoke. It gave him a sinister yet clownish look.

Then what was the point, I asked?

"My situation was compounded when you broke into Stephan Sarkesian's office." He deflected my question so matter-of-factly I almost didn't see what he was doing.

Then I realized what he'd said—and that he hadn't answered my question. But, so what if he knew. BFD. I didn't see what I'd done as a problem, and I said so.

Lapinov gazed at me the way drill instructors regard stinking trainees. "Your taking the documents pushed Sarkesian to act," he said slowly. "And we were not prepared for him to act. Not yet."

"What's this *we* shit, Oleg?"

"My government, and your government," Lapinov said. "We. Our governments. Acting in concert."

Now I have to admit, friends, that Oleg's second little info-shard also smacked me like the proverbial ton of brickskis. Except . . . now I realized what Major Ashley had been hinting at over the cell phone. And more to the point, why Chairman Crocker had groaned so long and loud when I'd told him what I'd done in Steve Sarkesian's office, and then insisted on learning every minute detail of my actions.

Are you confused, gentle reader? If so, let me explain.

What I'd done was insert *moi* right in the middle of a classic bait-the-trap scheme, jointly run by us, and, so it would now appear, the Russkies. And the target of this subtle joint exercise was . . . the Iranians. No wonder Jim Wink had been able to come up with so much nasty info about Steve Sarkesian so fast. He'd had the information right at his North Philadelphia fingertips. Because despite his bitching and moaning about operating blindfolded, and no assets, and all the other b.s. he'd handed me back in Washington, Christians In Action *was* obviously running an operation.

Not only were they running an op, they were running it jointly with their former adversaries, the Russkies. And left sitting out in the cold (along with me) about this little wrinkle to the plotski had been . . . our own fucking ambassador. Well, that made sense, too. If Madame Ambassador Madison was bolting Steve Sarkesian, there was no reason to bring her into the loop and risk a pillow-talk leak.

Meanwhile, both governments had allowed Steve Sarkesian to think he'd gotten his hands on inside information about what we (and the Russians) had planned for the Caspian region—i.e., the documents in his briefcase. But now that I thought about it, he'd obviously been carefully fed a diet of black data. Disinformation. That's the normal operating procedure in cases like this. And then, once the folks in Washington and Moscow were able to backtrack, and discover who Steve-o's sources were, and what his methods were, Christians In Action and Oleg's people would stage a series of coordinated ops, roll up his nets, shut down his agents, put Steve and his pals away, and take the Iranians out of the picture in this part of the world for the foreseeable future.

The more I thought about it, the more it made sense. While we and the Russkies weren't exactly buddy-buddy these days, both my government and Oleg's government had a vested interest in keeping Tehran out of the picture here in Azerbaijan, not to mention the Stans.

Except, my stealth mission had been compromised. Then I'd killed Sarkesian's POG, which alerted the sumbitch that I was coming after *him*. That was when he contrived the reception at the Foundation so he could lay eyes on me, see who I really was, and who I was working with. I guess the only thing he hadn't counted on was my ability to break into his office and steal his papers.

But that's exactly what I'd done. I'd stuck my big Slovak snout right into the mix. I'd burgled Steve's office—and taken his DIQs, assuming that they were the real thing. And whom did I leave the Sirzhik Foundation with? I left with the Ben Gals. So Steve Sarkesian put two and two together. He'd assumed I was working with the Israelis against him. Which was, of course partially correct.

Which was why he'd unleashed Ali Sherafi to kill Avi Ben Gal—and murdered Mikki in the attempt.

Now let me tell you that this sudden epiphany didn't do much to improve my mood. First of all, I was pissed at the Chairman for not telling me WTF was going on. If I'd known, I wouldn't have done the sneak & peek number on Steve's office. And Mikki Ben Gal would still be alive. It's one thing to bust your ass and lose lives for something important. It's another altogether to waste the life of a friend on something that doesn't matter. And that is exactly what had happened.

Okay, it was time for Oleg to give me some information I could put to good use. I looked at the big Ivan. "Where's Sherafi?"

I asked a simple question, I got a simple answer: "Back in Iran. He slipped across the border yesterday."

Shit. Well, sooner or later I'd find a way to get at him—and I'd take my revenge for Mikki Ben Gal's murder. But that would be then. This was now, and it was time to get back to my original question, which was, what the fuck was he getting at? I sat back down on the bench. So did Oleg Lapinov. "Okay, Oleg, spill. What's happened in the last thirty-six hours?"

Lapinov turned his face toward me and dropped the level of his voice, as if we could be overheard. "The Israelis sent a team to kill Sarkesian."

Hey, like I said, I wasn't in the mood for coy right now. *"And?"*

"My people in Moscow got advance warning and told the Azeris what was about to happen." He spat a mouthful of blood on the pavement. "I don't think the Azeris would have minded if the Israelis had come in and done it. But since we gave them official notice, there was very little they could do. So Araz Kurbanov put an end to it. The Israelis tried to slip in on a flight from Turkey. But they were stopped right at the airport by Araz's people. He escorted them back on the plane, and they returned to Tel Aviv by way of Ankara, no questions asked."

Y'know, friends, the Mossad just isn't the same organization it used to be. They fucked up the assassination of Haled Mesha'al, that Hamas official, in Amman, Jordan, a couple of years back. They got caught trying to bug a PLO apartment in Switzerland and got their operatives declared PNG. And now this.

Lapinov went on. "But Sarkesian has people at the airport, too. He learned he was about to be hit. And then . . ."

"And then? Let's get to the fuckin' point, Oleg."

"And then Sarkesian must have panicked."

"Must have panicked?"

"Must have. Because he ran. To his friends from the Armenian Mafiya—in Autonomous Karabakh. He asked to borrow your ambassador's helicopter for a site survey trip for his proposed pipeline, which runs through Armenia." The Russian spat more blood onto the hot pavement and digressed. "It will never happen, that pipeline. Not through Autonomous Karabakh."

Yeah? Maybe, maybe not. Anyway, right now, who the fuck cared where the goddam pipeline would be laid. "Oleg—"

He rubbed his big bald head and focused again on the matter at hand. "Yes, yes, yes," he went on. "And your ambassador, she is—" He pointed an index finger at the side of his bald head and wiggled it. "Not a lot of smart about people like Sarkesian. And so he convinced her at the last minute to go along to see where his pipeline would run. They filed a flight plan to fly from Ali Bajramly to Satlky," he said, as if I knew where he was talking about. He paused. "They made a cursory examination of the pipeline route, and then they flew to Naryndzlar for the weekend."

Naryndzlar? What the fuck was Naryndzlar? *Naryndzlar?* I couldn't even fucking pronounce it.

"Naryndzlar is an ancient Armenian fortress town, high in the Caucasus Mountains, at the very northern tip of Autonomous Karabakh," Lapinov explained, as didactically as if he were reading the words from a guide book. He spat another mouthful of blood onto the pavement. "It sits at an altitude of twenty-four hundred meters."

I did the math in my head and came up with almost eight thousand feet. Higher than Denver. Higher than Geneva. "That's where he took her."

"There is an old hotel at the top of the mountain," Lapinov said, wagging his head affirmatively, "made out from a fourteenth-century monastery. I have been there. It is isolated. It is impossible to get in and get out without people knowing. Besides, there, in that place, he has the protection of the local *lovrushniki*."[67]

---

[67]That's more Russian cop slang for the local Mafiya.

"You're telling me that Steve Sarkesian kidnapped the American ambassador, and nothing's been done about it."

"There were intercepts between Sarkesian and Tehran that have not been shared with your government."

"I thought we were working in concert."

Lapinov looked at me through hooded eyes. "Some things we prefer not to share—until absolutely necessary." The big Ivan pulled an envelope out of his pocket and handed it to me. I took it, opened the flap, and examined the contents. There were three sheets of official-looking paper, written in Cyrillic, with what I took to be TOP SECRET stamps on each sheet.

I shook the pages under the Russian's nose. "This shit does me no good at all, and you know it, Oleg."

Lapinov shrugged. "Your Major Evens reads Russian," he said. "Ask her."

I stood up and headed toward the hotel lobby. Five minutes later I was back. Ashley and I had huddled outside the hotel and she translated the Russkie to me. I had to admit that if the intercepts were genuine, Ambassador Marybeth Madison was in big trouble.

- The first intercept was a call from Steve Sarkesian to the hotel at Naryndzlar, requesting his usual suite, three rooms for his bodyguards, and two for the ambassador's pilots.
- The second intercept was a phone call between Ali Sherafi and Steve Sarkesian in which Sarkesian told Sherafi that the Great Satan's representative in Baku would be dealt with according to prearranged plan.
- And the third intercept was a cell phone call from Ali Sherafi to the headquarters of the IRGC,[68] reporting that

---

[68]Iranian Revolutionary Guard Corps

"the plan to deal with the American whore" was under way.

I returned to the bench and sat down, confused. Lapinov's expression was neutral. He said nothing. He was letting me figure it all out for myself. But it made no frigging sense, which is exactly what I told Oleg. You don't fucking kidnap an American ambassador. Not unless you want the whole goddam U.S. government beating you upside your head.

Lapinov nodded. "You are correct," he said. "But I do not think she believes she has been kidnapped, and therefore, there have been no alarms."

Let me describe the mental process that followed.

Whoa. Full stop.

Lightbulb.

Like, duh. *Hel-lo.* Wasn't I the one, only a few pages ago, who told you that Ambassador Madison and Steve Sarkesian were clandestinely doing the down-and-dirty? Didn't we see how she controlled Steve at the Sirzhik reception, leaving him sputtering as she made her exit? And finally, didn't we all see the Post-it note on Steve Sarkesian's draft message, which nicely but firmly told him to shove it—she wasn't gonna back him up on the Foundation thing, even though she really liked him?

So, it's not like, she was being *kidnapped.* It was like, she was going to go off for a day or two of 'site surveys' with Steve-o—at least that's what she thought. Steve obviously had other ideas. Maybe he was tired of being pussy-whipped. Maybe he had a new squeeze somewhere, and just wanted to end things with the ambassador. Maybe he'd only strung her along to get her to back his protection racket, and since she wasn't going to do that, he was going to dump her. Yeah: right out of the chopper. Whatever the case, he was obviously gonna take her for a one-way ride.

And by the time she realized what her situation really was—or maybe she wouldn't—well, anything could happen. Like, her chopper could go down in the mountains, with all hands lost. And who would be the wiser? This was an unstable region. A secretary of commerce had been lost over the Balkans. The president of the Georgian Republic barely survived three assassination attempts in the past year alone. If an American ambassador's chopper went down in the Caucasus Mountains, it would be a six-day story— two weeks at most. Why? Because Baku was not the center of the universe. It was expensive to keep news crews here, and besides, there'd be other crises to cover. And so, the story would simply evaporate. It would go away. And there would be unflattering news leaks—maybe even inflated ones—about her ambassadorial assignations. The dead, you see, can't sue for libel. And then, in due course, the U.S. government would replace Marybeth Madison—who may have been naive about where she got her nookie but did understand the awl bidness—with some striped pants apparatchik from Foggy Bottom who wouldn't know diddly-squat about either nookie or the awl bidness, and Steve Sarkesian and the people he was fronting for would ultimately prevail in this region.

Prevail how, you ask. Good question. One of the most basic truths about geopolitics is that things are never black and white. Absolutists and moralists make lousy secretaries of state and foreign ministers, because statecraft is sometimes amoral. Not immoral, let me remind you, but amoral. There's a difference. And in making statecraft, shading is important. Things are seldom black and white, but gray.

So, Steve Sarkesian would prevail because even though both the United States and Russia knew he was dirty, they'd still deal with him, because he'd retain a considerable degree of control over this region by the use of his huge financial and human resources to nudge things in the direction he wanted them nudged. Remember how he told me that the Sirzhik Foundation was, in its own way, a diplomatic entity just like the United States?

Well, he may have been delusional. But there's no doubt he was serious. So what came next? I'd told him the truth: that without military power to back up his economic clout, Sirzhik was an empty shell. So, did he start assembling military power by going after some of the pocket nukes I knew were floating around this part of the world and using them as diplomatic collateral? Did he recruit some broke Russkie scientist to build him a bomb and declare the Sirzhik Foundation a nuclear power? Did he take over the subsidizing of transnational terrorism where Khaled Bin Abdullah had left off after I'd waxed his royal ass?

Frankly, friends, I didn't know—and I didn't care. As I have said before, I make a lousy diplomat. I am an absolutist, and I am a moralist. What I knew I could sum up in a series of simple declarative sentences.

- Steve Sarkesian killed my friend's wife.

- Steve Sarkesian was my enemy.

- Steve Sarkesian was dead meat.

The fact that I could now kill him and do it at government expense was icing on the cake.

I looked over at Oleg. His expression told me he knew what had to be done, and that we had to act quickly. "I know the region," he said. "You have the men."

I had the men? But I *didn't* have the men—at least not enough men to take down a fucking fortified town. My people were all chewed up from the Iran hit. And Araz and his troops hadn't had but just over a week of training, and besides, this wasn't their fight—nor should it be.

Taking Azeri troops into what Oleg called Autonomous Karabakh would be as misguided as trying to take Israeli troops into Syria—it would complicate things, not solve any problems. Besides, there were twenty-five thousand Russian troops scattered through Armenia and Autonomous Karabakh.

According to my pre-JCET intel, a good percentage of them were special operations shooters. I suggested that, since we were all being so buddy-buddy these days, maybe we should stage a joint op with some of Oleg's Spetsnaz boys to show the folks back in Moscow and Washington how well we could all work together.

"It is impossible. We cannot use my assets," Lapinov said, when I suggested the Russkie option.

I do not recognize the word *impossible*, and that's what I told Oleg.

The big Ivan pursed his lips and kept silent.

I wasn't about to lose the opportunity to give him a shiv in the ribs. "What's the problem, Oleg? Your Russkies a little rusty in hostage rescue these days?"

Lapinov looked at me with murder in his eyes. Then he sighed a big Russkie sigh, and said, "You will recall, Captain, that we and the Azeris no longer have a mutual security agreement. This means all our forces have been pulled back across the border of the Russian Federation."

He was right. I had forgotten. "But you could arrange to infiltrate a Spetsnaz battalion—because that's what we'd need. To do the job."

"Not possible," the Russian growled, a nasty look creeping across his round face.

I don't like the *N*-word. A Roguish edge crept into my voice. "Why not possible, Oleg?"

He swallowed hard, his face growing more flushed with each passing second, then spoke. "Because if we did what you suggest, word would immediately escape to the wrong people, and your ambassador would be killed out of hand."

Geezus. He was telling me that the Russkies had no Op-Sec.

He was saying that his forces had been completely infiltrated by the Russian and Caucasian Mafiyas.

I looked at Oleg's expression. The rueful demeanor betrayed the fact that he wasn't happy about what he'd just confessed to me.

Now, I understood exactly where he was coming from. It would cause me great pain to have to admit that I didn't trust my own troops.

"There is no alternative in this," Oleg Lapinov said, a pathetic tone to his voice. "We must use your people to do the job." He paused, and gave me a piercing look. "It is your ambassador who is in danger, after all. But I will support you any way I can."

Oh, fuck—he was right. The birds were crapping, and all the merde was falling on my shoulders. Which meant that, yet again, it was about to be Doom on Dickie time.

I massaged my knee. It hurt like hell. My shoulder wasn't in good shape, either, and a pinched nerve in my neck throbbed, sending electric jolts of pain into my brain.

I guess all the signs meant God loved me, and I was mission-ready. I stood up and stretched. "I have to talk to my people," I said. "Because we have a shitload of planning to do if we're going to actually move as fast as I think we have to move."

Chapter

17

OF COURSE, I CHECKED OUT OLEG'S STORY. LIKE I SAID, I TRUST RUSSKIES about as far as I can toss the Empire State Building. But Ashley vouched for much of what he'd told me concerning the chronology of the past couple of days. And she handed me a sealed envelope containing a backchannel fax from General Crocker that both reamed me a new asshole, and confirmed the bare outlines of what Oleg had said regarding the fact that we and the Ivans were cooperating on the Sarkesian problem.

"The Russians came to us about this particular problem," the Chairman wrote obliquely. *"And it was decided at the highest level— repeat: the highest level—to work jointly with them in this area, and this area alone, as they had an officer on-scene, and we did not. There is no wriggle room here, Dick. You will cooperate."*

The Chairman's words left no doubt in my mind that his orders came directly from the White House. And if that was true, then this had left the military sphere and entered the world of politics. And I didn't even want to begin thinking about the significance of it all. I mean, in this White House, where political contributions pave the way for national policy, anything could happen.

And that wasn't even the most depressing thought. The most

relevant passage of the Chairman's note was the part that told me we had no assets in the region. I mean, we are the world's only remaining superpower, and yet the Russkies put Oleg Lapinov in play in Baku, the Israelis send Avi Ben Gal, and we—we had no resources.

But there was no time to mourn the loss of American gumption. I turned to Ashley. "Okay, what about Ambassador Madison?"

"What about what about Ambassador Madison?" Ashley asked rhetorically.

I didn't need smart-ass right then, and I let her know it. I needed information. Who at the embassy knew what? Who in Washington knew what? This entire op was going to have to be off the books, unless we wanted Delta Force, the FBI HRT, and the fucking State Department SWAT team all on-scene, followed by ABC, CBS, NBC, CNN, and the rest of the media circus.

Ashley looked at me, a rueful expression on her face. "Gotcha," she said. "Sorry." And then she gave me the sit-rep I needed. The good news was that we had some time on our side. There was nothing unusual about Ambassador Madison going off with Steve Sarkesian. She'd done it before—taken her helicopter, too.

"What about her security detail?" I asked.

She'd used Sarkesian's people, Ashley reported. The RSO hadn't liked that, but he didn't get a vote. It was the ambassador's call—and she'd done what she pleased.

The DCM, a career FSO[69] was running things while she was gone. He knew from past experience she didn't like to be bothered while she took time away from the office for her social activities. So we had a small envelope of time with which to play.

Once I factored Ashley's sit-rep into the mix, it was off to work for Dickie. As usual, the situation was not good, and the clock was ticking. But before I started on Ambassador Madi-

---

[69]Foreign Service Officer

son's rescue, I had to deal with two other elements. The first was Rodent. Ashley took care of him: he was in the air, on his way to Rhine Main. The squidge would live. Second matter was the Fist of Allah targets we'd discovered in Iran. I turned all those materials over to Ashley, too, and told her to get DIA on it—real fast.

Then I began to deal with the problem at hand. Ambassador Madison had told the staff she'd be gone for three to four days. That had been roughly a day and a half ago. So my window of opportunity was somewhere in the realm of thirty-six hours. After that, I knew Steve Sarkesian would either kill her on the spot, or send her back to Baku with a lethal charge of Semtex explosive (or a reasonable facsimile thereof) hidden in her chopper.

Sarkesian had chosen his location well. Naryndzlar was accessible by a single, two-lane gravel road that wound up through the narrow mountain passes. The village itself contained no more than three, maybe four dozen homes, a tavern, and a small guest house. From the end of the main street, an old-fashioned funicular railway climbed one kilometer up the steep mountainside, to the hotel above.

Here's some background. During the heyday of the Soviet Union, Naryndzlar had been a retreat for top Soviet officials and heroes. Yuri Gagarin, the cosmonaut, had been given a two-week vacation at Naryndzlar as a reward for his record-breaking trip into space. Khrushchev, Brezhnev, Andropov—they'd all stayed there, too. So had Oleg, who'd been a regular guest throughout the 1970s and 1980s. These days, according to the major general, the place had become a vacation retreat for Russia's top *vory*—the organized crime bosses—and the financial oligarchs who were the real leaders of the Russian Federation. "It is run by the *chornye*,"[70] he said. "The best of everything money can buy." He

---

[70]Shorthand for *chornye smorodiny*, or Caucasian Mafiya (see footnote 49, page 133).

laughed bitterly. "And believe me, they have the money to buy the best of everything and everybody."

"When's the last time you were there?"

"Two months ago. I stayed a week," he growled. "I have been there eight, nine times in the last year and a half. It is a secure place for meetings with the *lovrushniki.* I know them all, too. The managers, and the assistants; the people in the dining room and the bar. Even the women. I know what clan they come from; what crime family they belong to. Who their *vory* are. How they think and what they do and how they do it. I know it all—everything." He caught me staring strangely at him. "It is my mission to get to know these people. I do not care what anyone thinks."

I had to hand it to him. His cover, if that's what it really was, was fucking effective, and I told him so. He'd managed to convince me—and I am the original skeptic.

"Spasiba," Lapinov said, his head bobbing once in my direction, then continuing as if he was speaking to himself. "On my last visit I was the guest of a Georgian *avtoritet* named Japridze."

"Avtoritet?"

Lapinov had to think before he could translate. "It is like a godfather, a *vor.* But in the economic area, not so much the criminal activities like drugs and women. The *avtoritet* controls banks and business."

I had Oleg make me sketches of the village, the funicular, and the hotel grounds as best he could remember them. There was no time to ask for satellite reconnaissance. More to the point, I didn't want to alert anyone back in Washington, even my own support network, about the specifics of what was about to happen.

Washington, after all, is like a huge machine. Once it has been started, the inertia alone makes it almost impossible to change course as quickly as necessary for an unconventional operation. Israel has kept its decision-making apparatus small. So it was able to launch an op like the Entebbe rescue without having it move through innumerable layers of military middle management. At USSOCOM,[71] there are so many strata to penetrate that it is nigh on impossible to run a small, surgical operation without alerting twenty-five layers of governmental managers and apparatchiks, and word leaking out to the press—or worse, the enemy. Oh, it can be done. But it's not easy. And it is especially not easy if the request for such an op is coming from that SpecWar officer so beloved by the bureaucracy, the old Rogue Warrior® himself.

So I knew all too well that if Washington discovered Ambassador Madison had been kidnapped, it would react as Washington always reacts. The Pentagon would do what the Pentagon does. State would do what State does. And any rescue mission would turn into a complete goatfuck.

No—I realized that the only way to handle these things was to KISS them off, and run 'em UNODIR. And keep it simple stupid is precisely what I planned to do.

The hotel itself had fifty or so rooms and eight suites, spread over two floors. The corridors fanned out along the natural ridge of a small plateau in a gentle crescent from the old monastery building, which served as the reception area and lobby, and housed the main dining room and bar area. On one side of the crescent—the inner side—the rooms looked down into the valley below. On the other, said Lapinov, the view was spectacular: you looked northeast, across a series of craggy mountain peaks that towered as high as three thousand meters.

From the lobby area, an old circular stone staircase wound down to the monastery basement, which Oleg said had been totally soundproofed, then converted into a disco. "We put out the story that Andropov liked Western music when he became premier,"

---

[71]The United States Special Operations COMmand, based at McDill Air Force Base in Tampa, Florida.

Oleg said derisively. "Andropov hated Western music. Andropov hated the West as much as Stalin." The big general turned toward me. "Andropov made them soundproof the basement so he couldn't hear even a hint of the Western music they played down there." Oleg's expression told me he approved thoroughly.

There were three other major structures on the plateau, which Oleg estimated was perhaps fifteen, maybe twenty acres in all. The first was a large, three-story dormitorylike affair, built at the very edge of the plateau on the southeast side so as not to disturb the view, which had housed the staff and security element during Soviet days. A second two-story structure contained the communications equipment and had more dorm space for a reinforced security force when Kremlin leaders were in residence. Finally, there was a good-size aircraft hangar, built to house the choppers that had ferried the VIPs from the big airports at the Armenian capital, Yerevan, 175 kliks to the west, the Republic of Georgia's capital city, T'bilisi, 240 kliks northwest, or the small, single-runway airfields at Stepanakert or Agdam. "Brezhnev wanted to build a runway," Oleg said. "But they convinced him it would spoil the view."

"What's the current security like?" I asked.

"Lots of *byki*," Oleg said, using the Ivan slang for *hoods*. "Maybe fifty, sixty guys. Plus the personal bodyguards of the guests." He thought about it a little longer. "And the staff, of course," he said. "Most of them are armed, too."

I had fifteen shooters. The odds were not great. But let me tell you the truth about situations like this one. Odds, my friends, are one thing. Winning is another. In point of fact, all special operations come down to a small, well-motivated force overcoming vastly superior odds to win through speed, surprise, and violence of action. That is true whether we are talking about a hostage rescue, an oil rig takedown, or a Viet Cong tax collector snatch.

The problem here was to insert all of my shooters as quickly as possible, overwhelm the *byki* and any of Sarkesian's security people with a huge volume of deadly, suppressive fire, pluck Madam Ambassador Madison's svelte behind from Steve Sarkesian's clutches, and then haul ourselves out as quickly as possible.

Easy to do—if you have an EC-130 gunship at your disposal. And a fleet of Pave Low Special Operations choppers. And all the goodies needed for a fast-rope insertion. And . . . well, you get the idea. I had no air support. I could not lay my hands on a single chopper. So, what time was it? It was Doom on Dickie Time, because I was certainly fuckee-fuckeed by circumstances.

But being a SpecWarrior means that you always—yes, always—overcome your circumstances. Being a SpecWarrior means that you control your environment—not the other way around. Being a SpecWarrior means that you always—yes always—dominate the situation, no matter what the odds may be.

Besides, it's not as if this kind of snatch op hadn't been done before, and done textbook successfully.

When was that, you ask?

In mid-September of 1943, before most of you were probably born, is when.

That was when a noxious, nasty Nazi major named Otto Skorzeny led a unit of *Jagdverbanden*—hotsy-totsy-fucking Nazi commandos—into the Campo Imperatore Hotel, which was built on a mountainside about 120 miles northeast of Rome, and rescued Benito Mussolini, the F³ (which stands for fat fascist fuck) known as Il Duce, from a bunch of anti-Fascist Italians. Skorzeny used a flight of gliders, which he crash-landed on the small plateau where the hotel was located. In the initial four minutes of the assault, Skorzeny and eight other commandos surprised a force of more than 250 Italian carabinieri and soldiers. Within fifteen minutes, the Italians had been overrun, and surrendered. Skorzeny's men took control of the hotel, commandeered the funicular, surprising the Italians at the base of the mountain by hitting 'em from behind, and then linked up with a heavily armed Kraut konvoy sent from Rome, and *ecco:* Mussolini the F³ was rescued.

Now, I didn't have gliders, and I certainly wasn't going to exfil by convoy. No—the ambassador had her Dauphin-2 at Naryndzlar, and I knew that we could squeeze twenty-plus people in the aircraft, if we dispensed with such niceties as the seats and the VIP interior. But, just like Skorzeny, I could use surprise and speed to overcome superior odds, in order to achieve RS—relative superiority, and WIN. I could also use two major elements of Skorzeny's plan.

- The German had taken a carabinieri general with him because he knew that the sight of the Italian would confuse the carabinieri guards about the true intent of the mission. I would have Oleg Lapinov with me. Oleg knew the *lovrushniki* who were in charge of Naryndzlar's security. They would recognize him—and they would hesitate before shooting.
- Skorzeny's main force arrived later than his initial assault team. That was good because the small number of men in the initial wave confused the Italians and allowed Skorzeny to overcome the POV—the point of vulnerability—quickly.

So, I would need two aircraft to make my assault: a small chopper that usually held no more than four people. And a big aircraft to launch my main assault force. I'd cram six of us into the chopper, and the rest would HAHO from the aircraft and fly in, hitting from the hotel's blind side a few minutes after I'd put the chopper down. They would disable the funicular, thus preventing any reinforcements from coming up the mountain before we achieved our Relative Superiority, and then we would overwhelm the guards, snatch the ambassador, and all of us would fly out on her chopper.

The potential goatfuck factor was high. As Oleg put it so genteelly, delicately, and accurately in Russkie SpecOps slang, *"Ya ve pidze,* Captain—we are about to be stuck in a very deep vagina."

He was right, too. Consider just a few of the nasty DV Factors I had to think about.

DVF One: The winds at Naryndzlar were unpredictable. They shifted quickly, which could blow my secondary force off course. Shit—they could be blown onto the next ridge, and then I'd be left with a six-man assault force, all of us holding little but our limp *szebs* in our hairy Froggish palms.

DVF Two: The altitude itself made jumping a problem. We had no oxygen supplies with us and none were available. That meant jumping at twenty thousand feet or less—and even that altitude was pushing the edge of the envelope given the operational situation.

DVF Three: a HAHO approach can be hazardous to the health if you are spotted coming in, because you are literally hanging out there alone. You cannot shoot effectively and steer a parachute at the same time, and so a single man on the ground with a submachine gun can wreak havoc on an incoming assault team. There were scores of bad guys with various kinds of automatic weapons at Naryndzlar.

DVF Four: we would have to jump during daylight hours, because the drop zone was U2 (unlighted and unfamiliar), and the Skorzeny ruse called for Oleg to make a Grand Entrance, something that could not be done at night.

DVF Five: We had no idea where within the huge Naryndzlar complex we would find Ambassador Madison. She could be in any of the fifty rooms. If we didn't get to her within six minutes of our wheels down on the hotel grounds, the denouement of this book would come a shitload sooner, and it wouldn't be a happy ending either.

But despite the depth of this particular tactical vagina, what I was planning was exactly the kind of keep it simple, stupid operation that defies the odds and succeeds. Why? Because in addition to being KISS, it was also BAD (Brilliant, Audacious, and Direct). Given those Roguish qualities, WE WOULD NOT FAIL.

Chapter

18

THE TOUGHEST ELEMENT OF MY BIG, BAD PLAN WOULD BE GETTING our hands on two aircraft and a bunch of workable chutes. That responsibility fell to Oleg and Araz, who knew the place and the people a shitload better than yours truly. Oleg said he'd be able to cumshaw an old Aérospatiale LAMA. The LAMA sits three plus a pilot. It's not much of a chopper, but it's better than nothing.

As for a jump craft, well, Araz said he had an idea or two, but that every one of his ideas would cost money.

That didn't bother me. I understand that nothing comes for free in this part of the world. Besides, I had the proverbial suitcase full of cash left over from my last op, and since none of it was taxpayer money, I didn't give a shit how Araz spent it, except that he'd better come back with a plane. I got a Rogue-size wad of hundreds out of the box, counted out fifty, and gave them to Araz. "Will that help?"

He looked at the bills. "I thought you wanted an aircraft, Captain Dickie."

"I do. Isn't that enough?"

Araz raised his hands in mock surrender. "Enough? Enough? There is enough here to buy a whole air force," he said earnestly.

I do so love the third and fourth world, where the almighty

dollar still goes a long, long way. "Then you should be able to . . . expedite a decent plane, right?"

He grinned at my vocabulary, and saluted. "Abso*lut.*"

Cash-enhanced, Araz and Oleg went off in one of Araz's big trucks to scour the landscape. Me, I took the Russkie's sketches and worked 'em over with the help of Randy, Boomerang, and Ashley.

Ashley? Yeah, Ashley. She was working as hard as anybody I'd ever seen. While I'd been working the Marybeth Madison problem, she'd gone to the mat with Defense Imaging Agency headquarters back at Bolling Air Force Base just outside Washington, and talked 'em into putting those supercomputers to *work* for a change, instead of just playing solitaire and minesweeper games.

First, she had the computer dweebs input all the stake diagrams I'd lifted from the FA camp in Iran into the Defense Imaging Agency's computers. Then she had them try to match the outlines with the millions of surveillance photographs from satellites, U-2 overflights, and HUMINT target assessment photos available online. Within six hours, she'd wrung a thick sheaf of computer-enhanced, correctly sized photographs out of the intel squirrels at the Agency, which is buried inconspicuously amongst the warehouses, barracks, and office buildings at Bolling Air Force Base. The squirrels had been able to use their computer magic to overlay the stake patterns I'd brought out of Iran atop actual photographic images of buildings and installations. Once they sent us the results, it was like, *eureka.* We were now able to see just where Steve Sarkesian's Fist of Allah tango allies were planning to strike.

And knowing what he planned to hit gave me the outline of Sarkesian's overall scheme. Let's see what you think. The American embassy in Baku was at the top of his list. Then came U.S. embassies in Qatar, Abu Dhabi, and London. His other targets included the corporate headquarters of Exxon, BP, and Shell, two Paris-based banks, and the Turkish Foreign Ministry. He also planned to hit the ARAMCO oil pumping station at Al-Hufuf, Saudi Arabia.

Can you connect the dots? I certainly could—and the key word here was going to be the late and unlamented Roscoe Grogan's favorite squeaky-wheel-gets-the-grease word, *expedite.*

Steve Sarkesian's diplomatic targets were also prime objectives of half a dozen state-supported transnational terrorist groups. He could hit 'em. But guess who'd be blamed: Islamic Jihad, or Hezb'allah, or one of Khaled Bin Sultan's many fundamentalist allies, upset with the United States for sending Khaled on that one-way magic carpet ride to Allah's side, courtesy of *moi.* But Steve was hitting our embassies because he wanted to send a not-so-subtle message back to Washington, i.e., that he was just as powerful as the United States, and he could hit us anytime and anyplace he wanted. In fact, I'd be willing to bet that he'd made contact at each of those diplomatic locations recently to offer his foundation's services as a geopolitical "expediter."

The corporate targets were being hit because they'd resisted Steve Sarkesian's entreaties to use the Sirzhik Foundation to help them "expedite" matters in their oil-exploration programs in this part of the world. How did I know that? Because I'd heard it from Jim Wink (and so had you) when he'd briefed me about Steve Sarkesian and the Sirzhik Foundation. The French banks? They'd recently "bounced" Sarkesian's checks by limiting his line of credit, and he wanted to get even.

And the Turkish foreign ministry? He was going after it because the Turks were allied with Israel (Oleg told me that the Mossad hit team coming after Steve Sarkesian had flown in from Ankara). The Turks also helped the Israelis keep an eye on Steve Sarkesian's Armenian and Iranian allies, allowing them to use Turkish bases for their overflights and eavesdropping. Moreover, any strike against the Turks could conveniently be laid off on any one of half a dozen Kurdish nationalist terrorist groups.

That left the ARAMCO pumping station at Al-Hufuf, Saudi Arabia. Y'know what, friends? I believed that Steve-o was gonna hit it out of pure meanness. Either that, or maybe his Iranian friends had added it to the list without telling him. I say that because it was the one target that didn't fit the pattern.

Time to get moving. Ashley made sure that her people at the Defense Intelligence Agency alerted the folks in the field, and the embassy here in Baku. And because I like redundant systems (less chance for Mister Murphy to show his ugly puss) I got on the secure cellular and made half a dozen phone calls to my own security network back in the States. I called my *copain* Jacques Lillis at DST in Paris to warn him about the hits on the Frog banks. Then I got on the line to a longtime shoot-and-loot ally named Ricky Fewell, who was currently RSO in Abu Dhabi, told him to keep his eyes open, and told him to pass the word to Qatar and Riyadh. When I asked if he'd heard from anyone at Sirzhik, Ricky laughed and said that they'd made an offer to supply weekly strategic risk assessments at what he called a truly outrageous price. "It was a protection racket, pure and simple, Rotten Richard," Ricky said. "I tossed their crooked asses out into the fuckin' sand."

Have I ever mentioned that it is bad karma to bet against da Rogue? Okay, now that the messages had been received and were being acted upon, I knew it wouldn't take long for the FA to take on a whole new and improved organizational name. From here on out, they would be known to one and all as the Fucked Assholes.

Ashley had more to contribute. She'd heard Ambassador Madison describe the fancy accommodations she'd had during a weekend at Naryndzlar six or seven months before. Now that we all knew who she'd been spending her time with, I spent an hour and a half trying to drag as many ambassadorial details out of the major as she could recall.

Ashley remembered that Madison told her she'd had a wonderful view of the mountains. That would have put her on the north side of the hotel. She'd also mentioned that she'd had a corner suite, which allowed her to close the curtains against the morning sun but still have a great view of the mountains. That put her on the northernmost corner of the hotel. I looked at Oleg's sketches. There was one corner suite on each floor.

Now, if you are anything like I am, when you stay at a hotel more than once, and you have loved the room in which you've stayed, you ask for it again. And if you are Steve Sarkesian, and you have the American ambassador in tow, you get that room. I made an executive decision that the ambassador would be in the corner suite on the north side of the hotel. And that point would be the focus of our initial assault.

Making it to that suite without getting ourselves killed was the problem. From the chopper pad to the hotel was 250 yards of open ground. The hotel itself had one main entrance—the old monastery. The two-story structure had been turned into a huge lobby and reception area. Directly at twelve o'clock was the hotel's main dining room. The reception desk was at nine o'clock; the bar at three. We'd have to make it to the main desk, get past the guards in the lobby, take the two quick ninety-degree turns at flank speed, which would get us into the north wing. And we had to accomplish it all without raising anyone's suspicions. Until it was too late, that is.

Rotten Randy came up with the solution. "Remember what the Israelis did at Entebbe?" he asked, massaging his sore knee.

Well, the Israelis had done a shitload at Entebbe, where they rescued a bunch of Israeli hostages from a hijacked Air France flight by flying more than three thousand miles in a flight of C-130s, to kill the terrorists and bring their hostages home. It was an almost perfectly planned and executed SpecOps mission.

But what Randy was talking about was the deception. To cause confusion among the Palestinian and Baader-Meinhof tangos and their Ugandan allies, the first Israelis on the ground were dressed in Ugandan uniforms. And they had with them a Mercedes limo very much like the one Ugandan president Idi Amin drove around in, and a couple of jeeps, just like Idi-baby used as his escort vehicles.

The C-130 flight leader, a lieutenant colonel nicknamed Shiki, landed sans lights and dropped his ramp. The Mercedes and the jeeps, filled with Israeli shooters, drove straight up to the terminal where the hostages were being held. The commandos used suppressed weapons to wax the confused Ugandan guards before they could react. Then the Israelis stormed the terminal, killed most of the tangos (and took the others prisoner), and freed their countrymen, with the loss of only one commando and three hostages.

"We'll need some Russkie uniforms," Randy said. "And some Russkie weapons."

That made great sense, and I liked his way of thinking. I looked at Randy. "Handle it."

"Aye, aye, sir."

Ashley said, "It's almost workable."

"What do you mean 'almost?' "

"It's still a straight assault," she said. "The deception will only last until you get close to the hotel. And if someone starts barking Russian or Armenian at your guys, it's all going to turn to you-know-what real fast."

I looked at her. I hadn't known Ashley very long, but I knew her pretty well by now. "What's your point?"

"The point is that you need one more element of deception."

"And that would be?"

"That would be me," she said.

I gave her my answer quickly and succinctly. "No fucking way," is what I told her.

"You haven't heard me out."

"You haven't heard *me* out. No fucking way."

"You're being redundant."

"I'm being realistic. The only chopper we can lay our hands on is built for four—three passengers and a pilot. I'm going to try to cram six people inside and still fly the fucking aircraft at a higher goddam altitude than it was built to take with that kind of payload. This is not a male/female thing, Ashley, there is simply no room for you because I need all the fucking firepower I can get."

"Bullshit." She gave me a dirty look. "I know Pick and Nigel can both fly helicopters," she said. "So don't try to tell me you won't have enough shooters, because even your pilot'll be a shooter. Besides, if Oleg shows up with *me,* they'll be paying more attention to my tits and my ass than they will to you and your frigging SEALs." Ashley crossed her arms. "You know I'm right," she said. "Women make great distractions."

No argument there. Some of the world's most effective terrorist operations used women to achieve distraction. And in the realm of world-class villains, Leila Khaled, the PLO tango, is right up atop the list with Abu Nidal, George Habash, and Carlos da Jackal. I thought about it for maybe a minute. I did some mental arithmetic. I looked at Ashley. "Maybe," I said. "Maybe. First I gotta see what kind of chopper Oleg came up with."

"You said he had a LAMA."

Fuck, but she had a good memory. "That's what he said," I parried. "But I haven't seen it yet, so I can't assume it is a LAMA. For all I know it could be a baby Bell, and we'd be crammed inside like fucking fraternity dweebs in a phone booth."

Ashley was having none of my argument. "You know I'm right, Dick. So cut the crap. I want in."

"I said 'maybe.' I meant 'maybe.' Let's see what Oleg comes up with."

I see you all out there. You're thinking, like this is the fuckin' Rogue and he's gone politically correct on us. Next thing you know he's gonna tell us there should be lady SEALs and Rangerettes.

Hey, assholes, fuck you. When you wear the Budweiser or the Tab, you can talk the talk. Until then, keep your fuckin' mouths shut. Women can do a lot in the military. No, not as SEALs or

Rangers. Let's leave that to bad Hollywood movies. But they can work the begeezus out of intelligence assignments. They can serve as military attachés. They can do almost anything except fight as a part of elite and combat units.

The problem is that today's military sees itself as a social, not a fighting, organization. So we end up with situations like the Navy does, in which 18 percent of all females serving at sea get pregnant, and cannot perform their duties. That is no way to make war. And believe me, if we had to go to war with all those pregnant sailorettes aboard, their mommies and daddies would be screaming at their congressmen and senators to get their daughters out of the line of fire.

One way to begin to solve the problem would be to follow the Marine Corps example of keeping men and women separated. If that practice were followed in the Army, Navy, and Air Farce, there would be far fewer problems. But that is unlikely to happen with the current Pentagon mind-set, which is the product of leaders who have never had to shoulder the responsibility of leading other men into battle. Indeed, the majority of our leaders, both in the administration and in Congress, have never served in the military, and therefore see it as an alien culture, something to be mistrusted.

Okay, enough with the sermons. There was work to be done.

Araz reported back. He'd found a plane. It was an Arava, which is a short, squat Israeli STOL aircraft, perfect for HAHO operations and SpecWar insertions. He told me that even as we were speaking, he had a mechanic checking the aircraft out. Then, he'd managed to commandeer us some parachutes. He dug in his pocket and brought out a baker's dozen hundred-dollar bills. "Here's your exchange," he said. "I told you—too much monies."

Meanwhile, he said, Oleg had gone off looking for something or other—he didn't know. That made me nervous. I still didn't trust the Ivan motherfucker, and the thought of Oleg out there prowling and growling with no one watching him was vaguely disturbing.

But there was nothing I could do about it right then, so I forgot about it and worried about more important things. Like trying to work out the HAHO HARP—high altitude release point—for the jumpers by using my Magellan GPS and overlaying the routing on my Defense Mapping Agency pilotage chart. Of course, I was doing all this planning totally blind. I had no idea, for example, about the wind conditions on the mountain. Under normal conditions, winds flow upslope on warm days in mountainous terrain. But there are also what's known as unpredictable "valley breezes," which create wind shears, violent updrafts, and unpredictable turbulence. Between the physical conditions and the fact that we were going to be jumping blind, my shooters were going to have to overcome a high DVF to reach the target on time, and en masse.

Now, if this were the Normandy landings, there'd be no questions about whether or not to go. Everyone would go. But this was different. This was a rogue mission. It wasn't officially sanctioned—and hence it could cause deleterious effects on the FITREPS of all concerned. So, I called a team meeting in my room. I laid out the mission parameters. I explained that we were operating UNODIR once again—and that going along could have serious repercussions on their careers. I told the guys we'd be working a lot more seat-of-the-pants than I like to work. And I added that there'd be no consequences if anybody wanted to sit this one out.

Nod stood up. Eddie DiCarlo doesn't say much, and I was surprised to see him want to talk first. "Skipper," Nod said, "I don't think that was necessary." And then he sat down.

Boomerang uncurled himself from the armchair in which he'd stowed his lanky frame and maneuvered onto his feet. Brian (that's his real name) looked around the room at his shipmates. "We've been through a shitload together," he said. "Some of it good, and a lot of it not so good. But we've always worked as a team."

"Amen, bro." That was Gator.

"So," Boomerang continued, addressing himself to me, "why

the fuck do you think we'd do anything to break up the team, Skipper? I mean, this is who we are. And what we do is break things and kill people." He scanned the room. "No one here just showed up, y'know? We all volunteered. We volunteered for BUD/S because we wanted to be the meanest, baddest killers on the face of the earth. We didn't volunteer for peacekeeping missions; we volunteered to make WAR. We didn't volunteer to be Boy Scouts, or traffic cops, or social workers. We volunteered because we wanted to become the best warriors on the face of this fuckin' earth. And that is exactly what we've become."

He looked at me, his eyes blazing. "So, listen, Boss Dude, don't dis us by giving us that shit about no consequences, and this mission is bad for our careers. I'll tell ya, man, if I was interested in my career I'd be a fucking cake-eating civilian NFL football player with fuckin' Denver, because that's what the pro scouts offered me. Shit, I was a second-round draft pick. But I became a SEAL instead. Because there's no fucking comparison between sacking a fucking quarterback, and sending some fucking tango on the magic carpet ride to Allah. This is real job satisfaction. But we do it together. Not on some fuckin' pick-and-choose basis. We all go . . . or we don't go." He 20/20'd the room. "Now, I say we all go." And then he sat down, to silence.

I have to tell you that I had tears in my eyes right then. If one is a Naval officer, one cannot receive a greater gift from God than to be given men like this to lead into battle. It is the ultimate experience. And I was honored, and humbled, by what had just happened in this place.

So, there was nothing to say but "Fuck each and every one of you cockbreaths very much, strong message follows," and get down to business.

I wanted to hit the hotel at 0900. Why? Because at 0900, the sun would work in my favor, blinding anyone looking directly eastward. And eastward is the direction from which my HAHO shooters would be coming. I looked at my watch. It was currently 1752, and my tick-tock was ticking away. I wasn't altogether sure we'd be able to make the hit on time, because there was a shit-load left to do, and not a lot of time in which to do shit.

1825. Randy showed up with two dozen Russkie uniforms. He'd bought them on the street. There were three officer's Class-A ensembles, and the rest were camouflage, fatigue-type blouses and trousers, along with belts and web gear. Perfect? No. But plenty good enough for government work.

1840. Oleg returned, in a Russkie major general's uniform, a canvas document case slung over his shoulder. I plucked Araz from in front of the TV, where he was drooling over some CNN screen candy. The three of us, along with Nigel and Pick, my pilots, drove out to the airport to inspect the aircraft.

1925. The Arava was in good condition. It was an Azeri government plane, well maintained and shipshape. Pick did the walk-around, and pronounced it ready to go. Araz had already had it towed to a remote corner of the airfield, and set it next to an APU, just in case it had problems starting. It had been fueled and topped off. Three of Araz's men stood guard so no one would mess with it. All we'd have to do was climb aboard and take off.

1955. The LAMA was a piece of shit, and I'm being charitable. It belonged to the Azeri oil consortium, and had been used (and used, and used) to fly people out to the drilling platform at the drilling and pumping complex known as Oily Rocks, which comprises 125 miles of crumbling roadways, streets, drilling rigs, der-ricks, and stowage tanks, all atop decaying pylons sunk onto the Caspian bed, sitting sixteen miles offshore of Baku. The LAMA was in worse shape than Oily Rocks. It was a late 1960s model that had been neglected until it became a rusted hulk, with a wheezing engine that wouldn't start, Plexiglas hatches that didn't close, a cracked windscreen, and rotted seats. There were mouse turds on the deck, pieces of the floorboards were missing, and the bolts that held the airframe together looked as if they were about to separate. Once upon a time it had been painted turquoise blue. Now, between the orange rust stains and the faded paint, I was back in the HoJo Zone again (and I thought that once a book was enough).

I used RUT to tell Oleg what I thought. He grunted, and said, "We can clean. We can paint. We can change oil and adjust engine timing."

I looked at him, my expression somewhere between bemusement and numbed shock. "As if that would do anything. Can't you find a better chopper, Oleg?"

He looked at me in the way generals look at junior officers who speak out of turn. Then he shrugged, and said, simply, *"Nyet."*

If this was what the Russkie had come up with for transportation, I didn't even want to begin to think about the chutes we'd find in this part of the world.

2020. We careened around the ten o'clock side of the airport, to a small hangar that had some undecipherable Cyrillic above the door, and two Azeri shooters posted outside, their subguns locked and loaded.

Oleg and Araz stood aside so I could be first in. I pushed through and flicked on the lights. Holy shit, I was in a real rigger's loft. The ceiling was high and unobstructed. There were five long tables for packing chutes. There were hardware boxes, and sewing supplies—all the goodies.

Araz beamed when he saw my expression. "The Baku Sport Jumping Club, Captain Dickie," he explained. "We built this to train during the transition period when we weren't sure"—he jerked a thumb in Oleg's direction—"if they were coming back. So we did it civilian. Now, some of the oil workers brought their own gear, and they jump regular."

He grinned, held his right hand up in front of his nose, and rubbed his thumb against his forefinger, making the universal sign for greasing palms with cash. "I have just . . . expedited."

Frankly I didn't give a shit how, or why, or how much. I was just happy to see this setup in place where I could use it.

"Let's look at the chutes," I said.

2055. There were three Vector tandems, six Ram-Airs, and half a dozen Russkie military chutes that sorta resembled the old round MC-3s we used when Christ was a mess cook and HAHO hadn't been invented.

I hefted the closest Ram-Air onto a rigging table. "Let's get to work."

2122. GNBN. The GN was that the three tandems were in pretty good shape. But one Ram-Air was totally unusable—a fair portion of the silk[72] in the right stabilizer was rotted. The chute would not be steerable. Worse, the harness had been eaten through in half a dozen places by mice. A second Ram-Air had also been used as dinner by Mickey Murphy, Minnie Murphy, or some suitable squeaking fucking facsimile thereof. A third had minor rips in the parasail. It could be sewn.

We left the chutes spread out, so my jumpers could examine and pack their own. You don't want to trust that kind of thing to anyone else, especially when the jump is going to be potentially lethal.

2200. We held a team meeting to make the assignments and hand out the uniforms Randy'd bought on the street. Oleg brought his own. The LAMA crew would be Oleg, and me, with Nigel flying in the pilot's seat. That was three. Then I figured we could squeeze three more, if they were small. On that basis, I chose Half Pint, Digger, and Nod. Which left just enough room for Ashley. I had to admit that her presence would give us five, maybe six more seconds of distraction, which could mean the dif-

---

[72]Yes, I know that Ram-Air chutes are actually not made of silk—in fact, no chutes are made of silk these days. But when I first threw myself out of a perfectly good aircraft, parachutes *were* made of silk. And "silk" is how I still refer to 'em. And if you don't like it, then go fuck yourself—and buy someone else's book.

ference between life and death.

Then it came time to assign the jump teams. Pick was recused. He had to pilot the Arava, because I didn't want some Azeri who didn't know fuck-all about HAHO jumping to be at the controls when my guys went over the rail. He grumbled and he groused, but that's the way it was gonna be. As for the rest, Rotten Randy's knee still hurt like hell—but there was no way he was being left behind. He and Duck Foot volunteered for one of the tandems. So did Hammer and Goober. So did Timex and Mustang. That made six.

Which was when Oleg, who'd just arrived, interrupted. "Give each tandem team a machine gun," he said. "It is how we train to provide . . ."—he screwed up his face, hunting for the right word, then smiled when he found it—"suppressive fire in hostile landing zones."

I thought about what he'd just said, and it actually wasn't a bad idea—even if it was terminally flawed. One of the down sides of a jump insertion is that you are vulnerable as you come in over the enemy, because it is impossible to steer a chute and shoot a weapon simultaneously. But if my jumpers were using tandem chutes, the bottom man might actually unharness his weapon and lay down suppressive fire while the top man steered as they dropped into the DIP.[73]

But jumping with a machine gun? That's something you might see in a Hollywood movie—not in real life. And even if the Russkies did jump with machine guns, Russkie jumps were normally performed off static lines, not free fall. Moreover, the Russians have never minded taking 80 percent casualties when they stage an assault. If half their jumpers went splatski, it was just too bad. SEALs would rather their opposition took that kind of casualty rate.

That was all on the one hand. On the other hand, if my guys

---

[73]Desired Impact Point.

came down using tandem chutes, and the bottom men were able to unharness their MP5s on final approach, the fucking technique might actually work. I looked over at Hammer and Randy. The smiles on their faces told me what they were thinking. Randy jumped to his feet—and winced. "I'm going to tape my fucking knee," he said, heading for his room where his personal and much beloved MP5 sat field-stripped in the locked box by his bedside.

I looked around the room and gave my people the rest of the good news. We had four operational Ram-Airs left and only three remaining jumpers. It's amazing how sometimes, things just work out.

Chapter

19

0400. WE TRUCKED OUT TO THE AIRPORT. ARAZ BROUGHT US AROUND through the back gate so we wouldn't attract any attention. I let my jumpers deal with their own chutes. Me, I wanted a good look at the chopper.

I had to admit it: Oleg had kept his word. The LAMA had been repainted in the anonymous dark OD of the Russian military. It wasn't a pretty job. Close up you could see blisters of rust beneath the fresh paint. But it would do. Nigel and Pick did a walk-around. Then Nigel climbed into the pilot's seat and played with the switches. He waved me over. "They all seem to be working, Skipper. I'm gonna try the engine."

I gave him an upturned thumb. He began the start sequence. The engine coughed and whined and protested, but the motherfucker turned over, the big blades moving slowly at first, then whirling faster and faster. Nigel's face was a study in concentration as he checked his instruments, and played with the controls. Then, the rotors at full pitch, he lifted off the ground, hovered at a height of six feet, then set the chopper back gently on the deck and shut everything down.

He climbed out, and looked critically at a dribble of oil that was running down the engine housing. "It'll fly," he said. "I don't know that I'd like to spend a long fucking time in this bird, Skipper. But for a single short hop, it'll do."

"It better."

He gave me his Serious Pilot Look. "It will."

0455. It is harder than it may seem to coordinate a two-pronged attack, especially one in which one of the prongs is jumping onto the target. Basically, the Arava would fly into a standoff position roughly twelve miles off the hotel. As the chopper approached, the jumpers would launch, form up, and fly in, hitting the ground two and a half minutes after the chopper touched down. That would give us another 3.5 minutes in which to find Ambassador Madison's butt. After six minutes, she'd probably be dead.

So, let's do the math. After launch, the jumpers forward speed would be twenty-six miles an hour, with no wind. If they hit headwinds, the schedule would have to be adjusted. If there were tailwinds, we'd speed things up. And if there were crosswinds, we'd simply be fucked.

Now, there's a mathematical formula for determining the HARP, or High Altitude Release Point, during jumps like these. That formula is known as the modified D=KAV, where D equals the gliding distance in nautical miles, K equals the canopy drift constant, A equals the altitude, and V equals the wind velocity in knots. But D=KAV doesn't do any good if you don't know the wind velocity, the gliding distance is variable, the altitude is give or take a couple of thousand feet, and the LZ conditions are unknown. So what was going to happen here was that my jumpmaster, Boomerang, was going to have to read the air currents and winds as the team came in, and make his adjustments accordingly. In training, you'll want at least a "3" safety factor for jumps like this. This morning, our safety factor would be somewhere in the minus two-digit column.

0548. Equipment check. We used our own web gear. It looked

a little strange with the Russkie uniforms, but at least we'd know where everything was. I'd assembled a Russian colonel's uniform. The sleeves were two inches too short and the trouser legs were three inches too long, but as they say, WTF. Since weight on the chopper was going to be a factor, we'd use our MP5-PDWs, which we could conceal under our uniform blouses if we had to. Each man would carry eight thirty-round mags of 9-mm, plus a USP in 9-mm, with five fifteen-round mags. Each man in the chopper assault team also carried three DefTec distraction devices, three concussion grenades, and three frags. Nod and Butch Wells each packed prefab door busters: triple-thick loops of det cord taped to sheets of plastic foam, fuse material, and nonelectric blasting caps, just in case we met any doors we didn't like. I shoved a portable scanner into my blouse pocket. You never know when you may want to listen in on the opposition.

Timex and Mustang, Tandem Team One, had rigged their sub-guns so they could jump with the weapons secured, then lock and load during the long glide to the target. Tandem Three, Hammer and Goober, came up with one of Araz's AKs, and three thirty-round mags. While they loaded mags and checked the weapons, I went over the flight plan with Pick and Nigel.

Naryndrlor was 316 klik from the runway at Baku as the bird flies. But the straight route put us in jeopardy, as it took us precariously close to a pair of Azeri radar sites that Oleg said were controlled by the *chornye*. If they spotted us, they might conceivably warn Steve Sarkesian. Did I know for sure that they would? *Nyet.* Was I willing to risk the op? *Nyet.* So, I decided we'd take a more southerly route. From Baku, we'd head southwest and overfly the sparsely populated Mughan Steppes, keeping low enough to avoid the Iranian radar site at Parsabad. At Bejlagan we'd vector in a northerly direction, skirt the army base at Aghdzabadi, start climbing the ridge at Aghdam, and then follow the single-lane unimproved road that led straight as an arrow from Syrchavand, through the medieval town of Vanklu, all the way up the mountain ridge to Naryndzlar.

The Arava, which has a range of just about 650 miles, would take off twenty minutes after the chopper did, pass it enroute, and circle, waiting our arrival, over the Aghgol Nature Reserve, well east of the border of mountainous Karabakh. We'd keep in touch by radio, and as we began our climb along the ridgeline, the plane would come in, line up on the same road we were following, launch the jumpers, then skedaddle back to Baku and wait for us to show up with the ambassador. The road ran more or less due east/west, so my jump teams could follow it easily. Best of all, they'd have the sun at their backs, so they'd be in full surprise mode as they came into the LZ. Piece of baklava, right? Sure it was—at least in my head.

0636. I was standing outside, running Murphy factors through my head when Ashley parked her blue and white Suburban next to Araz's truck and climbed out, showing a lot of leg—and more. I turned. I looked. I blinked. *"Geezus."*

"Like it?" She whirled, like one of those fashion models you see on TV.

I guess the best way to put it, was that Ashley was out of uniform. She was wearing Nike sandals and a turquoise blue spandex minidress. From my long experience with these sorts of things, I can tell you for a fact that although she was wearing socks with her sandals she hadn't bothered to put on very much underwear.

"If you don't throw on a pair of coveralls, you're gonna get drooled on by my whole crew."

"I'm way ahead of you." She reached back into the big Chevy, pulled out a regulation Nomex flight suit, and climbed into it. She zipped up. "Better?"

"No, but safer. Much safer."

As the men did the final load-out check, I took Araz aside and filled him in on Sarkesian's plan to attack the U.S. embassy. I told him the attack would probably come from one of Ali Sherafi's units. The Azeri's face turned grim. "I will handle this, Captain Dickie," he said.

From his determined expression, I knew that he would.

0640. I came back to discover Oleg huddled with my tandem jumpers. He took the MP5 from Randy, and attached the submachine gun's safety line to his own body. "Like this," he said. "And—" He tucked the buttstock close to his chest. "Even after chute opens, during glide, keep tight your hold. If you do it like this"—he let the butt slip forward—"it cuts into the airstream, and you will . . ." The Russkie's hand started to spiral and wobble.

"Corkscrew," Randy broke in.

Lapinov nodded. "*Da.* Corkscrew." He handed the weapon back to Randy. "No fun, corkscrew."

Randy, Mustang, and Hammer practiced tucking their weapons' buttstocks tightly against their chests, as they and their partners mimed free-fall maneuvers. Oleg watched critically, nodding, and correcting, until he was happy with what he saw.

He smacked Mustang on the shoulder, rocking the big SEAL back two feet into Timex. Mustang threw his chest out. "*Spasiba,* General."

"You will all do well," Oleg said to the tandem teams. "You learn fast." The Ivan's mustache twitched in the early morning heat. "And if not, you will go—" He clapped his hands explosively, turned, and walked away. "Boom," he said as he marched off. "Boom. So learn fast."

Loading the chopper was kind of like stuffing all those big tall clowns in the tiny circus car. Nigel had the pilot's seat. Nod and his MP5 took the front passenger seat, so we'd have firepower as we came in for a landing. We put Oleg on one side of the rear bench, and me on the other, to make sure the craft stayed in trim. Half Pint squeezed between us, and Ashley settled on his lap, making the squidge-size SEAL the happiest (and most politically erect) man on the flight. That left Digger O'Toole, who crammed himself onto the deck plates in front of Ashley's knees.

Then Nigel and Nod started handing our equipment to us. By the time they finished, we were completely wedged in.

Which is when I realized that somehow, Mister Murphy had managed to squeeze himself on board, too. I held up my hand. "Whoa," I told my troops, "this ain't working."

I mean, just think about it. Once we'd touched down up at Naryndzlar, we were going to have to scramble out of the fucking LAMA looking like a Russkie general's elite bodyguard unit, not a bunch of fucking circus clowns.

"Unload," I told Nigel. "We have to reconfigure."

He groaned and started to protest. "Oh, Gov—there's another chute. Just let Digger go in the Arava"

No fucking way. I wanted all four SEALs and their firepower when we dropped into Naryndzlar. So I stopped the little Brit short, reminding him that he didn't have to like it, he just had to do it.

0702. Time was as tight as Ashley's dress. But until I solved our exit-the-chopper problem, we weren't going anywhere. We unloaded, restowed, and tried again, and rehearsed jumping out. It wasn't perfect, but at least Oleg, Half Pint, Digger, and I weren't tripping over one another as we piled out of the LAMA onto the tarmac in orderly and combat-ready fashion.

0712. Wheels up. For the literalists among you I am speaking metaphorically because the LAMA we were using didn't have wheels but skids. But you know what I mean. Nigel increased his engine revs, changed the pitch of his rotors, and the LAMA shuddered, then tail first, lifted off the deck. The little Brit hovered, getting his bearings on the controls. The craft rose another six feet vertically and perhaps a dozen yards horizontally, when we came down—hard enough to rattle my teeth.

Nigel's narrow face turned toward me. "We got too much

weight aboard, Gov. I'm not gonna be able to hold 'er steady—and she's certainly not capable of making the altitude we'll need out by Naryndzlar."

Doom on me. I leaned in his direction and shouted to make myself heard above the engine noise. "How much weight are you talking about?"

He shrugged, fighting the controls as the chopper bounced up and down precariously. "From the way it feels, it could be a hundred pounds, it could be a couple hundred."

The LAMA settled back onto the deck and Nigel shut it down.

I pushed against Digger's back. "Everybody out."

Once we cleared, I examined the interior of the old chopper. There were two steel storage boxes bolted behind the passenger bench. I peered inside. They were filled with mechanic's tools. They both got unbolted and jettisoned. That was about a hundred pounds of weight saved—maybe more. I tossed the old Russkie fire extinguisher onto the deck. Ten pounds more. I unscrewed the Plexiglas hatch covers and left 'em on the tarmac. That was another thirty-five, maybe forty pounds. I hoped that Mister Murphy was among the things being left behind. He was the real dead weight we had to lose this morning.

Okay—now it was time to toot the motherfucker out. "Let's pile in and see how it flies."

0717. Wheels up. Nigel took the chopper up six feet, and then skimmed along the tarmac. He worked the controls and pedals, and the chopper rose. At about a hundred feet, he turned his head in my direction, said, "This'll do, Gov," and simultaneously gave me the upturned thumb confirming we were good to go.

Then it was back onto the deck to top off the fuel tank. Another six minutes consumed. I got on the radio to Pick. "We're gonna launch."

Pick knew we were way behind schedule, but he was gracious enough not to bring it up. "Roger-roger, Skipper. Good to hear it. Fair winds and following seas."

"Thanks, Pick—same to you guys." I tapped Nigel on the shoulder and pointed skyward. "Okay, Nige. As you Limeys like to say, "Tally-the fuck-ho."

Chapter

20

0739. WE FLEW VFR,[74] FOLLOWING THE RAILROAD LINE THAT RUNS FROM Baku to Bataga. Nigel kept the chopper at about twelve hundred feet. We were making just under 140 knots. I unzipped the pouch on my body armor and felt for the paper on which I'd done the flight calculations. The four legs of this flight totaled 462 miles. I peered down at the landscape below, and saw a narrow, winding river over which the twin spans of a railroad bridge and an elevated highway crossed, right in the center of a good-size town lying below us and just north.

I checked the map, confirmed we were over Ali Dajramly, did some mental calculations, and muttered a few rude imprecations in three languages at Mister Murphy. Doom on Dickie. Somehow, he'd managed to cram himself undetected into the far corner of the passenger compartment before we'd left Baku.

Shit. If I could have reached the sumbitch, I'd have tossed his ass out the hatch. But I couldn't. Besides, I was too busy revising the op plan. We had 280 miles left to go. We were traveling at 136 knots. You do the fucking math.

---

[74]Visual flight rules.

You say that you're no good at math and you need a calculator, and you don't want to do math—all you want to do is kick ass and take names? Well, here is a bit of truth for all you Rogue wannabes out there. Using the *F*-word in all its compound-complex forms does not make you a Rogue Warrior®, because being able to use profanity means nothing without the ability to deal with the real profanity of perplexing situations. Neither does acting pushy, or aggressive, or being able to recite the Ten Commandments of SpecWar[75] from memory. And you can talk about guns all you want, but talking about guns doesn't make you a Rogue Warrior® either. Guns, like knives, and parachutes, and even tanks and F-16s, are all simply TOWs—Tools of War. They are not icons, or collectibles, or trophies to be shown off.

Oh, sure, when I was a tadpole, school was unimportant to me. In fact, I dropped out of high school to join the Navy. But the closer I got to the Teams, the more important having an education became. Let me remind you that my platoon chief at UDT 21, Everett Emerson Barrett, kicked my enlisted butt until I completed my GED, and an admiral named Snyder made sure I completed college and even got a master's degree. Indeed, I have discovered that the real key to Warriordom can be reduced to three words: study, study, and study. You cannot be a SEAL and not know math. You cannot be a Ranger or a Delta shooter and not know math, because there ain't no room on the Teams for someone who can't solve complex formulae about everything from the HARP of your HAHO, to the use of shaped charges, to decompression after a long, deep dive.

Bottom line? You wanna be like me, then you better fucking learn math, and you better fucking learn it good. Because how the fuck can you plan missions if you can't fucking add, subtract,

---

[75]© 1994–2000, Richard Marcinko and John Weisman

multiply, and divide, not to mention do your fair share of alge-
bra, calculus, and trigonometry. Got it? Good.

Now, like most SEALs, I don't carry calculators with me. And
so I crunched my numbers the old-fashioned way: pencil on
paper. And the answer I came up with was that we had 1.96
hours of flying time left, and 1.2 hours until 0900, which as you
will recall, was the optimum time for our hit, given the sun's
position and the condition of the target. That put us three-quarters of an hour in the debit column timewise, and that was with a
perfect flight—no head winds, no engine problems, none of the
numerous possible screwups, fuckups, and mess-ups that the
great nineteenth-century military philosopher Carl von Clause-
witz lumped together as "the fog of war."

I tapped Nigel on the shoulder. "Any way to gain some time,
Nige?"

I didn't care much for his response. Basically, we were flying
this craft in overload as it was, and just getting to Naryndzlar
was going to be a problem.

Oleg reached over and pulled the chart out of my hand. He
peered at it, then stuck a stubby index finger on the creased sheet
of paper. "There," he said. "We should cut short the trip by flying
northwest now, not circling around."

I saw what he was getting at. My route had been circuitous, six
legs in all, to avoid being spotted. Oleg's was direct: only three
legs. But it took us over two Azeri military installations. I
brought the subject up to him.

He shrugged off any objections. "They will not pay attention,"
he said. "They will not care about us."

"How can you be so sure?"

"I cannot guarantee," he said, shouting over the wind and
engine noise to make himself understood, "but Azeris in the past
have not been effective militarily."

Ashley nodded in agreement. "I concur with that part of what

Oleg says," she yelled. "Frankly, Dick, it would save us a lot of time. At least half an hour."

I thought about it, handed the map to Nod, and showed him the new routing with my finger. Then I retrieved the GPS unit from my vest, unhooked it from its lanyard, and handed it to Nod. "Punch the new route into the GPS," I mouthed, my words getting lost in the ambient noise.

Nod didn't have to hear. He understood perfectly, gave me a thumbs-up, and went to work. Three minutes later, Nigel looked at the Magellan readout screen, and tally-fucking-ho'd the LAMA northward. Our time to ETA had just been reduced by two legs and twenty-seven minutes according to the little abacus that sits just fore of the bullshit detector and just left of the pussy-meter in my brain.

Plus, because we weren't going to be heading up into the hills for a while, we could increase our airspeed. Which would save us another four minutes. That brought us into an acceptable Murphy range—just over fifteen minutes behind schedule.

0752. I radioed Pick, gave him the news, and got a roger-roger. He'd be taking off any minute now, and heading toward his target, thirty miles east of Naryndzlar. I put my head back, rested it against the metal firewall, and closed my eyes. I've learned over several decades of Warriordom that you grab rest whenever you can get it. So this was as good a time as any for a Roguish combat nap.

0832. A change in the way we were flying awakened me with a start. I opened my eyes. It had grown much colder, and I looked groundward. Our airspeed had slowed considerably—down to seventy-five, maybe eighty knots from the look of things, and the engine didn't sound good.

We were climbing over a series of scrubby foothills, whose ridgelines rose perhaps fourteen or fifteen hundred feet above the valley floor. The air around the chopper had dropped into the fifties, and without the hatches, the wind chill made it seem twenty degrees colder than that. I looked over at Ashley, who was shivering.

I mouthed, "You okay?"

"It's no worse than it was at SERE[76] school," she answered, her jaw shuddering as she spoke. "I'll be okay."

Now? Maybe. But it was going to get a lot colder when we hit the mountains. Well, Ashley was tough. She'd be able to take it. If not, well, she'd be cold. I glanced over at Oleg. His arms were wrapped around the document case, its strap running under his right epaulette. His head was back, his mouth was open, and he was snoring away, oblivious to the slipstream that was making a prop out of the waxed tip of his long, white mustache.

Good. I extracted the secure cellular from my pocket, snuck another look at Oleg to make sure he wasn't watching me, then punched up the first of the numbers in my head. It rang twice, and was picked up.

I said, "Sit-rep," then I plugged my right ear with my index finger so I could hear what was being said on the other end.

I hung up after thirty seconds, called a second number, and more or less repeated the performance. My third call was to Jacques Lillis, and the fourth to Ricky Fewell. The news was all good: the targets Steve Sarkesian planned to hit had all been hardened against attack. Jacques Lillis's people had identified the TIQs in Paris, and were watching 'em closely. MI-5, the British security apparatus, was waiting in London to pounce on the Iranians Ali Sherafi had sent to hit our embassy there. The oil company HQs were being protected, and the FBI had been alerted. Bottom line? Within six hours, Steve Sarkesian's nets would all be scooped up—and the sumbitch would be out of business.

No, that's not quite accurate. He'd be dead. I switched off the

---

[76]Survival, Escape, Resistance, and Evasion

phone and slipped it back into my pocket, glancing over to make sure that Oleg was still snoring. He was.

With the other problems solved, I could pay attention to our situation. I tapped Nigel on the shoulder and asked for a sit-rep.

It wasn't good. "There's a flutter in the engine, Gov," he said.

Well, I knew that already. You could hear the goddam thing struggling. "Will she make it?"

He shrugged, keeping both hands on his controls. "I dropped speed, but it's a real fight, and we haven't begun to climb yet."

I looked over at Nod, who was mirroring Nigel's every move, flying the fucking LAMA by osmosis. "How we doing'?"

Nod came out of his trance, hit the Magellan's "on," switch and when the screen came alive, handed the gizmo to me.

I peered at the readout. We were about forty minutes out, as far as I could guesstimate, due east of Naryndzlar. Below us was a narrow, winding river that made a ninety-degree turn south, then flowed down a more or less northwest to southeasterly course. I grabbed the map and the GPS unit from Nod, laid the map over my legs, balanced the Magellan on my right knee, and tracked our progress with my right index finger.

I looked down at the sequence on the small GPS screen. Yup. We were flying over Mughanly now. Next town to the west should be Kurdlar. After Kurdlar, we'd reach the mountains—the outer edge of the Caucasus range, and things would start to get hairy. I reached for the Magellan to double-check.

Which was when Oleg came out of a nightmare with a series of snorts and starts, his body shaking like a big wet bear. Inadvertently, he swatted Ashley with his big fat Ivan elbow, sending her body up against mine, and the Magellan careening off my knee. The position finder bounced once on the deck plate, knocking the double-A battery cover off. Digger shoestring grabbed the batteries as they rolled toward the hatchway. I hit my quick-release shoulder harness and went for the GPS. I swooped forward to scoop it up just as Oleg smacked into Ashley again. Her foot connected with my injured knee, and I reacted badly, kicking the fucking Magellan out of the chopper.

I thought about going after it, because that's how stupid I had just been. I fell back onto the bench, secured myself with the safety harness, and looked down ruefully at the lanyard that should have been attached to the Magellan. I looked over at Oleg. He was back asleep, oblivious to what he'd done, his mustache fluttering in the slipstream, a small line of drool coming out of the corner of his mouth. Digger O'Toole, who has a very sarcastic streak in him, rolled his fucking eyes skyward, held the batteries in his palm, and proffered them toward me without saying a word.

He didn't have to. I used sign language to tell him he was a number-one sort of guy, which brought an uneven, malevolent grin to his pasty Mick face.

And Nod didn't make me feel any better by telling me that we could probably fly visual from here on, because the course was pretty much due westerly. Hey, I'd fucked up, and I knew it. But there was nothing to do but keep moving forward.

0847. Twenty miles to go. And then, there it was: the high Karabakh Khrebet ridge, looming in front of us like a big fucking wall. The narrow road we were following disappeared into a tunnel. Doom on us, because we didn't have that luxury. We were gonna have to muscle our way over the goddamn ridgeline meter by meter and come out on the far side without crashing.

Which result was not guaranteed, because the chopper was in rough shape, and vibrating badly. Nigel really had his work cut out for him now. He was up to it, though, hunched over the controls, his hands and feet planted firmly on sticks and pedals, the neckband of his Russkie uniform wet with sweat, even though the air was close to freezing.

And then suddenly, his head turned toward me, his face contorted with the stress. "I can't hold it, Gov—gotta set 'er down or we're history."

I gave him an absolute negatory. I didn't fucking care if we crash-landed on the goddam plateau at Naryndzlar. But if we set the LAMA down now, we'd never fucking get airborne again. I knew it, and so did Nigel, even though he chose to disregard the message in his gut.

"Just fly the fucking thing, Nige—"

"Aye-aye, Gov." His face showed new determination. Like all SEALs, Nigel knew he had to produce when the odds were all against him. Like all SEALs he knew he had no choice other than TO KEEP GOING. He'd just needed to get a little encouragement from someone else who was in the same boat—or chopper—as he was.

And so, newly dedicated to the battle, he flew not only by skill, but also by SHEER WILL and SHEER DETERMINATION. He kept us moving ahead, forcing the chopper higher and higher even though the LAMA was disintegrating as we climbed. Yet, it didn't matter. Why? Because we were ATTACKING, and in that mode, we'd take our fucking chances. More to the point, we'd keep going toward our objective.

0904. The chopper's airspeed was only thirty-five knots now, and dropping. I could hear the engine begin to consume itself as we strained up the fucking Karabakh ridgeline, not more than fifty, forty, thirty yards above the scruffy treetops.

I didn't want to hit the trees. I really didn't want to hit the trees.

And then, and then, and then, Nigel crested the ridge, and we saw what was beyond it.

I felt the way Moses must have felt as he looked down on the Land of Canaan. Below and to the west lay a narrow, fertile valley. It was completely clean and green, no more than a kilometer wide, and totally hidden from the outside world.

It was like being on another planet. No shear. No crosswinds.

Tranquil air. And pastoral bliss: cattle and sheep grazed peacefully below. I saw three—no, four—small farms, with postage stamp–size vegetable patches. It was as if we'd flown into a time warp.

The valley hadn't been on the map. Not the one I was using anyway. Maybe if we'd had a tactical pilotage chart, I would have seen it. But we'd been using a commercial map—and the scale was just too big to pick this place up.

I peered over Nigel's shoulder. To the north, a small lake on a northeast/southwest axis fed a series of mountain streams running off southward.

We progressed up the valley for three, maybe four kliks. The green disappeared, replaced by the gray-brown scrub of the Karabakh. I saw the road that would take us to Naryndzlar, and pointed it out to Nod, who nodded, tapped Nigel on the arm, and hand-signaled that he should drop down and follow it. The land got uneven, and desolate once more. We'd left Eden—and were in the mountains once again.

0909. New air currents started to affect the chopper. We got hit by crosswinds, blowing us off course even at our pitiful altitude. Nigel fought the controls, keeping us steady. We maneuvered about six kliks south of Syrchavand, where Pick was circling. I scanned the skies but couldn't see anything in the twilight morning light. Suddenly, we were buffeted by a nasty wind shear. That's the mountain air for you: unfuckingpredictable.

The chopper dropped sixty feet in half a second, giving us all a bit of a shock. Then Nigel banked away and found smoother air. He regained altitude, and came around a right-hand bend above the road. Off at two o'clock I saw a trio of oil storage tanks. Once, they had been camouflaged to match the vegetation. Now the green, gray, brown, and tan paint had mostly chipped away and the tanks sat unused, huge rusting hulks.

Oleg came alive. He pointed at the tanks. "Red Army built those," he growled.

I looked over at him. "Nice work," I said sardonically. I don't think he got it. So I turned my attention toward more important things. Like the condition of our aircraft. The LAMA's engine was still vibrating, but not as badly as it had been as we'd crested the ridgeline.

0913. We proceeded west through the narrow valley, the jagged Karabakh mountains towering above us on either side. Nigel had dropped us low, flying a mere hundred feet above the narrow, blacktop (actually it was browntop) road below. He pulled up slightly over Vanklu, giving us a look at the old church. Vanklu was only four kliks from Naryndzlar.

I got on the radio, told Pick we were on final approach, instructed him to launch the jumpers, and made sure I got a "roger-roger."

0914. Nigel banked into an oblique turn. The hotel was dead ahead, sitting atop the ridge. But running parallel with us, right along the north side of the ridge, ran a half-dozen high-tension power lines. They came out of the mountain, ran for about two kliks, supported by huge steel towers anchored onto the mountain side, then disappeared once more into the Karabakh. The power lines hadn't been on my fucking map either.

You couldn't see the towers or the lines from the hotel. But they would sure as shit fuck with my jumpers, who were flying in from the northeast. I was reaching for the transmit button on my radio when Pick's voice echoed in my ear. "Jumpers away," he told me.

It would be easy to say that they were fucked. But in point of fact, they weren't—nor would they be. Because I make sure that all the men under my command train for situations like these. The operational budget for today's SEALs is only 14 percent of what the Navy gets for its SpecWar forces. The biggest chunk of change goes for (of course) administration. Then comes equipment. Training is at the bottom of the totem pole. Doesn't make sense, does it? Maybe that's why SEALs are leaving the Navy in record numbers these days. My shooters, however, still get saturation training. I bend the rules—even break 'em if necessary—to make sure they can HAHO and HALO under the very worst of conditions, because that's the way they're gonna have to do it for real. Do the powers that be try to screw with me? You bet. But fuck 'em. My men are more important than some apparatchik with stars on his sleeve. So I've taken my guys through high-tension power lines. And forced 'em to make the kinds of hairy, last-minute adjustments that Mister Murphy drops on us at the worst of times. And because they've been through my Roguish crucible of pain, and forged themselves on my Warrior's anvil, they will survive to fight, no matter what the odds, or the situation.

But there was no time to ruminate about how good my Warriors are right now. Why? Because Nigel had the LAMA's nose up, and we were climbing the ridge. The hotel was getting closer, closer, closer.

As I peered through the windshield making my final mental calculations Ashley managed to smack me in the face as she shrugged out of her overalls. I deflected her elbow on the second pass, but she'd already caught me hard enough to make my eyes water. WTF—was she related to Boomerang?

0916. We limped in from the east, the sun at our backs, performed a pretty smooth admin flare for an aircraft in our condition, and dropped cleanly onto the number-one chopper pad on the south side of the hotel, 250 yards from the main entrance and 100 yards from the big hangar. There was no one within a hundred yards as Nigel shut down.

Even before he did, Digger was outside, his submachine gun up and ready. Nod hit the deck, too, standing at attention as Oleg climbed out, turned, and held his hand out so that Ashley could take it.

I rolled out of the chopper's port side into the brisk morning air, and inhaled a deep breath of exhaust fumes, so happy to be alive that I wanted to kill someone. I made sure all my equipment was ready to go, started the stopwatch, then withdrew my suppressed USP, held its muzzle down, close to my right leg, and headed for Oleg and Ashley, who'd already started toward the hotel entrance.

Chapter

21

00:00:25 THEY HADN'T BEEN EXPECTING US—WHICH WAS THE WHOLE idea. I could see the *byki* and hotel staff scrambling, confused. Oleg paid no attention. Just like the general he was, he hadn't waited until Nigel had shut down to climb out. He clambered from the starboard hatchway and adjusted the document case so it hung out of the way. He helped Ashley out, and then, like an old, dangerous Russkie bear, he wrapped his big left paw around her shoulder, and the two of them began to march in lockstep unison up the long macadam path toward the hotel.

00:00:31 My SEALs had to move fast to catch up. Once they did they fanned out in a diamond pattern around Oleg and Ashley, just like Alpha Team bodyguards. They carried their MP5s suspended horizontally around their necks, fingers indexed just above the trigger guards.

I was perhaps ten yards behind them when a bearded goon in a pair of brown velvet jogging pants and a UCLA T-shirt, with a big semiauto pistol in a shoulder holster came over a rise in the path and cut across Oleg's bow. The Goon had a concerned look on his face, and his eyes shifted back and forth between my guys, Oleg, and Ashley. Obviously something was not quite right. And

317

then I realized what it was: Alpha Team bodyguards do not carry MP5s. They carry AK-74s.

The Goon hesitated, which was GNBN for us. The bad news was that he blocked the path, and his right hand was already moving toward his shoulder holster. The GN was that he couldn't stop looking at Ashley, and therefore he didn't see me, ten yards back. So I brought the USP up in a two-handed grip, got a 20/20 sight picture, and double-tapped him before he had a chance to do anything dangerous.

Fucking textbook perfect, if I don't say so. Who says Mister Murphy is always sitting on my shoulder? The goon spun backward, half-turned to my left, then dropped onto the grass in a heap. I caught up with Oleg. Ashley's face was a mask. I think she was in shock. Like most youngsters, she's been taught that fights should be fair. You don't fire unless fired upon and all that crap. Well, that kind of mealy-mouthed philosophy may be okay if you are debating some pimple-faced asshole in your freshman ethics class. But it has no place on the battlefield. On the battlefield, you kill the enemy before he has a chance to kill you. Any way you can.

00:01:09 Oleg ushered Ashley around the goon's corpse and kept moving toward the front door. We'd landed on the south side of the plateau, below the crescent of rooms and suites. The path we were walking along ran basically south/north, cresting a series of low knolls. It had been landscaped so as to keep the approach to the hotel out of the sight line of the big double-door entrance.

That worked in our favor: the goon I'd wasted couldn't be seen by anyone coming out the front door.

00:01:31 We drew closer, still unchallenged. I could get a sense of the place's layout. My eyes went toward the north end of the hotel—the second-floor corner suite where I'd find Ambassador Madison.

I wanted to check the skies, too, but I wasn't about to do it, because my jumpers were up there, and I wasn't about to draw attention to 'em. I glanced at my watch. If they'd released on time, they'd be landing within three minutes.

But that would be then, and this was now. The big main double doors swung inward, the welcoming committee came through, and headed in our direction. Five *chornye* in bright jogging suits surrounding a tiny, olive-skinned figure with a pencil-line mustache, dressed in a shiny, single-breasted black suit, white shirt, and maroon tie, that gave him the absurd air of a 1960s-era William Morris agent.

"Do nothing," Oleg hissed. "Just keep quiet until I tell you."

Fuck him—this was my op, not his. But I dropped the USP out of sight behind my right leg. My trigger finger was indexed on the frame. The safety was off, and the pistol was cocked in single-action mode.

Oleg's face took on a big, wide grin. He loosed a torrent of rapid Russkie at the little guy, his left arm hugging Ashley close to him every second or third word.

The little guy understood what Oleg was saying—and so did Ashley, because she was reacting just right, laughing and making nicey-nicey, which—just as planned—distracted the *byki* as well as the little manager, who couldn't take his beady little eyes off her bright blue . . . dress. But the manager must have had good instincts too, because he didn't give up an inch of ground. As he held his position, so did the *chornye*. Not good.

00:02:00 There was an instant of absolute quiet right then. At which point my Roguish ears picked up the welcome sound of canopy flutter coming from my three o'clock. No, the sound of canopy flutter is *not* obvious to most people. But it is obvious to me, especially when I am looking to hear it.

And then, my instincts were confirmed, because someone on the other side of the hotel shouted "holy shit" in Russkie or maybe Armenian. Now I don't speak either Armenian or Russkie. But I know "holy shit" when I hear it, no matter what the language.

The shout was followed by staccato bursts of automatic weapons fire. Which meant that my jumpers were low enough to lay down some suppressive fire. From what my watch said, they were a full thirty seconds early, too.

00:02:06 This was no time to wait for Oleg to say anything. I brought the USP up and shot the two closest *byki* with a pair of rapid double-taps. The other three started to grab for their weapons.

It was already too late for them. Here is a lesson for all you people out there. If you want to be a bodyguard, don't carry your weapon inside your jogging suit where you can't get at it without undoing a bunch of zippers or Velcro closures. Nod shot two, and Nigel got the third before their Russkie paws were able to clear their weapons. Oleg had the little guy around the neck, his big hands shutting off the asshole's air supply. He broke the guy's neck one-handed and dropped the *chornye* corpse onto the ground.

00:02:11 "Let's go—" Oleg pulled a big semiauto pistol out of his waistband beneath his uniform blouse and charged into the hotel lobby.

I wasn't ready. Not yet. Not before giving Ashley some protection. "Nod, give her a pistol." I pushed Ashley behind me. Nod unholstered his USP and handed it to her.

I couldn't see where Oleg had gone. Well, he was doing his own thing right now. Me, I had to find Ambassador Madison, and I had about four and a half minutes to do it.

00:02:18 We made entry as a TEAM. I took point. Nigel and Nod were at my shoulder. Ashley behind them. Digger had rear guard. Fuck: the lobby was empty. Oleg was nowhere in sight.

00:02:26 *Scan. Breathe.* I saw no one behind the registration desk. Off on the far side of the desk, a narrow door led toward an office space. There were lights inside. I silent-signaled Digger and Nigel to check it out. Nod and I pushed Ashley between us and moved up the center of the lobby, weapons at low ready, scanning for threats.

The lobby itself was wide and deep. At the rear was the staircase leading down to the disco, and at each side a corridor. To the left was the registration desk. To the right, a narrow passageway led who knows where. It hadn't been on my sketch.

As we moved straight for the corridor leading to the north side of the hotel, Digger vaulted over the reception desk, followed by Nigel. I heard "Office clear" in Nigel's Limey accent.

He was cut off. "Skipper—twelve o'clock!" Nod's voice. Urgent.

A *byk*'s shaved head popped up the staircase at the back of the lobby, along with the snout of a machine pistol. I shoved Ashley to the deck as Nod's MP5 laid down a long burst of suppressive fire, and bullets and huge, sharp pieces of marble caught the sumbitch right in the face. His head disintegrated, and the rest of him went flying backward and disappeared from sight.

I grabbed Ashley by the back of her dress and pulled her along the floor as we moved toward the threat. She shook free of my hand and rolled away, then scrambled to her feet. "I'm okay, Dick—you do your work."

That was okay by me. I pulled a frag grenade from the pouch on my harness, pulled the pin, yelled, "Fire in the hole!" and let it bounce down the stairs. I dropped to my knees and got out of the way last. I heard it bounce one-two-three-four times on the stone, then it went off, sending shards of stone, metal, and wood everywhere. I pulled myself off the floor and checked the staircase.

Nothing moved. I shouted, "Clear," and we headed to our left, moving closer to the corridor.

Two *chornye* came through the hotel door, AK-74 miniguns up and firing. They were obviously of the "spray and pray" school, because they began shooting before they saw anybody. That's what tunnel vision does to you, friends.

"I got 'em—" I swung around to the first target, painted him with my front sight, squeezed off three shots—and missed him completely. Shit, I wasn't leading the s.o.b. by enough.

Well, if I was fucking up, Digger and Ashley could take care of business. She fired three times and slowed the motherfucker down. Digger let loose a full-auto burst of MP5 that cut the lead shooter in half. The second *chornye* was harder to hit, because he dove behind a heavy wood table. I swung my sights and fired half a dozen shots in his direction to keep his head down while Nod stitched the table with his MP5. You cannot hide from 147-grain Hydra-Shok slugs behind a table—or even most walls.

Ah: the welcome sound of silence. Nigel sprinted over to the far side of the lobby, put a double-tap in each of the *byki* to make sure they'd stay where they were, and took one of the *chornyes'* AKs for Ashley.

I could hear the welcome chatter of automatic weapons fire from outside, which meant my boys were landing and swarming. They knew where they had to go—the barracks and staff quarters—and what they had to do, which was to bottle things up and make sure no one got out and bothered my snatch team.

00:03:31 My watch told me we were currently way behind schedule. I gestured toward the corridor, and Nod's MP5. Nod's face told me he understood exactly want I wanted him to do. He dropped the mag out of his sub-gun, replaced it with a fresh one, and gave me an upturned thumb. He was good to go.

But where the fuck had Oleg gone? Well, shit, there was no time to worry about that now.

00:03:39 We all stacked at the end of the corridor. It was clear, the doors all closed. The stairway was maybe two yards from where we stacked, on my left. The door pulled outward. I rolled a DefTec into the corridor, and when it blew, we moved through the smoke to the doorway and I reached toward the handle.

The fucking thing was almost in my gloved hand when a withering burst of automatic weapons fire came through the door, sending me hurtling backward.

Fuck. I recovered and we pulled back. I returned fire through the door to keep whoever was behind it well back. Meanwhile, Nod knelt. He retrieved one of the tri-folds of plastic sheet and det-cord from his knapsack. He crawled along the corridor past the door, then pulled the tape, attached the plastic to the door on the hinge side, removed a six-foot length of wire, plugged it to a connector on the plastic, then rolled back to the wall, attached the wire, screamed, "Fire in the fuckin' hole," and blew the door.

The blast sent the big metal door inward. Digger charged through, his MP5 up and ready. I followed, my USP giving his blind side protection.

Scan. Breathe. The smoke was fucking opaque. I saw a shadow in the stairwell corner and put two quick shots into it. As I got closer I saw I'd just killed what was left of the door. The stairs went down as well as up. Well, fuck down—we'd have to take our chances. I changed mags, dropping the spent one, and started up the stairwell.

00:04:10 I hate stairwells. They are nasty places in which to have to fight. Bullets ricochet. Noise is amplified by the tight surroundings. The visibility is always bad. And whether you are going up or coming down, the bad guy always has the advantage, because he knows where he is and where your are, and you only know where you are. Stairwells are a goatfuck waiting to happen.

But as you can probably imagine, I didn't have to like this fucking stairwell, I just had to assault it. And assault it I did.

Back to the wall, I began the climb, one step at a time, pistol up and ready, scanning and breathing, looking for any telltale shadows or hints of shadows that might give the bad guys away.

I made it to the first landing without incident. Nod was behind me, his sub-gun covering my blind spot. Ashley had the third slot. Behind her, Digger filled the gap. And behind Digger, Nigel backed up the stairs one at a time, his spine against Digger's, working the rear guard slot so we wouldn't be surprised from behind.

The door was on my left. It opened inward. I waited until we were all in position, with Nigel covering the landing below, and the muzzle of Digger's MP5 pointed toward the blind spot above.

Nod tapped me on the left shoulder to tell me he was ready to go. I reached forward, toward the big door handle.

"Holy fuck—grenade." Digger's scream cut through my concentration. He fired past me, three quick three-round bursts.

But that wasn't the focus of my attention. I was searching for the fucking grenade that the Russkie had tossed. My peripheral vision picked it up as it bounced off the wall six feet above me, hit the lip of a step, and, like a stoopball Spaulding, bounced in a big, high trajectory over my head.

Frozen in time and space, I followed the fucking thing with my eyes. It floated slowly in the air. It had been well thrown, too: caromed off the wall above us, so it would hit the stairs and explode over our heads, impossible to catch and toss back. The fuses on these things run five and a half seconds. But I didn't know how long the motherfucker'd held on to it before he let it go.

Well, just in case I never told you, I was the stoopball king of New Brunswick, New Joyzey—and there was never a Spaulding I couldn't shag. I dropped the pistol and launched myself toward the grenade, using the closest step as a starting block and stretching as high as I could, because I knew that if I could get my hands on it, I could deflect it down the stairwell, which would reduce the damage the fucking thing was going to do to us.

It's more convenient when these things happen in Slo-Mo, because they are easier to describe. So here's what happened. I launched myself up and out, toward the grenade as if it were a Hail Mary pass, the wide receiver was about to grab it for the winning touchdown, and I was a free safety with my job on the line. My arms went out, my fingers stretched, and I tapped the grenade, slapping it down the stairwell, away from us, directing it toward the wall, so it would veer away, not settle in the corner of the stairwell and explode, which would be bad for Dickie's health, not to mention the rest of us.

I sent the fucking thing spinning down the stairwell. That was the good news. The bad news was that I was now moving in the same direction as the grenade, and given my weight, my speed, and the prevailing laws of physics, I had to change direction fast, or I'd become a grenade sponge. I hooked my left foot through the rail to catch a baluster and stop my forward motion. It worked. But it also brought Dickie-San to an abrupt halt.

Abrupt? Yeah, abrupt. Like a WWF *slam!* One of those tooth-jarring, bone-crunching, back-cracking moves the prime-time boys love to do. My Roguish toe snagged one of the balusters, I stopped cold and spun around, wrenching my already tender leg somewhere in the vicinity of 160 degrees in the process, then came down hard, washboard gut first, on the flat newel of the landing. My face made audible contact with the newel post.

Which is precisely when the fucking grenade exploded twenty feet below us. The concussion blew me back off the banister, and slammed me into the stairwell wall. I groaned. I spat a tooth chip. I wiped blood from my forehead. And then I pulled myself onto my knees, and from there onto my feet, and I struggled back up the stairs, carefully stepping over the corpse of the Ivan who'd tossed the fucking grenade, so we could continue our DV odyssey and Get There Already.

Have I owned up about the Big Lie in my life? Have I mentioned that GTINFFAA? I have? Good, because it is the truth, the whole fucking truth, and nothing but the fucking truth: Getting There Is No Fucking Fun At All. And we still had the blankety-blanking hallway to clear.

Chapter

22

00:04:13. OH, WE WERE WAY BEHIND SCHEDULE. I RETRIEVED MY PISTOL and attached it to the goddamn lanyard so I wouldn't lose it again. Then I hit the door, Nod behind me. Warily, I cut the pie, checking the hallway inch by inch as I eased around.

It was empty. But oh, fuck: one-two-three-four-five-six-seven-eight doors to the suite. They were all closed. Here is a rule of hallway clearing: you do not go past a closed door unless you can make sure it can't be opened. And since all these doors opened inward, we'd have to blow 'em all, so we could make sure that Steve-o hadn't stashed any *hyki* or *chornye* or other miscellaneous *badniki* to do us bodily harm.

And then, as so often happens in these kinds of books if the hero, i.e., *moi,* is a Very Good Rogue: the cavalry arrives. I heard Boomerang's distinctive voice as he led a trio of SEALs up the stairwell.

The lanky master chief was followed by Gator, Timex, and Mustang, and best of all, their automatic weapons.

"Yo, Boss Dude—funicular's blown and the help is all corralled, so I thought maybe you could use a little backup."

I am truly blessed, because God has given me men like these to command and lead into battle. But there was no time for either gratitude or small talk. I gave the orders I wanted carried out. I changed mags because, to be honest, I'd forgotten to count rounds—and I wasn't about to play this particular game with a half load. Then we stacked, we made ready, and then we moved out flank speed. I mean, the term "Dynamic Entry" took on a whole new meaning. The fucking thing was fluid. Blow the door. Toss the flashbang. With two-man clearing teams working opposite sides of the corridor, and Ashley fielding an MP5 as rear guard, we were slicker than shit. Obviously, Mister Murphy'd heard us coming and he'd snuck out of the building.

00:05:12. The big, heavy carved wood suite doors were in front of us. I gave Nod the high sign, and he affixed the plastic sheets, inserted the detonator, we took cover, and since we all knew there was about to be fire in the hole, he didn't have to tell us, so he simply dropped the hammer and blew the fucking doors off their hinges.

I tossed a pair of flashbangs into the smoke, let them detonate, and then charged, my USP up and ready. The DefTecs had blown a couple of windows, because the smoke was venting pretty fast.

Steve's French bodyguards were waiting. They were operators, too, because they'd known enough to take cover as the doors blew. And they'd obviously cross-trained with SEALs, or with Delta, at one point, because they knew how we'd make entry: first man moving to his left, second to his right, and third man covering the first.

I cleared the doorway, kept my back against the wall, and moved to my port side, my USP scanning.

Movement at seven o'clock, between the settee and corner table. Here's what you do: you advance toward the threat. You suck the air out of the target's living space. I moved forward and fired twice. There was the *thwock* of bullet shattering plaster as double-taps whistled past my right ear.

Getting shot at is less fucking fun than Getting There, and as you know, GTINFFAA. I dropped low and hurled myself at the settee, knocking it back into the corner table, taking away the Frog's ability to move. From behind me and to my right there was more firing. That would be Nod and Digger engaging, with Boomerang backing them up.

Well, they were big boys and they could take care of themselves. Me, I was currently occupied, too.

Shit—I finally saw his gun hand, and fired at it. Hit him, because I heard him scream, and the weapon fell away.

Now I pulled the couch clear of the wall and went after him. He was a little cocksucker in a double-breasted suit, and in the instant that I jumped his bones I knew that we'd surprised everybody because he wasn't carrying a sub-gun, just his everyday Walther P-99, seventeen shots of 9-mm joy in an ergonomic package. But since he'd lost his pistol, and the use of his right hand, he'd decided to bid me *bon jour, comment ça marche* with the very nasty folder in his left hand.

He slashed at me, knocking me ass over teakettle across the settee. Then he dove for the Walther.

Fuck, there was no time to fool around—or even aim. I cranked off four rapid shots from a shooting stance that might be called the pretzel position. Two missed him altogether. One caught him in the knee, sending him sprawling, and the last one slammed him through the cheek.

You say how come I didn't double-tap him with two pair of dead-on hit-the-three-by-five-card-every-single-fucking-time hammers right through the head? Hey, assholes, I'll take what I can get when I'm shooting for real and the other guy has a gun. It ain't my job to be a brain surgeon when it comes to combat shooting. Sloppy and messy is just fine with me, so long as it does the job.

Nod and Digger'd done their jobs: they were standing over corpses. That left Boomerang free to back me up. I shouted "Bedroom" in his direction. I checked my position. The bedroom would be the door on the right-hand side of the suite. We stacked, I hit the door with my shoulder, and the wood frame splintered.

As it did, a scream came from inside. *That* sound fucking spurred me on. I went in and headed left. Boomerang tight behind me went to the right.

Scanbreathe. Scanbreathe. Shit, I was hyperventilating. I caught myself in time and took a slow, even load of fresh air into my lungs. *Scan. Breathe.* Better. Now I forced my eyes to work, not tunnel; kept the front sight of the USP moving right/left, left/right.

And then: *threat at eight o'clock.* Steve Sarkesian. Standing in front of Ambassador Madison, his body pressing her tight, up against the wall, her hands hidden. But I could see his hands. There was a small stainless steel Walther pistol in them, held in an old-fashioned cup-and-saucer grip. The gun was pointed at the floor. Then he saw me—recognized me—and its muzzle started up, vaguely in my direction.

Here's the difference between Steve and me: he had to raise his pistol, and I could see his eyes tunneling, fixating on me, not seeing anything else but the bulk of my body as I closed on him, moving carefully, foot by foot by foot.

I held my front sight right on him. And if you don't mind a micromomentary digression at this point in time, I'd like to say I had a great sight picture, too.

I'd swung my pistol onto his left clavicle, because his left clavicle and shoulder were both completely clear of the ambassador's body. I could take him out anytime I wanted to. But I didn't want to. Not yet. Not until he knew that he was about to be closed down for good. "Yo, Steve—"

"You," he said. *"You!"* The pistol muzzle rose another two inches. He looked straight at me with his violet eyes. His hair was messy and his demeanor seemed confused. Now he shifted and put his body squarely between me and Marybeth Madison.

I kept my front sight on his left clavicle. "I've got news for you, Steve: you're out of the expediting bidness."

Now it was the ambassador's turn. She looked at me with undisguised loathing. "What the fuck are you doing here, Captain Marcinko?" I guess she really *was* confused.

I didn't have time to explain myself to her right now, because I had some killing to do first. So I ignored her excellency, and spoke to the asshole I'd come to kill. "I have your target list, Steve. Yours and Sherafi's. The embassies in Abu Dhabi, Qatar, and London—they're safe. The folks who were gonna blow up those banks in Paris are spilling their guts to DST.[77] So are the goons you ordered to hit the oil companies and the Turkish foreign ministry. Your nets are all rolled up, Steve. And even though the Israelis missed you, I'm not gonna miss you. You killed the wife of my friend. That makes you my enemy, and you're gonna die. As of now, Steve, the Sirzhik Foundation is going out of business for good."

He kept his weight against the ambassador's body and started to shrug, as if he didn't understand what I was getting at. Except . . . except . . . except, that the muzzle of his fucking pistol started moving in my direction again.

I wasn't about to wait for him to get the first shot in—besides, I knew he wasn't a trained shooter and he'd hesitate. And as much as I wanted to blow his head off right then, I wasn't about to do it with him standing directly in front of the ambassador. All I'd need was Mister Murphy to adjust the round's path—and we'd have a big fucking incident. I saw the headline in the *Washington Post* in my mind: NAVY SEAL KILLS U.S. AMBASSADOR TO AZERBAIJAN DURING BOTCHED HOSTAGE RESCUE ATTEMPT. And so, I closed the distance between us in a millisecond and was all over the motherfucker, just like stink on shit. I swatted him across the face with my

---

[77]Remember, that's the Directorate for the Surveillance of the Territory, France's internal security and counterintelligence organization.

pistol shattering his perfect teeth. The blow made him drop his Walther, which went clattering off to my left. Too bad for him.

The ambassador tried to insinuate herself between us, her hands clawing at my face. I thought about cold-cocking her, but it just wasn't an option. I looked around, saw a closet door six feet away, took her by the scruff of her neck, thrust her inside, and turned the key to make sure she'd stay out of the way.

Bad idea. That had left Steve-o alone long enough for him to go scrambling for his weapon.

I tackled him just as he was reaching out for it. I clubbed him in the face. Bit his ear. Kneed him in the balls. He tried to fight back, but it was impossible. The white heat of my rage was too hot; too intense; too concentrated, to allow him any kind of progress.

I slapped him silly, then rolled him over, straddled him, and sat on his chest.

"You scumbag." I raked the front sight of the USP over his eyes, ripping right through his eyelids. He screamed and flailed.

"You kill innocent women," I told him. "I don't like that." I raked the front sight over his eyes again.

Then he really started to protest, screaming about all kinds of shit, in all kinds of languages. Well, fuck him. I wasn't here to listen. I was here to take Old Testament revenge. I ended his monologue by forcing the muzzle of the USP into his mouth, breaking more teeth in the process.

I looked down at him. "Say good-bye, Steve."

Oh, he fought. He bucked his shoulders, and he tried to kick me in the back of my head, and he writhed like the fucking snake he was. But it did him absofuckinglutely no good at all.

I smiled down into his face, and pulled the trigger.

The back end of his skull exploded like a fucking ripe melon. Bits of brain and bone imprinted a nasty Rorschach on the suite's marble floor.

I pulled myself off Sarkesian's body, stood over him, and put three more shots into his corpse just to make sure he stayed as dead as he deserved to be.

Then I unlocked the closet door and retrieved Madame Ambassador so we could hustle her out and save her ass.

This was harder to accomplish than you might think, because once freed, the ambassador jumped my bones, swatting me around the head and shoulders, kicking at me with her bare feet, and was screaming her head off very undiplomatically about my being a goddamn fucking murderer and having me fucking arrested. Maybe it was because she'd slipped on some of the spatter and was now covered in Steve-o's blood. To be honest, I didn't give much of the old rusty *F*-word right now. We had to get her bundled up, bundled out, and back to Baku before the reinforcements arrived.

0925. I posted security while Ashley tried to calm the ambassador (but didn't have much luck, since she wasn't carrying any Ketamine with her today). I sent Digger scurrying to bring Ashley's coveralls. While he ran that errand we went through the suite and the surrounding rooms, which had been occupied by Steve-o's security force, checking to make sure there was no lose intel lying around.

I had to admit there wasn't much. It appeared to be exactly what ambassador Madison kept screaming it was, which is, "A private fucking assignation that you had no fucking right to stick your fucking nose in the middle of."

Hadn't anyone ever taught her that a preposition is not a word to end a sentence with?

0929. Syntactics be damned, we had to get our butts in gear, and fast. I tossed the scanner to Ashley, who spoke the local lingo, so she could monitor the situation. The LAMA was going to be no use at all, so I took Nigel, Hammer, and Gator out to the hangar to get Ambassador Madison's chopper prepped and ready to fly.

0932. We ran into Oleg in the lobby. "Where the fuck have you been?"

He shrugged noncommittally. "Looking for documents in the hotel safe."

"Yeah, well, we could have used you."

The Ivan's eyes flashed. "You had your work to do; I had mine." He paused. "Sarkesian?"

"Dead."

His face brightened. "That is good," he said. "And your ambassador?"

"She'll live."

In response he grunted, and turned away.

I wasn't about to wait for him. I had work to do. I turned to my guys. "Let's go."

0941. Gator used a tractor to ease the Dauphin-2 out of the hangar. Nigel and I pushed the fuel unit into position and topped off the tank. I dropped the hatchway and peered inside. It was going to be a fucking tight fit. Ambassador Madison had configured this chopper as a VIP craft, which meant it held only eight passengers. We were going to be more than double that number. Weight wasn't a problem because Dauphin-2s can hold twenty-two troops. But given the VIP configuration, interior space made fitting us all in impossible.

I looked over at Gator and Hammer. "Anything that Nigel says we don't need, you rip out."

0952. The ambassador had finally quieted down. But when I came back into the suite, the look she gave me wasn't very sociable. Ashley shook the scanner in my direction. "We got company coming," she reported. "Russians. Lots of 'em. They're traveling by chopper."

"Arrival time?"

"I'm not sure. The radio chatter says they just lifted off an airstrip near someplace called Uytash."

I looked over at Oleg. "What do you know, Oleg?"

In answer, the Russkie's arms opened wide. "Maybe the *byki* got a message out."

That was possible. "How far is Uytash?"

Oleg shrugged. "Maybe two hundred twenty-five miles. Maybe less, maybe more."

That gave us plenty of time to clean things up and get outta Dodge, because I didn't want to be around when the Ivans got here—too many questions, and not enough answers. We picked up every bit of intel we could lay our hands on, then we bundled everyone out of the hotel and moved down to the chopper pad.

Nigel was just finishing the walk-around. I looked at the pile of custom-made furnishings piled on the macadam and then over at him. "Ready?"

He gave me a thumbs-up. "Right on, Gov."

1019. I got Ambassador Madison, who was still in shock, loaded. My guys were ready to go. I looked over at the big Ivan. "Oleg, you coming?"

He shook his head. "I will wait for my people," he said. "This will take some explaining, and I want to make sure they get it right."

Well, they were his people and he could handle 'em. "That's your call, General."

He threw me an offhanded salute. "Your men did well today," he said. "They learn fast, Captain."

"*Spasiba*, Oleg. Thanks for all your help." I climbed aboard and pulled on the hatch cable to raise the steps. "*Poká*—see you later."

"*Schastlivovo putí*—bon voyage," the big Russian said, waving at me, a blank stare on his Mister Clean® face. Then he turned, hunching his shoulders against the prop wash, and headed back toward the hotel.

1021. The Russkies were about forty minutes out. It was time to haul ass. I looked into the cockpit where Nigel was waiting and gave him a "circle the wagons" gesture.

1022. The big chopper rose slowly into the morning sky. I looked around at my Warriors, who'd overcome the odds once more. They were true Samurai, who lived by a code that would not allow them to fail. They were better than Samurai: they were Warriors in my own image, and I loved them as only a Warrior can love his troops.

And then, as Nigel dipped the Dauphin's nose, and we turned east toward Baku, just as I started to stretch and relax, secure in the knowledge that we had not failed, the hair on the back of my neck stood straight up, and I suddenly understood that something was very, very wrong.

"Set this fucking thing down—*now!*" I shouted.

Nigel gave me a confused look, but he complied. Thirty-eight seconds later we were back on the deck. It wasn't a pretty landing. But it got us back on terra firma.

I dropped the hatch. "Out—everybody out."

My troops were confused. So was Ashley. So was the ambassador. But I didn't give a shit. When the hair on the back of my neck stands up straight, someone is trying to kill me.

Oleg had obviously heard the chopper return, because he was standing on the pad as I climbed out. "A problem, Captain?"

I scratched my beard. "Maybe. I'm not sure." And I wasn't sure. But the hair on the back of my neck had stood straight up. And in all my years of Warriordom, that danger signal had never been false. My instincts had told me something was wrong—and I always trust my instincts in situations like this one.

I thought about all the DVFs. Like the explosives Steve Sarkesian might have already planted on the Dauphin. I replayed the mental videotape of how Steve looked at me as I came through the door of his suite—and how he'd tried to protect Madame Ambassador with his own body before I tossed her into the closet and killed him.

And then, the truth, the whole truth, and nothing but the truth hit me like the proverbial ton o' bricks: *Steve Sarkesian may have been guilty of many things. But planning to assassinate Marybeth Madison wasn't one of them.*

I went into the hangar. I looked around. There was nothing that seemed out of the ordinary. So, I stopped. I sat on the cool concrete floor. I crossed my legs, and followed the Roy Boehm Zen precept of mind clearing. Then, newly focused, I stood up and started to look. *Really* look.

That is when I found the small rectangle of shiny paper that led me to believe someone had recently used a piece of two-faced tape. And then I discovered the canvas document case, stuffed way down in the bottom of the fifty-five-gallon oil drum the mechanics used as a garbage container. It was the very same document case Oleg Lapinov had been carrying.

I dug it out of the trash, rolled it in a shop towel, and jogged back to the chopper pad. Nigel had the engine idling. I took my right index finger and slashed it across my throat. "Shut it down."

I waited until I got close to Oleg before I let the case drop out of the shop towel. When he saw it, his expression told me all I had to know.

I didn't waste a millisecond. I started my sucker punch in the balls of my feet, let it build in my calves, thighs, and gut, felt it roll through my chest, shoulders, and right arm until I caught the big, ugly Ivan with a tsunami-size punch, right in his throat.

He went down like the shitload he was. I told you a few pages back that I don't trust Ivans. And Oleg Lapinov was the personification of why I don't.

But there's no time to ruminate about that now, because he is a strong motherfucker and he was already pulling himself to his feet, murder in his eyes. I kicked him in the head to keep him on the deck, but he rolled away just ahead of the blow, and scrambled to his knees, his face Commie-flag red, his eyes crossed in pain.

That was all the time I needed. I clapped him across the ears. His head snapped back. But he still managed to deliver a single punch, his big fist catching me right in the nuts.

Oh, that *hurt*. It took the wind right out of my sails. Instinctively, I bent forward. Which is when he hit me again. This was getting tiresome.

"Roll right, Boss Dude, roll right—" That was Boomerang's voice shouting through the ringing in my ears. I threw myself to starboard, catching a big Russkie foot on the side of my bad knee as I did. But I kept going, rolling, scrambling, clawing my way past Oleg's churning extremities.

And once I'd cleared far enough to give them a clear shot, Boomerang and Rotten Randy, who'd positioned themselves at right angles to Oleg, shot the sumbitch. They put enough rounds in his head to shut him down for good, and left Ivan brains all over the fucking chopper pad in the process.

I looked over at the bloody Rorschach pattern on the concrete, and told them, "Great fucking work." And it *was* great work, even though all you folks out there were probably waiting for me to do the deed myself.

Well, live and learn, tadpoles: only under Hollywood's stupid rules does the Big Hero have to kill the Big Villain at the end of the book. In real life, he who can take the shot had better take the shot, or the Big Hero's gonna get whacked and the Big Villain's gonna walk away unscathed.

But not today. And not in *this* book. I rolled Oleg's body over, and retrieved his radio transmitter—the one that he would have used to blow the Dauphin out of the sky. And then, we started crawling over the chopper like locusts until we found and disassembled the bomb made of half a pound of Semtex explosive he'd stowed in the oil cooler fan compartment. Oleg had done his homework: it wasn't a place you'd normally include in the ol' preflight check.

I had to admit—somewhat ruefully—that Oleg had done his homework about me, too. Why? Because he'd manufactured a scenario requiring exactly the sort of KISS operation I like to pull off. I mean, the kidnapping *almost* made perfect sense—the precise thing you want for one of these smoke-and-mirrors ops. And Oleg, being an operator, knew how to suck me in. He gave me the plot, he set the clock ticking, and then he let my Warrior instincts take over from there.

Well, I wasn't the only one he'd fooled. He'd made Ashley believe his story, too. And Ashley was about as easy to convince as *moi*. But that was the genius of his op. I mean, it was conceivable that Steve Sarkesian might have actually kidnapped Marybeth Madison. But the more I thought about what had just happened, the more I understood that the trio of intercepts Oleg had showed me had all been fakes. The kind of *dezinformatsia* the Soviets used to call "Active Measures," which is black information, made plausible by grains of truth planted within, and set into a believable context. Info land mines. The Sovs had been effective practitioners of *dezinformatsia* during the Cold War. And Oleg Lapinov hadn't lost the talent more than a decade later.

Besides, my guys hadn't found any explosives or the accoutrements thereof, in Steve's effects, his bodyguards' luggage—or anywhere in the hotel, or the hangar, for that matter. No. It was Oleg who'd wanted to blow Ambassador Madison's chopper out of the sky, because by doing so, he could rid himself of two adversaries: Ambassador Madison, and me.

But only after he'd used me to kill his double agent.

There was a kind of warped genius to his plan—because he'd built it around my Roguish personality, and my tendency to operate UNODIR. Once my men and I were corpses, he could claim that I'd jumped the gun again, just as I had when I'd burgled Sarkesian's office. He'd tell Washington I'd gone Rogue and killed Steve Sarkesian on my own, but fallen victim to Steve's preplanned hit on Ambassador Madison.

And if the scenario played itself out true to form, the American oil companies would reassess the situation, and the United States would downsize its relationship to Baku. Which would leave Oleg the last man standing. And Moscow would once again roll across the border, shut out the Iranians, and dominate Azerbaijan—and the rest of the Caucasus, too.

Is that confusing enough for you? It was certainly confusing enough for me. In fact, God save me from geopolitics—and the practitioners thereof. I'm happiest waxing tangos, sucking down a few cold brewskis, sipping some Bombay Sapphire, and taking a long, long soak between warm thighs every now and then. And since I'd just had my fill of waxing tangos, the other three sounded pretty fuckin' good.

1055. Time was getting tight. I looked over at Oleg's corpse. He was proof that, despite what the old Azeri adage says, the enemy of your enemy ain't always your friend. Well, I'd let the fucking Russians find him and puzzle things out for themselves. Me, *I* was gonna have a hell of a time explaining this little episode to the Chairman. But that would come later—after the brewskis, and the Bombay, and the long, long soak. I windmilled my right index finger, sending everyone toward the chopper. Oh yes, it was way past time to head for home.

Free Public Library of Monroe Township
306 S. Main Street
Williamstown, NJ 08094-1727

94483

Glossary

A²: aforementioned asshole.

A³: Anytime, Anyplace, Anywhere.

Admirals' Gestapo: what the secretary of defense's office calls the Naval Investigative Services Command. See: SHIT-FOR-BRAINS.

AK-47: 7.63 X 39 Kalashnikov automatic rifle. The most common assault weapon in the world.

APOC: A Piece Of Cake.

AVCNO: Assistant Vice Chief of Naval Operations.

Bandity: (Russian) Police slang for hoodlums.

BAW: Big Asshole Windbag.

BDUs: Battle Dress Uniforms. Now that's an oxymoron.

BFD: Big Fuckin' Deal.

BFH: Big Fuckin' Help.

BIQ: Bitch-In-Question.

BJB: Leader of the Free World.

BOHICA: Bend Over—Here It Comes Again!

BTDT: Been There, Done That.

BUPERS: Naval BUreau of PERSonnel.

BUWEPS: Naval BUreau of WEaPonS.

C-130: Lockheed's ubiquitous Hercules.

C-141: Lockheed's ubiquitous StarLifter aircraft, soon to be moth-balled.

C-4: plastic explosive. You can mold it like clay. You can even use it to light your fires. Just don't stamp on it.

C²CO: Can't Cunt Commanding Officer. Too many of these in Navy SpecWar today. They won't support their men or take chances because they're afraid it'll ruin their chances for promotion.

CALOW: Coastal And Limited-Objective Warfare. Very fashion-able acronym at the Pentagon in these days of increased low-intensity conflict.

cannon fodder: See FNG.

Christians in Action: SpecWar slang for the Central Intelligence Agency.

CINC: Commander-IN-Chief.

CINCUSNAVEUR: Commander IN Chief, U.S. Naval forces, EURope.

clusterfuck: See: FUBAR

CNO: Chief of Naval Operations.

cockbreath: SEAL term of endearment used for those who pay only lip service. See: SAP/BJ.

CONUS: CONtinental United States.

CQC: Close Quarters Combat—i.e., killing that's up close and personal.

CT: CounterTerrorism.

DADT: Don't Ask, Don't Tell.

DEA: Drug Enforcement Administration.

DEFCON: DEFense CONdition.

DEVGRP: Naval Special Warfare DEVelopment GRouP. Current U.S. Navy appellation for SEAL Team Six.

detasheet: olive-drab, ten-by-twenty-inch flexible PETN-based plastic explosive used as a cutting or breaching charge.

DIA: Defense Intelligence Agency. Spook heaven based in Arlington, Virginia, and Bolling Air Force Base.

Diplo-dink: no-load fudge-cutting, cookie-pushing diplomat.

DIPSEC: DIPlomatic SECurity. SEAL shorthand for the Diplomatic Security Service, the Department of State's special agent shoot-and-looters.

Dipshit: can't cunt numb-nutted pencil-dicked asshole.

DIQ (pronounced *dik,* except in France, where it's pronounced *deek*): Document-In-Question. You can have sensitive DIQs, big, thick DIQs, or even tiny, penciled DIQs. But if you drop your DIQ into a puddle of water, you'll end up with a limp DIQ.

Do-ma-nhieu (Vietnamese): Go fuck yourself. See: DOOM ON YOU.

doom on you: American version of Vietnamese phonetic for *go fuck yourself.*

dweeb: no-load shit-for-brains geeky asshole, usually shackled to a computer.

EC-130: Electronic warfare–outfitted C-130.

EEI: Essential Element of Information. The info-nuggets on which a mission is planned and executed.

EEO: Equal Employment Opportunity. (The Rogue Warrior® always treats 'em all alike—just like shit.)

ELINT: ELectronic INTelligence.

EOD: Explosive Ordnance Disposal.

flashbang: disorientation device used by hostage rescue teams.

FLFC: Fucking Loud and Fucking Clear.

FLIR: Forward Looking InfraRed.

FNG: Fucking New Guy. See: CANNON FODDER.

Four-striper: Captain. All too often, a C²CO.

frags: fragmentation grenades.

FUBAR: Fucked Up Beyond All Repair.

Glock: Reliable 9-mm pistols made by Glock in Austria. They're great for SEALs because they don't require as much care as Sig Sauers.

GNBN: Good News/Bad News.

goatfuck: What the Navy likes to do to the Rogue Warrior. See: FUBAR.

GSG-9: Grenzchutzgruppe-9. Top German CT unit.

HAHO: High-Altitude, High-Opening parachute jump.

HALO: High-Altitude, Low-Opening parachute jump.

HICs: Head-In-Cement syndrome. Condition common to high-ranking officers. Symptoms include pigheadedness and inability to change opinions when presented with new information.

HK: ultrareliable pistol, assault rifle, or submachine gun made by Heckler & Koch, a firm based in Oberndorf, Germany. SEALs use H&K MP5 submachine guns in various configurations, as well as P7 9-mm, and USP 9-mm, .40- or .45-caliber pistols.

HKTB: Hot Knife Through Butter.

HUMINT: HUMan INTelligence.

humongous: Marcinko dick.

Hydra-Shok: extremely lethal hollowpoint ammunition manufactured by Federal Cartridge Company.

IBS: Inflatable Boat, Small—the basic unit of SEAL transportation.

IED: Improvised Explosive Device.

Japs: bad guys.

Jarheads: Marines. The Corps. Formally, USMC (Uncle Sam's Misguided Children).

JSOC: Joint Special Operations Command.

KATN: Kick Ass and Take Names. Roguish avocation.

KH: KeyHole. Designation for NRO's spy-in-the-sky satellites, as in KH-12s.

KISS: Keep It Simple, Stupid. The basic premise for all special operations.

KTFM: Keep The Fuck Moving.

klik: One kilometer, equaling six-tenths of a mile.

Kuz emeq (Arabic): Roguespeak for "Up your mother's cunt."

LANTFLT: atLANTic FLeeT.

LBFM: Little Brown Fucking Machine.

LTWS: Lower Than Whale Shit.

M³: Massively motivated motherfuckers.

M-16: Basic U.S. .223-caliber weapon, used by the armed forces.

Mark-I Mod-0: basic unit.

MILCRAFT: Pentagonese for MILitary airCRAFT.

Mossad (Short form of *Ha-Mossad hamerkazi Lemodi'in Vetafkidim Meychadim*, or Central Institute for Intelligence and Special Tasks): Israeli spy service. Not as good as it used to be.

MOTI: Russian Ministry of the Interior.

NAVAIR: NAVy AIR Command.

NAVSEA: NAVy SEA Command.

NAVSPECWARGRU: NAVal SPECial WARfare GRoUp.

Navyspeak: redundant, bureaucratic naval nomenclature, either in written nonoral, or nonwritten oral modes, indecipherable by nonmilitary (conventional) or military (unconventional) individuals during normal interfacing configuration conformations.

NILO: Naval Intelligence Liaison Officer.

NIS: Naval Investigative Service Command, also known as the Admirals' Gestapo. See: SHIT-FOR-BRAINS.

NMN: No Middle Name.

NRO: National Reconnaissance Office. Established August 25, 1960, to administer and coordinate satellite development and operations for U.S. intelligence community. Very spooky place.

NSA: National Security Agency, known within the SpecWar community as No Such Agency.

NSD: National Security Directive.

NYL: Nubile Young Lovely.

OBE: Overtaken By Events—usually because of the bureaucracy.

OFACW: Only Fucking Asshole Carrying Wire cutters.

OOD: Officer Of the Deck (he who drives the big gray monster).

OPSEC: OPerational SECurity

OSINT: Open Source INTelligence.

PDMP: Pretty Dangerous Motherfucking People.

PIC: Pissed, Irritated, and Confused.

PIQ: Pussy In Question.

POTUS: President Of The United States.

RDL: Real Dirty Look.

RIB: Rigid Inflatable Boat. SEALcraft used for clandestine insertions and extractions.

RPG: Rocket-Propelled Grenade.

RSO: Regional Security Officer. State Department's diplomat with a gun.

R^{2}D^2: Ritualistic, Rehearsed, Disciplined Drills.

RUMINT: RUMor INTelligence. Urinal gossip. Generally, the information is of piss-poor quality.

S^1: Square one.

S²: Sit the fuck down and shut the fuck up.

SADM: Special Atomic Demolition Device. Man-portable nuke.

SAP/BJ: Special Assistant to the President for Blow Jobs.

SAS: Special Air Service. Britain's top CT unit.

SATCOM: SATellite COMmunication.

SCIF: Sensitive Compartmented Information Facility. A bug-proof room.

SEAL: U.S. Navy SEa-Air-Land SpecWarrior. A hop-and-popping shoot-and-looting hairy-assed Frogman who gives a shit. The acronym *really* stands for Sleep, Eat, And Live it up.

Semtex: Czechoslovakian C-4 type plastique explosive. Can be used to cancel Czechs.

SERE: Survival, Evasion, Resistance, and Escape school.

SES: Shit-Eating Smile.

shit-for-brains: any no-load, pus-nutted, pencil-dicked asshole.

SIGINT: SIGnals INTelligence.

SMG: SubMachine Gun

SNAFU: Situation Normal—All Fucked Up.

SNAILS: Slow, Nerdy Assholes In Ludicrous Shoes.

SOF: Special Operations Force.

SpecWarrior: One who gives a fuck.

SSN: nuclear attack sub, commonly known as sewer pipe.

SUC: Smart, Unpredictable, and Cunning

SWAT: Special Weapons And Tactics police teams. All too often they do not train enough, and become SQUAT teams.

szeb (Arabic): dickhead.

TAD: Temporary Additional Duty (SEALs refer to it as Traveling Around Drunk).

Tailhook: the convention of weenie-waggers, gropesters, and pressed-ham-on-glass devotees that put air brakes on NAVAIR.

TARFU: Things Are Really Fucked Up.

TBW: Tired But Wired.

TECHINT: TECHnical INTelligence.

TFB: Too Fucking Bad.

THREATCON: THREAT CONdition.

Tigerstripes: The only stripes that SEALS will wear.

TIQ (pronounced *tick* and just as apt to bite you on the ass): Tango-In-Question.

TTS: Tap 'em, Tie 'em, and Stash 'em.

U$_2$: Ugly and Unfamiliar.

UNODIR: UNless Otherwise DIRected. That's how the Rogue operates when he's surrounded by can't cunts.

USSOCOM: United States Special Operations COMmand, located at MacDill Air Force Base, Tampa, Florida.

VDS: Very Direct Stare.

vor: Russkie godfather.

VTVE: Very Thorough Visual Exam.

wannabes: the misguided assholes you tend to meet at *Soldier of Fortune* conventions.

weenies: pussy-ass can't cunts and no-loads.

Whiskey-Numbers: NSA's 1999–2000 code word designator for highest priority intercepts.

WHUTA: Wild Hair Up The Ass.

WTF: What The Fuck.

ZULU: Universal time designator used in formal military communications. Formerly called Greenwich Mean Time (GMT).

Index

All entries preceded by an asterisk (*) are pseudonyms.